THE LAST VALLEY

BOOKS BY A. B. GUTHRIE, JR.

THE BIG SKY
THE WAY WEST
THESE THOUSAND HILLS
THE BIG IT AND OTHER STORIES
THE BLUE HEN'S CHICK
ARFIVE
ONCE UPON A POND
(for children)
THE LAST VALLEY

THE
LAST VALLEY

◇ ◇ ◇

A. B. GUTHRIE, JR.

Houghton Mifflin Company Boston

1975

Library of Congress Cataloging in Publication Data

Guthrie, Alfred Bertram, 1901–
   The last valley.

   I. Title.
PZ3.G95876Las [PS3513.U855] 813'.5'2 75-17598
ISBN 0-395-21899-3

PRINTED IN THE UNITED STATES OF AMERICA

V 10 9 8 7 6 5 4 3 2 1

The author is grateful to Farrar, Straus & Giroux, Inc.
for permission to quote from *The Poems of
Trumbull Stickney*, edited by Amberys R. Whittle.
Copyright © 1966, 1969, 1972 by Amberys R. Whittle

FOR CAROL

Author's Note

THE CHARACTERS in this book are real. That is, they are real to me after long association, as I dare hope they will become real to readers. Should anyone look for them outside my pages, he will be disappointed, for they have no substance elsewhere and no intended resemblance to actual persons, living or dead. (Amendment: There are two exceptions that a few old-timers may spot.)

Readers may fault me for liberties taken with thing, place and chronology. For the sake of shape I have had to combine and condense. The dam on the imagined Breast River is almost equally imaginary, being a composite of two actual structures, widely separated, and of others. The great flood in Montana occurred in 1964, not 1946, as I am well aware. The hanging dealt with here is a year off the true date. So far as I can determine, saline seep, now a big and growing problem, wasn't recognized, or, if recognized, was not identified, until a decade, more or less, after 1946.

These violences to the record seemed necessary and do not, I hope, blur or distort the overall course of developments.

I am grateful for aid to one organization and several individuals. The organization is the Montana Historical Society, always the ready helper of writers. Among the individuals are Cap Peterson, once prominent member of the sheriff's office and participant in the hanging written about, whom my deputy does not resemble; Olga Monkman, historian of Teton County; Richard H. Kennedy, veteran of the Bureau of Reclamation, who, contrary to what I had been led to expect of the Bureau, answered questions readily and without evasion; June Thornton, meticulous typist and spotter of my errors; my wife, Carol, always the loyal and uncommonly perceptive critic, and my stepson, Bill Luthin, whom I abominate fondly because he is too wise for his years.

PART I

1

"I CALL THIS a pretty fair plant," Ben Tate said, knowing he exaggerated. He had just completed a tour of it.

The publisher sat back behind his desk. There were cigar ashes on the vest that his belly strained and the smell of whiskey on his breath. "Sure. Sure," he answered. "All I need are a few little things, like a new flat-bed press and a new building. Minor items."

"I like the town, too. I'd say it had a future."

"Right again. People been saying that for seventy-five years. That's proof enough for you."

The words, Ben thought, were mere fringes to the air of defeat about this old man with the stained and uneven mustache. There came from him the impression of things long lost if ever attained, of feelings numbed and hope receded. One age-spotted hand moved a sign on the desk that was cluttered with scissorings, paste pot and exchange papers. The sign, burned on a board, read MACALESTER CLEVELAND.

"A one-cow rancher branded my John Hancock on this slat," Cleveland said. "In lieu of a subscription, you understand. That was ten years ago. High-priced name-plate."

Ben kept silent.

"So you think you want to buy me out?" Cleveland said, at last getting back to the subject. "What gave you the idea I want to sell?"

"I thought you might, from asking around."

But they weren't talking like buyer and seller, Ben thought. What prospective buyer praised the possible purchase? What seller discredited it?

Cleveland heaved himself up and closed the door of his small office. It had only the desk in it, a pigeon-hole file, a couple of chairs and an obsolete Oliver typewriter in addition to the desk's accumulation. From just outside came the measured thump of a job press.

Cleveland pulled open a drawer of the desk, took out a pint bottle of whiskey and drank from its mouth. Afterwards, seating himself, he asked, "Care for a bracer?"

"Thanks. No."

"Not recommended for Bright's disease, not by old Doc Crabtree, but nothing is, so what the hell?"

"Hard to come by?" Ben asked.

"Whiskey? In Montana? Boy, you don't know the state. We voted Prohibition for others, not us. Federal agents come here from afar to get a good drink. People who can't afford red whiskey drink moonshine. Must be ten stills in the county." The mustache moved to a one-sided smile. "Of course, playing safe, my paper is dry, but everybody knows me. Evens things up."

"Now about selling the paper —"

"Times are hard enough without giving up booze," Cleveland went on, perhaps to put words between himself and the issue, perhaps to indulge himself in old man's talk. "The ranchers are broke. Wheat ranchers, livestock men, all broke. Wall Street's on the up, I see, but that doesn't mean shit in short-grass country. You a Republican?"

"Nominally."

"Better so, if you want the county printing."

"That means you're ready to talk business?"

Cleveland belched, wiped his mustache and waved the subject away. "All my life, nearly, I've been a booster, not to say a boozer. Why, one time — must have been before 1920 — after we had a good rain just in the nick of time, I ran a headline, 'Now Is the Winter of Our Discontent Made Glorious.' Prof Collingsworth knew I was quoting Shakespeare. So did Mort Ewing. Wise old farts, though not ancient, either. Tell you about them. How do I say it? Not the spirit of the town. Not the guts. Oh, they have been, they are still, you might say, the head and the hoof and the haunch and the hump. That's from Kipling, young man. Not politicians, either, they aren't, and not particular friends of mine, but they're what Kipling said."

"Interesting. People I'll want to know. Provided —"

"And another time," the old man continued, "I wrote an editorial — that was in about 1920, hard times — and I captioned my piece, 'Nothing Was Ever Lost by Enduring Faith in Montana.'"

He sighed then, remembering, and added, "Bullshit. Pure bullshit. How many homesteaders dried up and blew away? How many claims did the land and loan people have to take over? Any idea?"

"None."

Cleveland took another drink.

Ben said, "Look. I don't want to take up all your time."

"Doesn't matter. Paper came out yesterday, on time, too. No, I tell you, young man, hope, not love, is the only bow on life's dark cloud. That's paraphrasing Ingersoll, if you don't know it. By the way, you got an education?"

"B.A. degree. I worked, part-time, as a two-thirder in a composing room while getting it."

"Good. Your old-time country editor was an educated man. When he retired, he sold to his faithful printer, who didn't know a pluperfect from a passenger pigeon. Sorry state of affairs."

Cleveland fumbled for the one cigar in his vest pocket and took pains in lighting it with a kitchen match. The smell of it mingled with the smell of whiskey. The job press still beat its measure in the room.

Maybe now the man was getting back on the track, Ben thought, until he said, "So you got to be a booster. Success springs from the manure pile, though who am I to say so, not being rich? Still and all, I've made out in my years here. Before that I owned a weekly across the mountains. No go with those apple-knockers. Took me a long time to learn the secret of success." He smiled a smile with no mirth in it. "A young fellow like you brings a high mind to publishing. After a while he learns the first duty of a newspaper is to make money."

"Are you trying to discourage me?" Ben asked. "Remember, I love this state. I have, ever since as a kid I hopped bells in Yellowstone Park."

"Belles with an *e?*" Cleveland said.

The question didn't deserve a reply.

"Great state for hunting and fishing, not to mention scenery," Cleveland went on. "Don't blame you, young man."

"All that. That and the youth of the country."

"Youth?" Cleveland said and let the question lie in him. "Youth?" It was as if he were trying to summon his early years, to recall the old drive and dreams dusted over by years. Then, abruptly, dismissing the attempt, he asked, "What's your proposition?"

"What's yours?"

"I don't remember suggesting one."

"All right. I can put ten thousand dollars, cash, down. The rest would depend on an examination of the books, inventory, appraisal of equipment."

Cleveland made a little movement with his cigar, and ash fell on his vest. "Ten thousand? So much? So much for a young man?"

"I saved every cent I could in the army."

"Saw service, huh? What rank?"

"Captain, and I saw more than enough service."

"And don't want to talk about it?"

"No." He knew his tone was abrupt, but who, knowing them, wanted to talk about death and guts and stink and fear? "I saved my money, as I said. I had some to begin with, earned as a journeyman printer in Ohio before I volunteered. Then, after the war, with government help I took a few courses at Harvard and in my spare time worked at my trade."

Ben stopped. Why did he feel he had to explain to this sad old wreck of a man?

"You would fit in," Cleveland said. "This town is shot in the ass with patriotism. Sees bolshevikis everywhere. You a member of the American Legion?"

"No."

"Better be. It's strong here. Pine-tree patriots, meaning they served their time at Camp Lewis or somewhere west and never got within moon length of a Hun. No matter. They're true-blue Americans and damn the First Amendment." Cleveland looked up out of his veined eyes and asked, "No offense?"

"Not particularly."

"I've been wanting to say that for a long time," he said, his eyes still on Ben. "I guess I can speak out now."

"If you sell." Spoken, the words seemed regrettably cynical.

"Declaration of independence, huh?" Cleveland answered without heat. He picked up the bottle and took his third drink. "Still say no?" he asked afterwards.

Ben regarded the bottle and the old mouth that had sucked on it. The mouth said, "I got a glass somewhere." Cleveland shuffled his desk papers and found it.

"A short one, then." Cleveland poured a stout drink, and Ben raised his glass and said, "To a sale?"

"Hold it," Cleveland answered and drank from the bottle and added, "I must give thought to the matter."

But, going out into the bright sunshine of July, breathing air as fresh as on the first day of earth, seeing the high sky kind and all-encompassing, Ben felt sure he had bought himself a weekly newspaper.

2

AFTER BEN TATE HAD GONE, Cleveland sat in his chair and let the minutes drift by. All right and goodbye, he would sell to this young fellow. How often in these skimpy days did any man come up with ten thousand dollars in cash? Having sold, he would go to California or someplace and get out of the wind and the cold and the pitiless, dry days of July and August.

Get out of them? But cold had been his companion and the wind a good enemy, and on sun-struck days a man able-bodied could laze along a trout stream and let the fool world go by. He would miss the seasons, though more and more they tended to merge in his mind. Spring, summer, fall, winter, spring — they slid into one another, became a stream that carried a man along, forgetful of the changed waters. Yet, sometimes even now, his old blood rose to the warm wind of the chinook, and his eye loved the first dandelion.

Cleveland looked at the bottle on his desk. There was still a heel in it, and he drank it.

In the time of youth a shot or two or three did things for a man. They brought to flower a spirit in which the sap already ran strong. They opened it to the full sun of promise, and its answer to that sure light was unmixed jubilation. Not so anymore. Old bastards drank so as to ignore and forget, to harden the hide against the slings and arrows of regret and the damn general sameness of day by day and year by year. They drank against the withered hope, hastening, if they knew that much, the arrival of the coffin, which would take them even earlier if they had Bright's disease.

The job press ceased thumping, and footsteps sounded, and

Cleveland slipped the empty bottle into his desk drawer. Just as well not to invite that look of reproof. Okay Myers opened the office door. Okay for Oscar Knapp, if anyone cared. "I could still get those dodgers run off," Myers said.

"Never mind. Time to knock off."

"There's some orders piled up."

"I know, but never mind. We'll get to them."

As if doubtful, Myers turned around to go out.

"Leave the door open," Cleveland said. "I'll stay on a few minutes."

Okay Myers, the faithful printer, the upright, reliable temperance man, who always pushed to get the *Advocate* published on time. As if time were of the essence, as it ought to be in the newspaper business. Okay, who was Catholic and had eight dull kids and so had uckfayed himself close to the wolf. Okay, who nevertheless could probably raise a down payment on his reputation alone and by rights should be sold the business. By rights? Okay an editor? Ask him about Cicero, and he would be likely to answer it was a town close to Chicago.

Was there in himself still, Cleveland wondered, some clinging vision of what a newspaper could and should be. A reporter of all the news, and let the chips fly? An informed and literate organ? A molder of opinion? A community influence, a good one?

Save on exceptional days, days of stray sparks, he hadn't been an editor himself but only a printer of chitchat and advertising. He could have spoken out against the Ku Kluxers, that bunch of bigots who had seduced some good men but at last appeared to be losing their drive. Right now he could editorialize about evolution, the Scopes trial and the true-believing monkey minds who walked with God. He could inveigh against Prohibition, that failure foredoomed at the outset, that noble-minded, simple-minded *Verboten* endorsed by old ladies, anxious parents, reformed drunks, and men who feared that one honest jolt would unbutton their pants. And the Red scare, the Red hunt, fueled by that lunatic patriot, Attorney General A. Mitchell Palmer. It was coming late but with full force to Montana, as most crazes did. Full force because the tail-ender thought it was still a part of the parade.

He had dodged and was dodging subjects like these and would do so again, given the option. Out of timidity? No. Out of expedience? Yes, in degree. Out of fatigue or more likely laziness? Take your choice. It had come to be that almost nothing was important enough to justify effort, let alone controversy.

He heard the outer door open and called out, "Come in."

By the limp of the footsteps he knew his visitor was Billie Gayle, who moved in a shuffle and had difficulty directing his hands. A birth injury, rumor had it. Billie ran the Arfive Club, where a man could buy tobacco, cigars, cigarettes, near beer and pop, or engage in a small game at one of the two tables in the rear.

"Well, hello, Billie," Cleveland said, knowing his tone was cordial, wanting it to be.

Billie dragged himself toward the desk. His mouth smiled a smile that his maimed face would hardly allow. "I thought I'd pay my bill," he said.

"No hurry, Billie," Cleveland answered. "I never worry about you."

Billie tried his crooked smile again. "But I do." He got his hand inside his pocket and brought out three silver dollars, some smaller coins and the crumpled charge statement. The cash must have amounted to half a day's take, maybe more. Cleveland counted out the amount owed and receipted the bill. Taking money from a cripple and an uncomplaining one at that!

He listened to the halting step and half-step of Billie's exit and wished he had a drink.

Not one drink, he thought, but enough drinks to be comfortable. What did it matter? Earlier, when he realized he was on the downgrade, he had wondered whether booze was being his undoing. Or had the decline of purpose led to the booze? Or had they joined forces? Or had compromise caused them both? But why wonder now? It was too late to find a newer world and smite the sounding furrows with Ulysses.

He was about to get up when the front door opened again and

Peter Sears entered the office at Cleveland's greeting. Peter ran the town's principal and almost only department store and so, of course, was often called Roebuck.

"What's on your mind, Peter?" Cleveland asked.

"Just hair, and it's disappearing."

It was, all right, though Peter was young and spoke in the strong tones of youth. "Have a seat."

"Just on my way home, but I wondered — well, I guess you know the Bureau of Reclamation and maybe the Army Engineers are taking a look at the Breast River, thinking to dam it at the mouth of the canyon?"

"Routine," Cleveland answered. "Long way off. They're looking at every river in the country. But why in hell don't you read the paper? Piece appeared yesterday."

"Oh. Sorry. I haven't even had time to open the mail. First I knew, an engineer visited the store this morning."

"Call him a scout."

"You know, though, Mack, it could be a great thing. Lots of land to be irrigated that can't be dry-farmed worth peanuts."

"There are other dams, on the Medicine, for instance, and settlers have had to scrabble."

"But they'll make it. It's hard times for everyone now. And think of the business the dam crews would mean."

"No doubt about that."

"I was thinking a little newspaper promotion would help. Might hurry things up. It would get people interested and in back of the Bureau."

There was a question in the words, and for an instant Cleveland was tempted to say he was selling out. Instead, he answered, "It's a long, long way off. But, Pete, you ever know me not to boost for the town and county? Time's ripe, I will."

Peter said, "Sure, Mack. I know. We all do," and rose and walked out. Before he reached the front door, he was humming some tune that was probably popular.

For a moment there sounded in Cleveland's ears the old voices singing, the young voices sure of themselves, now silenced or reduced to the cackle of dotty ancients who crippled from county rest home to post office, if they could make it that far. For a fact, they were all dead or deadened, the old, young friends, the old, good times, the singing that said dreams come true.

And he didn't care. That was the thing. He wasn't able to care. The town was not his town anymore, the world not his world, life not his life. "This, too, shall pass away," someone, maybe Lincoln, had said, ignoring the fact that cheer and hope and friends disappeared along with the troubles referred to. And age couldn't bring itself to feel or to care. The final subtraction before death itself.

He got up then. He could go home and listen to the squawk of his Radiola. He could go to Billie's Arfive Club and play pinochle. But first he would have a drink or a dozen. He would go to the drugstore, where Spence Green would fix him up with a prescription and bottle, thanks for the prescription to old Doc Crabtree, who left his booze pad at the store and wouldn't charge anything. Good old Doc Crabtree.

The bottle secured, he would go to the Club, not Billie's, where men with time on their hands, as well as some with none, went to talk and to smoke over drinks.

All right, then, go, he told himself, and went to the door and locked it behind him. For a moment he looked to the west, where the sun played fire on the late-afternoon clouds.

He heard a whimper and scratching behind him and realized he had forgotten his dog, who liked to lie by the window in the shop and let the sun warm his old bones, but only when Cleveland was close by.

Cleveland let the dog out, who gave thanks with one tail wag, and looked at the run-down building in which he had spent his years. The building wouldn't miss him. Neither would Okay Myers. Neither would anybody except for one goddamn old dog.

3

EMERGING FROM the odors of printer's ink, newspaper and job stock, cigar smoke and the whiskey he couldn't smell after having a drink, Ben Tate considered a casual stroll, casual droppings-in on the storekeepers and shopkeepers who would be his advertisers when and if the paper was his. He had met a few of them already, more or less by accident as he reconnoitered the town.

All right, it could be called a one-gut town, counting only the business places — stores and shops, two banks, two hotels, commercial garages, abstract office, real estate and insurance, farm implements, some others. Not too many of any, but enough for a going newspaper energetically managed.

Standing on the walk, he looked toward the west, toward a sunset such as a man didn't see in the East. The clouds flamed behind the purple humps and spires of the Rockies. They rested like sea vessels, in shades and hues and brilliances not known to rainbows or dictionaries. Behind them the sun showed only a part of its face, like an eye drooping toward sleep.

Whenever he walked, undetermined as to direction, Thoreau had written, his feet always took him west and southwest. And that was good enough. West he had come, Ben thought, and west he would remain, and now let his feet march him to a clearer view of one of the reasons he'd found.

After half a mile he was out of the town. He came to a wire fence and bent through it and halted in a field given over to coarse grass and low brush and saw a cow looking toward him, a cow full in the bag, her head lifted, her eyes patient and curious, perhaps wondering whether he had come to ease the strain on her udder.

He sat down on a bald hummock and gazed at the clouds, at the harsh lift of the mountains, at the sun close to sleep now. At either side of him, far off, the valley lifted into benchlands, bright yellow in the last sun but bare and unshadowed as yet. Closer, in front of him, meandering to left and to right, the trees of the Breast River bordered its shores. The cow had gone back to grazing.

There were words for this land and these sights, empty and editorial words, words like space and peace and freedom and majesty. He tried them on his tongue, seeking better ones, and felt a tide running in him. He was awake and asleep both and in both states alive, in both aware and receptive to the far and close presences of sky, cloud, and earth.

A newspaper, then a marriage and children and a house built to order — he could think of them now. At twenty-eight he could think of them. A girl faithful and lovely and tenderly eager, a girl distilled pure from all the women he'd known or imagined. For a moment he lay with her, his hand admiring her contours — and felt a swelling in his trousers and got up abruptly and brushed himself off.

"First things first," he said aloud and saw the cow gazing at him.

The sun had gone down when he got back to town, but the long light lingered. It was time and past time to eat, and he decided to forego the indifferent fare of the Arfive House and try the food at the cafe called Eva Fox's.

A woman in unspotted white welcomed him and showed him to a table. At this late hour there were few customers, none of whom he had met. The woman took his sailor straw hat and glanced at his Oxford-bag trousers and coat and made him aware that he was an outlander. Save for the business and professional people, most of whom wore full suits, with ties, men hereabouts dressed in jeans or plain pants, open shirts and vests not covered by coats. For headgear they preferred western hats made of felt.

The woman handed him a menu and waited and said without other comment, "What may I bring you, stranger?"

Before he could make up his mind, a man entered and called out, "How, Eva."

She said, "Mort!" and left Ben. "Long time no see. How's the family?"

"Fine but out gallivanting. No time for a saddle tramp."

She made quite a business of seating him. He was a man of perhaps fifty-five, maybe more, though he bore himself with an easy confidence that belied age. He had the wind and the West in his face, Ben thought, and he wore the clothes of a stockman. His cowpuncher heels clumped as he went to the table.

"What's in the cook shack?" he asked after seating himself. "Got a good steak, Eva?"

"Did I ever let you down?"

"No, ma'am. Scald me one then."

She came over to Ben. "Sorry. Now, what will you have?"

"The same as your friend."

"Fine," she said, seeming to hesitate, as if perhaps he'd asked what was reserved for the few, or the one only. She disappeared and came back, bringing water.

Mort? The name dodged around in his head, and on impulse he asked, low-voiced, "Would that be Mr. Ewing?"

Her head lifted, and she looked toward the man, smiling, and called to him, "Mort, there's a stranger here knows you."

The man's eyes examined Ben briefly. They were not unfriendly. "That's sure a horse on me," he said and rose and came toward Ben's table. His smile touched his eyes. "Mind a pardner?" he said. "I hate to graze alone."

"Of course. Please sit down."

Seated, the man said, "Seems you know my name. Mort Ewing."

"I've heard it mentioned."

Ewing was silent.

"Oh, sorry. I'm Ben Tate." He felt his hand grasped by one that was rougher, maybe tougher, than his.

"Easy brand to remember," Ewing said.

"Not in full," Ben answered, wondering why, in the presence of this strange man, he felt inclined to say more. "I was christened Benjamin Aswell Tate."

"Quite a handle," Ewing said. The over-all smile came again, the smile that was more than politeness. His eyes, responding to it, appeared to see near and far both, as if beyond detail he looked into distance. Sun had darkened his face and wind left its marks on it. Life had been good to this man, Ben thought, or he had made it be good and found fun in the doing.

"I'm not out on the town much," Ewing said after a pause. "Don't hanker to be."

He was silent again, and Ben suspected a question had been put, though unasked. "I'm just drifting around, I guess you could say," he answered to it. "And I guess you could say I'm from Ohio. Born there, anyway, in a little town known as Leesburg."

"So," Ewing said as if that matter were settled. "Most of us came here from someplace. Except for some young bucks just feelin' their oats and the small fry, of course, we're shy on native stock. Live here twenty years and you're an old-timer."

In looks the man rated as an old-timer doubled. He might have been born in the open and exposed to the sculpturing western weather on his first day of life. And yet he was set apart from his fellows. His clothing, though western, was clean and better in quality than common run. His boots had a shine. His vest had seen cleanser and iron.

The woman brought them each a steak, a baked potato, a dish of corn and a radish salad in some kind of dressing and, for their common use, a basket of hot rolls. Ewing asked for black coffee, and Ben ordered the same.

The food was excellent, far better than he had been served elsewhere in the West, where, Ben judged from experience, the best steak available had been cut from some scrawny cow. The rolls were delicious, and the salad had a sweet bite.

They ate in silence. For an old cowboy type — and surely he was that — Ewing had uncommon good manners at table, good enough for Ben's mother if only he wore a coat.

After dessert Ewing said as he fashioned a cigarette, "Kind of dull here for you, I reckon. Nights, anyhow."

"I can always read."

Ewing lighted his cigarette and blew out a thin plume of smoke.

"Yeah. I feel sorry for them that don't read. Where you puttin' up?"

"Right now at the Arfive House."

"Used to be a good bar there, before Prohibition turned it into a rot-gut restaurant." Ewing considered. " 'Course, there's always the picture show but generally so full of shot and shell and men dead and dyin', you wonder there was anyone left to settle the West."

"They're true to the outside impression, the movies, I mean."

"And about as close to true as instant salvation of sinners."

A suggestion seemed to come and be debated in Ewing's eyes before he spoke again. "The stranger, the Book says, is a man to be taken in. Say so if you don't, but you want to come with me to the Club?"

"Well, thanks, Mr. Ewing, but I don't like —"

"No imposition. It's just up the street. Some of the boys drift there, and we can have a drink if that don't run against your current."

"It doesn't. Sure, then, and thanks again."

The Club was a basement room in one of the only two two-story buildings in town. Scattered in it were a dozen or so chairs and three round tables with decks of cards on them. A row of lockers flanked one end, close to a shelf lined with glasses above a water basin. There were only two men in the Club now, one a stranger to Ben, the other Macalester Cleveland, who lifted a hand in a tired salute from a far corner of the room.

"Sit down," Ewing said. "We got two drinks here, straight bourbon and bourbon with ditch water. Which?"

"About half and half."

Ewing went to the lockers, opened one, mixed two drinks and brought them to the table. "How," he said, once seated, and lifted his glass.

Ben drank with him.

Ewing studied the bright toe of one boot, lifted as he sat with crossed legs. "I didn't know I was so famous, bein' named to a tourist."

There was the unput question again.

"I said you were mentioned. I don't really feel free to tell you the circumstances. But your name came up and that of — let's see — Collingsworth."

"Prof, you mean. One hell of a good man. My friend, even if we don't always track the same trail."

"I was just inquiring around, thinking I might stay for a while."

Ewing said, "So."

There were clatters on the steps, and voices, and three young men came in, yelling greetings as they made for the lockers. "Long time between drinks," one said, and another answered, "A long fifteen minutes."

They fixed drinks, took their bottles and went to sit at a vacant table and, noisy with nothings, kept sizing Ben up.

In this setting he felt conspicuous and a trifle ridiculous, felt like a show-off in trousers so baggy that one leg was roomy enough for both of his own. On the eastern seaboard they had been quite the thing.

More footsteps sounded, and more voices descended with them, and two more young men came in, followed by an older one evidently not of their party. The older one waited while the others got drinks and, bantering, went to join those already seated. Then, methodically, he prepared his own mixture and came to sit with Ewing and Ben uninvited.

Ewing said, "How, Doc? How's the weather with you?"

"Unchanged, same as usual."

"Meet Benjamin Aswell Tate." Ewing's eyes showed a quick glint of amusement, no doubt at this proof of unexpected remembrance. "Doctor Crabtree, Ben."

They shook hands.

Doctor Crabtree might have been put together with long scraps of left-over lumber, wired at the joints by a child. His face was lean and hard, as if shaped and forged by felt suffering.

Ewing listened to the noise from the other table and presently said above it, "Good intentions always get kicked in the ass."

"What did you expect?" Crabtree asked, as if knowing without explanation to what Ewing referred.

"My idea was to have a club for us old and lonesome stags, like you and Mack Cleveland for instance, where we could have a quiet drink and quiet talk and a quiet game if the notion hit us."

"This is what you got. What you might have expected."

"What's to do for lonesome old bucks?" Ewing appeared to sigh, noiseless in the noise. "Drop in at the barbershop. Visit Billie Gayle's. In good weather laze on the street, hopin' to strike up a conversation. Go to the post office and not get any mail. Anything to put between themselves and the boneyard and nothing to find. That was my idea, a gatherin' ground for old bulls." He had to speak louder. "Not this, though I got nothing against youth except it's so young."

Crabtree turned to Ben. "Mort's not so lonesome and not so sour as he's saying. He could shut up the club right now. Hell, he owns the whole goddamn building and leaves this room open for free."

Cleveland had heaved himself out of his chair and with stiff care was pouring himself another drink. Behind the chair a grizzled dog lay watching.

Now, as Ben's table fell silent, a hard voice rose at the other and word by word won attention. "So it was just a scare, huh? A Red scare, they call it. A scare, my ass." The speaker had an intent, unlined face, as if truth had ironed out every wrinkle. "I tell you these shit bolshevikis are everywhere. Right here to find in this town if you look."

"I been suspecting you, Mort," Crabtree said. A grin turned up one corner of his mouth.

"And me you. That's the ticket. No one to trust, savin' yourself."

For the moment the speaker seemed to have exhausted his steam, or to be overwhelmed by the extent of his knowledge. He looked at his hands, held still on the table, as if picking and choosing what next to say while awaiting energy appropriate to it. The men around him were slow to pick up their idled talk. They passed a bottle and studied Ben, not quite openly except for one man who stared at him. He was a big man with a big face that suggested it had been plowed, and he appeared close to drunk.

Mere curiosity, not suspicion of his being subversive, Ben thought. He was an outlander in an outlandish outfit. He could wish he were behind the table and not at the side, where his clothing was in open sight.

"Sacco and Vanzetti, if that's their real names. Yeah, that Sacco and Vanzetti." The speaker had made his choice and found fresh strength. "Still alive, those dirty bastards, found guilty but still alive. And what does that prove? It proves weak minds and foreign influence. If loyal Americans had had their way, they'd have been strung up the minute the jury reported, if not before."

The big man with the plowed face said, "We're with you, Earl, one hundred percent, but me, I got to mosey on home or get throwed out to the dog. My woman can lecture even fiercer than you."

The man left his chair, made toward the door, caught sight of Ben again and halted before him. "I do say," he said, "those are the goddamndest pants ever I saw. Goin' to buy a couple of wool sacks and have a pair for myself." He waited for an answer and went on, "Big enough in one leg for me and my old lady and a picnic lunch."

He waited again and, as if the silence had diverted his train of thought, asked abruptly, "You a member of the American Legion?" His eyes began to show a dull animosity.

Ben didn't reply.

"Not an ex-serviceman, huh?"

To the unasked questions of Ewing, he had felt obliged to reply. To these blunt questions, no. He knew he could get up and assume the old pose of authority, could voice the old tones of command and so, by such cheap dramatics, and subsequent explanations, put himself in good grace. He could fight the man. He kept still. The room was still, too.

"A goddamn dodger, I bet."

"Get some air, Brobeck." Ewing was speaking, soft-voiced but all the more effective for that. His thumb jerked toward the door. "Go cool off and come back mindin' your manners. It's my friend you are tryin' to rag."

The man opened his mouth, said nothing and went out. One by one the others followed. As they filed by, Ewing said, "Not to say you're not welcome, boys."

One of them answered, "We know, Mort, but it was one of our party went wrong. Sorry."

When they had gone, Ben said, "My fault, I guess. It's hard to know how to act. But he was just drunk. He didn't have a mean face."

"No, not Brobeck," Ewing answered. "He's not mean." He reflected and added, "Not that one."

Mack Cleveland scraped back his chair, got up with effort and came to the table, watching each step. "A buck private," he said, his mustache fanning to his breath. "That's all he ever was — no, a buck private busted from sergeant and never moved back." He put one hand on Ewing's shoulder and leaned close for emphasis. "Do you know he was talking to a captain, one that saw more overseas service than all that bunch put together?"

The man was enlarging on what Ben had told him.

"No," Ewing said, "but I know when a man knows enough to keep a tight rein. Ben here could have taken him, too, or I'm way off the mark."

With one hand on Ewing's shoulder and the other one pointing, Cleveland said, "It could be you'll see a lot of this young fellow."

A quick speculation showed in Ewing's face. He answered, "I wouldn't object."

"Good enough." Cleveland turned toward the corner in which he'd been sitting and called out, "Here, Bluster," before he found the old dog at heel.

They went out slowly, old man and old dog, one as stiff in step as the other, if not for the same reasons.

4

" 'Jacta alea est,' meaning the die is cast, if you know your Latin," Cleveland said. "But just in case signs and seals, legalisms and lawyers don't bind the deal, let's shake hands on it and have a drink by way of hello and goodbye."

They were in the *Advocate* office again, and again the time was afternoon. Ben took the extended hand.

"It's my bounden duty, as they used to say, to take you around and get you acquainted, but, hell, duty is the cargo of the weak vessel."

"There's no need for that," Ben said.

"I'll put out the goodbye issue this Thursday and introduce you in it, but the word's in the wind already." A smile touched the mouth under the shag of mustache. "Reminds me of the time — I was just a kid — I wrote, 'Lawyer Murchy moved from where he was to where he is now on Tuesday,' and even that much didn't need to be printed."

Cleveland pushed himself back from the desk and felt for a cigar. His breath moved the hairs of his mustache and rose and fell low in his chest. The veins of his nose were like trickles from the flow of his heart.

"But damme, boy, I forgot. Out of character, too." He pulled a drawer open and took out a pint bottle from which a nip or two had already been drunk. He poured into two clean glasses on his desk, which had been put into some kind of order, but seemed in no hurry to drink. He studied his whiskey. Studying it, he drew on his unlighted cigar, then bit the end off.

"You know the sources," he said then and went on as if visiting them one by one in his mind. "Courthouse, of course. Deeds and transfers. Suits filed. Marriage licenses. Court when it sits. County agent will give out hot news like how to bait gophers with the new batch of poison he's mixed. Sheriff's office. Once in a while, to show his heart's in the right place even if his tastes aren't, he knocks off a still or chases booze run in from Canada. Undertaker, the end of the train but no small caboose."

Ben said, "I know."

"Mayor's office," Cleveland continued as if uninterrupted. "Forest Service, which puts out fires and then sells off the trees that it's saved. But most of them come to me with the news." He lighted his cigar and blew out a puff of remembering smoke. "I got a high-school kid meets the train for local items, distributes leads and slugs and melts, skims and molds Linotype metal in off hours besides covering school news and sports. He's not much, but here's his name."

Cleveland scribbled on a pad and passed the sheet over. As Ben nodded his thanks, he went on. "You can save a lot of wear and tear, such as covering local concerts and plays and Chautauqua and such boons to culture by enlisting local talent. I have quite a corps of people willing to work just so they can say they wrote this or that. And a by-line! Good God, for a by-line they would investigate hell. Want their names?"

"Later I may ask you for them."

Now Cleveland drank, not as a toast, and, with his glass drained, poured another. He sat slumped and quiet as if waiting for a flame to rise from the embers. As he took the cigar from his mouth, his worn eyes rolled up to Ben. "You're in no hurry?"

"None at all, Mr. Cleveland."

"You can go if you want or waste time with my prattle. Sin of old age, son, prattle is. A man with age on him maybe thinks if he twitters he can stave off the end. Or maybe the old fool thinks years give importance to ignorance. But it's all just mewling and puking, thanks to Shakespeare."

Ash dropped unnoticed on Cleveland's open vest. Ben's nod was meant to mean go ahead.

Cleveland sighed. "But I tell you, Ben, when the string is run out, a man wonders. Here I'm thinking now about where to go, where on God's earth to go. Used to be, right up to the time we made our deal, I swore I'd get out of here before the next winter came. Yeah, sunshine and no wind and maybe the seashore, and an old man can still look at pretty girls, remembering."

One hand closed in a loose fist, as if it would strike at something not clearly seen. "But, damn it, I'm grounded in this country, snubbed up and hog-tied, and blind, you might say, to other suns and other skies. A by-God Eskimo homesick away from his ice house."

The little-rivered eyes looked into distance, and the old words slowed. "The country gets into a man." Cleveland paused, like a writer hunting for the right phrases to type. "Yes. The man bends to the wind, knowing calm days will be better for it. He shivers in the cold, and part of that shiver is the shiver of summer to come."

Again the stop-to-think pause. Again the man at the typewriter, fingers waiting on brain.

"He looks to the mountains, blue-cold and bleak as on the first and last days." The fingers of his voice went idle, then busied themselves. "He looks to the hills from whence cometh, not the biblical help, but the seen float of distance and the sense of endurance."

Cleveland broke off and said abruptly, "Shit and goddamn!"

Ben didn't speak at once. When he did, it was to say, "Thank you."

"Humph. Whiskey talking." Cleveland finished his drink and seemed to debate about pouring another. His side lost, for the moment at least.

"You said I must meet two men," Ben said, not as a change of subject but as the beginning of a new one.

"Yeah, I guess I did. Mort Ewing and Prof Collingsworth. You've already met Ewing."

"And liked him."

"I don't know just why I sicced you onto those two men.

They're not what you could call close friends or good customers."
Cleveland spoke again after reflection. "Well, candor compels me
to state — that's my editorial style coming out — that they have
stood and still stand for something."

Now Cleveland poured himself another drink and replenished
Ben's glass. His voice was suddenly harsh. "They stood for something, goddamn it! Stand for something. You understand?"

"Not entirely."

Cleveland straightened in his chair. He seemed to bristle.
"Not that I have any regrets," he said with what Ben took to be
aged defiance. "Not one goddamn stinking regret." He raised his
glass. "And now, young man, the deal is done. Drink up, and so
long."

5

OUTSIDE, Ben turned to look at the shop. So the building was false-fronted? Weren't most of the buildings in town? So the paint was peeling, and even the *Advocate* sign, once black on white, suggested no more than a gray advocacy. So the windows were dirty, and the concrete step-up from sidewalk to door crumbled at either corner.

No matter. It was his, all his, though subject to a mortgage that time and hard work would pay off. All his, do or don't, make or break. His perfect if imperfect baby. Yes, sir, that's my baby — the song sang itself — No, sir, don't mean maybe . . .

He could see part of himself reflected in the one big, dirty window. No Oxford bags now, but the conservative trousers of a suit just bought at Shannon's Men's Wear, an advertiser. His sailor straw hat would have to be accepted as a small eccentricity.

As he was about to go on, a dusty pickup pulled up at the curb, and a man got out. He came to be the big man with the plowed face. Brobeck, Ewing had called him. The deep ruts of his face went wide with a smile. "Cap'n," he said, "I'm beggin' pardon for the other night. I had you all wrong. Care to shake my paw?"

Ben shook it.

"It was them big as by-Jesus britches. Them and the whiskey I'd drunk."

"It's all right." Ben was returning the smile.

"Not without I own up. Drunk in the privy, and I fell through the hole. Get caught shitty, I say, and the only soap is excuse me all to hell."

"You're excused. I'm glad to know you."

"Brobeck's the name, hitched onto Frank. Frank Brobeck."

"Ben Tate," Ben answered, taking the hand again, "and in case you or your friends wondered, I'm not a foreign agent, bolshevik or remote sympathizer."

"Hell, no, Cap'n. It was the pants sidetracked me. Earl Kilmer — he's a lawyer — it's him and a couple of others dream Red, just maybe with some footin' in fact. But the rest of us men in the Legion, we don't pay 'em much mind. It ain't often, even, we go to meetin's. Let them three, them three officers, see the country is safe."

"What's wrong with that?" Ben said. On this closer look, the man's face showed that the plow had cut furrows of open good nature in it.

"Me, workin' on the roads for the county, I got my own dirt to dig." Brobeck's eyes went from Ben to the shop and back to Ben again. "Hope you're goin' to be around for a while," he said as if knowing the answer. "Right now I've got to shove off."

"First, can you tell me where Professor Collingsworth lives?"

"Sure. I went to school to him for a while, and it ain't his fault if it didn't take, I don't care what anyone says. Just head out on Main Street," he said, pointing. "In about half a mile or less you'll see it, a pretty big house, white, to your left."

After Brobeck had gone on, Ben crossed the street to his Hupmobile, parked in front of the Arfive House. Four o'clock, an hour suitable enough for a call if the call itself suited sense. He sat in the car for a while.

The two-story house stood behind a flanking of cottonwoods. Back of it, at the side, an open garage covered a Ford touring car, the like of which was not being produced anymore. In the looping turnabout that the drive made, a new Reo was parked. Company, then, and too late, once he'd turned in, to beat a retreat.

Across the front of the house ran a porch, so darkened by screening as to veil easy sight, though Ben sensed presences in it. He tapped on the door.

It opened, and a man said, "Good afternoon." He was a man of square build, not tall, and straight in the shoulders. The hair was whitening, brushed to the side above a face that was square, too, and dusky rather than sallow. Ben noted this much as he said, "Good afternoon. My name is Ben Tate. You are Professor Collingsworth?"

"Yes?"

From behind Collingsworth a voice called, "How, Ben."

"Come in, won't you?" Collingsworth offered his hand.

Mort Ewing rose from a two-seat swing suspended by chains from the ceiling and shook hands. On the porch were three chairs, two easy, one straight, and all worn.

As they were seating themselves, Ewing said, "Prof, I aimed to tell you about Ben before my mind went off chasin' rabbits. Met him the other night. If you want to work the full handle, it's Benjamin Aswell Tate." His eyes were amused.

Inside the house, turned low, a Victrola was playing.

"Born in Ohio," Ewing went on. "That's about all I know for a fact, but not all I might swing a loop at. Eh, Ben?"

Collingsworth's expression was questioning.

Ben said, "I guess it can't hurt to tell now, since the rumor's around and everything is agreed on. I am buying the *Arfive Advocate*, to take effect the first of the week."

"Oh," Collingsworth answered and nodded as if in endorsement.

"That's one of the reasons I'm here."

"I doubt I understand."

"Mr. Cleveland told me I must meet you. He said you and Mr. Ewing were the head and the hoof and the haunch and the hump of Arfive, if I remember correctly."

"How's that for top grade, Prof?" Ewing asked.

"Correct in regard to Kipling at any rate," Collingsworth said. Of a sudden he smiled an incredulous smile. It transformed him, making sunny an expression that had seemed habitually sober. "Cleveland said that! Cleveland did?"

"He did."

"Mort, you never know, do you?"

The music from inside came to an end, and a girl appeared in the doorway, a woman perhaps in her mid-twenties, but a girl for all that.

"Come out, Mary Jess," Collingsworth told her. "Mr. Tate, Mary Jess, my daughter."

The girl nodded gravely and said in a voice meant for singing but muted, "How do you do, Mr. Tate?"

She stepped to a chair and sat down. In her movements was that sure economy known as grace. Her hair was coiled at the back of her head, up and away from a brow that had room for thought. It would have dismayed an up-to-date girl, Ben thought, to wear a dress well below the knee, to show a waistline where the waist was, or to leave even a modest suggestion of bust. Her eyes were brown, or, in better light, possibly hazel-green.

"That music you were playing?" Ben said.

"It's an old, old song, 'Whispering Hope.' "

"I know, yet I always thought of it as a, well, as a sort of last wail of hope, as a kind of sticky despair. But those voices!"

"Alma Gluck and Louise Homer," Mary Jess said. Her words came out softly but finally, not to be added to, their meaning contained by simplicity; and it struck Ben, looking at her, that here might be a girl of patient containment, of containment that patience made pitiful.

"The head and the hoof," Collingsworth was saying. "Would that imply wisdom?" He didn't expect an answer. "Like Thoreau, I wonder if the wisest man has learned anything of absolute value by living."

"But he did himself, or seems to have thought so," Ben answered.

Collingsworth cast him a quick glance, as if admitting a surprising addition to his measure. "Yes, Mr. Tate, but he warned by what he added. He wrote that in thirty years he had not heard the first syllable of valuable or even earnest advice from his seniors."

"Father," Mary Jess said in that voice of songs unsung, "if you believed that, you wouldn't be teaching."

His smile appeared to have sadness in it. "I suppose not, my dear."

"Much as I like him," Ben put in, "I find Thoreau full of ambivalences."

"And every one of them true, or — shall we say? — supportable."

Ewing had rolled and lighted a cigarette. "The trouble with Henry David is," he said, "you got to look hard for his best hits on account of all the birdshot."

Here was strange conversation, Ben thought, book conversation in what some might consider a mere outpost of civilization. It had an eastern or at least a midwestern flavor, and here was an old cowboy type joining in. His surprise must have been evident, for Ewing said in an aside, "You stick around bookworms, and you get kind of wormy yourself."

"I did a term paper on Thoreau, if that qualifies me."

Ewing continued, speaking to all, "I reckon any man, any man alone, could live Thoreau-style, that's if he chose to. But what's left out of the tally is woman, man and woman, and young ones when it comes to that. Embarrassin' to mention, but there's a little item called love, and where was that in his build? Left out? Docked off? And don't tell me his love was the love of mankind, for he was shy in that department to boot. That drum he marched to beat his own selfish time." Ewing broke off and laughed, apparently at himself. "Excuse me, you all. I'm just a lay reader."

A door slammed at the rear of the house, and a young voice called, "Mary Jess!"

She got up, saying as she was leaving the porch, "That's the boys, and they'll be hungry no doubt." Again she moved with controlled, unaffected certainty that a man could only call style, as different from stylish.

"Bring them here first, will you please?" Collingsworth asked. "We want them to meet Mr. Tate."

She returned and ushered the boys through the door. One was a thin boy with large, inquiring eyes, the other sturdy and smiling. Both were about eight years old, by guess. "Son," Collingsworth said, speaking to the thin boy, "I want you to know Mr. Tate. My son, Charles, Mr. Tate."

Ben rose and took the hand gravely offered.

"And Mr. Ewing's boy, Morton — young Mort, as we call him."

"We've been to the slough, seeing about muskrats," the Ewing boy said.

"Mr. Tate is the new owner of the *Arfive Advocate*," Collingsworth told the two.

"Well, that's good." Young Mort turned toward his father. "There's a lot of them there — muskrats, I mean."

"And Charlie's been looking to see how they live and build houses, and you, young'n, have been thinking about when furs will come prime."

"They ought to bring a dollar apiece."

"And how will you get back and forth from the ranch to your trap line?"

"I can stay some nights with Charlie."

Charlie said, "Of course you can."

"Any time, Mort." Mary Jess motioned toward the door. "Come along to the kitchen now, boys. I've made cookies."

On their leaving, Collingsworth fell to gazing into distance, or into himself, his gray eyes fixed and unblinking. At last he said, "If I dare to give one bit of advice, Mr. Tate, it is this: be chary that you don't assume the coloration of the community."

"The community isn't bad?"

"Oh, no. Only provincial, only parochial, as are other communities, little or big, in their way."

"I see," Ben said, not sure of how much he saw. "Can a man avoid that?"

"I've managed to keep intact some of my prejudices." The sudden smile came again, touching the whole face, the whole personality.

"My chunk of advice ain't so weighty," Ewing said. "It's just watch out for progress because you can't backtrack."

Collingsworth had risen to peer through the screen toward the drive. "More visitors. Why, it's old Mr. Greenwood."

With the screen open, Ben could see an ancient horse, an ancient buggy, and an ancient man who stepped stiffly down. The man left the horse untied and hobbled toward the entrance. "Well, hello, Mr. Greenwood," Collingsworth called. Then, "A pleasure to see you. Do come in."

"If I'm not intruding." Between the cracks in the old voice, a resonance sounded. "God bless you."

"No intrusion whatever. You know Mr. Ewing. And here is Mr. Tate, Mr. Greenwood. Mr. Tate is a newcomer to town."

Greenwood said, "Bless you, Mort," shook hands with Ben and looked him over. A faded friendliness and the innocent blank inquiry of age showed behind eyeglasses worn askew. His dry hand had no grip. He had a fine-haired, white beard that descended over his throat, and he wore a long-skirted, black coat such as preachers once did. He made his way to a chair and sat down and put his dusty black hat on the floor.

"Mr. Tate is the new owner of the *Advocate*," Collingsworth told him.

"So," Greenwood answered and put a veined hand to his beard. "Good fortune, Mr. Tate. But poor Mr. Cleveland. Hard on him to give up, I imagine." To Collingsworth he said, "He's really not a bad man, Professor."

Ewing had been listening, not speaking, while he smoked. Now he put in, "Reverend, I reckon nobody weighs plumb bad on your scales."

"Does anybody, Mort? Truly, does anybody?"

"I've seen some it wouldn't bother me to be pallbearer to."

"Mort. Mort." Greenwood strung out the name in shaky reproof.

"All the same, it would bear hard on me to be so kind to someone who thought I was out of my mind." Ewing had spoken with a quizzical smile.

What was meant for a chuckle moved the white beard. "Many think that of me. No doubt you do yourself. But should I condemn Mr. Cleveland for his opinions? Mort Ewing, you're stickering me."

Ewing laughed. "Reverend, you always come nice to the bait."

Greenwood turned to Ben. "You see, Mr. Tate, I'm a preacher turned farmer and Socialist." The voice, by turns cackling and resonant, went on as if in senile compulsion to confession. "The pulpit has no room for one of my conscience. I believe in my soul that land ownership originated in theft and so is intolerable to justice. The good Lord made the earth for man, not men."

Collingsworth considered, his brow wrinkled. "But I can't get it out of my head that that's the talk of the anarchists, the believers in wild revolution and not much beyond that."

The white beard moved up and down, sadly, it seemed. "I know, and you've heard me. I say, if patriotism is the last refuge of the scoundrel, then the refuge of the mindless is violence. But because one part of a belief is false, does it follow that no part can be true?"

"Sayin' you're right, which is as may be," Ewing said, "how do you unbrand the land?"

"We can begin by recognizing the truth. Then we can pray for guidance in asserting the truth. In God's good time, with faith, we shall see the way."

Mary Jess came from the house quietly, ending discussion, and set up a folding table. "I thought you might enjoy some iced tea," she said. She went back into the house and returned with a tray on which she had placed a full pitcher, glasses, sugar and spoons. On a second trip she brought a plate of cookies.

After Greenwood had sipped at his glass and taken a cookie, he said, "You are married, Mr. Tate?"

"No, sir. Never married."

With what seemed old familiarity, Mary Jess had sat down beside Ewing, who gave her shoulder a pat.

"Then I am reminded," Greenwood continued, illustrating with the cookie. "If you haven't arranged for lodging or meals — please excuse my presumption — you couldn't do better than to see Bertha Anderson — Mrs. Anderson, that is. I do believe she has a vacancy." He looked around as if for endorsement.

Ewing said, "Good woman. Good cook, too," and Collingsworth followed with, "Amen." Mary Jess didn't say anything.

"Fine, Mr. Greenwood. I might just do that. And thanks."

For a time they were silent. The cool of the afternoon drifted into the porch, harmonious with the chill of the tea. Greenwood wiped his beard with one of the napkins Mary Jess had supplied, put napkin and glass on the tray with a hand slightly palsied and said, "Thank you for the refreshment and company. I must be getting home. My old horse, though an internal-combustion machine of a sort, doesn't quite make the time of mechanized models." He rose creakily.

Collingsworth went to him, took his arm and saw him to the door and beyond it to the buggy, leaving the door open. He helped the old man to his seat, all the while treating him as he might have treated an heirloom, an antique, a piece of Hepplewhite in need of glue. Until Greenwood spoke and slapped it with the reins, the old horse had stood where it had stopped, as if nothing less than new works would get it going again.

Back in the porch, Collingsworth said, "I fear Mr. Greenwood isn't long for this world. I should have helped him when he arrived."

"I fear he isn't even in it," Ewing answered. "It's passin' strange I like him, cracked as he is."

"No, Mort. Not strange. He's a good man, too good for some people to understand or accept. You appreciate him because you appreciate goodness."

Into the pause that followed, Ben said his thanks and goodbye. On him as he spoke were the eyes in the still face of the girl.

He thought of that face as he drove back to town. A face with the look of waiting in it. A fine face too pensive, remembered as if seen through an enveloping mist. And the voice, the song not sung, listened for over far waters. Whispering hope.

6

HE WASN'T quite up to dinner yet, he thought as he parked his car. The tea and cookies had dulled the edge of appetite. A drink or two, then, but where? Without a bottle he could hardly visit Mort Ewing's club. Neither did he feel well known enough to proposition the drugstore.

He walked to Billie Gayle's place. Three old men were playing cards at a table in the rear of it. Billie limped up the far side of the counter and asked what he'd have, his misshapen mouth uttering the words at one side.

"Near beer, please."

Billie produced bottle and glass with one uncertain hand, making two movements where one would have done had he used both. The other arm did a small, nervous dance at his side. "You are Mr. Tate?" he said. His expression was friendly, all the friendlier because of the ruined face.

"Yes. Ben Tate." It was courteous not to offer his hand. "I've seen you a time or two, but not to speak to."

"One of the town's curiosities." The slow mouth worked at the words but said them without self-pity or bitterness, as if he had learned to accept himself as he was.

"Oh, and give me a pack of Camels, too, please," Ben said, knowing he was abrupt. But infirmities, talked of firsthand, made a man, any man, uncomfortable.

Billie looked at him, as if understanding, said, "Sure, Ben," and shuffled for cigarettes. He put them on the counter, managed to make change, said, "Sorry," and moved back to the card players.

Ben drank his drink slowly, puffed at a cigarette, then another,

wanting neither, and went out wishing that somehow he had been
more adroit in talking to Billie.

He went to his room in the Arfive House, washed hands and
face in the one bathroom on the floor, then changed shirt and tie.
Possibly he would, possibly wouldn't, call on the rooming-house
lady tonight.

He had dinner at Eva Fox's, which at this tardy hour had only a
couple of customers, one of whom he might have seen before.
Eva had recommended beef stew, with good reason.

After the two customers had gone, Eva Fox came to his table
and asked, "New broom, huh? When does it sweep?"

"Won't you sit down, Mrs. — or is it Miss? — Fox?"

"Just Eva. Plain Eva," she answered, taking a seat across from
him. "I asked when?"

"If you mean what I think you do, it's Monday."

"No change in rates?"

"Not to my knowledge. I don't know yet."

"Better not be," she said, smiling. She was a big woman and
struck him as motherly. Her hair, dressed without one hair out of
place, was turning white. "I'm a regular advertiser. Six main
dishes on Sunday, all freshly cooked, and steamed clams or fresh
oysters for extras. But the prices I have to pay and to charge!
That's why I asked about space rates."

"Be at ease for now, anyhow."

"Sixty cents for a T-bone steak — can you imagine that? — and
the country crawling with beef that won't net a rancher enough for
a consolation bottle. Wheat's worse, what there'll be of it. This
is the driest July known to man, or almost."

She pushed back as if to go, saying, "Sing a song of sixpence but
no pocket full of rye."

He said, before she could leave, "Now that's out of your system,
any advice to a cub newspaperman?"

"Advice?"

"I've been getting some."

"Such as?"

"Professor Collingsworth told me to beware of becoming too

much like the community. It was thought and attitude he referred
to, I'm sure. No reflection on the town, though. I think he
meant imprisonment in locality, wherever it was."

Eva nodded. "Hard thing to do, Ben. Bias and ignorance kind
of creep into you. Not that Mr. Collingsworth hasn't some bias
himself, but God knows he imported it. Still, he's a brainy man
and an honest one, not to be led by the nose. What else?"

"Mr. Ewing said to watch out for progress because you couldn't
go back."

"That's Mort for you. He has spells, I bet, when he deplores
the invention of the flush toilet. But sometimes, so to speak,
don't we all?"

"Now," he said, "what do you have to add to the maxims?"

"Smart boy, using 'maxims.' " She thought for a moment and
rose and smiled. Out of her motherly face came, "Keep in mind,
sinnin' is fun."

"Wait a minute, now. Wait a minute, Eva. One other thing."
He looked up at her, standing. "For accommodations it's been
suggested that I see one Mrs. Bertha Anderson."

"Damnation, man, I've lost a customer. That old biddy sets a
good table, everyone says."

"So?"

"Well, see her. You won't be sorry. But, Ben, remember I'll
still be in business. You, your nice clothes and all, add a ca-
chet — that's in exchange for your 'maxims' — to my place, besides putting cash in the till."

"Mostly I'll eat out, I think, and I'll remember, I promise."

"Promise filed. Go two blocks west and one north, and you'll
find her house, white and green, two-story, on the northwest corner. Her widowed daughter lives with her, but don't get ideas.
They'll be dashed."

A stillness hung over the town, over the whole land, wherever
stars shone or would shine, for the twilight was too light for stars
yet, save for one low in the west that kept a kind eye on the mountains. The quiet air came into the lungs as if of itself, as if by itself making sure that he prospered, free even of the tiny effort of

breathing. Under this sky, in this silence a man felt — a man knew — possibilities infinite.

The Anderson house rose clean against the horizon. It was an old-fashioned house, its open front porch scalloped and furbelowed. A couple of chairs stood on the porch. High in one corner some small bird had nested.

A woman of perhaps thirty answered Ben's knock. "Good evening," he said. "You're not Mrs. Anderson?"

She had fair hair, cut rather short, and one of those fair faces so open as to suggest no underneath artifice.

"No. I'm sorry. It's Mother's night for auction." Her generous mouth was wide with a smile.

"Auction?"

"All right." Her voice was pleasant. "Auction bridge, then. Successor to five hundred. I'm Mattie Murchison."

"I see. I'm Ben Tate. I wanted to ask her about lodging and, possibly, board."

"Won't you sit down? I'll play Mother's little substitute." She motioned toward a chair and took one herself.

She wore a full skirt too long for flappers and a white blouse, and her step was more nearly a stride, an easy, free-flowing movement. A self-sufficient woman, he thought, a business type probably.

A car came to a stop in front of the house, and she said, "Well, I believe that's Mother now. What in Sam Hill?"

A figure emerged from the car and became a small, quick woman with gloves and a hat on. "I do declare," she said as she approached, "if I didn't forget my glasses."

"Mother! Again? I'll find them, but do meet Mr. Tate, Mr. Ben Tate."

"Hurry, then. I had to beg a ride. How do you do, Mr. Tate?"

She sat down as if briefly, a rather old woman dressed in a style certainly old except for a cloche hat fixed to her head with precision.

"I'm looking for lodging and perhaps a few meals, Mrs. Anderson," he said in the daughter's absence. "Rather permanent, I think. Mr. Greenwood advised me to try here."

"He must have liked you." Her small smile seemed to suggest that Mr. Greenwood's liking was sufficient for her. "It happens I have a room, one of those rare ones with a bath of its own. Of course it comes higher." Her eyes questioned him about that.

"Good."

Mrs. Murchison reappeared. "Here are your glasses, Mother."

"Thank you. And now what about meals, Mr. Tate? We serve breakfast at seven-thirty."

"That's fine. And just a couple of evening meals? Let me see. Not Wednesday or Thursday. First press run is Wednesday and paper day's Thursday, and I might have to work late. What about Tuesday and Saturday?"

"Oh, dear. Tuesday's my bridge night."

"What does it matter, Mother?" Mrs. Murchison put in. "We have to eat anyhow. Ferd expects his supper, and I'll be here right after work."

"I just didn't want to burden you. But all right. Let me figure, Mr. Tate. If the room pleases you, would you think it excessive if I asked fifteen dollars a week?"

"Not at all."

"Will you show him the room then, Mattie? I do have to run." She bustled up and, bustling, went to the waiting car.

"Call me Mattie," Mrs. Murchison said. "Our only other roomer and boarder won't bother you. Ferd Montjoy is his name. He keeps books."

"It's Ben then."

"Ben it is. Ferd's quite a gentleman. His only vice, I guess you could say, is panguingue."

"That sounds like a cardinal sin. What is it?"

"Pan for short. A glorified rummy game, as I understand, that runs into money. They play it ferociously at both of our fair city's pool halls. But come on. I'll show you the room."

Moving ahead of him, she took him upstairs, snapping light switches on as she went. She was, he thought, a bit angular — but angles could have their own grace, couldn't they? The downstairs, from what he had time to see of it, appeared well-furnished and tidy. The room was large and airy, equipped with a chiffonier, a long table, a straight and an easy chair, a double bed with a blue counterpane and, unexpectedly, a large bookcase awaiting his books. Three gay scatter rugs lay on the polished floor. A door to a small bathroom was open.

"Some people prefer an eastern exposure. But here," she said, standing before a large window, "you can look west toward the mountains."

"Yes."

"You'll be warm enough. Just last year, when the gas line was laid, we converted our coal furnace."

He said, "Yes," again.

"Ferd's room is across and down the hall, next door to the other bathroom. Mother and I live downstairs in the back. We won't bother you or you us. We won't even hear you. And the front door's never locked." She turned her head to look at him. "Well, Ben, what's the verdict?"

"What it has to be. Home again. Mattie, it's just right. The one question is: when may I move in?"

"Any time."

"Tomorrow, then?"

"Yes. Mother will be home all day. And later I'll be on hand to help if you need me, after I get through at the treasurer's office."

"Count it settled then."

She preceded him down the stairway, her loose-knit body moving with that swift freedom he'd noted before.

He took her hand before he left. It was a square, warm hand, appropriate to a face that must hold secrets because it appeared to hold none.

7

BEN LEANED FORWARD in his chair, set his elbows on the desk and let his head rest in his hands. Two weeks as a publisher, and he already felt old, and here it was Tuesday, a light day comparatively. Late afternoon, and he ought to get up, take his hat and walk to Mrs. Anderson's table, where company and food were equally good, if a man had the appetite for either. Or the will to move.

To prosper, a country newspaperman had to hustle at the expense of what he most wanted to do. Selling advertising, taking orders for job work and lending a hand in the shop, keeping books, collecting bills, meeting callers, jotting down personal items — these and a score of other chores stood in the way of good editorship. And, good Lord, the scrambled accounts Cleveland had bequeathed him! Night work in his room, where he had installed his portable typewriter, a stack of copy paper beside it? Sure, except for a little item called energy. He had had barely enough of it to take stabs at his reading.

There was nothing else for it: he would have to hire someone to assist in the office, someone with brains enough to answer the phone, take orders, write personals and make sense of the books.

But who? Yeah, who. Not one of the fussy old widows or busybody clubwomen who so loved good literature. Not a high-school student, no matter how promising, because of the hours demanded by classes. Not a man — he couldn't afford it. And not Mattie Murchison, whose job in the treasurer's office was better than the one he could offer.

But Mort Ewing might have an idea.

He roused himself to lift the phone and call the ranch. A surprisingly pleasant voice answered.

"Mrs. Ewing?"

"Yes."

"This is Ben Tate. May I speak to Mr. Ewing?"

"Oh, hello, Mr. Tate. Mort has talked about you. But he's in town on business. Possibly he's in the Club now, improving his appetite." The laugh was like the flutter of a wing.

He thanked her and hung up and then called the Anderson residence. Mattie answered.

"Sorry, Mattie," he said, "but don't count on me for dinner tonight. Business."

"And it gives beef roast and Yorkshire pudding and fresh apple pie. Shame on you."

"Mort Ewing's in town, and I want to see him."

"Oh, all right." She added, "Don't let it suggest anything, sir, but the stove has made me too hot to handle, anyway. It's Mother's bridge night, you know."

"I want to talk to you, too."

"Now?"

"You can be thinking about it. I need help in the office, probably female, someone to spare me at least part of the routine. Any ideas?"

"I'll put my mind to it."

Afterwards, he got up, put on his hat and went out, feeling better at the prospect of help. A couple of weeks more, and the season for sailor straws would have passed.

The day was cooling off now at six o'clock, and the shadows of the west-side buildings lay long on the street. Not a breath of breeze stirred the leaves of the flanking cottonwoods, but the air was new, recovered and buoyant after the afternoon heat. It was the hour to gaze at the sun-setting sky, if a man had the time.

Ewing was not at the club. Neither was anyone else, save for old Macalester Cleveland and his dog, the one drinking, the other drowsing. Cleveland said, "Hi, Ben. How's the veteran editor?"

"All right, Mr. Mack. Hope you are. Mort Ewing been in?"

"Not lately. I just got here myself. Have a drink."

"I guess not. Anyhow, I have my own bottle."

"Aw, come on and sit, goddamn it. Drink on me. I could howl like a coyote for lonesomeness."

Ben took a glass and water and sat down at Cleveland's table. "Mrs. Ewing said Mort would be in."

Cleveland poured into both glasses, his breath sounding from the small effort. "All newspapermen drink," he said. "To put it another way, the men who drink are the men who think."

"What would you say, after seeing two issues? Have I been thinking enough? Any suggestions?"

"Not exactly, Ben." Cleveland lit a cigar and blew smoke through his mustache.

"Not exactly?"

Cleveland heaved back, his vest open, his belly pouched over his vest. "You're doing well enough, better than I did at the last." His eyes went blank, considering the roll of the years, back to the young days of his newspapermaking. He might not have known he took another turn at his glass. "The facts of life," he said as if to himself. "They're not all romp."

"Not the birds and the bees and then the blissful bed, huh?"

"Forget it. Just let me get drunk. Tell me to shut up."

"All right, Mr. Mack, but forget what?"

"Forget it's adjustment, not divinity, that shapes our ends, Mr. Shakespeare."

He fell silent, his head back, his eyes on the ceiling, as if alone. His belly, rather than his chest, rose and fell with his breath.

When Ben spoke, it was just to rouse him. "A Mr. Stoneman called at the office today."

"Yeah?"

"Jerry Stoneman."

"Copper man. Representative of the Anaconda. Slick lobbyist."

"You know him then?"

"Who doesn't?"

"He seemed like a nice enough man."

"They're all nice guys, nicest on earth if you're nice to them. Mean sons of bitches."

"He made no bones about his connections."

Cleveland straightened now and drank to bring himself back to the present. "The company has its goddamn finger in every pie. Go against it, for instance, and you lose the county printing, without which you can't get along."

"Lose it how?"

"The company will see you're underbid. Besides, it will manage to take advertising away from you. And if you want financial help? Not likely. The banks are the company's friends. Hell of a note, Ben. We'll drink to it."

"And the people put up with it?"

"The fact is," Cleveland said, ignoring the question, "that a newspaper can't survive in Montana if it bucks the company. I ought to know. I tried it on the other slope."

"I asked about the people."

"The people, shit!"

Cleveland began growling low in his throat, the tired growl of failure. "No need to go on. Christ!"

"Don't then, if you don't want to, but I'm interested."

"Just remember, Ben, the company always confuses the issues. During the war it was patriotism, to cover honest labor troubles and fair taxation. Still is patriotism, if not as strong as before, but the enemy's not Germans or pro-Germans but socialists alias bolsheviks."

"I can't believe the people can be hoodwinked all the time."

"No? The company has a stable, state-wide, of retainers and favorites. Watch that pluperfect patriot, Earl Kilmer. I bet he's being groomed for the legislature."

Cleveland downed the last of his drink and got up to go. A sudden, embered anger showed in his old features. "The people voted Joe Dixon out of the governor's chair, thanks to Anaconda and the owned or bought or pressured help of damn near every big and scrawny newspaper in the state. I was on that shit list."

He took a step toward the lockers, the heel of whiskey in his hand, then turned and brandished his chewed cigar. "But don't you think, by God, I was too tame. I skated a thin edge from start to finish."

The embered anger died. The cigar went into a spittoon. "Old men talk too much. With me as an editor, Ben, it was go somewhere or nowhere. I wanted to go somewhere, if it was only to the bank with a deposit."

He put the bottle in a locker. "Grub's ready at my house. Come on, Bluster. Good luck, Ben." The old dog followed him out just as Mort Ewing came in.

"How, Ben," Ewing said. "I been reading the paper. Looks to me like you're tailing it up."

"Thanks."

"Have a drink."

"On me this time." Ben stepped to the locker and took out his unopened bottle, drew half-portions of water into glasses and followed Ewing to a table. "Mr. Mack has been singing the blues."

"So would you, under that tormentin' burden of booze."

"I'd say that's not all that torments him, but I wanted to talk to you about something else."

"Sing away."

"I need office help, part-time anyway. I'm thinking of a woman because, well, I doubt I could pay enough to attract a good man."

Ben had opened the bottle and now offered it to Ewing, who poured for them both and said, "Skoal."

"To the northland."

"Skoal. But don't fall on your spear."

Ben had time to think that this cow-country rancher must have read everything.

"You don't want some skitty filly?" Ewing asked.

"God help me, no."

"Someone educated and not broke down. You said part- or full-time?"

"Either one, I guess."

Ewing considered, then said in a drawl, "Well, from this distance I kind of think I see one critter in the corral."

"Take a closer look."

"Scared to, kind of, but, on inspection, it might hold some promise." Abruptly he added, "How about Mary Jess Collingsworth?"

"Good Lord, do you think there's a chance?" Ben asked, but already he was hearing that muted, musical voice answering the telephone, already seeing that grave, controlled girl handling visitors.

"Might be." Ewing put his glass to his lips and then went on. "She's well-educated and young, and she's living her life just for her dad and young brother, and Charlie's old enough now not to need a ma all the time." He broke off long enough to roll a cigarette and get it lighted. "It's this way, Ben, as you would find out in a little while anyhow. Mrs. Collingsworth — May, she was, and as fine a woman as you'll ever see — she died when Charlie was born. We took care of the baby, along with our own, and he's lived off and on with us ever since — that is, until Mary Jess got out of college and made a home for Prof and him. A good boy, Charlie. But it's time Mary Jess struck out more or less on her own. Not fair to her just to be housekeeper, and her young and unmarried."

"Would Mr. Collingsworth take kindly to the idea?"

Ewing examined his empty glass. "Is it thirty on the whiskey, Ben?"

"No, not to a man who talks newspaper talk," Ben answered as he passed the bottle.

"Now, assumin' you're agreeable, you want me to sound out Mary Jess and her dad?"

"Would you? I'm more than agreeable."

"Sure thing. Maybe tonight since I'm already in town. You goin' to be home?"

"Bound home in a few minutes."

"I'll report." Ewing took his drink in a gulp. "That's that, then. Now for the feedbag. Want to join me?"

"Thanks. I think I'll wait."

He waited only a few minutes after Ewing had gone, then got up and went out and walked home. He didn't have to eat supper. Good food for good thought was supper enough.

Mattie met him at the door. "Come on into the dining room. I've kept things warm, some things anyway. I just got back from taking Mother to her bridge club."

"You didn't have to think about me."

"No, but I did. Come on."

His place was set. She brought in a platter and bowls and sat opposite him and waited until he had taken the edge off the appetite he hadn't known he had. Between bites he kept looking up at her, at the fair, open face with eyes wide apart. Not a vulnerable face, surely, but one that seemed to share and reflect the undisclosed feelings of others.

"Well," she said, "did an idea come to you?"

"One came to Mort Ewing."

"Secret?"

"It's a maybe, a secret maybe so far. He suggested Mary Jess Collingsworth."

She sat silent for a moment, her fine eyes examining him. "Yes. She would do."

"Except?"

"Well, out with it, Ben. I suspect you're stuck on that girl. You've talked about her. I've seen you walking and talking to her after church. Is that the reason you go?"

"I was brought up that way."

"Fiddlededee, and coarser words to that effect. You're stuck on her."

"Thanks for telling me."

"I don't blame you. She's a lovely, if a cool and remote one."

"I have eyes."

"Sure you do, and what do they see? They see that look of pure innocence, of everlasting virtue, that every man wants to defile."

"Mattie!"

"To rectify, then."

"You know everything."

She gave him her wide-mouthed smile. "Not everything. Not the answer to this, for instance: how would romance go with the job?"

"I'll make my own matches, Mattie."

"Don't be cross. What makes you so cross?"

"Too much work."

"I suppose," she said, as if she didn't altogether agree. "But, Ben, I endorse the nomination. Ignore my misgivings."

"Thanks, Mattie, and thanks for keeping things warm." He watched her full-skirted stride as she returned the dishes to the kitchen. "If you'll excuse me, I have some typing to do."

But the typewriter balked, and a face and a figure kept floating over the print when he tried to read.

It was near midnight before Ewing called. "Get on your horse, Ben," he said.

8

"How about going to the Eversole auction?" Ben asked. "Take the afternoon off?"

"I haven't finished making out bills," Mary Jess said, "let alone done the posting." Papers and blanks and the account book before her, she was seated at the flat desk he had installed, thus crowding the office. Grave as always, competent as proven, direct of eye, he thought as he looked at her. Somehow someone sometime would add vivacity to her credentials.

"You forget it's Saturday, and afternoon at that. Okay can take care of the callers, if any."

"By the time we get there the auction will be over, or almost."

"No. Big stuff first. The crowd will stick around to see the pots and pans go."

She sighed, as if slightly vexed at leaving chores undone, and rose from her chair, her actions neat and controlled as he had learned to expect. "All right, I guess, if the boss says so."

"Just a minute, then." He ducked into the shop, where Okay Myers was methodically distributing type. "Can you watch the office, Okay?"

"I'll listen." The unsmiling face held a question.

A good man, Myers, if somewhat grouchy, a man destined to spend his life at type boxes, chases and presses until time tossed him into the hell box. To the unasked question Ben said, "Yes?"

"I been thinking. My oldest boy — he's twelve now — he could be helping out. Putting away leads and slugs, swamping out, melting and skimming off Linotype metal, and the like of that?"

The idea was good, though open to slight suspicion. Myers hadn't been given a chance to purchase the plant: now his disappointment, his view of himself, demanded this trifling concession.

Ben answered, "Sure. We'll fix it up. We can talk about pay later."

"No need to. After school, all day Saturday, Sunday if needed. I can teach him in off hours. Dollar a week is enough to start."

A good man, Myers.

Ben led Mary Jess to the Hupmobile. They rode east, toward the hill that rose to the bench. "You know the Eversoles?" Ben asked when they were under way.

"Slightly. Enough to feel sorry for them. He owns, or did own before the foreclosure, perhaps a thousand acres of land."

"That sounds like enough."

"But it's poor land, Father and Mort Ewing say, and it's not irrigated, as some of the benchland is. Also, you know the price of wheat. Fifteen years according to Father, and nothing earned besides callouses."

"All these foreclosures, all these auctions," he said.

"Look on the bright side," she answered, her gaze turned down. "They bring you legal notices and display advertising."

"I will be damned!"

"But solvent."

She ought to be told that, solvent, he could continue to be an employer. She ought to be told that a country beset by foreclosures and auctions was in a bad way. She ought to be told, she ought to know, that no decent man could rejoice if he survived by the wreckage of others. She ought to be told a lot of things. But one of them was not how to write.

They rode on silently, a wall between them, until he said, "Change of subject, but that coyote piece was simply beautiful, as I've told you before."

"Thank you, Ben."

"Beautiful," he repeated and thought about it. The piece, run as an editorial signed by her, had been prompted by the news that a federal hunter had been hired to put an end to the coyotes that roamed near the Breast River, a few miles north and west of the town. He had titled it "Coyote Song or Lamb Blat?" It was a sort of hymn to wilderness, to loneliness and the cry that came from it, and it included the point, in expert, accented prose, that sheep killings, blamed on coyotes, were as often or oftener than not the work of town and ranch dogs. The detection of a guilty dog two days after the paper came out had modified criticism.

"I expected more kicks than I got," he said. "Few from stockmen. The chief kicker was your Mr. Kilmer."

"Mine!"

"He and Hank Stutemeyer and Alvor Torgerson, and of them only Stutemeyer owns sheep, and it a small band."

"They're certainly not friends of ours. You may not know that Kilmer has vowed to get Father, to have him voted down by the board: they're your Legion friends."

"All right. I joined the Legion, but they're not buddies of mine. The Legion does do something. It can contribute more. I joined it to help."

"I would think an objective newspaperman should be on the outside looking in, not on the inside looking out."

"Two points of view," he answered. "You take yours, I'll take mine."

"Obviously."

A hell of a way to spend an otherwise pleasant afternoon, volleying a cactus with a pretty girl — no, a lovely and fetching one whose nature and name were cantankerous. He wanted to penetrate her — wrong word but, all right, right, too — to understand her and to be understood, to come to amiable terms that would lead to more than amiability, but here they were, as much at odds as a couple about to divorce.

He drove up the hill, not speaking, and saw the flatlands swimming to the shores of the sky, broken here and there by a house or barn and little huddles of despairing trees.

She said, "Would you mind turning off for a minute, ahead and there to the left?"

He took a dirt trail that branched from the gravel road. It brought them to a point of land overlooking the valley. The sun was beginning to slant down toward the mountains. Now, in late

September, after the snowy and unsettled weather of the equinox, it shone, not hot, but kindly, and it mellowed the fields, trees and town buildings below. With the car engine shut off, a great silence came, a great stillness, and it struck him that, if a pebble were dropped in the valley, quiet ripples would lap to the edges of sight and beyond.

After a silence she said, her eyes lost in looking, "Look, Ben. Just look."

He could see the canyon of the Breast River, purple with distance, and the meandering, tree-fringed flow of the stream, and the buttes and foothills that separated mountains and river, and it seemed to him that all bore the unchanging face of forever.

"Father, the tool of progress, remains half-antiquarian." Her voice came from far away, from whatever her eyes saw, with the muted music in it so much expected as sometimes not to be heard.

"There would be tepees in the big bend of the river," she went on, "and smoke rising straight from the smokeholes and the horse herd nearby and buffalo on the ridge to the south. And no one would foreclose or compel others to sell what little they had."

The singing, not-singing voice, the words painting pictures, the girl as far beyond reach as the times spoken of — they went together and together raised from the dust an unreal and sad hunger. He could see buffalo now and white lodges and wild grasses saluting the breeze, and a squaw, a certain squaw, in this free land welcoming her man to the tepee. She let him take her hand.

"But no telephones, though," he said to break his own spell. "No electric lights or power. No radios. No automobiles."

"But no ugly fences, no torn earth and no buying and selling and counting the cost or the profit."

"No newspapers."

"No newspapers, just smoke signals."

"That's a pretty fancy. Borrowed from Mr. Greenwood?"

"Call it a fancy, but don't say it's borrowed."

"I'll say it's unrealistic. We have to live in the now time. We must live in that time and work for the future."

"Whatever it is."

"I can hope it's a better way of life. I can pin my faith on that.

A better, more comfortable, more prosperous way. With prosperity people wouldn't have to sell out. This reaching for the past has its charms, but it's sentimental, not practical. You know that."

She said, "I wonder what practicality is."

"At least we know that progress doesn't reside in a tepee."

"Is its home in the bank?"

"Come off it, Mary Jess."

She stirred, drew her limp hand from his and shook her head, as if, he thought, to shake the subject out. She pointed ahead of them. "That little heap of rocks at the brow of the hill?"

"I see it."

"An Indian is buried there on the point, a half-Indian, a friend."

"Oh?"

"His name was Smoky Moreau. He was born too late for true and free tribal life, but from around dying council fires and talks with the old ones he learned what that once-life was."

"And followed it?"

"As best he could. He hunted and roamed and enjoyed himself, if he did, with the dead. Sometimes I think he thought the white men would all blow away. He certainly thought the homesteaders would, as some or many are doing. But he was a gentle man, a gentle, sad man."

"What happened to him?"

"He and Father used to get together. They went out, just the two of them, to stream and field and mountain. But they never talked much, not that I heard. It was as if they knew each other without speech. I guess you could say they had a communion of silence."

"What happened to him?"

"He died on the reservation. I don't know from what, but probably some white man's disease. Father gave the funeral oration, surrounded by full bloods with braided hair and skin britches. But Smoky wanted to be buried here." She made an encompassing gesture. "Here, where he could overlook the valley he knew and see his old visions." She paused and went on as if she were saying nothing strange, "Father often comes here to talk to him."

He didn't have an answer. He couldn't say that only people well along in years talked about the good old times. He couldn't question her about the oddities of her father. He started the engine, put the car in gear and turned around.

The auction was well along, attended by perhaps a hundred men and women together with children and conducted by a man named Baker, by custom referred to as "Colonel." In scatters and groups stood farm machinery, three horses, saddles and harnesses on sawbucks, furniture, and on tables the considerable, small miscellanies of housekeeping.

Frank Brobeck, half-listening to the auctioneer, said from the edge of the crowd, "Hi, Ben. Hi, Miss Collingsworth." A smile stretched the seams of his face.

"Buying, Frank?"

"A few tools. Nothing like an auction to get them dirt-cheap. Brought my old truck along in case I bought more, but some bids weren't dirt-cheap but high as a flagstaff."

Ben made way through the crowd for Mary Jess and himself. Mr. Collingsworth sat at a table, pen in hand, a journal before him. He often served as clerk at auctions and doubtless more often was asked to. People knew he was honest. He nodded to Mary Jess and Ben, the briefest of smiles touching his mouth.

Colonel Baker, flushed from whiskey, the sun or his work or all three, had his hand on a saddle horse. "Now, folks," he was saying, "soon as we get this here fine animal sold, we'll get to what you good ladies came for. Now here's a prize mare. Gentle as a dog and dog-smart to boot. A family horse, this is, right for the missus, the kids or the old man himself. Good with stock. Knows a cow's mind better than the cow its own self. What am I bid. Fifty? Fifty?"

The mare sold for forty dollars.

A couple stood at the back door of the house, a couple not old but bent and expressionless, as if years of effort, coming to naught, had brought them to the same place. Before he asked Mary Jess, Ben knew they were the Eversoles. She greeted them with a small wave of her hand, her lips moving in a smile of regret.

He turned and let his gaze travel over the furniture and, with her at his side, walked toward it.

"I hate this," she said, her tone pitched for his ears alone. "It's picking over their bones."

"But it has to be, Mary Jess. They need every cent they can scrape up."

"The rags and tags of living, of having lived. Just junk, and soon not even their own."

"Is it?" he asked and tried to check a growing enthusiasm. "Do you think it is?" He laid his hand on a chest.

Her eyes studied him and went to the chest. "It's been painted and repainted and painted again. Pitiful. Hardly worth the effort. I've seen a hundred like it."

He knew better. He took a knife from his pocket and scraped a patch bare at the far edge of the chest. "Cherry," he told her, "or I'm blind. A swell-front cherry chest."

"And is that so unusual?"

"It's better than good. And look at that stand table. Hepplewhite, or I don't know the first thing about styles. See those lovely, tapered legs."

He was talking outside of her knowledge. "They're antiques, Mary Jess," he tried to explain. "The real thing. Perhaps as much as a hundred years old, maybe older." He pulled out a drawer of the chest. "Look at the dovetailing. You won't see such work in modern furniture. We'll inquire."

He steered her back toward the Eversoles. "I'm Ben Tate. You are Mr. and Mrs. Eversole?"

The man nodded tardily, as if even his name might be gone. The woman stared through Ben and past him.

"I wonder if you could tell me something about the chest of drawers there and the table alongside?"

"They're there," Mr. Eversole said. "See for yourself."

"Yes. I was looking. You've had them for a long time?"

Now Mrs. Eversole spoke, her mouth twisted. "Too long. Should have ditched them — but no money for new things."

"You didn't get them in Montana?"

Mr. Eversole said, "They was handed down. Hand-me-downs, that's what they are."

"From where?"

"Tennessee or somewhere. That's where Effie's granddaddy came from."

"That's interesting."

"Maybe. Came by steamboat to Fort Benton. That's the story I git."

"You ask me," Mrs. Eversole said, "I wished many a time, while sloppin' paint on, they'd been pitched in the river."

"At least they have a story to tell."

Mr. Eversole turned and spit and said through a mouth that managed to turn up. "Yep. Sad story."

They left the two waiting impassively, hardly listening to the auctioneer's spiel. Two old people, Ben thought, two middle-aged people made old by event, by toil and soil and weather and the price that wheat brought.

"You don't like old things, Ben," Mary Jess said when they had drawn aside. "Progress, ho!"

"They don't make things like that anymore. I've hardly seen a decent stick of furniture in Montana. The best is bad, bulky Victorian. Simple explanation: family pieces went by the great waterways. Too clumsy for wagons, too heavy for ox teams."

"You might extend your admiration for old furniture."

"All right," he said, letting the words be stiff. "Call me inconsistent, eccentric, anything, but leave it at that."

They waited, wordless, until the auctioneer and the crowd came around, and the furniture was put up for bids.

Ben got the chest for eight dollars and the table for two—giveaways both, honest-to-God bargains, Ben thought, dismissing the stares of people who no doubt were wondering how soon he and Mary Jess would become housekeepers. Let them wonder.

He found Brobeck at his side and said to him, "Frank, you have room in your truck for what I just bought?"

"Why, sure, Ben. And where would you want them delivered?" His gaze went to Mary Jess, and mischief came into his eyes. "There?"

"Just drop them off in back of the shop."

Mr. and Mrs. Eversole were standing as before, except, Ben thought, that with each purchase it was as if a layer of themselves had been peeled. They would be left naked, in their hands money enough maybe to serve as fig leaves. Adam and Eve, about to be cast, wild and alone, from an unhappy garden. He saw Mrs. Eversole put a hand to her mouth as a highchair was sold. No tears, no open lamenting, just surrender to fact. And he had a swell-front and a Hepplewhite.

Without explanation he left Mary Jess and went to the Eversoles. The auctioneer and the crowd had moved a few yards away. "I didn't pay enough for the chest and the table," he said to the unrevealing faces.

"A deal's a deal," Eversole answered.

"And cheating is cheating. I'll give the pieces back or pay what I think is a fair price."

Eversole's eyes were cold. "Mister," he said, "I don't know what your game is, for I never seen the like of it. Like I say, a deal's a deal, and you can damn well get in your head that we ain't on charity yet. Understand!"

Ben turned away, to find Mary Jess right behind him. They walked to the Hupmobile.

Then she said, singing, a new look in her eyes, "Ben, I'm sorry."

9

MACALESTER CLEVELAND put the latest issue of the *Advocate* aside, took his watch from a vest pocket and flipped the lid open. Christ, not quite four o'clock, and Mag Egstrom frowned and went silent if he took off for the Club quite that early. Mag for Nag.

He picked up the paper again. That boy, Ben Tate, was doing all right. Last week he had published a comprehensive article on summer fallowing of dry land, which was pretty new in this section yet but by proof was far more profitable than seeding the same acreage season on season. Hope for Montana and the county in that. And here was an interview with that spokesman for the Bureau of Reclamation, which wanted to dam the Breast River and irrigate land otherwise unproductive except for what little in native grasses it grew. And Ben hadn't been satisfied with that statement alone. He'd consulted the state college, which said that the full fruits of irrigation couldn't be realized by the first generation of farmers. It took a second or a third before the uses of soil and the ways of water were learned. Small comfort for the first generation on the Medicine project, but hope for its sons.

Anyhow, the articles weren't just county-agent handouts or commercial-club crap. And it wasn't crap but a boost to the town and the paper that a J. C. Penney store soon would start operations. And it was true that better roads were sore-needed.

He could hear Mag fussing around in the kitchen, where, like as not, she was preparing Swedish meatballs or some other dish dear to the Scandinavian palate. A fussy, fat old lady. It was hard to believe that once, having employed her as housekeeper after his wife's death, he used to take her to bed. The very thought was enough to give a man the droops, if they weren't chronic already. Wasn't it some ancient Greek, grown old, who said to a joking question about his sex life, "Young man, every day I thank the gods for having delivered me from that savage and insatiable monster"? Huh. Well, huh.

Mag came to the door to ask, "Wouldn't you like some tea and cookies, Mack?" What she had left of hair was drawn back from her forehead, over a face that showed wear.

"No," he said as usual. Tardily he added, "Thanks."

"Why don't you turn on the radio?" she asked. She was always trying to delay his departure.

"Just because they've quit playing, 'Yes, We Have No Bananas'?"

She made a noise in her throat and retired.

There was always some damn pesky, well-meaning person around when a man grew too old for anything but the chair and a bottle. Always trying to temper his habits, to see his diet was wholesome, to keep him alive, when all he wanted was to spend what life he had left in any manner he chose. As if his occupying space meant a damn! Still, wasn't that his own way with the dog, nursing it along when it ought to be dead? The dog slept at the side of his chair, too far gone to whimper at the dream of a rabbit or perhaps to have dreams at all. He just slept and farted in sleep, making a stench against which a cigar was protection. That was the way of age, to drowse and break wind and not dream.

Cleveland got up and went to the wardrobe and got a bottle from the scuffed cowboy boot in which he had cached it. Empty, of course, as he knew it would be. Problem: how to dispose of the empty. He put it back in the boot, for the time being.

He sat down again and again looked at his watch. Still too early if he wanted to avoid Mag's displeasure.

He fiddled with the stack of magazines in the rack at his side. The *Saturday Evening Post*, *Harper's*, the *Nation*, the *American Mercury*. Except for the *Post*, they would put the dander up in the patriots — but that man, Mencken, knew how to flay boobs. So, in a different way, did Sinclair Lewis. A losing battle,

though. Too many boobs, too many heads with paralyzed cere-
brums.

He returned the magazines to the rack, lit a cigar and leaned
back. In sight on the dresser was a picture of his wife, his wife
long dead and a stranger to him now. He didn't know why he
kept it. The likeness stirred no dear memories. So time healed
all wounds, did it? And left only vacancy, a vague sense of loss
and the sore wish to care again. Even to care for Mag, the old
fool. She had been with him fifteen years, slept with him for five
or so and still concerned herself with his health. Once people had
talked, he knew, but there was a thing you could say in their favor.
For a while they conjectured, they gossiped, they professed to be
scandalized, but after a time they took an enduring illicit relationship as a matter of course. And when you grew too old for
sinning, they thought the relationship nice. All forgiven if ever
truly condemned.

He rose and drew on his hat. "Come on, you potlicker," he
said, nudging the dog with the toe of his shoe.

Mag heard him and came again to the door. "Oh, are you
going out?" she asked.

"Looks like it, doesn't it?"

"Well?"

"The good ladies of the Methodist church are giving a dinner,"
he said. "I just can't miss that."

"Your dinner will be ready at six-thirty. Please don't be late."

"Make it seven, Mag."

"Well, then," she said, reluctance in her voice. "But you're
not going out without an overcoat." She disappeared through the
door and came out with it. He heard that noise in her throat as
he walked outside.

His old Velie stood at the side of the street, parked crookedly, as
if he had been unsteady last night, forsooth. He lifted the dog inside, got in himself, started the engine and pulled away, not
changing gears. Low gear all the way. That was the gear for him,
low.

He parked by the drugstore and went in. Spence Green knew

what he wanted and handed it over. Only three dollars, kindness of old Doc Crabtree again. Outside, he helped the dog from the car, walked to the steps of the Club and went down, the dog slow at his slow heels.

The Club was deserted. He took a glass and water and sat down at his accustomed place. The dog dropped at his place and fell asleep. The first drink of the day had to be a jolt. A jolt, yes. That was the medicine. Nerve medicine. A man got so he had to drink for his nerves, among other good reasons.

What the hell had he told young Ben Tate not so long ago? How to run a newspaper, huh? Big joke. He downed the jolt and poured a bartender's drink. All those years, the good years. When he met Saint Peter, assuming the old boy still guarded the assumed portals, he would have to say, "Pete, old pard, I did my best," and Pete would answer, "No room for liars, Mack."

"But, in the name of your boss, Pete, there were mitigations."

"We call them excuses."

"You're a hard man."

"Saints don't get there by compromise. We've no room for slackers, either."

"No one but a fool ever called me a slacker."

"Defined as one who has not made the most of what he's been given. In short, life's malingerers. Sorry."

"All right. I'll go to hell and have a drink."

Then, if Saint Peter were a decent son of a bitch, as not all his certified residents were, he would say, "Hold it, Mack. Slow day today. I'll lock the joint up and have a shot with you."

The conversation was interrupted by the entrance of Doc Crabtree, Hank Stutemeyer, and Earl Kilmer, who could be relied on to show up at about this time of day.

Doc Crabtree said, "Hi, Mack. How's retirement?" The others gave their hellos.

"Looking up, last few minutes."

The door came open again and admitted Peter Sears, who looked satisfied with the day's department-store sales. He gave a bright, "How you, gang?"

"You want to pile cirrhosis on top of Bright's disease?" Doc Crabtree asked Cleveland.

Sears took a seat and sipped at his whiskey.

"Why not?" Cleveland answered. "It's a way of euthanasia."

"Hardly a pleasant one, but it's your choice, old friend."

"Me," Earl Kilmer said, "I wish you were still at the helm of the paper." It was as if dedication had purified his face, removing the wrinkles and warts of uncertainty.

"Me, too," Stutemeyer said. He was a rangy galoot with no back to his head. Don't beware the lean and hungry look, Caesar. Beware the want of occiput.

"Young Tate's doing all right," Cleveland said. "More news in the paper now."

"I thought that piece about the dam and irrigation was good," Sears broke in to say. He was safe enough in so saying. Otherwise he wouldn't have spoken. Businessmen had to fight shy of controversy.

"That crap about coyotes written by the Collingsworth girl," Stutemeyer said.

"Yeah." It was Kilmer speaking. "She ought to be called the coyote girl."

"Didn't you beau her around for a while?" Cleveland asked.

"I had just a couple of dates with her. Come to find out I couldn't stand her."

"That's the way it was?" Cleveland said, not quite asking.

"That's the way it was."

"Thanks for telling us."

"I said that's the way it was. What do you expect of a Collingsworth?"

"Honesty."

"Shit!" The blood rose in Kilmer's face. Cleveland imagined that if Kilmer had any expression other than that of carved consecration he would have worn it. "Screwy honesty, if you can say that much for it. Tate will learn better, I hope. Right now he turns down most of the news the Legion gives him."

"Let the Legion do something. He'll report it."

Kilmer seemed to consider before he asked, "Just what do you mean by that?"

"I've seen some of your so-called news. I even ran some of it, but only to fill up the page and keep you off my neck." Cleveland poured himself another drink and saw that his hand was steady. "You want the *Advocate* to reprint the witch-hunting stuff you read in the rags you subscribe to. As a professional man you ought to know it's not news."

Doc Crabtree got in, "Dickens says the law is an ass."

Kilmer ignored the remark, saying to Cleveland, "I never heard you talk this way before."

"Never did, before I signed my declaration of independence."

Kilmer fixed him with his eye. "Independence of what?"

"Of corsets. Of corsets and stays," Cleveland answered and felt so pleased with his impromptu reply that he decided to embroider it. He took a breath, feeling most of it go to his belt level. Age made for short-windedness. "Never told you before, but I was born in Russia. Great friend of young Tzar Nicholas. Used to skate with him. That was before the revolution, of course."

"Funny, funny. And then you helped overthrow him, I suppose?"

"Sure. My real sympathy was with the masses."

"Quit it! Goddamn it, Cleveland, you're just leading me on." The tone of the orator came into his voice. "You know I stand for a loyal and enduring America, for my country and tried and true principles, just as you do."

Cleveland looked at Kilmer, knowing he could never penetrate that dedicated, casehardened skull. "Strange to say," he said, "I do."

"Then let up on that pink stuff. Quit talking that fake bolshevik talk."

Cleveland got up slowly, somehow feeling both tranquil and sour. He said to Crabtree, "Let's move to another table, Doc. I just can't seem to piss red, white and blue."

10

THE WIND WAS BLOWING, so hard that a man, driving, kept having to fight it. Firm hand on the tiller against the push of the tide, quick hand against the blind, rocking waves.

It was cold, too, as cold, an old-timer had said, as a western wind ever got. The cold squeezed in through door frames and drove up from the floor. No frost on the windshield, though, not in this dry, speeding air. The wind swept tumbleweeds over the road. The weeds charged the car, clawing for entrance.

Ben glanced at Mattie and said, "I feel like a tumbleweed myself."

"It's not far now."

True daughter of Montana, he thought, heir to the spirit that disregarded the weather. As she had come to the car, dressed rather lightly, weather considered, the wind had attacked her, blowing her hair wild, clamping her clothes against the hollows and curves of her body, and, with the close of the door, she had laughed as if somehow exultant. She sat beside him now, a robe over her lap and knees, as serene as the weather was not.

True daughter of Montana. No matter some grumbling, what was storm but a change of the seasons, to be expected and stood against? What was distance? Montanans climbed in their cars and took off, sure of themselves though arrival might be unsure. Freighters, wagon drivers, horse riders at heart if unknowingly, they regarded machines as old ones had regarded their animals. All distances could be tackled, all weather challenged, even if sheepherders had been known to perish in blizzards. Good men, they stayed with the sheep, didn't they?

They were on the bench now, and the valley lay down from them to the left, the windswept valley, barren of the last leaf. The wild tan grasses ran with the wind. Beyond the mountains white wind clouds, unmoving themselves, sent their wild forces, like headquarters generals. But below were houses that stood fast and people not prey to dismay.

The bench streamed with weeds and dust from the fallow fields scattered in plots forsaken and ugly. It was hard to believe they would be reborn ever and stand rich with green and ripening grain.

"Your mother will blow away, walking to the Collingsworths'," he said.

"Don't worry about Mother. She won't be worried herself. Right now she's probably writing a composed little note, telling Ferd Montjoy how to warm up the stew. It's not so far anyhow, and she may get a ride." Mattie pointed ahead. "Turn right at the next corner, Ben."

The turn put the wind behind them, and the car rolled at low throttle.

"Who all's going to be there?" he asked.

"In addition to us, I would imagine the Ewings."

"Mary Jess didn't tell me."

He could see Mary Jess again, standing there in the office, a seeming diffidence in her manner as she asked him to dinner.

"Why, thanks. Of course," he had said.

"I wanted to ask you first."

"You have. I accept."

"What about Tuesday, then? Wednesday and Thursday are our busy days. Friday or Saturday hardly suit Father. And —"

"Tuesday's fine."

"And since I work just half time —" Her grave eyes completed the question.

"Half-time pay. Full-time work. I'm going to see about that. Oh, you want Tuesday off?"

"Just the afternoon."

"Take the whole day."

"Maybe. And do you suppose you could run out and get Mr. Greenwood?"

"Glad to. With you?"

"The cook will be busy." She added without inflection or change of expression, "Why don't you ask Mattie Murchison, Ben, if it happens that the date suits everybody? She knows the way, and she'll be invited, she and her mother."

So, he thought, if you can't have first choice, take second. Arguments both ways. The first was challenge, dreamed destination glimpsed from afar. The second was comfort, was ease. Toss a coin and look to see if it didn't come up Mary Jess.

"Turn right again," Mattie said. "You can see the place, there, with the trees."

"Good ranch?"

"Yes, but call it a farm. It's irrigated. Mr. Greenwood rents it out, on shares I imagine, but lives in the house along with the couple that rent it. She cooks and watches out for him."

Ben braked to a halt in front of the house. A fading green, it had a front porch and small windows covered by storm sashes. A couple of cottonwoods and a tangled growth of willows, bare now and wind-bent, adorned the grounds. A solitary cow, brooding on the hard ways of nature, looked out of a barn door to the side and rear of the house. Chickens, if any, must have been blown to Dakota.

"You stay here and keep warm," Ben told Mattie. He opened the car door, careful lest the wind snatch it out of his hand and tear it loose from its hinges. He had to wrestle it closed.

Mr. Greenwood met him at the door, a stooped figure in a long coat and a cap with ear flaps pulled down. The coat might have fit him before the years shrank him. He pulled off a mitten to shake hands. The hand seemed as fragile as ash. "Brother Tate," he said, his voice sounding small in the wind. "How good of you to come for me." The old eyes slitted for better sight. "And who's that in the car? Oh, Mattie, dear Mattie."

Ben took hold of his arm. If he lost his grip on it, he thought as they leaned into the wind, Mr. Greenwood would soar like a discarded page of the *Advocate* or roll like a tumbleweed. To shield him, Ben stepped a bit to the front, still holding his arm.

On the way back to town, with three in the seat, Mattie was pressed close to him. He could feel the length of her upper arm and the touch of her thigh. It would be rudeness to inch away.

◆

Mary Jess opened the stove door. The three stuffed chickens were browning well. She basted them. Potatoes still to be mashed, molded salad, chocolate pie and whipped cream in the new electric icebox, peas in the pan to be heated, sweet potatoes baking, rolls ready for the oven, and oh, yes, the scalloped oysters, first of the season.

Above the renewed hum of the refrigerator the wind sounded outside, musical or fearsome according to mood. Through the window the caragana hedge in the rear of the house looked forlorn, as if ready to lie down at last and let the wind have its will, and far beyond it rose Elephant Ear Butte, the indomitable upthrust, penetrator of the whipped sky.

But the wood range had quit smoking and burned with a steady heat now. Thank heavens for two ovens, the just-bought natural-gas one and the other in the old range that had been kept as accessory and, more important, as heater of the kitchen in winter in a house minus a furnace.

She was getting some dirty utensils out of the way when her father came from the living room. "Anything I can do, dear?" he asked, his small smile admitting there wasn't.

"Nothing, Father. The table's all set, and I'll have the food ready on time. You might see about the stoves, though, and be prepared to meet company."

Poor, helpless Father. Moody, difficult, pitiful Father, largely withdrawn and solitary except in the presence of special company. Never quite the same, confirmed and advanced in retreat, since Mother had died bringing Charles into the world.

The wind, it was always the wild wind that sang Mother's last cries. "You take good care of your father, dear," and "Oh, Benton, whatever will you do?"

A fine time to be heeding the wind, when she had to be composed, to make sure all was just right. A fine time to be thinking about pregnancy and the death that resulted. Both acts of nature. Acts of nature nothing. You didn't have to. No one commanded that you enter the valley of the shadow. For any reason, all right, fear included, a woman could say, "Not for me."

She tested the boiling potatoes. Not ready quite yet.

It was Father's idea. It was Father's party. And if Ben Tate came to think she had suggested his name, he would learn better. It had been a mistake even to go to the auction with him. Men imagined too much. People were too quick to make matches.

Ben Tate and Mattie and Mrs. Anderson, and the Ewings, as well as old Mr. Greenwood — they'd be arriving before long. She would put them out of her mind, all of them, each and every one of them, while she concentrated on cooking, while she scorned the wind that tried in vain to thrust in. Soon enough Ben would find she was his employee and no more than that.

She put her hand to her head. It must be the damned moon, her damned time of the damned moon. Pardon, Father.

As she put the rolls in the oven, the doorbell rang and bright and hearty voices rose in helloes and how-are-yous, louder than refrigerator and wind. Mattie breezed into the kitchen. "Hi, Mary Jess. Where's an apron? Tell me where I can lend a hand."

A blowy girl, Mary Jess thought, a generous, outward girl who might have been carried in by the wind.

"Mattie, thanks. Everything's about done."

She felt Mattie's eyes on her. She felt Mattie's hand on her arm. "Why, Mary Jess," Mattie said, "no cause to get rattled about a little old meal."

◆

Ben found himself seated between Mort and Mrs. Ewing — Julie, everyone seemed to call her. Mr. Collingsworth sat at the

faith, renounced old values. I don't defend fundamentalism by any means. But I do think religion is important, and it's losing out."

Mr. Greenwood put in, "Perhaps because the real truths of Jesus have been misinterpreted, ignored and distorted."

"Look at our young people." Mr. Collingsworth shook his head. "They all chew gum," he said, as if that practice were condemnation enough. "In public or private they chew it, but not in my classrooms, you can be sure."

"Give me a good chaw of tobacco anytime," Ewing said.

"Now, Mort." It was Mrs. Ewing who spoke. "Don't make light of it."

Mattie and Mary Jess were smiling at Mort.

A grin touched Mr. Collingsworth's mouth and disappeared.

"Soon enough, youth will change," Mr. Greenwood said, as if, reaching to the limit of memory, he could recall he was young once.

"They'll live through it, I suppose," Mr. Collingsworth said, "but will the rest of us? Rolled stockings, bare knees, face paint and bobbed hair."

"Oh, Mr. Collingsworth," Julie Ewing said, pretending outrage, "you can't say you disapprove of shorter hair. I had my own cut."

"Yep," Ewing said, his smile warm, "woman's crowning glory got itself docked."

"To your everlasting mortification."

"Yep, again. Haven't showed my face since."

"At least," Mattie said, speaking almost for the first time and shaking hair that fell well short of her neck line, "I had no one to mortify, not even Mother, who's thinking she might do the same thing. It does save a lot of bother."

Mrs. Anderson accompanied her nod with, "It seems to make sense."

"I've been thinking —" Mary Jess said and looked at her father and let the sentence die. Her hair was coiled, beautifully, Ben thought, at the back of her head.

He studied the two girls when they weren't looking. If either had used lipstick or rouge, it was so little as merely to enhance, not travesty, nature. Probably, for Mary Jess, the stove had brought color enough to her face. Largely silent, a little flushed, she was something to see and to think about. He sensed Mattie's eyes were on him and glanced away.

"Ben," Mattie said, catching the table's attention, "you've hardly said a word. Now what's your opinion, about short skirts and short hair and makeup and all that? Do you approve or not? Speak out, boy."

Their scrutiny, their waiting, pressed on him. "I like a bit of decorum," he managed to get out. "Quite a bit." He cast around in his mind for something more. "As for the rest, well, I heard about a man who went to one of those psychoanalysts, and the psychoanalyst said, 'If I'm right, your trouble is that you can't make up your mind. Is that so?' And the patient answered, 'Well, yes and no.' "

They were laughing when Mr. Greenwood broke in to say, as if his words were germane, "I believe in saying yes to life. Right, Brother Ewing?"

"Sure. It will give you a crop of some sort. Noes don't germinate."

"What exasperates me most of all," Mr. Collingsworth said, as though unwilling to let go of the subject he had brought up, "what is really irritating is not just the abandonment of good taste and good manners. It is the assumption of superior wisdom by the young. They know everything. No use to tell them that wisdom comes from hard thought and long experience. New knowledge, new insights, as well as discards and enforcements of old ways, they don't burst forth. They're not miraculous. They are the fruit of the years."

Mr. Greenwood said quietly, "There was Jesus."

No one answered. No one spoke at all. It was as if a hand had been clamped over discussion.

Mattie broke the silence, her gaze on Ben. "What were you about to say?"

"Nothing at all."

"But you were. I could see it. After Mr. Greenwood hushed us, I could see it."

"Nothing original. It's been said before."

Mary Jess's fine eyes came to him. "Can't you quote it?"

"All right. I forget the author, but he wrote, 'Nothing is so fatal to conversation as an authoritative utterance.' "

For an instant they seemed to think, and then they laughed, all of them except Mr. Collingsworth. That grin that transformed him, that changed his expression from sober to merry, came on his face. He said, "Good boy."

After they had finished dessert and the men, save Mr. Greenwood, had smoked in the living room while the women did up the dishes, Mrs. Anderson said, "I do hope you'll excuse me. I mustn't be late for my bridge club." She looked toward Mattie and Ben.

"Of course, Mother. And Mr. Greenwood —"

"We'll drop him off," Ewing said. "It's no more'n two lopes away. Besides, I want to convert him." He turned to Mrs. Ewing. "And besides that, it's time we got back to the ranch, hopin' Charlie and young Mort haven't burned down the house."

"That would be kind of you, Brother Ewing," Mr. Greenwood said.

They gave their thanks then and made more excuses, and Ben went along with Ewing to help old Mr. Greenwood into the Reo.

The wind was a little less fierce. Taking Mattie and Mrs. Anderson to the car, Ben looked back and saw Mary Jess, framed in light, at the porch door.

Mattie said, tugging, "Come along, Romeo."

11

BEN BRAKED his car in front of the Anderson house.

"Aren't you coming in?" Mattie asked before getting out.

"It's only a little after eight o'clock. Too early for me tonight."

"There ought to be a club for women," she said.

He felt obliged to ask, "Do you want to ride around for a while?"

"Thanks, no, Ben."

He took her to the door, their heads turned away from the wind, and, back in the car, set off for the center of town. But nix on a visit to the Club. There'd be only talk there and a couple of drinks that would blur or distort the paths of memory and wish. And nix on the picture show, where he would see Jack Holt or Ken Maynard in something foreign to fact as well as counter to mood. Besides, it was too late for the opening scenes.

Just drive around. Drive by the Collingsworth house and see a shadow in a lighted frame, hear the remembered voice. Drive around, while imagination bloomed. A man had a right to be foolish, if dreams and desire were foolish.

The wind had renewed itself, if from harsh to harsher could be termed renewal. He felt its pushing hands on the Hupmobile and welcomed its strength as he defied it. In a certain mood a man was glad of contest. In the west a full moon declined, shining bright and brave through the wind, and he found himself humming a new song, "Does your mother know you're out, Cecilia?" Cecilia was in, casting brief shadows against the blind of a lighted window. She was in and sheltered from storm, free of all but its cry.

He turned around and drove back and saw old Mr. Mack and

his dog, who might make it down the steps to the Club. Mr. Mack had a package, a fresh bottle, no doubt, in one hand.

He stopped in front of Billie Gayle's place and for a moment sat motionless, letting himself feel the good cold. He went in and asked for cigarettes and a near beer. No other customers, not in this weather.

"Wind's fierce," he said to the misshapen face. He and Billie had come to good terms.

"You learn to live with it, Ben." The mouth had to take time with the words.

Yes, to live with it, to live regardless.

"Hard to manage against it," Ben said, not wanting to put the bald question.

"No trouble, Ben. Living upstairs, I just have to make it from my outside door to the next." The eyes in the crooked face were straight eyes, gentle but not wishful of help or of pity.

Ben answered, "Fine," stubbed his cigarette and gulped his beer. "I'll see you, Billie."

A drive, a cigarette, an approach to beer — and there was nothing else for him but home and bed. The post office, though. He walked to it in the wind, expecting nothing much except perhaps something locally posted, and found nothing.

The house seemed empty when he entered, though Mattie would be somewhere around, perhaps preparing for bed or already in it. He went upstairs quietly.

A bath and then a book, he thought. Work could wait till tomorrow. Bathed and dried, he put on pajamas and looked for something to read. Novel or not? Fiction or exposition? Nothing very new in his little collection of books. William Dean Howells? No. Walter Hines Page? No. Floyd Dell, the moon calf? No. Not Sinclair Lewis tonight, either. But here was John Burroughs, kin to Thoreau. Here was *The Summit of the Years*, which was good on rereading.

In bed, he was just starting the book, savoring, "The longer I live the more my mind dwells on the beauty and the wonder of the world," when a bare rap came at the door.

He sat up and said, "Come in." What could Ferd Montjoy, the dried-up bookkeeper and pan player, be wanting?

The door opened quietly, revealing Mattie clothed in a dressing gown.

"What's wrong, Mattie?"

"Me." She hesitated and then asked with a directness he had learned to expect, "Do you want to turn off the light and move over?"

He looked at her, seeing the frank eyes and wide mouth — the girl without secrets.

"Don't gasp. You have the right to refuse," she said softly.

He was numb, all of him but the rising eagerness under the blanket. It commanded him to turn off the light.

For an instant, in the filtered moonlight, he saw her naked, the gown dropped, saw her naked, slim-waisted, fruitful-hipped, proud-breasted, the breasts somehow pitiful, enough to make the heart ache.

No time for more talk. No time but for one thing. He felt the warmth of her, the dear femininity, and kissed her and mounted. It had been so long. One thrust, three, half-a-dozen — and it burst in his mind as he was about to burst that people so blessed by sensation could ask nothing more. Let the climax of dying come with the climax of love. Like this. Like this. And then it was fading to after-beats, to cherished remembrances.

For long minutes afterwards she lay next to him, her head on his arm, her breath in the hollow of his throat. The wind sang outside, the great, wild, seeking wind. And here, safe and completed, they rested.

She said then, "I'm not promiscuous, Ben." She might have been talking to the room, to the moonlight.

"A few things I do know. That's one. Another is that I don't want you to get that reputation. Aren't we taking a chance now?"

"Mother will call me when she's ready to come home. Ferd will play pan until midnight at least. So it's just us, and you won't talk. Not you, Ben Tate. Your reputation counts, too."

"At any rate I won't talk, except to rejoice to myself."

"I've had plenty of opportunities, if you can call them that," she said. "Earl Kilmer and Ferd have been trying for years."

"Kilmer's married."

"Of course, you innocent. Loyal to one flag and the whole world of females. I refuse to be infiltrated by divided loyalty." Her small laugh sounded wry.

"And Ferd?"

"He would have entered it on his books under profit or loss, probably both for the sake of his balance sheet."

"I'm the lucky one, then?"

"I had a good man once, Ben," she said. "The only man, until you, who's ever known me. He was a wonderful, thoughtful, kind husband, and he died in the service but not in combat. The damn flu killed him. That hellish flu."

"I'm sorry, but you haven't explained about me."

"You're a good man, too, Ben. That's why I came to you, a hussy in the night. But let's have one thing understood: I don't love you, and you don't love me. Right now I'm your girl of the evening, but I'm not your girl. If you asked me to marry you, thinking to play the gentleman, I would say never. Even if you imagined you loved me, the answer would still be the same."

"You don't mean just this one time, this one time tonight, and never again?"

"I didn't say that. Biology is insistent."

"The old animal impulse."

"Don't make it cheap. Say it's impulse directed by discrimination. We're friends in need, no more and no less than that. Call us prey to biology, but wary and selective prey. Careful, too, of getting our emotions involved."

He put up a hand and stroked her hair back from her forehead. She had a good brow. "All right, Mattie. Not love, but certainly liking."

She was such a nice girl, and nice girls came to a man only in dreams, girls somehow wonderfully innocent of commandments and warnings. The avowed code removed and elevated the sex, so that a man might think girls occupied a separate world and spoke a language different and esoteric. How often in uneasy sleep had he sought the good but compassionate girl who recognized and relieved his torment! And how seldom had he found her, catching at the last only the far flutter of a skirt!

She stirred and said, "You haven't had much experience with women, Ben. Isn't that so?"

"Some."

"I would have thought those French girls —"

"I pretty well shied away from them."

"Afraid of women or of disease?"

"Both, I guess. Hell, I was a victim of Methodist morality. Still am, I suppose. Anyhow, I don't like bought sex, and a trip to a prophylactic station was enough to chill me."

She patted his chest. "Ben, you don't know a damn thing about making love."

"I'm ready to try again."

"Not yet." She was silent for a minute. "I hate to think how many marriages are spoiled by the men."

"How do you know?"

"I hear the girls talking. They do talk, you know."

"And tell the truth?"

"Oh, women are liars, one to another, but I'm sure some of the truth is there. To a lot of them sex is a bore or worse. One told me — and I believe her — that she thought out her grocery list while submitting."

"Why fault the men? I hear plenty of women are frigid."

"Mostly the result of men's ignorance, young men's in particular. Or of their indifference. One thing for sure, Ben, if you and Mary Jess are to be happily married, you have to learn a few things."

"I can't even date her. Talk about marriage!"

"Don't get on the prod. You'll be married."

"So teach me."

"Sure, dummy," she said in a voice that took away any sting. "Write it in your skull that a woman is not just a railroad station, where you get on and get off."

"Play on words there."

"Smart boy. Men are all for satisfying themselves. If a wife happens to find enjoyment, I suppose there wouldn't be any objection, though that's not the point of the exercise. True of you just a while ago, too."

"I'm afraid you're right. I took your reaction for granted, anyhow. But go on."

"Oh, hell, Ben, it sounds so damn clinical. It'll forever cool you towards me."

"Let's see."

"Did you know that suckling a baby gives a mother a sensual pleasure next door to sex or even closer?"

"You've never had a baby. Oh, good God, Mattie, I never thought. I didn't take any precautions. Did you?"

"Don't jump out of bed and run. I'm not planning to trap you. I can't have a baby. I'm barren. Two doctors have said so, to the disappointment of my poor husband and me."

He didn't mean to sigh. He couldn't say it was too bad, not now. He said, "Back to my instruction then, Mattie."

"I just told you a mother gets a sensual pleasure from suckling her baby."

"And I was about to ask how did you know."

She held up her answer and then said quietly, "It doesn't have to be a baby, Ben."

"I see," he said, wondering about what he did see.

"And you don't exactly abandon yourself when you kiss."

"Shall I practice?"

"Listen, instead. A woman needs preliminaries. She's not as fast as a man. Damn again to this clinical stuff, but you won't learn it from preachers."

"I learned enough there. Sex is nasty to them, except that they always seem to have plenty of kids. Hell, I was reared that way. Sex is nasty."

"You'll think it nastier yet, what I have to tell you."

"Tell me and see, teacher."

"The teacher says a woman has a little, inside thing. Here, give me your hand. For goodness' sake, it's not perversion."

He gave her his hand.

"There," she said, guiding a finger. "There. Now gently, gently. Remember what else."

Of a sudden she clutched him and pulled him over to her spread thighs and steered him home and, thrust and thrust, and her body arched to him, and heels and hands pulled him deeper, and throat sounds came from her panting mouth.

And then it was over, and she said, "There, Ben."

"Yes," he said. "Yes and yes."

They rested, wordless, until she said, "Now I must get dressed and be ready to go get Mother."

"Want me to go along? Be glad to."

"Then I might be known as your girl, if not something more."

In the moonlight he watched her put on her robe, saw her cover the brave breasts, the slim waist, the pelvis over the shadowed triangle where he had just been. "See you, Ben," she said as she closed the door.

He asked, "Next Tuesday?" knowing she couldn't hear.

He lay, listening to the wind, whither it bloweth, and it blew in Mary Jess.

Bird in the hand. Bird in the bush.

12

IN THESE DAYS just before Christmas it was cold, so cold that in windswept places the snow cried under heel like dormant life stepped on and, where drifted, crunched under foot. The air, if unstrained by cloth, bit at the lungs. The migrating geese had honked south long since, and a man walking bundled up along the shore of the Breast saw only stray magpies, stray chickadees and perhaps a horned owl, all of them hunched and forlorn as if, in short lifetimes, spring was too distant for hope.

Ben walked in his heavy coat, overshoes, ear-flapped cap and gloves inside mittens, his nose and mouth covered with a muffler that froze with his breath. A cold time but a good one, he thought. A man rose to the weather. In it he proved his leather. Sunday, the day of rest, and the far sun shone, companioned by sundogs, and dazzled the eyes, and God looked on His work and called it good.

What would Thoreau have said? Or Walt Whitman? Men of an older, gentler clime, as a poet had written? The westward-looking men, the westward-yearning, doomed never to see the West? Would their prose have been finer had they known it, their songs more full-throated? The answer had to be yes. Yes to the cold, yes to the far sky, yes to the solitary owl and to the numbed thicket and yes to the man alone.

A good time, this, and a right day to rest, if walking were resting. The days in the office had merged into nights, and the office more often than not had led to the shop, where job work, private and county, had swamped Okay Myers. Stationery, business cards, invitations, dodgers for this and that, admission and membership tickets and official forms for the sheriff and clerk — all these and more and the business of setting advertising and news type for the paper had been too much for one man, even with the limited help of a printer's devil who happened to be his son.

But thank the Lord for business, Ben thought, walking on. Thanks for job work and increased advertising. And thanks that he knew where to hang his own hat in a shop, how to set type by machine or hand, how to justify a page, how to operate presses. Hard on the hands but nice to the purse.

A little bunch of mallards, seeing him, flew up and away from a short stretch of open water where the Breast proved there was life in it yet. Greenheads among them, maybe all greenheads, arrayed in advance for their spring courting. He watched them circle against the blued sky and moved away and saw them start to wing back. A long wait until mating if they only knew, but nature, knowing, could wait and prepare.

Nature could wait — with assistance on Tuesday nights. The assistance had become custom and a matter of almost week-long expectation, canceled just once by the regularity of Mattie's rhythm. Tuesday was just two nights away.

No good to think of that now. Think of the paper. Think of Mary Jess, promoted to full-time as she should have been earlier. With her help he was finding enough copy to fill up the news space and didn't have to plug holes with syndicate boiler plate. In time he could hope to discard another crutch — newspaper stock preprinted on one side and supplied free or almost because the supplier pocketed the national-advertising returns. Some good historical stuff in those pages, though.

No, he told himself, don't think about Mary Jess. Put her out of mind. A man moonstruck was just half a man, reduced in independence and purpose. But she insisted on intrusion. She was at a dance she had let him take her to, graceful and female in spite of a shapeless, low-waisted dress, duplicate of those other young women wore, as if contours were deformities. She sat next to him at a picture show. She was across from him at Eva Fox's table. She let him feel the bare touch of her lips in their quick good-nights. Competent, even gifted, she was working with him in the same office, as near as the next desk and as far away as the edge of the world.

He shook his head against remembrance and daydream. He would go home now and shed his rough clothes and go out to eat, by wheel if his car would start, by foot if it wouldn't. The cluster of town a mile distant looked huddled, too, like the birds. Less than a mile, and a jack rabbit leaped up and loped off, a patch of snow moving on the unmoving snow. It could have stayed safe under its tangle of cinquefoil.

Mattie met him at the door, on her face such an expression of strain that he said, "What?" before she could speak.

"Will your car start?"

"I can see. Why?"

"Please do. It's for Mother."

He stepped inside and slammed the door against the cold clouding in. "Your mother?"

"Not her. It's Mr. Greenwood. He's dead."

"Dead? I don't see —"

"Found dead. By Mrs. Broquist. Nels drove a buggy to town. His phone wouldn't work. Car either."

"Wait, Mattie. Does Lawrence Chiles know, and Doc Crabtree?"

"They're on the way in an ambulance."

"Then your mother —?" He let the question hang.

"She insists on going out there." She moved to him and took his arms in her hands, her face upturned. "She's one of his oldest friends. Please, Ben. She has old ideas."

"Not to the point of laying him out?"

"Not quite. She thinks he would want company now. She'll pick out his burial clothes."

"Where is she?"

"Getting ready. She's bound to go somehow."

"Watch to see if the car starts. You'll need blankets, your mother and you."

The sullen engine, disturbed in its hibernation, groaned over. It was too much for machines, this weather far below zero. It fired and died and fired and died again and at repeated rousings, began a hit-and-miss beat until finally all cylinders awakened.

He got out and helped Mrs. Anderson in, and then Mattie. Mrs. Anderson's face was tight. There was a duty to perform, and she would perform it, and it struck him that women, most women, faced illness and death as men didn't and couldn't. It was the impulse and compulsion of men to remove themselves from the sick and dead bed. Ben saw to it that the robes protected his passengers.

There had been little traffic on the hill to the bench and little up on the flat, where snowdrifts occurred helter-skelter. He squinted against the bounce of the sun on the snow and heard Mattie say, "Here."

She took off one glove, poked in her purse, found a pair of dark glasses and fitted them on him. "All right?" she asked.

"Fine, but they're not mine. I didn't have any."

"You do now. I was saving them for your Christmas stocking."

For thanks he reached over and patted the bare hand.

He steered the car in the trail rutted out by the ambulance and arrived at the Greenwood house just as Crabtree, Chiles and Broquist were entering. Chiles was carrying a folded litter.

Mrs. Anderson hurried Mattie from her seat and marched to the door with Mattie following. Ben took time to lay one of the robes over the hood of the car. The engine would grow cold soon enough even so.

The body of Mr. Greenwood lay on a couch, just as found, Ben supposed. A sheet had been drawn down to his waist. Doc Crabtree straightened up and, returning his stethoscope to his bag, shook his head. Mrs. Anderson, her fingers light on the old, dead face, was saying, "Nathaniel." Mattie sat straight in a chair, her fair face blank, as if, like Mr. Greenwood, she had lost the capacity to feel.

Mrs. Broquist, standing aside, said, "He liked to nap. I took it he was sleepin', you know, until —"

Broquist, near her, put in, "Then she called me, and I saw it wasn't no use."

Doc Crabtree was still looking down. He uttered one word, almost under his breath. "Dignity."

"Then I drawn the sheet over him," Broquist said. "Poor old feller."

Mrs. Anderson's voice took on a soft sharpness. "He doesn't want pity. That's an affront. Yes, Nathaniel?"

Ben touched Mattie's unmoving shoulder. There was nothing in him to say. Let others speak while he listened and looked. The Broquists, awkward now, two country people, probably second-generation Americans, the sturdy yeomen in fact. Lawrence Chiles with the lugubrious look of all undertakers when on scene. Doc Crabtree being Doc Crabtree. Mrs. Anderson comforting death. And Mr. Greenwood lying serene, his white beard fine and prophetic below the age-withered cheeks.

"Can I take him now, Doctor?" Chiles asked.

"No, indeed." Mrs. Anderson was speaking. "I must get out clothes suitable for the funeral. And look, Mattie." She pointed to a table on which rested a leather-bound Bible closed with a brass clamp. "In there somewhere you'll find the family history, date of birth, parents and all. I know he had no living relatives."

At Mattie's look of loss, Ben unbuttoned his coat and took out some copy paper and a pencil. She moved to the table with them.

Mrs. Anderson had gone into the next room, a bedroom presumably, directed there by Mrs. Broquist, who followed her.

While they waited and Mattie took notes, Doc Crabtree said, "Just the burden of the years. It wears a man down, to the grave finally. But, not like most, there's peace on this face or I never saw it."

"I should have thought of those vital statistics," Chiles said. "With an old man like him, where else but in the family Bible?" He sounded put out, perhaps because Mrs. Anderson had remembered. "Broquist, it's near as cold in here as outside."

"I didn't see no need of buildin' the fire up." Broquist gestured. "He don't care."

Mattie had finished her note-taking by the time Mrs. Anderson and Mrs. Broquist returned carrying things. "Small clothes,"

Mrs. Anderson said, laying articles on a chair as she inventoried. "His frock coat, and it's clean. Shirt. Tie. His best trousers, matching the coat. And shoes. He always kept his shoes shined. Mrs. Broquist, please hand me the hangers and bag."

"You best leave the shoes," Chiles said.

"What?"

"It's not customary. Besides, it would be a waste."

It took Mrs. Anderson a minute to understand. "It's customary with him, I can tell you. Nathaniel would as soon be buried face down as without shoes. Right, Nathaniel? I'll see they're put on myself if I have to."

Chiles said, "So be it, ma'am," and beat a retreat to Doc Crabtree. "Now?"

"I would imagine so."

Chiles began arranging the litter. Here, Ben thought, here at last was something to do, and he stepped forward, forestalling Broquist.

With the litter arranged, they lifted the frail body to it and covered it with a sheet. Ben helped on the way to the ambulance, knowing at least one pair of eyes was on them.

Once the body was inside, Chiles said, daring a smile as he faced away from the house, "Old boy's light, isn't he? Use the beard for a tail, and you could fly him like a kite. Now, Ben, I didn't mean anything. It's just in my business a man's got to keep his sense of humor."

Ben sidestepped and went back into the house and then helped with the little luggage and saw Mrs. Anderson and Mattie to the car.

The quick winter night was falling as they rolled homeward. Into a long silence Mrs. Anderson said, "There's supper yet to get, Mattie, for Ferd and us."

"Why don't you all come and eat with me somewhere?" Ben asked.

"Not at a time like this. Thanks."

After another silence Mattie leaned forward and spoke across Mrs. Anderson. "Yes, Ben? Something troubling you?"

It was a part of intimacy, he supposed, a development from it, that she should know his humor and ask about it. "I was thinking about the obituary. I can write it, of course, the usual cut-and-dried thing, but it ought to be by someone who knew him better. That's what would be fitting."

Mrs. Anderson answered, "There's Mort Ewing and —"

"No, Mother. Not Mort and not you, if you meant to suggest it."

"That's outlandish."

"I don't think Mary Jess," Ben said. "Too young really, to know him."

"That leaves Mr. Collingsworth." Mattie added, "He's the right person."

"That's who I had in mind," Mrs. Anderson said.

"I, too," Ben told them. "If he'll do it."

Mattie said, "You can ask."

"All right. I'll drop you off at the house, take your notes, Mattie, and run out there."

Mary Jess came to meet him. Through the glass he had seen her coming from the kitchen, an apron on. "Why, Ben," she said, "come in out of the cold. Stay for dinner?"

"Thanks, no, Mary Jess. I'm not riding the grub-line tonight. You know about Mr. Greenwood? This time it's your father I want to see."

"Yes. We heard earlier. Father's in the living room."

Mr. Collingsworth put down a book as they entered. It joined a pile of other books on a library table. "Welcome, Ben," he said, rising. "Have off your things."

"I mustn't stay."

"Sit down, anyhow. No purpose in standing." The smile on Mr. Collingsworth's face went away, leaving it darkly sober as usual. On his feet he wore congress gaiters and over his shirt an old smoking jacket.

"It's about Mr. Greenwood."

"Yes," Mr. Collingsworth said, nodding his head. "A sad thing."

"I want to impose on you, Mr. Collingsworth."

"Oh?"

"Would you write his obituary for the paper?"

Mr. Collingsworth looked down at his folded hands. "I dislike to refuse you, Ben, but —"

"You've known him a long time. You could do him justice — you alone, Mr. Collingsworth. Please."

"I would offend the newspaper rule of objectivity."

"I would hope so."

Mr. Collingsworth kept studying his hands. After a while he said, "A man of gentle righteousness," and Ben felt sure he was writing the obituary in his mind.

Quickly Ben drew off a glove and reached in his pocket. "I have some biographical notes, taken from the family Bible. Here."

Mr. Collingsworth took them absently, hardly raising his eyes.

"I'm ever so grateful," Ben said. It seemed best to go before time brought a change of mind, and he turned and almost collided with Mary Jess, who stood silent at the dining-room entry. On his way out, he heard Mr. Collingsworth saying, "Gentle righteousness."

Mary Jess stepped out on the chill porch with him, half-closing the door behind her. She gave him her quick kiss, and, for the first time, he felt her back tremble under his bare hand.

Well, it was cold enough to make anyone shake.

13

WITH A CHINOOK WIND breathing out of the west, the car would run again. Cleveland waited until the engine worked evenly.

That was the way of weather in Montana, a day or a week or two weeks so cold that a man was drawn in to the faint core of life, all appendages numbed and shrunken to the little stove of his guts, and then a time so breezily balmy that fingers and feet found themselves, and the man could almost hear the spring birds.

It was at times like today, Cleveland thought, that he knew why he had settled and stayed in Montana. A land without seasons would taste flat. No seasons, no seasoning. Which was a way of saying that good and bad existed only by contrast, dependent one on the other for appreciation and name.

He put the Velie in low gear and let it growl along. Pursue that value-by-contrast idea, and it gave value to sinners, for what was virtue without its opposite? What was sobriety if no man took a drink? Too early yet for a drink, though, except for the one he had taken to start off the day. A man in retirement had to watch out, else boredom intensified and extended his drinking hours from get-up to good-night.

Off to the west the mountains stood clear, twenty miles distant and as close as his hand and, hanging low and beyond them, hovered the dark clouds, senders of the chinook. More bad weather was coming, of course, for February was a notional month, not to mention March, April and even May. But today was today, and he should feel content to let the grass think of growing.

The streets were slushy, and water ran on the inclines, but the sidewalks were bare. Chalk one up for progress — sidewalks. When, long ago, he had courted his wife, more than once he had gone to her house wearing gum boots. Muddy teams and saddle horses had stood at the hitching racks then, and now just one rack remained and it on a side street and seldom used. The fragrance of horse manure had given way to the stink of exhausts. And was that progress? "Skunk wagons," the old Indians, themselves smelling of willow smoke, had called automobiles. He had been part of it all, part and promoter of change; and change was the rule of things, and he had had no choice and now was just indulging an old man's regrets.

Look on the bright side. Natural gas to cook and heat by. Reliable electric lights to read by. More than hit-and-miss telephone service. Two dairies, a creamery, and milk, for those who liked milk, available bottled, whereas, not so long ago, a mother and cook had had to use the canned stuff or rely on a neighbor who kept a cow, and a child of the house had gone to get it carrying an empty lard pail. All these and more on the bright side, and all encouraged and supported by him as *Advocate* editor.

He drove around the block and parked his car in front of the *Advocate* office. Mostly he had stayed away, not wanting to intrude, wanting to break out of old habit and adjust to the habit of nothing.

Ben Tate met him with a smile and, rising, told him to take his old seat.

"Where's the editorial helper?" Cleveland asked as he sat down and took out a cigar.

"She's gone to the courthouse."

"Pity I never had a good-looking girl in the office."

A look came to Ben's face, a faraway look if you could classify looks. "Competent, too," he said, as if just recalling that quality.

"Sure. What's going on, Ben? Funny for me to have to ask that."

"Not much besides job work. Plenty of it."

"Good." Cleveland lit his cigar. "But I always said it was a shame to man and God that a country paper couldn't make out on its own, independent of the damn shop." He blew smoke at the ceiling and added what Ben surely knew. "Of course, it kind of evens up. No paper, no county printing under the law, and the shop would lose out on job work. But still I say it's a shame."

Ben shrugged, and no wonder. All this fool maundering, this taking the time of a busy man who had a half-typed sheet in his typewriter. To hell with it.

Before he could get up, Ben said, gesturing toward loose pages on his desk, "The Legion's bringing in a speaker, nationally known and high-powered, so Earl Kilmer says. Two weeks from yesterday, and he'd like two front-page stories, this week and next. There's the stuff on the man."

"Ever hear of him?"

"No. His name's Mark McBride. You ever heard?"

"No."

"Plenty of recommendations by civic groups here and there."

"One thing for certain, the flag will fly on God's mast."

"So let him speak. I'll run the stories. It doesn't matter."

Cleveland rose from his chair now. "Free speech, free press, yes, Ben. Being free, though, we have to make sure we don't make free with freedom." He had to smile, at himself and at the look on Ben's face. "Whatever that means."

He stepped to the door, said, "So long," and went out.

Nothing to do. That was the hell of having nothing to do — nothing to do. Picking his way through the graveled slush, he walked across the street and leaned against the wall of the Arfive House.

Here was what old men did when the weather was nice — they backed up to a wall and watched cars and people go by. Here was their goodbye, watching things go by. And if the old men found a projecting column or corner or door frame, they leaned against it and stropped their backs, for the years had made their skins itchy. When two or more of them met, they talked of nothing while they soaked up the weather and subtracted these minutes from the small total left them.

Change came to a town almost unnoticed, until a man cast

head of the table with Mrs. Anderson on his right. Next to her was Mr. Greenwood and next to him Mattie. Mary Jess sat at the end of the table, when she did sit. She was forever going to the kitchen for more coffee, hot rolls, or other replenishments. She looked somewhat flushed, no doubt from her labors over the stove, and all the lovelier for it.

He hadn't met Mrs. Ewing before, at least not for more than a quick introduction. An extraordinary woman, he thought, glancing again at her — friendly and fresh-looking. She was young yet, perhaps in her mid-thirties, younger than Mort, but did not seem too much younger, for Mort bore his years lightly.

Ben mostly kept silent while the talk swung, rather idly, from mahjong, which was just catching on in Arfive, to Floyd Collins, dead in his cave in Kentucky, to last year's presidential election. They were subjects old in the news. Let Ewing and Mr. Collingsworth, assisted by Mr. Greenwood, carry on. The ladies also seemed content just to listen.

"Evolution and that Tennessee trial," Mr. Collingsworth said when discussion lagged. Another stale topic by newspaper standards, Ben thought, if stale by only two or three months. Newspaper, even weeklies limited in scope and made tardy by periodicity, addressed themselves to the immediate and future. But communication was sketchy and slow in Montana, and events filed away elsewhere were still talked of here.

"I was glad to see that trial come to an end," Mr. Collingsworth said. "A cheap circus, they made of it."

"And that big bang of guilty came out just a squeak," Ewing added.

"William Jennings Bryan always was a fool," Mr. Collingsworth said, not as if he expected dispute.

"Anyone talks that much always shows up a fool," Ewing told the table. "But, take it another way, silence don't prove a turnip is smart." He smiled. "Now, Prof, who said I was referrin' to President Coolidge?"

"All the same, it is disturbing," Mr. Collingsworth said as if uninterrupted. "These days are disturbing. People have lost back and thought. A death here, a death there, a family move to another location, all were noted, regretted or met with indifference, but seldom summed up. People came and went. The ways of life shed them. The body of the town acquired a new skin, like a snake, but was unconscious of it. Not so long ago he would have seen Jay Ross or Merc Marsh or Fatty Adlam or Nick Brudd or Hank Howie, good men and bad, and all dead and gone or simply gone now. Even their names were growing dim even to those who had known them, family names with no families to claim them, for time had sent their young away, too.

Mary Jess Collingsworth was walking on the other side of the street, head up, step precise, destination in mind. Destination: *Advocate* office. Neat girl, Mary Jess. If Ben Tate didn't have an eye for her, he stood in need of a white cane. She gave a little wave and went on.

Peter Sears passed on foot, bound for the post office, and to his salesman's bright, "Fine day, Mr. Mack," Cleveland grunted a greeting. Up the street Billie Gayle stood crippled at the door of his place, smelling the fresh air, if the sense of smell had been given him. And here came Mattie Murchison, striding a good, natural stride, unfettered by notions of how a woman should walk.

She stopped and asked, "How are you, Mr. Mack?"

"Better than I deserve. You playing hooky from the office? Say, what's the matter?"

"I worked through the noon hour." The words came quietly, but the face was flushed and the blue eyes had the held gleam of anger. Abruptly she said, "Would you have a cup of coffee with me, Mr. Mack?"

"I'd like the company, but coffee?" A further look at her led him to say, "You want someone to talk to. Anyone, huh?"

"Not just anyone. Honestly, I wasn't looking for you, but you'll do. Please."

He heard a whining moan and, glancing across the street, saw his dog, the anxious head of his dog raised to the half-opened window of his car. He gave it what was meant to be a reassuring hand signal.

The Arfive House dining room, which had a poor patronage at the best of times, had none at all now. Cleveland ordered coffee for two and, at Mattie's refusal, a single doughnut.

"You? A doughnut?" she asked with a lift of her eyes.

"Wait and see. And wait on your talk."

He took the doughnut after it and the coffee arrived and said, "A man's got to tend to dumb animals." He excused himself and carried it over to the dog. More than the doughnut the dog seemed to appreciate a couple of pats on the head.

Seated in the restaurant again, Cleveland said, "Out with it, Mattie." He added, "I'm listening keen as I can, though a high-ball would help."

"The will hasn't been filed, but I've seen it. Except for a thousand dollars to the Broquists, Mr. Greenwood left Mother all that he had."

"Farm included?"

"Yes, and about three thousand dollars in cash. You know he didn't have any expenses to speak of."

"Good for him."

"I wish it wouldn't get known."

"Why, Mattie?"

"Because people are so suspicious. They'll say there's more here than meets the eye. That's what they'll say, and no basis for it whatever. I wish the paper —" She didn't need to finish the sentence.

"Now look here, Mattie. It's damn rare and only in mighty big or contested cases that the paper prints how a man left his property."

"The farm would show up in the report of deeds and transfers, wouldn't it?"

"Maybe, but what of it? Now here's your mother, a fine, by-God woman, respected all around in spite of the tough times she's had. I know about them. Oldest friend Mr. Greenwood had, probably, and he without kith or kin. Who — whom, Mattie — would he leave his estate to except to his old, thoughtful friend? To a stranger? To an enemy? To God Almighty, Who has more than He needs?"

She managed to smile and said, "Go on, Mr. Mack."

"I can understand, having no relatives myself. I know your mother. In the old days, best forgotten, she never turned her head away from me the way a lot of Christly people did. Gossip can't hurt her. Let 'em talk."

"I suppose you're right."

"And look again. It's what a paper suppresses that gets talked about most, and talked about wilder and crazier and longer than it would be if revealed publicly. If there was something whispered about that I was involved in and that I wanted to be over and done with, I would say, 'Print it.' "

She took a sip of her coffee and put the cup down and gazed at him, and the glint of anger was still in her eyes.

He said, "That's not really it, is it, Mattie?"

"Fools!" she burst out. "Fools! I hate all fools."

"That gives you a wide range. Worldwide. It must be there's an immediate fool who put you on the warpath. Or don't you want to say?"

While she considered, he studied her. A damn good-looking girl with her honest face and fair hair, and, like Mary Jess, a good girl besides. Maybe a year or so too old for Ben Tate and by all accounts not interested in marriage, either, but any man would take more than one look at her.

"It's Jim Quinn," she said. "I wish I didn't have to work in the office with him. I wish he'd go to the devil."

"Jim Quinn," he answered. "Uh-huh."

"You know what he's like." Her eyes asked him to say.

"Yep. Bottled-in-bond American. Maybe stronger than that. I guess, like Earl Kilmer, he would test one hundred and fifty proof."

"Along with Earl and a few others with Earl as their leader."

"So?" he said, sure that she would go on.

"It involves old Mr. Greenwood again. It came up over him — I mean, the dispute."

"For an old man dead and buried, he seems pretty live."

"Don't try to be funny."

"For God's sake, Mattie!"

"I'm sorry. It was that obituary, printed days ago, that set him off. Especially that description that called Mr. Greenwood a man of gentle righteousness. He's hot over that. He sneered when he said it."

"And you gave him what-for. Hot against whom, Mattie?"

"I don't know, Mr. Mack. First of all that the words should be printed at all, I suppose. Then maybe Ben, though Ben wasn't the author."

"I didn't think so. Give me one guess, and I'd say Mr. Collingsworth."

"It was. I know that for sure. Ben asked him."

"How many know it was Collingsworth?"

"It can't be much of a secret." She put her hands to her face and interrupted herself with, "Poor Mr. Greenwood. Gently righteous he was."

"No argument there."

She put her hands in front of her, then remembered her coffee and, after sipping, sat straight. "If Ben got compliments on that obituary — and I'm sure he did — he wouldn't claim credit. He's not that kind of a man. He'd name the author."

"And if he got kicks?"

"He'd take the blame. You must not know him very well, Mr. Mack."

"Just wanted a second for my motion. Now, hell, forget it, girl. You're outnumbered as against fools."

"But that's not all. Jim Quinn said, with a kind of sly and devilish glee, that the Legion was bringing in a speaker."

"So it is. He didn't reveal more than that?"

"He left the rest to my imagination. Anyhow, I took off. I didn't want to hear anymore."

Cleveland sighed and thought about a drink. It was high time for one. He patted Mattie on the hand and said, "Now you've got that off your chest, feeling better?"

"Believe me, I am. And thanks, Mr. Mack. It's a relief, having you to talk to."

She did look better, he thought, not so flushed, not so stormy-eyed. "If that's it, it's past my time for the Club."

As they rose, he touched her arm to add, "Be of cheer, girl. Not many things are really worth fuming about. Whatever comes, it'll blow over. I promise you it will blow over."

Slushing across the street to get his dog, he heard the echo of his last words. It would blow over, he had told her. Yeah. Everything blew over — given enough time.

He guessed he still had connections enough to get a line on one Mark McBride.

14

"I DON'T LIKE this parking, Ben. It's cheap. We're not high-schoolers."

"But how, then, do I see you alone?"

"You see enough of me, at the office and at home," Mary Jess answered.

"You call that private? At your house your father is always around — he or Charles, or both of them."

"It's their home, too."

"Granted. But you sound as if you were glad to have them there when I call on you."

To answer honestly would be to agree, if not wholly. She would not admit to the unbidden impulses, the sudden wishes, she had to fight against. She kept silent.

They were parked on a rough country road that skirted the flank of Breast Butte. Below them lay the town with its sprinkle of lights and to the west shone the faint, goodnight gleam of the sun.

"The days are getting longer," she said. "Every evening after the solstice I mark the sunsets. The mountains make a good yardstick."

He moved closer to her, saying, "You're just putting conversation in the way of the real subject. Now, look here, Mary Jess, you know I love you. I've said it over and over. You know I want us to get married."

"Yes, Ben, and I'm complimented, but suppose I don't want to talk about that yet. Suppose I want to talk weather. We're enjoying a false spring. February can turn brutal."

"And suppose I want to talk about you and me. We'd make a fine team, in our private lives and in business. Can't you see what we could make of the paper? Can't you see the town and country grow and us helping it grow, us having a hand in the shaping of it? I can picture a healthy and prosperous community, land put to use that's of little use now. Think what a dam on the Breast River would mean?"

"The old garden idea, Ben. I shrink from it."

"Why?"

"There used to be a slough on the edge of town, and there were frogs and garter snakes and minnows in it. I fished for the minnows with bent pins."

"I'm surprised you came that close to nature." He allowed her time for the implication and then added, "But that's off the subject."

"A fine spring made the slough, but the town cemented it over and now pumps its water to the tank up on the hill. That's a gain, I suppose?"

He put an arm across her shoulder, and she let it rest there, resisting its pull. "The town has water at least," he said.

"And in the daytime, looking down from here, you can still see buffalo grass and wild growth waving and maybe a prairie-chicken hen and her brood. In time, I'm afraid, they'll all go the way of the buffalo that used to graze there."

"So what? Old things do go away. They must when they stand in the way of men's needs. You wouldn't put a stop to progress if you could."

"I wonder. Anyhow, I feel set against change. I would cry for what went away. That's a reason we wouldn't make a good team."

"Nonsense. We'd have balance. You'd keep me from pushing too hard. A governor, that's what you would be."

His arm increased its pressure, and a wayward excitement rose in her. "Is it," he asked with a quiet, upsetting humility, "that I'm not the right man?"

But he was the right man if there was one, if there ever could be one. What more than he was could a woman ask? A sudden demand of honesty, a sudden sense of unworthiness, made her say, "I do love you, Ben."

She heard his quick intake of breath. He said, "I want to jump out of the car and yell hurrah to the sky."

Instead, he seized her, and his mouth found hers, and she felt his hand sliding toward her waiting breast and on her thigh the hard, male thrust of him, and she squirmed and cried into his mouth, "No, Ben! Please!" Even as she spoke she came to wonder whether she was resisting Ben or herself or the brute facts of love and its sequel.

Once she had wrenched free, he said, his breath fast, "All right, honey. But if we're agreed on marriage, please set the date and set it soon."

"I'll do my best, but be patient, Ben." One thing more she must say, and she said it in a voice that made itself small. "It's just I'm afraid, Ben. I'm afraid." It was out then, it was acknowledged and faced, this fear that rode her.

"For goodness' sake —" he began.

"Don't ask me why. Don't ask me what. Please, just start the car."

◆

"I warned you I'd be late," Mattie said as she slipped off her robe and let it drop to the floor.

Getting ready for bed, lying in it, Ben had been divided in mind. Did he or didn't he want her tonight, hardly an hour after he had left Mary Jess? Should he or shouldn't he? Now, as he glimpsed her outline in the dark of the room and saw the well-set head, the good breasts and the thighs that had delighted and comforted him, his body erased the doubt.

"I haven't been waiting long," he said. "Come to bed."

She stretched out beside him, saying, "It will have to be a short session."

"Devoted to business."

"What else?"

He made haste with her, more haste than time demanded, knowing he was less than a satisfactory lover. A man with a woman ought to be single in purpose, intent on the one act, not weakened and hurried by contemplations beyond the limits of bed.

But she seemed not to mind. She lay largely passive, as if distracted herself.

At least, he thought and rejected the thought as crude and unworthy, by this act he had rid himself of the stone ache. Mary Jess could have no idea of what sex excitement, unsatisfied, did to a man.

Afterwards, resting beside him, Mattie said, "There are things ahead of you, Ben."

"I would hope so."

"Not that kind of things."

"Name a few."

"You'd better be prepared for fireworks when that speaker comes to town next week. The Legion, or those men who maneuver it, have plastered the town with posters."

"Sure. I printed them for them."

"Well, look out. What if you are a target?"

"What if I am? People aren't taken in by the likes of those men."

"Wait till the speaking."

"You scare me. Now, what's next, what dreadful thing?"

"This household is about to break up, and the good thing you had on the side will be gone."

"Wait. What do you mean?"

"I mean me. I'm leaving town."

He had to think before he spoke. "That is dreadful. You're sure?"

"It's like this. Mr. Greenwood left his farm to Mother. She's moving out there. She likes the country, and besides — Ben, can I tell you something?"

"Anything, private or public."

"Quite private. It explains Mother, Ben. I'm a bastard."

"Nobody better say so." But did she mean what she said?

"But I am. A true and literal bastard and glad of it." She paused and put in, "I don't know why I'm telling you all this unless it's because we've made love and I trust you and won't be seeing you very much longer."

He said, "Thank you, Mattie — for all but the last."

"My reputed father was a drunk, a whorer, a brawler, a wife-beater. Name the worst, and you have him. He got shot while Mother was carrying me, but I know."

"Who shot him?"

"He shot himself, by accident. Shot most of his head off. He was drunk and went hunting and crawled through a wire fence and tried to pull his shotgun through after him. It had the good sense to go off."

He said, "Yes," and waited.

"Before his death Mother had wanted a child, but not by him certainly. More and more she wanted it, and finally she decided to have an illegitimate one. It stood a better chance, it could hold its head higher than any product of his. I suppose you can guess the rest."

"I can't believe what I'm guessing."

"All the same, she chose Mr. Greenwood, or they got together somehow, by design plus love or whatever. Who knows the all of it? Mr. Greenwood was already a widower."

"And your mother told you?"

"Yes. She wanted me to be proud of my parentage, even if half of it had to be secret. Better for me to know, she figured, than to think my father was a damn scoundrel."

"And Mr. Greenwood? Did he know?"

"She never told him, and I didn't, of course. She may have thought that the burdens of a true Christian were already heavy enough." Mattie spoke without disparagement. "She wouldn't have wanted to add to them."

"Knowing this much about your mother, I can begin to account for you, Mattie."

"Not the baby part. I don't want one."

"And you don't need to worry, one way or the other."

She was silent, and he had time to wonder what would happen to reputations if the public knew. Where would go the esteem in which Mrs. Anderson was held? Where the gentle righteousness of Mr. Greenwood? They shouldn't be altered one damn bit, but they would be. Secrecy here ruled out revelation.

"Strange they never got married," he said.

"I can only guess that possibly Mother thought marriage to her would demean him, considering the kind of man she had lived with. Or maybe the fires, if there were any, went out. Or maybe he wanted to remain single-minded in his devotions. At any rate they remained good and close friends, no doubt remembering."

"All right, then. Let's get back to the subject. The household is breaking up, but why must you leave?"

"Mother's independent enough now, and I'm not going to rattle around and grow old in a small town."

"You'd better think about it, Mattie. The town's not so bad, and, besides, where would you go? What would you do?"

"To Minneapolis, where some relatives live. And I can do more than you know. I'm not just a secretary. I'm trained as a legal secretary, too, and I can keep books."

"I don't want you to leave, if that counts."

"You mean not leave just yet. After your marriage you wouldn't be comfortable with me still in town."

His hand stroked her flank, enjoying the sleek nakedness of it, and he felt the beginnings of renewed desire, but she took the hand away and held it in both of her own.

"Ben," she asked, "has Mary Jess consented to marry you?"

"Well, yes."

"Good. Make it soon for the sake of you both."

"She hasn't consented to the point of setting a date."

"Nevertheless —" she began. Then she said, "You weren't very ardent tonight, were you? You didn't want me very much?"

"That's not true."

"Yes, Ben. You're engaged, and you're feeling disloyal and guilty. Tell me the truth."

"A little, then."

She moved away from him. "I know, Ben. I know you."

"But that doesn't mean —"

She rose and sat on the edge of the bed and groped for her robe. "Don't finish the sentence, Ben. It has no right ending, not for you. I understand." She added quietly in what could have been pity or acceptance, "It's no use to tell you that an engagement is not a vow of fidelity. No use, Ben."

With her robe on, she stooped and kissed him lightly. He tried to hold her, but she pushed his arms back.

"Please, Mattie," he said, "please don't go."

She stepped away and put her hand on the knob and turned back to say, still in that quiet tone, "You won't have to feel ashamed again — not because of me, Ben."

He saw her shape in the darkness, saw her go out and heard the door close gently but firmly, as firmly, he thought, as any door ever closed.

15

FEBRUARY WEATHER, Cleveland thought while staking no claim on originality, was best compared to a woman who was all warm compliance one day and all frosty rejection the next. Today was its day of frigidity — ten below, his thermometer said — and his car wouldn't start, and he had to go to that speaking tonight. He could stay home and no one would fault him, but, damn it, he had to go. Blame Mattie Murchison for that, Mattie and his vague suspicion of mischief afoot.

He sat in his easy chair, a drink and a bottle beside him, and looked out the window into the gray twilight and thought it was a good time to die but a bad time to be buried. A man laid away wouldn't be pushing up daisies soon, not with the sod snow-covered and frozen stiffer than the corpse it would receive. The sum of cheer was that the wind wasn't blowing.

Mag came in from the kitchen, saw him lifting his glass and said, "You hardly ate at all tonight, and now you're drowning what nourishment I got into you."

"Drink and think," he answered. "It's food that would addle my brains."

"Humph. And curdle your liver." That said, she withdrew, and he felt a mean sense of victory in this open defiance of her objections to his nursing a bottle at home. He had another bottle in his clothes closet if she only knew it.

"Damn you, Bluster," he said to the dog that lay at his feet. "I wish you'd control your wind or anyhow sweeten it." He lit a cigar. The dog didn't even wiggle an ear.

A drink and a smoke. It had come down to that — which was

better than nothing. But where were the old days of the young nights, of music and fragrances and girls, the eternal wonder, the eternal promise? Eroded, worn away, shriveled along with his balls.

Still, there was hope for virility, if a man could believe the official sages who were afraid of it. Listen to that new-fangled wailer, the saxophone, and rediscover concupiscence. Right there — his eyes went to the pile of newspapers stacked at his side — right there it said the City of Washington had declared any sax music immoral. No mention of the violin and Fritz Kreisler, who were a better bet to put lead in your pencil.

He filled his glass and knew he was filling in time, diverting his mind from his major concern. Something didn't smell right about that meeting tonight. Some stink was in the wind, some odor different from the patriotic bullshit the speaker's title suggested. "America Evermore."

And where was the dope on the speaker, this Major Mark McBride, about whom he'd asked in a telegram? Bill Scobee, living on his pension in Washington, should have answered already. A man's service record couldn't be that hard to dig out, not hard at all for a man who had been a general. And now it was too late to turn to anyone else.

On the chance he had missed a call, Cleveland got up, went to the phone and got hold of Pinkie Adams at the Great Northern station. "Cleveland," he said. "Any wires for me, Pinkie?"

"Nope. Might as well say Western Union's gone out of business, Mr. Mack. Say, if one comes, you want I should deliver it in person?"

"It depends. I'm going to that speaking tonight."

"Be glad to, Mr. Mack. Your home or the auditorium, either, you being an old friend and anxious, I know, to hear."

"Thank you, Pinkie."

Cleveland went back to his chair, stretched to turn on a light and finished his drink. Why all this damned foolish concern, he asked himself? Why nag himself into going? He had listened to enough speeches, by windy politicians, flag-wavers and oracular

Prohibitionists. And why walk, when Ben Tate or any number of others would pick him up if he asked? No matter. By God, he would walk. He was man enough yet.

The late light had surrendered to dark, gray dark, if a man could see out. Later the stars might shine, distant beyond the stretch of the mind, frosty as eternal indifference, but now the night brooded in a smother of cold.

Six blocks to the high-school auditorium, a little less by the shortcuts. Just six blocks. Christ, in days gone by he could have hopped there in his shirt sleeves and arrived with breath in his lungs and warmth in his body. That was where a man noticed age first — in his footing. Once, asking no recognition, his legs had carried him gaily: nowadays their joints creaked, and their muscles prayed for relief after a minute of exercise. Then the lungs atrophied, and any day the heart might ask what was the use.

But, by God, he would walk! "Daniel Webster," he said to the sleeping dog, "sink or swim, live or die, survive or perish, I give my hand and heart to this vote."

Time to go, with allowance for a short drink. After swallowing it, he went to the corner of the room where the hatrack and his overshoes stood, sat down and began buckling the overshoes on. How much of a man's life went into buckling and unbuckling, buttoning and unbuttoning? Brushing teeth if he had them, going to the bathroom, bathing, changing clothes? A by-Christ weary routine.

He stood up, blowing, and put on muffler and overcoat and was about to clamp on ear pads and hat when Mag came out of her room to see he was togged out all right.

"I am going to take a walk, Mag," he told her.

"Dog, too?"

"I don't know —?"

"He'll cry all the time you are gone, you know that."

"Up, Bluster!" he called. "Come on, you wind-breaking hound. Oh, here you are. All right, you're a privileged character. They'll let you in. And if I can stir my stumps, so can you." The dog couldn't hear much anymore. He gazed up sadly.

"I'm not bound for the Club, Mag. I'm going to enjoy oratory."

She didn't believe him, and he couldn't blame her. On a sudden, fool impulse he kissed her wrinkled forehead, then saw tears coming to the old eyes. "Goodbye," he said. "Back soon. Goodbye." He pushed the dog out with his foot and closed the door behind him.

Outside, the air burned his nostrils and lungs. A cold fury, he thought, taking some credit for a fresh use of an old phrase. Unaided by wind, it thrust its dead fingers into his clothes. The night was still, frozen motionless, its breath locked. His own puffs of breath bloomed white before him. He held up while the dog, barely able to lift a leg, took a leak.

He went on, picking his steps in the churned and trodden snow and damning the muscles that had started to ache. Had he chosen another way, a car might have picked him up, but there was no hope for a lift on these side streets and shortcuts. Hurrah for his choice, then.

He was a little more than halfway to the school when he heard crying whimpers behind him. There was Bluster, down in the snow, scrambling and failing to get his legs under him.

Cleveland walked back, saying, "You poor old son of a bitch." He set the dog upright, positioning his legs and, watching, took a few steps away. The dog tried to follow but went down again.

"Oh, Christ!" Cleveland said on his return. "Mean I have to carry you when I can hardly carry myself?"

The dog's sad eyes apologized.

Cleveland cradled the dog in one arm. Fifteen more pounds, then, and almost half the way still to go. He stood still, willing the ache in his legs to ease up. Mind over matter, and how a man felt was determined by thought. The fool dog tried to lick his face.

Here were the steps to the entry at last, and Cleveland paused and panted, wondering whether his legs would lift him the half-dozen risers, let alone the first one. Frank Brobeck and his ugly face were about to go in. "Trouble, Mr. Mack?" Brobeck asked.

"No. I made it, didn't I?"

"Sure, you did, Mr. Mack, but it looks like your dog didn't. Here, give him to me."

There couldn't be a look of concern on Brobeck's seamed face. He took the dog and moved aside to let people pass. Cleveland unbuttoned his overcoat. Christ, he was hot, cold out or not, hot and out of breath and ready to drop. He felt a tug on his arm.

"Here you are, Mr. Mack," Pinkie Adams was saying. "Western Union and yours truly on the job."

He heard himself wheeze, "Thanks, Pinkie," and stuffed the telegram in his suit pocket.

"Won't hurt to blow a little," Brobeck said, still with a sort of asking look in his face. "I feel kind of winded myself." After a minute or two he added, "Ready now?"

Brobeck found a seat for him in the front row near the exit, set the dog to one side, folded Cleveland's overcoat, placed overcoat and hat on the floor under the chair and reset the dog at his feet.

"I could have done that myself," Cleveland said.

Brobeck moved away, saying, "Take it easy now."

After his breath and heart steadied, Cleveland looked around. He could see Mattie and Mrs. Anderson, Mr. Collingsworth and Mary Jess and, next to her, Ben Tate, who held sheets of copy paper and a yellow pencil in his lap. There were the Legion boys — Hank Stutemeyer, Alvor Torgerson, Jim Quinn, torch-bearers for true America. In the front row to his left sat Earl Kilmer and a spruced-up stranger who must be the speaker. Just behind him were Mort Ewing, his wife beside him.

If he had to, Cleveland thought, he could name everyone present. That was the way of small towns — no strangers. Opponents, even enemies, but no strangers. And it was the way of small towns to go to meetings, good and bad, exciting and dull, anything to relieve day-by-days. The hall, which would hold a hundred and more, was filling up. At the front of it rose a stage with a flag on it, but the arrangements committee apparently had decided on a lectern and desk, presumably to bring the truth nearer the people.

After the last of the audience had trickled in, Kilmer walked to the lectern. A smooth, unsmiling bird, Kilmer. Commitment and its air of sincerity left no room for humor in him and no door to argument.

Kilmer welcomed the audience and went on, saying, "A good friend has suggested to me that our American Legion post do more, that, in a sense, it quit hiding its light under a bushel. Tonight we are acting on that good advice."

Cleveland felt himself squirming. Though he could hardly qualify as a good friend, he was the one who had said that the Legion must make news if it wanted newspaper notice.

"Yes," Kilmer was saying, "we are doing something tonight, I am sure everyone will agree, something fitting and proper on the part of men who have fought for our country and who, by fighting, have manifested and increased their everlasting loyalty to the greatest nation on earth and to the principles on which it stands."

With that, he introduced the speaker, a man, he said, widely known and respected, a staunch upholder of the American way. And a lot of other damn things. It was his pleasure and privilege to present Major Mark McBride.

McBride was smooth, too, smiling smooth, and the privilege was in reverse. It was his privilege to address so large and generous an audience.

Flowered bullshit so far.

McBride half-turned and pointed to the flag on the stage and told how it was begot and what glory had attended its waving.

The flag, the flags of all nations, Cleveland reflected, should have been listed along with the graven images men should not bow down before. What were they but pieces of bunting exalting to the farthest reaches of heaven good and bad both? Respect for the flag was one thing, worship another.

Bluster had let wind again. By rights he ought to share honors with the orator. On either side of Cleveland people put on a show of not sniffing. Like children in school they sneaked glances one at another, trying to detect who was guilty.

McBride had come to the outrages perpetrated by enemies

against public order and national safety, to shootings and bomb-
ings, to Centralia, Seattle, Atlanta, Washington, and Wall Street.
Radicals were at the heart of the trouble, radicals, socialists, syn-
dicalists, all adding to bolshevists, all threatening the structure, the
very spirit of what was America.

The outrages were real enough, Cleveland thought, but pretty
old stuff if you ignored the case of Vanzetti and Sacco, which was
still being argued. Of course McBride wouldn't mention excesses
on the other side, since they were justified, patriotic manifesta-
tions. Neither would he mention labor, which had been conveniently consigned to the ranks of the radicals because some unions
had rebelled against sure-enough grievances.

"And now," McBride was saying, "we come to the question of
what the individual can do, how the honest and loyal citizen can
work to save our society from the manifold perils besetting us.
Oh, he is sly, that enemy of ours. He is devious. By subtle
means he subverts our aims. A word here, a word there, out-
wardly innocent, a phrase, a paragraph inserted in otherwise in-
nocuous print, a belittling and polluting of the moral standards
honored through ages, an avowal of righteousness where little ex-
ists — by such means does he undo us, for we are a gracious people, too quick in these dangerous times to ignore, forget and
forgive."

Cleveland straightened. The man was getting his teeth into
something and doing it in that professional manner that held and
persuaded most of those who listened and looked. The considered
modulations of tone, the practiced gestures, the projection of earnestness against the threatening evil — these were his stock in
trade, and they worked. The son of a bitch was good, that was all.

Turning, Cleveland saw that Mr. Collingsworth's dusky face
had gone rigid. If he didn't watch out, that smart-ass at the lectern would get a poke in the jaw.

McBride seemed to be winding up as he spoke again. "Believe
me, my friends, I speak without prejudice and without suspicion.
I do not know what is taught in your schools. But do you? That
is the question. In this very school perhaps? Have you examined

the textbooks? They can be enemy instruments. Do you know what is in the library? *Main Street*, for instance, that defamer of village life? A library can be the nesting place of sedition, and of perdition, if you please. What magazines are subscribed to? The *Nation?* The *New Republic?* The *Survey? Harper's?* The *Scholastic*, which parades as an educational organ?

"Oh, I tell you, good and loyal citizens, much that encourages the bolshevists and promotes their cause is to be found in these areas. If I had the power I would excise offending passages. Some publications I would order — forgive me — to hell."

The damn dog had offended again, but now no one noticed. They were caught up, these people, and held. Cleveland felt a slow fire in his guts. He wished he had whiskey to feed it.

"I am powerless here, my friends," McBride was continuing, "but you are not. You can appoint screening committees. You can examine the textbooks, the library books, the publications, and through your board have offensive material deleted or banned and through the board, too, investigate those who are guilty or suspect. Our children, yours and mine, must not be corrupted. They won't be if we exercise vigilance."

Only propriety, only the decency to let the man finish, was holding Collingsworth back, Cleveland thought as he turned again. But it still wouldn't do. Collingsworth wouldn't do. He wouldn't explain. He wouldn't debate. He would march up and swing. Mort Ewing in rebuttal? Nope. It wasn't Mort's dish. Whose then? That damn fire in his belly tormented him.

"So," McBride said, now for sure in conclusion, "let us give our loyal thoughts, our faithful hearts, our dedicated efforts to the cause of America. God bless our country, and God bless us all."

Almost as one man the crowd rose and applauded. The fools. The damned idiots. Shot in the ass by evangelism. Only the hammer of a spike in the skull could restore them. Collingsworth was pushing to the front, his eyes aimed like a rifle.

Cleveland wrenched to his feet, went to take a step and fell over his dog. He got up by himself, gave the dog one quick pat and lurched to the lectern.

"O ye of little faith," he tried to shout. His lungs were in his belly. Somebody snickered. Slowly people sat down. Collingsworth was finding a vacant chair.

"O ye of little faith in America." He had found some voice now.

A man — Alvor Torgerson it was — called, "Drunk again."

"Not drunk in the manner you are," Cleveland said, pointing. "Not befuddled by the fumes of the phony. You, I suppose, judge yourself fit to decide what is fit to be read." That ought to hold them. It seemed to. Torgerson had flunked out of high school.

" 'Decipimur specie recti.' That's Latin, Mr. Torgerson, for 'We are deceived by what seems virtuous.' In truth we are deceived."

Earl Kilmer interrupted. "Did you ever fight for your country? Ever bear arms for America?"

"I will come to that in due time, if you'll have the courtesy to hear me." He looked out and around, seeing the faces blurred, more curious than intent, more eager for a ruckus than for rebuttal. "Will you listen, you people among whom I've spent more years than some of you can count in your lifetimes? Will you hear me, knowing I am not socialist, syndicalist, bolshevist or anything but American?"

He had found wind and voice now and his tones rumbled in his ears. "How long, how long, has man fought to be himself? How long for the right to think his own thoughts and speak his own words? We go back, back through the centuries to Stephen Langton and King John and the eventual Magna Carta, the Great Charter, and before then to the mists of history, back and forth, following the brave efforts of brave men against the oppressive monarch, the priest, the tyrant under whatever guise, under whatever name. Among others, that name includes bolshevism." All his adult life he had been ready with words, and he knew something of history, yet he had never been a public speaker and never tried to be, but it struck him as he gestured that he was getting some of the hang of it now, managing some imitation of McBride's finesse — the changing resonances, the pauses where useful, the right movements of head and arms. And it was all a cheap act, or it would have been but for the burn in him.

"Long ago, in the year 1791, our forefathers, drawing on the experiences of men before them, drew up our own Bill of Rights. The First Amendment gave and gives us freedom of religion, of speech, and of the press, and the freedom to assemble in peace and to petition the government for a redress of grievances. Those freedoms, though sometimes denied us in hysterical times, have made America. Do you remember the words of one of the first of Americans and one of the greatest? Thomas Jefferson said, 'I have sworn upon the altar of God eternal hostility against every form of tyranny over the mind of man.' "

He wished he had a drink, if only of water, but thoughts kept spouting.

He pointed to McBride. "You, sir, don't agree with Mr. Jefferson. You don't believe in the rights of man. You would have us all think alike, 'alike' meaning like you. You would control and channel our thought and our speech, even as Russia, though at the other end of the political pole, controls and channels its people. Given enough power, sir, men like you would put men like me before firing squads."

McBride jumped half up from his seat, crying, "Now you wait just a minute!" and then slammed back in his chair, clapped there by the hands on his shoulders. The hands were Mort Ewing's. Ewing told him, speaking loud, "You set there, mister! We listened to you."

Cleveland nodded his thank-you. "We here have had our own guardians of freedom, largely unsung. You will remember the war years. You will remember the councils of defense and some of their idiotic excesses. In certain areas of the state — indeed, nearly all — men were joined in suspicion, one of another. The acceptance of slander and hearsay and unfounded or silly charges of disloyalty and pro-Germanism usurped the place of calm reason. It was almost enough to have been born abroad, or to be closely descended from those born abroad, to be under the dark of suspicion. Even some of you here tonight, I know, though you probably don't, were named as disloyal."

He thought he could see an uneasiness in some of the faces, in those of first- and second-generation Americans. He took a breath and called on what strength he had.

"Nothing came of all that in our county, except that one man and one only was persuaded to shut up and put up for Liberty bonds. Other reports were found to be false or malicious. Why, I ask you, why? It was because, in those times of fever, our fevered governor by accident appointed to our county council of defense two men of good judgment. Those men, as you know, were Mort Ewing and Professor Collingsworth, against one of whom you have heard slurs tonight."

There wasn't much more to say, Cleveland thought, but there was more, and he would try to say it, though there were trembles in the hand and arm that supported him on the desk. The faces before him were blurring again.

"Now, to go back. There are limits, necessary limits, to freedom of speech. You may not traduce a man with impunity. You may not bear false witness. You may not calumniate or malign. And it has been rightly and sensibly said that no man may cry fire in a crowded theater when there is no fire."

Of a sudden he was lost, lost for words, mind collapsed and body about to go, too. His mouth tasted pasty. He fumbled for his handkerchief, and his hand felt the telegram he had forgotten. He took it out and opened it, willing his shaky hands to be still, hoping the crowd would indulge him while he made the pretense of having still more on his mind. Then he had it in plenty.

"You, sir," he said, pointing to McBride again, "have come close to traducement. Into this peaceful assemblage, into our loyal community, you have yelled fire when there is no fire."

It was Earl Kilmer who tried to get to his feet now, and again it was Mort Ewing, reaching over, who yanked him back.

"A final point," Cleveland went on, unsure that he could make it. "It has been asked if I ever fought for my country. Earl Kilmer has asked me, implying that one who never bore arms had no right to speak. I am not a professional patriot. I have almost never mentioned my record and never leaned on it as some do, but I rode with Teddy Roosevelt's Rough Riders."

He held the telegram up and looked at McBride. "Major, did you ever fight for your country?"

"I was in service throughout the war." The answer came clearly but as if from some too-bold assumption of confidence.

"An unresponsive reply, Major McBride. I asked if you ever fought for your country, and I will answer for you." Cleveland brought the telegram to full view. "You never bore arms. During the war, throughout the war, you occupied a cushy place in the department of the judge advocate. Do you deny it?"

McBride didn't reply, except to mutter, "It wasn't so cushy."

"By Mr. Kilmer's standards, then, you have no right to speak, though I grant you the right. Yet I wonder what springs feed your polluted stream. Is one, and the only one, hatred? Is one, and the only one, ignorance of the stuff of America? Is one, and the only one, secret payments to you by companies that seek to raise false issues to the neglect of the real? Do I traduce you? Sue me if so."

They were all swimming now, McBride, Kilmer, Ewing, Tate, Mary Jess, all of them, their faces flowing and changing place while the hall rocked. But one final utterance, one final blow, then rest after a drink.

"You are a self-appointed censor, McBride. You are a book-burner at heart. In you, deep in you, is the tyrant. We bid you goodbye, sir. We ask you to leave."

The lectern turned from him. The desk went away. A strange leg thrust out, numb to command. People seemed to be on their feet. They seemed to be clapping. They seemed to cheer.

A hand grabbed his arm. He thought he said, "Thanks, Frank," but it wasn't Frank Brobeck. It was Ben Tate. Tate was getting him into his outdoor gear. Tate was saying, "Oh, you left your overshoes on." Tate was lifting old Bluster. Tate was asking, "Got your car, Mr. Mack? I'll drive you home then."

The doorway was just behind them, and he thought he heard a hoarse voice sounding above other voices. It had to be Brobeck's. "Now see here, folks, it wasn't the Legion done this, not the whole —"

So he was home at last, and the place looked steady, looked fixed. The world had decided to settle down.

At the door Ben said, "I'm afraid your dog is on his last legs." His eyes weren't on Bluster.

"We're all right," Cleveland said. "Set him down. A long rest is what he needs."

"Can't walk," Ben said, stooping. "I'll take him in."

"Be quiet. Mag's sleeping." Cleveland went ahead, fumbling for light switches, trying not to totter.

Ben put the dog down on the bedroom floor, at the place Cleveland designated. The dog crumpled and went to sleep or into a coma.

It was a fine way to thank Ben — to wish he'd get the hell out and leave him to his bottle.

Ben gave him a long look. "You're all right?"

"Sure."

"Then I'll go. I'll turn off the lights." He put out his hand. There seemed to be a strange twist to the young mouth. "Mr. Mack," he said and appeared to hunt for more words, "Mr. Mack, damn it all, thank you." He left then.

Cleveland got the fresh bottle out of the closet. The infernal thing didn't want to be opened. He drank from its mouth. After a minute, sitting on the bed, he felt a weak spread of strength. A big man, he was, a god-damned rousing success, declarer of independence for one and all. Let heaven sing his praise.

Anyhow, his hand had steadied, and he would do what he had to do. He eased himself up and went to his chiffonier and from a drawer took a very small bottle and brush and stepped to the dog that lay with one eye half-open, unseeing, unhearing, closed to all dreams. He brushed the dog's lips with the liquid. He said, "Goodbye, Bluster. Won't hurt, Doc Crabtree said." The dog's tongue came out and licked and licked again and then didn't lick.

Cleveland returned the poison and went back to sit on the bed. He took another drink and sat, bottle in hand, and there was nothing in his head, not one thought, not one remembrance to be regretted or savored. He ought to feel something, he told himself, even maybe a little pride, but all he could do was sit and think he was thinking.

He lifted the bottle again and drank and lowered it and felt it slip from his hand and knew he was falling.

PART II

16

OUTSIDE THE OFFICE, construction trucks rumbled, carrying explosives, cement, sand, lumber, machinery parts, gasoline. If he stepped outside, Ben knew, he would see other traffic and men on the sidewalks walking with purpose, from office to office and shop to shop. He would find carpenters and masons working and people snatching time to look on. Not for the first time he said to himself, "Some difference." President Roosevelt might be an opportunist, a hasty improviser, a grandstander, but he had put men to work.

He pecked away at an editorial, aware of without being distracted by the sounds of activity in the shop, where both Okay Myers and his son worked steadily now as journeyman printers. Yes, due credit to Roosevelt, credit for his public concern, his optimism, his work programs, good or indifferent, and credit for the great dam being built on the Breast. Especially hereabouts for the dam, which the *Advocate* had argued for over the years, Mary Jess notwithstanding. Mary Jess was an antiquarian.

The editorial completed, he typed "30" on the sheet of copy paper and said to her, "I think I'll go sound him out anyhow."

She sat at her desk, busy with figures. The years hadn't changed her, unless a certain drawn refinement of features was change. They hadn't changed her, and neither had wifehood. She remained beautiful and, somehow, untouched.

She looked up and answered, "You know I think you're being impulsive."

"Of course you do, but you know as well as anybody that we need a new building."

"It seems so right now. Will it later?"

He knew she was thinking of the lean times fresh in memory, of unpaid subscriptions, unpaid bills, scant advertising and dribbles of job work. It had been a struggle just to survive.

"Later, after the dam is finished, there'll be thousands of acres more of irrigated land. I keep telling you that."

"You keep telling me that."

"Damn it, Mary Jess, nothing ventured, nothing gained, as they say."

"They also speak about having all your eggs in one basket."

"It's the only basket we have."

He got up and stood at the window. There was no purpose in argument. He ought to know that much by now. She would be unchanged forever, firm in first opinion, touched seldom in bed, the virgin deflowered but still virginal.

He said, "See you."

Dust hung in the street, and dust dirtied the store windows, but in this time of boom nobody cared. Strangers on the street, too, newly-come businessmen and men drawn to Arfive from eastern Montana, where drought, wind and low prices had forced some farm families to subsist on jack rabbit and gopher, plus what little garden stuff they might be able to grow, and to cut for their scrawny livestock the inedible Russian thistle that they called Hoover hay.

Stricken though the immediate region had been, Ben thought as he walked along, Arfive and the county had known nothing that bad. No real dust storms, at their worst in the dust bowl but bad enough in eastern Montana, which blew the good earth away and buried farm buildings. No storms like that, although the county agent was advising strip farming as an answer to the blown loss of soil. No men of his knowledge so poor that housewives canned rodents, provided there was ammunition to shoot them. Lines, but not long lines, for handouts. Drought, yes. Hardship, yes. Forced departures for the West Coast, yes, some. Yet the county had fared better than most.

Peter Sears was putting a new front on his building and remodeling inside, spurred to do so by competition from Penney's. There was enough business for both. Billie Gayle was still eking along, thanks to soft drinks, tobacco and cards, and despite the brisk trade done by two so-called beer parlors.

In his mind, as he made for the bank, ran the proofs of revival, most of them in sight on Main Street. A new hardware store, a new automobile dealership, two new gas stations, a new women's store, three new restaurants, none so good as Eva Fox had once run. Spence Green was enlarging his drugstore, even though given more shelf space now that his whiskey business was ended. The state liquor store had taken over the trade. The old Club, Mort Ewing's club, was a barbershop.

Like its one rival, the bank building where he transacted his business had had its face scrubbed. ARFIVE STATE BANK shone on its front in bright metal. Stanton Rivers sat at his desk behind a waist-high partition, his attention alternating between the papers before him and the entrances and departures of depositors. He lifted a hand and said, "Afternoon, Ben. Come in. Have a seat."

Ben passed through the swinging gate and took a chair.

Rivers asked about Mary Jess, commented on the weather, spoke about the dam and then asked, "Something special on your mind, Ben?" He sat erect, just as he always stood erect. His dark face looked healthy. On it he grew a trim mustache that showed some gray.

"Nothing immediate, Stan, but not too long delayed, either. I'm putting out feelers. You know I'm outgrowing my place?"

"I would imagine."

"It was an old building when I bought it. What's more, there's no room in it for the small engraving plant I want to buy and no room at all for more editorial help. I'll have to have more. I need it now."

"Yes, I see." Rivers' eyes were alert and friendly.

"I thought, given encouragement, I'd have some plans drawn. I already have my eye on a building site. But it all depends on financing. I can't handle it without help."

Rivers flattened his cared-for hands on the desk. His mustache moved to a smile. "Ben, I wouldn't worry. Go ahead and have the plans drawn. You don't have any figures, even tentative, of course?"

"No. It's too early."

"When you have, come around. I'll have to consult the directors, naturally, but —" His hand dismissed the directors.

Ben rose and shook hands with him, saying, "Thanks, Stan," and went through the gate and out the door, feeling pleased. A good reputation was almost like money in the bank.

On the street he nearly collided with Frank Brobeck, who said, "Watch out there, Ben, running high-headed and blind like a loco horse."

"Hi, Frank. How goes it?"

Brobeck wore frontier pants, a fitted western shirt, a big hat and cowboy boots and carried a revolver in a hip holster. He looked like the sheriff he had come to be.

"Good enough," Brobeck said and took him by the arm. "Got time to jaw a while?"

"Sure."

They walked to a worn street bench between two cottonwood trees, a good place to sit but for the dust and the hazard of birds overhead.

"I'm thinking, Ben," Brobeck said and gave himself time to think. He had come a long way, Ben reflected, since those first days of acquaintance. Road crewman, deputy sheriff, then sheriff, and, along with political progress, a growing confidence of manner, a reputation for reason and honesty, an improvement in speech. With the years, his big, furrowed face had become almost handsome.

"First off and by the way," Brobeck said, "how about going hunting this fall? For elk, I mean? We could get up a party."

Ben answered, "Well, maybe. We'll see."

"You'll be needing a vacation. So will I, and that's the God's truth." He sighed. "Ben, you got no idea."

"That depends on the subject."

"The subject is these shanty towns roundabout — three of

'em — and the men and women the dam has brought in. Christ!"

Traffic flowed on the street, and foot traffic sounded behind them, and Ben said, "I've seen them. I know."

"But you really don't. Oh, let 'em have their beer and their outlaw booze and their young floozies and their old slum whores. Gambling, too. Who cares?"

"You seem to."

"And what it all brings on. That's what I care about. Fights every night, bad fights, and they have to be busted up. Then no one will bring a charge or appear as a witness. And that road to and from Burtville, it's death alley. You do know that. In Burtville, in all three towns, we try to restore order, but, hell, how you going to restore it when it wasn't there in the first place? My staff works its ass off, and what's to show for it? No cases, that's what."

Brobeck sighed again and put a hand to his cheek. "And the kids in those shacks, the poor, goddamn kids. Some run wild. Some go hungry and wonder whereabouts are their folks. Quite a few get sick, and no one to nurse them. And, Ben, some go to whoring right after being toilet-trained."

"The paper speaks its mind, week after week."

"Sure. I got no reason at all to criticize you. It's just that there's nothing to be done, and I get tired of it."

"You're not thinking of resigning, Frank? You couldn't be."

"It's not in my mind, but I could resign and live for a while on my sudden wealth. Sure, I got quite a pile for the old homestead that the dam will flood. But I'm hanging on, hell or high water."

"Good for you. Good for all of us."

Now Brobeck smiled his crinkled smile. "That's really what I wanted to talk to you about. Close to it." Abruptly the face sobered. "Ben, I wouldn't want to go against you. I wouldn't do it."

"What in the world are you talking about?"

"The state senate. Or the house. Higher office. I hear people say you would be a good man, and there's no doubt about that." There was a question in the big face.

"That's nonsense, nonsense because I won't run," Ben said. "I'm the outsider looking in and always will be." Did Mary Jess remember those words?

"You're sure?"

"Positive." Ben grinned. "You know, the paper might even support you."

Brobeck thrust out a sudden hand. "Ben," he said, "thanks. I just might need you."

They got up and walked on, and Ben crossed the street to the office. "I think I'll run out to the construction site," he said to Mary Jess, who had switched to her typewriter. "Want to come with me?"

"No thanks. I'm swamped."

He said, "So be it," and was sorry immediately. A good share of the personality of the paper, a good share of credit for its survival, was hers.

He stepped over and kissed the brow that she lifted.

"Don't hurry. You might eat out tonight, Ben. I'm going to get a scratch supper for Father, then hurry off to that meeting tonight."

"You work too hard."

"As if you hadn't been working every night of the week. Besides, I enjoy it."

And so she did, he thought. Enjoyed work too much. Enjoyed it at the cost of what might and should be. "All right," he said.

He went to the car and wheeled off. The day, at least, was fine. The afternoon sun smiled on the work of man. The breeze held its breath, and so the dust hung like a long banner on the road to the dam. It was like a big, torpid snake, kept alive as moving wheels fed it. Through the dust, along the meanders of the Breast River, he could see the winding growths of willow and cottonwood. They stood still, satisfied in the sun's rays.

Had Mary Jess been Mattie Murchison, she would be at his side. If he were to suggest they turn off to the woods and make love, she would smile and be willing. But Mattie was married now, to a second cousin of her first husband, and had a son, both events announced in jocular little notes. Wasn't it convenient, she had asked, that she hadn't had to change her name? But it had been a long time since he'd heard from her, a long time since those Tuesday nights.

A jack rabbit lay mashed in the road. A couple of magpies flew up from it. Farther along lay a dead porcupine, then a skunk. The odor of skunk filled the Buick.

The dam site was a confusion of machinery and men, of noise and dust, of moving and unmoving equipment. He pulled his car off to the side and watched, regretful of his ignorance about construction. But he had a right to feel that the dam was his, some part of its being was his, a little, mixed with the shares due the PWA and the President. The unacknowledged editor still was entitled to some satisfaction in self.

A road of sorts led around the construction site and on into the canyon. He started his car, tooled it along the road and after a mile or so stopped at a small mountain park where the walled mountains widened and the river ran free, as if never to be stopped in its course.

Here was no dust, and the noises from downstream came muted, sounding under the river's soft murmur. A patch of broad-leafed fireweed shone like a spangle on the near shore. He left the car and sat close to the bank and saw a trout jump in a pool where the stream turned. The sun, declining, touched one shoulder and the side of his face.

A voice from behind him asked, "How's the quill driver? Hey, don't jump through your collar."

"Oh, hi, Jap. Didn't hear you. Lots of room to sit down."

Jasper York sat, saying, "You city fellers got no ears." He was a man of perhaps fifty-five, his skin darkened by sun, his eyes squinted by it. When he wasn't trapping or guiding anglers and hunters, he bached it in town, where he was known for an occasional thirst and an oblique way of expressing opinions.

"How are you, Jap?"

"The happy loafer on horseback, that's me. Horse is grazin'

over yonder. But how am I for a fact?" The rumble of blasting came from downstream, and Ben could feel a quiver of earth. "I'm thinkin' the Bible played hell when it said the earth was made for man. That's how I am."

York got out a pipe, crumbled tobacco in his palm and lit up. The stream talked, and a breath of breeze played with a leaf. "Make the most of it while you can," York said. His eyes rose to the mountain side and lifted to the clear sky.

"This here," York went on, waving his pipe stem. "This grass, them trees, them posies along the bank, brutes, big and little, the mountains theirselves." His head moved in a slow shake. "That Jesus Christ dam!"

"You have to think of men."

"Men. Yeah, men. I had a pet onct, a cub bear, just the one, and I cared a heap for him. But bears by the bushel, bear after bear in bear country, why, I guide dudes to shoot 'em and don't cry a tear. If only one dandelion grew, you'd have to add to the grandstand."

"But men have to eat. You do yourself."

"I can make out without riskin' my life warrin' on prairie dogs. I see where nine million of 'em was done for last year in Montana. Didn't say how many men owed their room and board to that fight. And now for relief, so men can eat, as you say, we got a general program for rodent control. Goodbye, all ground squirrels and bunnies and such. Eat hearty, men."

Ben grinned, as he imagined York wanted him to. "But, Jap," he said, "you can't stand in the way of things. In your own lifetime you've seen a lot of changes."

"Can't call to mind any good ones right now." York fell silent, then added, "Hell, I know I'm a lost coyote, the last coyote cryin' to the last moon. 'Jap York. Jap York.' Don't that sound like a bark?"

York faced toward him, and Ben saw sadness in his eyes, the sadness of goodbye said by him or the world.

"Sorry for my jabber," York said, getting up. He knocked the ashes from his pipe on the heel of his hand and put the pipe in his pocket. "You don't feel it like me and you don't agree, but that's all right, Ben."

He walked away, as silently as he had come.

In the west the sun had vanished beyond a cloud bank, leaving only the fire of its going by the time Ben returned to his car. To detour by way of Burtville, which Brobeck's talk had suggested, meant only an extra five miles, and Mary Jess wouldn't be waiting him. Some distance before he came to the squatting of shacks, he saw and picked up the girl.

17

AT FIRST, in the fading light, he thought she was a boy, an under-sized boy who dragged one lame foot in the roadside dust and ap-peared as lonely as the last of the race. But when she raised a hes-itant thumb, he saw she was a girl dressed in a blouse and jeans.

He braked the car, steered to the side and asked, "Town?" As she approached, he leaned over and opened the door, seeing a young, lonely face with the look of haunt in it. She pulled herself inside and pushed back her long hair. Her brow was good. She said, "Thanks, Mister."

"You've hurt yourself?"

"I sprained my dumb ankle. That's why I thumbed you."

He let the motor idle, not shifting into gear. "You'd better see a doctor, don't you think?"

"It'll heal by itself. I got no money for doctors." Her voice was soft and matter-of-fact.

As if to answer the question he hadn't posed, she added, "It's my old man's fault. We had a big row and I went for a walk to cool off."

"Your father?"

"Who else? He's the only old man I got, not that he's someone to brag on. Two years ago or somewhere near, Ma, she took off with another man. I can't blame her one bit."

A car went by, and someone, probably a drunk, called out, and the call settled and died along with the raised dust.

"You're ready to go home now, I suppose."

"Got to, havin' lamed myself up. The old man's likely got

some liquor in him by this time, enough so's he can serve beer without sloshin' it all out."

He studied her, feeling pity. She couldn't be more than fifteen or sixteen or, at most, a small seventeen. Without embarrassment she let him look, like a child innocently open to scrutiny.

"You live in Burtville, then?"

"Upstairs over Smitty's beer parlor, my old man and I, if you can call it livin'. The old man, he tends bar and swamps out when he's sober enough."

"I see. And you're the cook?"

"Sometimes. When there's somep'n to cook. Mostly we live on pretzels and crackers and maybe a piece of smoked sausage or cheese or pickled stuff that the old man sneaks from the bar. He ain't got much appetite."

And so it was all accounted for, the lean features, the slim boyishness, even the look of haunt.

She asked, "Want to feel my ribs?"

"No." He waited until two more cars passed and then switched the car lights on, dimming them. "What's your name?"

"Beulah. It's supposed to be Beulah Sanders, only I ain't sure if my old man's my old man or not. When he's mad, he says damn if I'm any blood kin of his, for a true Sanders has got more to him than me. Mostly he's mad when he's drinkin'."

"And most of the time he drinks?"

"That's where ever' cent goes, on booze. Lookit here." She showed the worn cuff of her blouse. "I have to wash it all the time, it bein' one of just two, which is all I got to my name."

Cars were wheeling in from the dam site now, more and more of them, their lights striking through the Buick and going on. He rolled his window tight against the dust. He should drive on, he knew, but her matter-of-fact, childish candor held him, and she must have still more to tell. Something had to be done for her.

"So you and your father quarreled?"

"I already said so."

"Care to tell me what about?"

"You ask a lot of questions, mister, but I don't mind. It wasn't about booze we had our fight. He's so damn moral, if that's what you call it. Goody-goody, I call it. Wants me in my cage starvin', just so's I got a rag to cover myself."

"So?"

"I was goin' to Big Lil's and make a nice livin'."

"Good Lord! Big Lil's!" To men she was known as Big Tit Lil, madam of the main whorehouse in Burtville.

"If she'll take me, that's where I'm goin' onct my ankle's all right."

"You know what she does? What her girls do?"

"Sure. Even if I ain't practiced, I can learn. I can be broke in. Anything's better than nothin'. That's what I told the old man, and he got on his high horse, sayin' no Sanders ever went chippie."

"You could look for work — other work."

"What? Washin' dishes for my meals and a poor penny extra? Mister, some of those girls at Big Lil's make twenty-five dollars a night, maybe more. Besides, there's no dish-washin' jobs around that I know of."

How tell this girl? How explain to this child? How make her see age ahead of her, age and blowsiness and bloat? To her the future was twenty-five dollars a night and a square meal. He asked her, "How old are you?"

"Old enough. You can see." With one quick movement she bared a breast. In the dim light it looked as round and as plump and as fresh as a peach just picked.

He kept his hands on the steering wheel and said, "Cover up!"

"I was just provin' it to you."

"Cover up!"

"Sure, mister. I didn't mean to be dumb, but dumber girls than me work at Big Lil's, I bet."

"I'm sure of that. But, look! Before you tackle Big Lil for a place, let me scout around. There's sure to be other work for you. There's bound to be something better."

"Anything's better than the shape I'm in now. Hungry and ragged and broke. That's me."

"I'll try to help you. I'm going to give you some money right here."

"I wasn't hintin' at that."

"I know you weren't. I'm going to give it to you provided you don't try for Big Lil's."

"For how long?"

"Just until we see."

"Well?"

He took out his wallet. It had two bills in it, a ten and a five. He held them out to her.

"Mister," she said, not taking them, "I ain't on charity, but I got only one thing to give. You just have to say yes or no."

She turned her face to him, the young, lean, sober face which now held the look of pleading as if she hoped to be spared but still would consent. This for that, tit for tat, it for fifteen dollars if he insisted.

He thrust the bills in her hand, put the car in gear and said, "No, Beulah."

In Burtville she pointed. "There's where I live. At Smitty's. Over the beer joint."

He pulled to the side and stopped. There were customers and lights in the beer joint. A man with whiskers and alcoholic ruin in his face stood behind the bar and tried to squint through the window.

"He's lookin' for me, but he can't see nothin'," Beulah said. "My old man. Pretty, ain't he, mister?"

"Remember your promise," he told her.

As if in grateful goodbye she flung her young body against his and kissed him. Of themselves his hands and arms tightened on her, and he abruptly pushed her away. She said, "That was my thanks, mister."

"All right. Go now."

She let herself out and limped for a step or two, the bills upheld and forgotten in her hand, and watched him as he drove away. Big Lil's house — a sort of cluster of shacks — came to his eye. Beulah would have been in demand at Big Lil's.

He ate a late and solitary supper and, eating, happened to think of that new woman appointed to the federal emergency relief office. Her name? Herlihy, wasn't it? Patricia Herlihy. She would be a good one to see about Beulah.

The house was dark when he entered, but Mr. Collingsworth called from his bedroom, "That you, Ben?"

"Yes, governor. Good night."

He undressed in the bathroom. Mary Jess would be asleep — or pretending to be.

18

MR. COLLINGSWORTH placed his knife and fork on his plate, used his napkin, sighed with satisfaction and said, "A good meal, Mary Jess, dear." It was, Ben thought, an often-expressed judgment and a true one, though only the Lord knew how she found time for cooking.

To his "Amen" Mary Jess answered, "Thank you both."

"I've hardly had time to tell you that we got a letter from Charles today," Mr. Collingsworth said.

Mary Jess asked, "Any special news?"

"No. You can read it, of course. Between the lines it appears he continues to do splendidly, especially in English and music."

"Not homesick?"

"Never once, apparently. You would have thought he would return home for vacation rather than take summer courses. Astonishing, isn't it, that this country seems to have no hold on him at all?"

"He hears Thoreau's different drummer," Ben put in.

"I suppose, but I feel sure I couldn't live in New York, not for a king's ransom, though I'd like to be able to say I was a graduate of Columbia." He paused and went on, an edge of regret in his voice, "The different drummer. Two boys reared in the same place, in much the same manner, but young Mort seems to be pleased with our state college. I was speaking to his father today."

The talk went on as Mr. Collingsworth liked it to after dinner. Talk and more talk. Discussions about matters both big and small. Chit-chat. Personal reports. Questions about the pronunciations and meanings of words. References to the dictionary

kept ready to hand on a stand at the side of the room. It was quite
a well-furnished room, it and the whole house for that matter.
For Montana, the furniture, some of it, was elegant. By any standards the best pieces were very good, though shaded by the presence of the old upright piano Charles used to practice on.

Mary Jess had been the principal collector. Through him she
had developed an interest in antiques that exceeded his own, and
in off hours during those dead days before work began on the dam
had scoured the country, going to auctions and junk shops, storage
sheds and battered homes. Once in a while she had picked up for
pittances the good pieces that owners, hard put for cash, had thrust
aside even in better times. A Hepplewhite to go along with the
one he had bought years ago. A Chippendale chest. An inlaid,
mahogany, half-moon table. Some of the better Victorian stuff.
Probably it was all made by ancient American craftsmen, not imported, but it was all good, fine in line, shape and substance, and
it was all old. She rejoiced in finding and having each piece. All
right, Ben thought. Better to have one passion than none at all.
And he had enjoyed the refinishing, taken pleasure in working
with the old, whispering cherry and walnut and mahogany.

Mr. Collingsworth had gone silent. A frown creased his forehead, and lines deepened at the sides of his mouth. No doubt he
was thinking about some vexation the day had brought, and, like
as not, he would speak next with blind heat, in hard, leveled
tones, addressing his dissatisfaction to a found substitute. You
never could tell. He was that way.

They were awkward, even disturbing, these sudden and fugitive
rages, but they were best ignored, best let pass. They were excused by Mr. Collingsworth's general worth, his stout intentions,
by the sun that followed the heat lightning. And if keeping still
made the listener feel somewhat like second fiddler, what of it?
Besides, Mary Jess wouldn't want her father disputed.

Ben pushed back from the table, saying, "I have to go out for a
while."

"Not work again?" Mary Jess asked.

"Call it an errand of mercy," he said and got to his feet. She
wouldn't care to hear about Big Tit Lil and a poor girl who

thought she could learn how to earn twenty-five dollars a night. "Be home early." He walked to the rack, put on his hat and went out to their goodbyes.

The late summer night welcomed him. It breathed the assurance of well done and all right, though the day had seen little done. Overhead the stars waited the rise of the full moon. To the west he could see the vague line of the Rockies, gentled by distance and night.

It was a short drive to the two-story apartment building, once given over to a cheap store and cheap offices, where Patricia Herlihy had suggested he come, thus avoiding her constant workaday interruptions. He climbed to the second floor and knocked at her door. She opened it at once. She said, "You're punctual, Mr. Tate. Do come in."

She was a small, erect girl, on the edge of plump, who could have been twenty-six years old. A neat package, Frank Brobeck had called her. She had substituted a flowered housecoat for the suits Ben had seen her wear. "Take that chair," she said after he had acknowledged her greeting and entered. "It's reasonably comfortable."

The room was small but tasteful enough. Its size seemed to suit her, as did the tidy furnishings. Yes, a small neatness all round. Her face, he figured, was Irish — bright blue eyes, very fair complexion, nose small and a little upturned, and that appearance of wit and impudence that could readily turn to belligerence.

"Wouldn't you like a beer to start things off?" she asked.

"It's really not necessary, and I promise not to take much of your time."

"Wouldn't you?"

"Well, yes, thanks."

She disappeared and came back with two tall glasses and after serving him sat down, unaware or heedless that the housecoat spread open from above her knee to her ankle. The exposed leg was good, he saw, before her glance drove his eyes away. She lit a cigarette.

"You said the business was personal." A smile went with the words. Her teeth were good, too. After drinking, she went on,

"Rather short acquaintance for personal things." She smiled again. "Tell me."

"Personal," he said, feeling a little on guard, "but hardly as the words might suggest."

"Yes," she answered and listened, her eyes on him as she sipped at her beer.

He told her about Beulah Sanders, how he had happened to meet her, what she had said, how she had impressed him, and why he had come here.

Miss Herlihy, not interrupting, had finished her drink by the time he was done. "We can't let that happen to her, can we?" she said. Her smile struck him as somewhat at odds with the sentiment.

"I hope not."

"Apparently this girl made quite an impression on you?"

"She was so young."

"How old?"

"Surely not more than seventeen. She wouldn't tell me her age. She just said she was old enough."

"Of course she is. Our sex gets that way early. Out of mothers' arms into men's." She made a small face. "Who wrote *The Way of All Flesh*? The title at least is wonderful."

"I don't know, but —"

"Yes, Mr. Tate. Back to the subject." Her smile lightened her blue eyes, as if by sudden infusion. "But would you think ill of me, sir, if I suggested we had an honest drink first? My grandfather always said beer was a beverage for brats."

"No objection, but I didn't come here to drink up your inventory."

"Inventory, one bottle," she answered and took their glasses and went to the kitchen. She returned briskly after a minute, handed him a glass and sat down. "Now to business."

He took a swallow, watching her do the same, and, when he could, asked, "Did you add any water at all?"

"Some. Enough for me. If it's too strong, the tap's in the kitchen."

"No. It's all right after the first shock."

"Drink, then." She followed her own order, taking a gulp that he found hard to equal. Mort Ewing would have said the drink was as strong as Kentucky studhorse piss.

"Speaking of books —" she began.

"Who's speaking of books?"

"I was, just a minute ago. How are you coming along?"

"With what?"

"Your book. Every newspaperman has a book in him, though he seldom gives birth. Right?"

The whiskey felt good in his stomach. He took another swallow. "Once I was going to," he said.

"And never have?"

"Never a decent line. Hardly any lines at all."

"Why?"

It was none of her business.

"In the ten years I've been here, it's been a struggle. Only lately have things begun to look up."

"But still you won't write your book?" She tilted her glass.

"Excuse me if I say you're an inquisitive miss. But all right. In the beginning I thought I'd write about the war, as soon, that is, as I could bear to think about it. Time went on, and other men wrote about it, better by far than I ever could do. So now?"

Sure enough, he thought to himself, once he had thought he might write a book or perhaps a series of books. There would be time for them later, after he had established himself, for time spread forever ahead. But the years passed, closing doors. They took with them some part of energy, some part of ambition, some part of hope, even some part of regret at things left undone. That was the final loss, the slipping away of regret. But these were old-man thoughts. Hell, he was only thirty-eight.

She had allowed him time for reflection, which he ended by saying, "What's wrong with a good newspaper?"

"Nothing, but aren't there stories everywhere, even in way stations like Arfive? Men live and work and dream and love and suffer and die."

"Agreed, but don't knock our town. It's home."

"I didn't and won't. Here's how! Home to the sailor." She was a greedy drinker. He had to keep gulping to keep up.

The whiskey had brought a light flush to her cheeks. If possible, it made her eyes brighter. Without too much effort a man could think of a blossom waiting for pollination.

She said, lifting her glass, "I like to drink, if that's news for your paper. You can also report that I'm up and at 'em every morning and keep up the pace through the day. Don't you enjoy wetting your nose?"

"Yes, but it's hardly compatible with circumstance."

It was as if she were studying him and the words, seeking conclusions, and he felt himself shy away from the possibility that she might press him for explanation. In the presence of a woman like this one, what man cared to admit that he largely abstained because of his wife and her father? A man liked to appear to be his own man, and it struck him, not for the first time, that in some ways he was not. He felt the good strength of the whiskey in his blood stream.

"Under the circumstances," she said, "let's have another. Come on. Mix your own poison."

He followed her to the small kitchen. She got out an ice tray and put cubes in their glasses. In this close space his nose opened to her perfume. It caught the faint, good, woman smell of her. "Say when," she said, pouring from a bottle labeled Bottoms Up.

Back in the living room she said, "I'm garrulous. That's because I seldom have company. But don't think I've forgotten the purpose of your visit. To save a poor girl from a life of shame."

"And the miseries that go with it."

"Frankly," she said with a sudden businesslike air, "I hardly see how our office can be of help."

"Why?"

"We're involved in programs, relief programs, to be sure, but they're not directed so much to individuals as to groups and masses. Our object is to give work to men, to restore pride through self-sufficiency."

The inappropriate smile touched her face. "Your girl apparently will have no trouble finding work, work of her choice. For the self-supporting we have no program."

"It's not work she would choose, if you can call it work. It's not work anyone would choose for her."

"Oh, yes, men would choose it for her. Without men she wouldn't have work. But, even so, as it is she has food and shelter."

"Of a sort."

"Better than a lot of people. But, as I said, we try to provide work for men out of work, and for impoverished boys, too, as in the Civilian Conservation Corps. I'm afraid not much attention has been paid to women, though we have one in the cabinet. Men are the breadwinners. Hence men are the masters."

"But surely —"

"Oh, I'll see this girl of yours, since you asked me to. I'll try to do something." She took a sip from her glass. "But, tell me, Mr. Tate, just what is so wrong with prostitution?"

"You can't be serious."

"Can't I?"

"She's just a kid."

"And my office is not a vice squad, thank God. Your kid is big enough, as she told you. She can make herself self-supporting, and that's the whole aim of the programs — self-support."

"No matter how. That's what you're telling me?"

"I'm telling you this. Through the trickle-down process — no pun — when men have work, prostitutes can be self-supporting. They don't need us. But you avoid the main question. What really is so wrong with prostitution?"

The imp in her face asked for an argument, but all he said was, "You know as well as I do."

"I know that every woman has regarded prostitution with some measure of fascination. If she hasn't, I bet she'd be a poor wife. Now I'll mix the drinks, since you seem a little upset."

When she returned, he asked, "You've been married?"

"Briefly. The bottle was my man's single devotion, but I would have made a pretty fair wife. But have you ever thought about what I just said?"

"If I have, it's just now."

She drank, thoughtfully rather than thirstily. Then she turned the smile on again. "This may shock you, Mr. Tate, but if I had one piece of advice to give a young girl it would be this: Beware of the man who seeks to protect your virtue. What he means is, save it for me."

"That's not true in my case."

"No, Mr. Tate?"

"Doubt me if you will."

"Perhaps you may come to doubt yourself."

"You're really spoiling for an argument."

"Really, I'm not." She drank again, and he, too, lifted his glass. "I'm saying — I don't mean to offend your delicate sensibilities — if your little girl wants to be a whore, she'll be one, and I'm asking what's wrong with that?"

"But you will see her?"

"I said I would, and I will."

"And try to do something for her?"

"Something you think should be done for her. I yield to your noble principles." She finished her drink. "End of argument. End of interview."

At the door she took his arm. "I'm really quite moral," she said. "I don't believe in charging for what is my pleasure, too." She gave him a sudden, full-mouthed kiss and then pushed him away and demanded, "Begone!"

A teaser, he thought as he went to his car. He found himself striding. A mere teaser, or more than that?

He undressed quietly and got into bed and reached out for Mary Jess. Drowsily, without heat, in her soft-singing voice she said, "You stink of whiskey," and moved away from him.

How did it happen, where was the why of it, that Mr. Collingsworth should have sired and reared a daughter both sterile and frigid and a son whose masculinity just might be open to doubt?

Patricia Herlihy was really quite moral.

19

BED WAS A GOOD PLACE to be — or could be. He lay in it, alongside Mary Jess, and let a side thought go to Beulah Sanders. Surely, after two days, Pat Herlihy would have found time to see her. They appeared in his mind, the lonely, the haunted face that had talked about whoring, and the impudent, Irish face that had seen nothing wrong in it. And into their company came Mattie Murchison. How long, how long since they had found relief in each other? How long since those Tuesday nights when they had made love without loving involvement? Body to body, with Beulah Sanders, with Pat Herlihy, with Mattie Murchison. Any of them.

It was faithless to dwell on them, to feel himself swelling with memory and impossible prospect.

He moved closer to Mary Jess and put his arm over her and pressed himself against her seat. There was always the chance, the slim chance.

She said, her voice as always somehow seductive, "Please, Ben, not tonight. I'm tired out. Won't you move back?"

"Lord, Lord," he answered and, when she didn't reply, asked, "Why not, Mary Jess? Why are you always too tired?"

"Please don't exaggerate."

"All right. Nearly always too tired? Or something?"

"It's you, Ben, if you'd only admit it. I'm a perfectly normal woman."

He shifted away from her, knowing embrace and the push of his body were of no use, asking as he moved, "Who is the judge of that?"

Mattie had said in that long ago that women were liars, one to another, unwilling to admit normal appetites to those of the same sex. And wasn't his own experience, though limited, enough to prove Mary Jess wrong?

He said, "So all marriages are frustrating to men?"

She turned face to face to him then, her knees drawn up like barriers. "I suppose you can speak for all men?" The lovely voice had the strain of anger in it.

"Just as you can speak for all women."

Ten years, he thought, ten years since their marriage, and he had believed then that the nagging, the aching urgencies would be quieted, that love would be answered with acts of love, that all would be well — husband's needs satisfied, wife happy to satisfy them. Out of bed in the morning and brave for the world. And all of it only a dream that reality shattered. Only a damn dream dreamed in ignorant youth.

She said, "Look at yourself." The omission of "Ben" in her words was significant. "Understand yourself."

"Sure. I'm a sex fiend."

"At any rate you're insatiable."

"Am I? Two times a month if I'm lucky. You ration it out like limited calories."

"I won't argue with you. I said I was tired."

"It's a sort of tyranny, the way you use sex. Give the boy one cookie if you must and afterwards expect him to be a good boy to the point of death by starvation."

"I won't listen to any more."

"Don't, then, for Christ's sake."

"Your swear words entice me."

"Fine, goddamn it."

"You'll wake up Father."

"I'll bet he had it better than I do."

The bed moved to her sudden rigidity. He heard her breathing. At last she said, "If I'm not woman enough for you, find another."

"Divorce you, you mean?" he answered unbelieving. "Not that."

"No. Just sleep in other beds if you must, but be discreet. As a couple we have a reputation to maintain." The last words sounded wry.

"I don't want to lie in other beds." He was close enough to the truth to justify what he said.

"I give you your freedom. I just don't care. Only be discreet."

"That's exactly what I might do," he replied and felt lost, lost to the lost dream, lost to the bonds he respected, lost to all save the free future and a new, slow anger. To save them she had to give so very little of self. She had only to yield, only to goddamn yield. So little to ask.

He rolled to his side of the bed, saying shortly, "Good night."

He lay awake wanting her, wanting her to the total exclusion of any others, he told himself. It was so little to give, he thought, so great to get and so hard to come by.

And now it served her right if she had to cry.

◆

Were all men like Ben, she asked herself? The answer was probably. It might be that most of them actually were. Men. Barnyard roosters, happy only in a harem of hens. Nature's way for the race to perpetuate itself, as if child after human child mattered.

She had no wish to perpetuate herself. God knew her mother and father had done enough of that. Pregnancy on pregnancy until Mother died of pregnancies; and the end result, the token reward was a bundle of red wrinkles that grew up to be Charles. Thank heavens Brother Charles showed no outward interest in sex.

She was probably sterile and should be glad. Accused, Ben had confessed to times he hadn't taken precautions, but nothing had happened except the long dread of pregnancy. She didn't, she wouldn't, mess with precautions herself. Those ugly preparations were up to Ben, and he had promised not to forget or ignore them. Sterility, and it was just as well, an added insurance, though, more than ever, it made the act of sex empty. The act of love, it was known as, as if love couldn't exist without the coarse seal of performance.

The coarse seal, nearly always unwelcome, never invited. Most women must think and feel as she did, and, if they didn't, nevertheless here she was, incapable of keeping Ben satisfied, incapable really of ever finding joy and release in the act.

She wouldn't cry, she told herself! The hand on which her head rested closed into a fist. She wouldn't cry. The problem was Ben's, and he couldn't help himself, either. Why cry?

Once or twice Ben had tried his little tricks, thinking to arouse her while he pushed hard on her body; and the tricks had been bestial, rude as any animal's preliminary behavior.

Father had had it better than Ben, Ben had said with thoughtless or thoughtful cruelty, touching on circumstances best never thought about. She had ceased trying to understand the physical woman who had been her mother. And no longer did she feel any grievance toward Father. Maybe it was because in his long, wifeless years he had never shown an interest in another woman. Not once had he. Pictures of Mother, six of them, stood arrayed in his bedroom, and, sometimes, entering, she had caught him studying them with what seemed to be and must be devotion. And sometimes, unknown to him, she had heard him singing, "No rose in all the world until you came." The one woman in his life, the abused, cherished woman, loved beyond all. It was unlikely men like Ben ever could understand.

But Ben was such a good man. Give him credit. List his qualities, forgetting his animal appetite. Industry. Patience. Thoughtfulness. Intelligence. Gentleness. He was kind to Father. He overlooked, he dismissed Father's senseless bursts of temper. He didn't argue. He didn't disagree, and he didn't concede. He just kept silent, even when Father needed rebuke. She should be glad he restrained himself, even if it made him seem, well, rather pale, even if she wished he'd talk back as she had learned not to do.

Only a time or two had Ben suggested, mildly suggested, that they buy or build their own house and vacate the old premises. He had understood, then, that she couldn't leave Father, couldn't possibly leave him. For his sake, they couldn't. Forget Ben's. Forget hers. Think of Father. He wouldn't be happy without them. He wouldn't be happy anywhere else. Here was home.

A patient man, Ben. A cheerful man. A successful one. A mild man, tolerating in his house another of more outspoken and heated opinion.

And she had given this good man her permission for illicit rutting. Now pray that no other woman came into his life. Pray for constancy. Pray against anything that would mar or ruin their marriage. She could see him lying with some willing partner. She could hear them whispering confidences. And a sudden fury came on her and turned into hurt.

Such a good man, and if he asked her now, she would come to him. If only he put his arm around her and told her he loved her. But, freed, he lay still, far away from her, a great divide between them, the divide she had erected, hard and impassable. Move to me, Ben! Ask and it shall be given you.

It was then that she couldn't keep from crying.

20

THEY DROVE to the office together, as wordless, it seemed to Ben, as two strangers passing on opposite sides of the street. There came a time when talk ended, a time when talk threw up a wall between talkers that more talk couldn't climb. Concession could do it, but who would concede? Not Mary Jess, that was sure. And not he, that was just as sure. It gave a man a certain, a rightful satisfaction to reach a position from which he wouldn't budge.

Only when they were in the office did he say, "Don't count on me today. Sportsmen's Club meeting at noon, Lions Club meeting tonight."

"Very well. You can have the car. Father will pick me up."

"No need to. One of the boys will drive me home."

"Very well."

He looked in the shop and found the men busy, without need of directions, and gathered some copy paper and overdue bills and went out.

Dust was a price of progress. It rose and hung and settled down on the town only to rise again, whipped up by trucks and pickups and passenger cars. Just a year, maybe two years ago, it would have lain undisturbed except now and then for the passage of a vehicle whose owner had a piece of rare business and the price of a gallon of gas.

Hurrah for progress, then, but it was time the town paved its streets. It could afford to. There was a subject for an overdue editorial. And the old cottonwoods, dusted over now, that shaded Main Street. Some of them were dying, and more had been cut down. The damn birds, you know, and, what's more, a businessman wants his sign to be seen, not lost in a bunch of branches, the guilty parties had argued, ignoring the fact that the trees gave the town a pleasing individuality that most high-plains settlements lacked. There was another editorial, one for Mary Jess, if and when.

He dropped into Billie Gayle's place for a package of cigarettes, and Billie said gently, while an ungentle fate agitated his hands, "Morning, Ben. Fatimas again?"

"Fine morning, Billie. Yes, please."

"Every morning is a fine morning," the tortured mouth said. "To wake up to any morning is fine. To know you're still here."

"You sound pretty doleful."

"Oh, no. It's just I wouldn't want to come to the end of my days and not have good things to look back on. Like mornings."

There, for Billie, was the sum of it all, Ben thought, all that he asked for, all perhaps that he wanted, plus, of course, enough money to supply his few needs. Any mornings fine and all mornings good to remember. Let the world wake to light, struggle from bed, fumble into clothes with hands and feet that wouldn't take orders, and rejoice for the dawn.

"Sure, Billie," Ben said, touched by a sense of shame, "I'm with you." He took his change from the trembling, uncomplaining hand and walked back to the street.

He went to the Forest Service office and found that no fires burned now and all danger was past, or almost, after a combined loss for which the ranger would supply figures tomorrow. He learned at the offices of the Corps of Engineers that work on the dam was abreast of schedule or even ahead of it. Penney's spoke for a full-page ad, Peter Sears wanted a half one, and Spence Green one of two columns. The new man at the new lumberyard paid up, with apologies.

Patricia Herlihy was walking up the street as he came out of the lumberyard office. She wore a businesslike suit, a little severe for place and weather, but above the close neck of it her face seemed to bloom.

He said, "Good morning, Miss Herlihy."

"Since when, Ben?"

"Since when what?"

"Since when Miss Herlihy?"

"All right, Patricia or Pat. Still, good morning."

"A busy one," she said. "Busy days, all of them."

"Too busy for what we talked about?"

"To talk about now, yes, but I haven't forgotten."

"Or done anything?"

She frowned and said, "Just a little. I'm afraid it needs discussion."

"All right. When?"

"I'll have some office news for you, too."

"That's good. When again?"

The frown turned into her impudent smile. "Would it compromise the editor to come to see me tonight? I'll be home." At his hesitation she added, "For the sake of appearances you could bring your briefcase."

It came on him to say, "And a bottle?"

"Why not?" She clicked off in her high heels, her face smiling as she looked over her shoulder.

So Pat Herlihy hadn't exercised herself to help Beulah Sanders. It was doubtful she would. The roguish and provocative face faded into that of a lean, little girl with disappointment in it, the sad eyes fixed on Big Lil's. Where else could she turn?

But not there. By all that was holy, not there. And it struck him that what she would sell was the very thing that his groin demanded, though not from her. No, not from her. Put that base thought aside. Bury it. But so things went — good intentions, untoward and sneaky impulses, and no answers that satisfied both. No answers. That was the answer to life. No answers.

Yet he could go to the post office, scribble a hopeful note to Beulah and enclose a few dollars and thus weigh in for rectitude.

The note written, in care of Smitty's, and fifteen dollars enclosed, he felt better. He would feel still better if Frank Brobeck canvassed the courthouse on the chance there was a job for her there.

Skeeter Jerome, so named because he resembled a gnat, sat in the outer office, telephone to his ear, and with a thumb motioned Ben back.

Brobeck was at his desk, papers before him and a mangled cigar in his mouth. He took the cigar out and said, "Hi, Horace Greeley."

"Howdy, high sheriff."

"Glad to see you, Ben, but I got nothin' much for your news nose today. Have a seat."

"Fine morning."

"Yeah, but by the looks of you you didn't come to talk about weather. Something on your mind, Ben? Something weighty?"

"Something you might help with."

"Yours truly. Spill it."

Ben looked toward the connecting door and saw that he'd closed it and then told about Beulah Sanders. "I wondered," he said in conclusion, "if maybe you could scout up a job for her here?"

Brobeck had listened, his cigar held still in his teeth, his ugly, not-ugly face grooved as always. Then he said, "What's the lady's name?"

"Did I forget that?"

"Shit, Ben. What is it? You protectin' her fair reputation?"

"It's Beulah Sanders."

Brobeck took the cigar from his mouth, shook his head, bowed it in his hands and shook it some more. "Jesus loves me," he said.

"Why say that?"

"Beulah Sanders!"

"You know her?"

"Innocence is a trap, Ben, and maybe a sin."

"You're speaking of her?"

"No, for God's sake! You." Brobeck shook his head again. A smile that might have been rueful touched his mouth. "Bawlin' Beulah. Little bawlin' Beulah. She hooked you. Been hookin' the innocent right along. You're a sucker, Ben."

"Thanks."

"You're welcome. But back to the case. That poor, little, innocent girl that tore your heart so, she's been whorin' at Big Tit Lil's for more'n a year. Now, when trade gets slow, she hoofs off up the road and plays sorrowful. The locals know her and pass her up, but they don't spread the word, because that would jinx a legitimate business."

Ben looked away. He heard a sigh go out of him that was more like an exhaustion of lungs.

"Now," Brobeck went on, "them as don't know, like you, pick her up and get sympathetic, bein' she's so alone in the world and so close to sin. Way it winds up, most of 'em fuck her in the interests of purity, give her a nice piece of money and tell her now to be a good girl — until they come by again, that is."

Brobeck's eyes peered from their fretwork of wrinkles. "No, I guess you didn't, Ben."

"I didn't."

"I believe you. But you gave her money. Even sent her a note today. Signed, too, I bet."

Ben nodded.

"Want your money back, and the note to boot?"

"Forget it!"

"You don't have to look like the holy temple was wrecked. It's just your innocence suffers."

"I'm a sucker."

"But a good sucker, Ben. Don't forget it."

"Why don't you shut down all the houses?"

"Now, now, Ben. Don't get riled. There's arguments both ways. No one's payin' me to let 'em stay open. Best of a bad choice is what I say."

Skeeter Jerome stuck his head in the door. "Sheriff, you made a note to remind you of that Sportsmen's Club feed."

"Thanks, Skeeter. I'll be there."

After Jerome had closed the door, Ben said, "I know you're not being paid."

"Well, the hell with the whole subject then. You remember when I talked about huntin'?"

"Some time ago."

"It's all set up now. Jap York will outfit and guide us. None better. Middle of next month, season opens. Spence Green wants to go, and there's you and me, and then our friend, Mr. Earl Kilmer. How does that strike you?"

"All right."

"You don't even hear me."

"I said all right. It's your party."

"Aw, let the son of a bitch come along. Can't hurt, even if we both got our eyes on the Senate."

"I'm not sure I'll go. I don't care about killing."

"Who says you have to shoot anythin'. Just tail along."

"Maybe."

"Make it yes. Ben, I can see things are gnawin' on you. Your face has forgot how to smile. You have to get away, by God, and look at the sky and feel the breeze and fill your belly with camp food and get a taste of freedom from all shitty fret."

"Lecture ended?"

"Nigh onto. Yeah, things are gnawin' on you, I'm smart enough to see that, and it's not just Beulah Sanders and your bleedin' innocence, but I ain't curious. What I want is the old Ben." He looked at his watch. "Time we went to that lunch."

Walking to the Arfive House, Ben felt demeaned and betrayed and, more than that, foolish. A smart man, he was, a knowledge-able editor, a contributor to rectitude where no rectitude was. A silly son of a bitch, full of innocence, brimming with sperm, thinking of Mary Jess, thinking of Pat Herlihy, a man with no an-swers and no right to opinions.

But he could act. Tonight he would skip the Lions Club, buy a bottle and, briefcase in hand, call on Pat Herlihy. She might think him witless but conclude he had other credentials.

◆

He slid into bed, trying not to disturb Mary Jess. But she moved closer to him and murmured, "Ben," and didn't remark on the odor of whiskey, and he knew she was willing to make her belated concession. His mind could hear Pat Herlihy saying, "Skip the preliminaries, Ben. I'm a self-starter." And later in the night she was saying, with emphasis on the last word, "Good God, Ben, don't you ever get any?"

He patted Mary Jess's shoulder and moved away. And now it was he who could say, and say truly, with a pleasure that pained him, "I'm too tired tonight, dear."

21

MR. COLLINGSWORTH placed a red queen on a black king and let the deck rest in his hand. He had never liked card games, in fact had avoided them, but someone — who was it now? — had taught him Klondike, which he said was one version of solitaire, and it was a way to pass quiet hours.

In one picture at the back of the flat desk on which he played, May was smiling on him. Her mouth was gently amused, as if about to say, "Having fun, Benton?" The other pictures, standing on dresser and shelf where he could see them from his bed, showed gentleness, too, but not so much of amusement.

"Burning daylight, Maysie," he said to himself. "That's what Jack London would call it."

He ought to be making preparations for the beginning of school. There were still things to be done, but a full staff had been engaged, had arrived and been interviewed, and he had no stomach for detail today. Better to sit quiet and fool away time with the cards.

The summer days were always quiet, what with no school to attend and Ben and Mary Jess out of the house. In older times he would have had a fishing rod in his hand and his eyes on a trout hole, but fishing was, after all, only fishing, and good roads and automobiles and more anglers made decent catches infrequent.

Another picture was chiding him, saying, "Now, Benton," as if mere laziness kept him in his chair. He answered in silence, "But, Maysie, I'm older. Things aren't what they were. No, not with me and not with the country. It used to be good fishing was only a short hike away. Used to be."

He slid a card from the deck, saw there was no play and again held the deck idle.

Change, he thought. Years. Time. There was never a now to seize and hold still. It slipped past the tongue and became then in the moment of saying. A man trying to grasp it felt it slide through his hands and hook him and carry him into new nows that weren't nows because now never was. The world was a world of thens, of back-whens, of used-to-bes. Time swept on, hurrying a man along with it, and the only beacons he sighted were those long left behind.

The long afternoon sunlight shone through the west window. It, too, would be gone, was going even as he observed it. Night would return, but it would be a new night, different from all nights before. And the unsettled weather of the equinox would return, not as it ever had been.

There was no play for the red four or the black. Pity for them to be buried when the prospect was good.

"Sorry thinking," he said without words and went on thinking. The smiling face on the desk understood.

Time was the great thief, the slow, sure taker of all. Of the school board that had hired him in those green years of long ago only Mort Ewing survived. The others — old Mr. Sterling McLaine, Jay Ross, Merc Marsh — one by one they had been subtracted from days remembered. Friends, the old, certain friends beside whom later ones paled? The Stuart Alexanders were gone, and their great house to the west of town stood blind and vacant, its lower floor the retreat of horses and cattle in bad weather and fly time. Old Mr. Greenwood had been taken, rightfully, if right existed, to the socialist world that he believed Jesus Christ preached. Smoky Moreau, the mystic Indian, drawn off to the happy hunting grounds. And Macalester Cleveland, the neglected, whose removal time had celebrated with a blaze of pure light. A man could even regret the loss of his enemies. Almost alone of old friends, besides Ewing, Doctor Crabtree remained, weathered as a piece of discarded harness.

He gathered the deck and shuffled, saying but not saying, "Just one more, Maysie."

There had been laughter in those days, laughter and hearty talk and feasts to founder a man. It was then as if everything were at the beginning and ahead lay the ripe world.

Thirty-four years, he thought while he surveyed the new layout of cards. Thirty-four years of trying to teach simple manners and excite intellectual curiosity in incurious rowdies, in gum-chewers and bubblegum-blowers and glandular showoffs. Was the cultural level elevated as a result of his labors? How many, given the start, pursued knowledge? Maybe to the first question. A few, a dear few, to the second. They were the great and scanty reward.

He made a play. The downing sun shone longer in the room.

" 'The years that the locust hath eaten,' " he said, not aloud, to a photograph on the shelf.

He rose and stepped to the west window, the unturned cards in his hand, and looked to the mountains. The base of Elephant Ear Butte, which ignorant upstarts were calling Ear Mountain these days, lay shadowed by its own height under the sinking sun, but the summit was crowned with light. How often had he looked at it, finding some kind of assurance there, knowing that at least one thing endured? Let people, seeing him, wonder at this attraction to stone. He wouldn't explain, if he could. It was there, and he was here, close by, a partner to what the locusts couldn't devour.

So, he thought, sitting down again with the cards, I laze away the quiet summer days. There are sunup and high noon and evening star and night. A placid, tranquil life, easing along to the end.

There was a slow vexation. Tranquillity. A tranquil house, a tranquil daughter, a tranquil son-in-law. Even were Charles back from Columbia, he would only add to the unrelieved atmosphere. There were no storms in this house and no aftermaths of sweet calm. Lives cruised along at dead level. Once he had had a temper and had exercised it, to both his regret and gratification. He was still edgy and always would be, but his temper, so easily fired in past years, had given way to a controlled irritation. Call him tranquil, too.

He turned the ace of spades and put it up.

This dead house needed children, no matter how pesky. It

needed shouts and thumps and tears and laughter. Children to love and enjoy, to share living with, to direct and shape and forge and be proud of. "Where are the babies, Maysie?" he asked a picture. Where, Mary Jess? Where, Ben? Are careers so important? Is your love not love, then?

"Maysie," he said silently while his gaze went from picture to picture, "We knew, didn't we? We had a better life, didn't we? Tell me it's so. If only you hadn't had to go on!"

Now, aloud, he said, "I loved you so, Maysie."

For an instant, in the lowering beam of the sun, Doctor Crabtree appeared, stern as God, and May lay dead in their bed. Doctor Crabtree was asking, "How many pregnancies, Mr. Collingsworth? How many live births? How many miscarriages?"

Then the stern mouth, suddenly torn, said, "I wore out one wife myself."

Mr. Collingsworth seized a handful of cards and flung back his hand to throw into the shaft of sun. Then he placed them quietly on his desk, got up and marched out.

22

"LITTLE FROSTY these mornings," Frank Brobeck said.

"Fine weather, though," Ben answered.

"Yeah, but not for elk hunting. No snow, no tracks."

They rode in Brobeck's pickup, which was loaded with hunting-trip gear. The first light was just striking the high tips of the mountains, and Brobeck switched off the car lights and switched them back on, for the morning's mist hovered low. Snow showed on the peaks and in the high crevices twenty miles to the west, but lower down the Rockies were dark, for this little time holding their secrets against the eye of the sun. No wind stirred, and the dust of the day before had settled, not to be disturbed again until workers started out for the dam.

"I bet those damn two, Kilmer and Green, will hang back until the horses are packed," Brobeck said. His face showed good humor, though the dawn light shadowed its furrows. "Don't matter, though. Jap York and I can get the string ready."

"I'll help where I can."

"Sure. Sure." Brobeck turned to smile. "But you're just along for the ride. Which reminds me, just why did you bring that light rifle? No open season on deer this year."

"I told you it was the only one in the house. Some rancher, gone broke, gave it to Mr. Collingsworth for clerking an auction."

"Which don't exactly answer my question, since you don't intend to shoot anything."

"That's for the others to find out, but everyone will have a gun, everyone on this trip."

Brobeck smiled again. "Didn't want to be plumb out of style, huh?"

"Something like that."

"Like goin' to a birthday party with nothin' in hand? Like bein' found bare-assed at a fancy-dress ball?"

"All right, Frank."

In the distance, at the dam site, the great earth movers stood outlined. One light gleamed from a crane. The sunshine was inching down the slopes now, and the humps and gashes of construction loomed dark, like giant animals stricken, Ben thought, like creatures, gouged, that lived before man.

Looking, Brobeck said, "Say, Ben, you heart and soul, so to speak, for the dam? Hundred percent, I mean?"

"You ought to know. I've been plugging it long enough."

"Yeah, for irrigation to begin with. But this ain't for irrigation. Just flood control, and it don't hold up to argument."

"Irrigation will follow, don't you worry. Meantime men have work."

"Oh, sure, and I'm all for that, and you know it. It's a poor dish, empty bellies are. But still the dam means sayin' so long, so long to the runs and holes we used to fish, so long to huntin' grounds and campin' grounds and pretty places we knew once."

"But if every change is goodbye to what was, it's hello to something new and something better. At least we can believe so. You've got me preaching now, but we can't say no to the future. If the first men in the West had said no, there'd be no Montana, no Arfive."

"Which, I guess, wouldn't have bothered them much. Remember, I'm with you, but you run a newspaper and so got to be up in the collar."

Brobeck was right enough. A good newspaper stood against stagnancy. It had to concern itself with community welfare, to look ahead, to encourage, to promote. To back President Roosevelt, if it came to that. To support the authorities and administrations he had brought into being, makeshift and disorganized and in need of refinement as they might be. The man aimed at the general good.

Into his thought Brobeck said, as a by-the-way, "The Indians tried to say no."

"And couldn't. Neither can we, and we shouldn't want to. Sure, the past has its charms, but the future is what we make of it and can be better than anything yet, but we can't make anything of it by balking at change."

"You're preaching, sure enough. All right, no balk."

And yet, Ben thought, and yet. It was a sorry condition of life that change always had to tow a trailer of goodbye, that every gain entailed a loss. It was sorrier yet that every choice, big or little, had to be burdened with regret. Or with a load of guilt.

Take himself, he thought as the pickup bumped along. Only with Mattie Murchison had he felt free of guilt, but there had been a choice there, a choice of marriage no matter what she said, and he had made the choice and come to know a lingering regret. Which might be why he seldom made a point of calling on her mother. Last time he saw her, months ago, she told him Mattie had a good job but had lost her husband.

Or take himself and Patricia Herlihy. Freed by Mary Jess, he had lain with Pat by choice, not once but often, and as a consequence had become an undemanding husband, and Mary Jess was happy with him, perhaps suspecting but not knowing why the change. There was a gain of sorts. But gain or not and freedom or not, the choice had burdened him with guilt, as recollection of it did this minute. To sneak up back stairways! To feign business meetings! To arrange secret pickups at dark corners and take furtive drives! Great conduct for a married man with respect for the proprieties. It was some small comfort to have learned that guilt piled on guilt made the first inconsequential and the last less onerous.

He hitched in his seat. He couldn't make that choice again or feel that latest guilt again, for Pat was leaving town, appointed to a better station at Butte. Good! Good?

Brobeck steered around the southward footing of the dam and remembered to turn off his head lamps. The light on the crane had gone out. The fury of the day — roar and clatter of machinery, voices, dust, blasts in resisting stone, gouged and tumbling earth — would begin soon. Now the monsters of machinery slept, and the only noise was the noise of the pickup, the only dust the dust stirred by its wheels, the only voices his and Frank's when they chose to speak.

Brobeck said, "Kind of spooky, isn't it? Like ghosts, those machines are, but nights are the time for ghosts. These start rattlin' their chains with the sun."

Above the dam site, away from the noise and movement to be, York had the horses tied up, five saddled and ten under pack harness. He said, "Howdy. Where you been all day? And where's the rest?" His eyes had the bright, squinted gleam of a man, shaped and colored by weather and space, who could see game where others couldn't.

"Comin' along," Brobeck answered. "We got the gear with us, or most of it."

"You won't get it unloaded, sittin' there at the wheel. We can mante up."

From the pickup Brobeck and Ben took sleeping bags, food, ammunition, their rifles in scabbards, binoculars, heavy clothes, camp utensils, a tent, a folded-up camp stove. Some of the items made York remark, "Jesus Christ, why all the plunder? I said bring clothes, grub, glasses and your rifles. Think I'm a two-bit outfitter?"

Brobeck gave him his plowed-face smile. "Just afraid you might be runnin' shy, Jap. If it was just you, you'd make your fire with a couple of sticks, cook your meat on a willow stick, feed your face by hand, rump up on a rock for a bed and howl at the moon."

York went to a horse and returned with ropes and canvasses. He said, "Help mante up, you smart-ass sheriff as never caught anything but the clap."

They assorted the items and, save for rifles, ammunition and binoculars, laid them on canvas squares and wrapped and roped them with a dexterity Ben could only watch and admire. Then, with equal dexterity, they lifted the packs to the pack horses, balanced the loads and made their hitches.

They had just finished when Spence Green and Earl Kilmer

drove up. After greetings they brought their own rifles, ammunition, extra clothing and glasses from the car and with them a carton that held half a case of whiskey.

"Well, now," York said, seeing the whiskey, "we'll call it square, your bein' late, seein' as you brung a necessity. I'll even thank you, for it gets boresome waitin' at the still."

Kilmer was uncorking a bottle. He said, "You ought to know." The reference was to York's reputation as a moonshiner during Prohibition.

York took the bottle and drank. "It was thirsts like yours drove me to it."

When the bottle got back to Kilmer, he lifted it and said, "Here's to the one good thing I can say for the New Deal. Repeal. But if Roosevelt cuts the dollar any lower, it's back to the still for you, Jap."

York shook his head. "Too deep for me, boys. Spendin' ourselves broke so as to be prosperous." While he made a pack of the whiskey and extra clothes the two men had brought and hitched it on a horse, the others waited.

Since those days of ten years ago Earl Kilmer's face, once so smooth and pure in the possession of right, had grown a fine fret of wrinkles. They gave him the appearance of a quizzical humor until you looked in his eyes, which were unsmiling and fixed on unrevealed goals. Time hadn't changed the essential man, Ben reflected, except to add a waiting and shrewd calculation. Spence Green appeared to be what he was, a pharmacist and drugstore owner careful with prescriptions both medical and financial. A good enough man, pale from his store's shelter and grown a little too fat.

" 'Bout ready," York called as he examined the packs.

Here, down in the canyon, the night's chill hung on, untouched yet by the sunshine on the shouldering mountains. The mountains rose all around, their bases blue-dark in the gathering light. A growth of aspens strung along a ridge began to gleam in dull gold. Except for clumps of wild daisies the flowers of summer were gone, the broad-leaf fireweed along the bank shrunken to a tangle of stems. Some chokecherries hung purple on a bush that had lost most of its leaves. Where grass grew, the frost whitened it. An old man's stubble of beard on the face of Mother Earth, Ben thought, feeling the chill push through his clothes. He moved, and the stubble crunched under foot.

"Climb on," York said after assigning each man his saddle horse, and Brobeck said to Ben, "Tenderfoot, see your cinch is snug and try out your stirrups for length."

Ben answered, "Thanks, Frank," though he knew that much without being told.

They set off, York in the lead with a string of five pack horses, then Brobeck with five, then Kilmer, then Green. Ben was well content to be at the tail.

Looking behind him to see all was in order, York called to Ben, "Just twelve–fourteen miles. Stick ass to saddle, boy."

The trail led through willows, through cottonwoods, through pines, through little clearings, rising and falling, leaving the stream and returning. The sun climbed over the mountains and shone gently at first, then so hot that Ben, like the others ahead, pulled to a stop, dismounted, took off his coat and tied it in back of the saddle.

Mile by slow mile the stream dwindled. Where the trail ran close to it, trout moved in silver-black flashes, weasel-swift in alarm. Then there was no more stream but a swampy spring and near it bright falls of water from last winter's snow pack. They let the horses drink there.

Above the spring they came to a mountain of coarse shale, an unsurmountable mountain, so high that a man had to arch his back and strain his neck to see its top; and the trail tackled it by switchbacks, narrow switchback on switchback, the hairpin turns so acute that each horse almost had to double back on itself. Gazing down while he let his horse choose its footing, Ben could imagine a slide, one that would tumble man and horse down and bury them and bury the spring and rumble to rest, damming the canyon without help of machine.

Here, near the summit, he could look eastward over the tops of the mountains they had snaked through and see the sunny plains stretching to the horizon and their small dottings of homesteads and wheat elevators.

At the summit York held up his string. His eyes roamed the canyoned valley from which they had climbed, and his mouth moved, saying words that Ben couldn't make out. Were they, "Look well. Look well while you can"?

Ben looked, to the meanders of the stream, to the small parks, to the brush and trees that, wanting water, drank from the river and in time would be drowned. From this height all appeared diminished, delicate and dear as a child's careful construction, not to be disturbed by the meddling of grownups.

Even so. Even so. Better to restore bounce to life than to leave things as they were because they were what they were. Better to spend yourself broke so as to be prosperous. If you could do so. If only you could. Decision again. Choice again. And again loss.

The horses were getting their wind back. They were wet and lathered with sweat, and the smell of it seemed almost visible.

They angled down the divide into the drainage of the Medicine. How many more miles? Ben found himself asking himself. How much longer? His seat felt raw, and his knees permanently sprung by the stretch of the saddle. But it was plod after plod after tormenting plod, and his head thudded to the steps of his horse; and this was vacation, all this, vacation from work, time off from troubles, time on for high spirits.

Then the horses quickened pace, and at last they arrived at a pole corral beside which lay a few canvas-covered bundles of what must be hay. Off to the side was an irregular circle of fire-blackened stones. The sun had made its swing and, gentle again, shone from the west, just above farther mountains.

York rode his horse to a pole, dismounted and tied up. He and Brobeck knew what to do with the packs and horses, and Kilmer stood ready to help. After unsaddling his horse and freeing it inside the corral, Ben started rustling firewood. From one of the lashings Green had taken an ax. He breathed hard as he used it.

With the packs on the ground, York led the unsaddled horses inside the corral, let them roll, hobbled a couple, hung bells on two more and let down the gate. Stooping to light the fire, Ben heard the thump and clump of hooves and the jangling of bells as the bunch surged out to graze.

Once the packs were brought close to the fire, York rummaged and took out the bottle they had drunk from before. "Tea time," he said, uncorking it. "Tea time if only you, Ben, would run to the crick and get a bucket of water. The straight stuff closes my pipes."

There was nothing like a good drink, once it settled, to straighten sprung knees, Ben thought as he passed the tin cup.

York scanned the sky and said, "No snow tonight, but we best pitch a tent. It's a sucker's game, bettin' with nature that holds all the aces. Want to lend a hand?"

"I'll cook. How about it?" Ben said.

"Good. You know where the grub is."

They ate fried potatoes and onions, steaks broiled on an open grill, and drank coffee that Ben had let boil, knowing they wanted it strong. Chocolate bars did for dessert. York took whiskey instead.

Afterwards they sat around the fire, smoking, occasionally feeding the little blaze, feeling the night's chill enclose them now that the sun had gone down. The moon bulged the eastern horizon and grew into a great, golden disc, and the camp and the mountains assumed outline and detail.

"The way it is," York said, "us outfitters each of us got our territories pretty well fixed. Not strict, you understand, but still more or less. That don't mean that outside parties can't hunt here, amateur parties, I mean, but most of them are too busy makin' heap big wages at the dam and catchin' up on debts to their bellies."

Ben saw the men nod, as if what had been said was no news to them.

"What you don't know," York continued, "is that this year, not like last year or the years before, the elk voted for my territory. Or more'n a few did on account of the graze, not bein' grazed off, had got better here. It'll take careful huntin', but there's elk around."

"I'm heading up the Medicine in the morning," Kilmer said, not as if he desired company. "I know where." The moonlight and firelight exaggerated the fine fret of his wrinkles.

"I'll take out for Beaver Creek," Brobeck announced. "How about it, Spence?"

"Sure, but that leaves Ben."

"I'll tend camp," Ben said.

"Me'n you both," York put in. "Now I've got whiskey and found me a cook, I figure to loaf."

Brobeck edged a few sticks into the fire. The moon in its rise had turned from gold to silver. The step-by-step ring of the horse bells sounded soft in the night.

"One other thing," York said, his eyes on the fire. "There's an old she-grizzly around. I hope you remember we're not huntin' bears."

Kilmer asked, "Why not? It's legal."

"She come here last year from the Yellowstone country or maybe the Flathead with a gimp in her leg where somebody shot her, and she's old and alone, and there ain't many of her kind around anywhere anymore — not anymore — and I guess she don't see much future before her. It all makes her pretty short in her temper."

"What's that got to do with it?" Kilmer asked.

York kept looking at the fire, and it struck Ben that he might be equating himself with the bear as the losing survivor of change.

"Last year," York said, "she treed an assistant ranger and kept him up on a limb for two or three hours. And he wasn't doin' anything to get up her dander except he caught her unaware-like. He had took off from the station — you know, Ben, Gates Park, maybe four miles from here — " York gestured with a back-slant-ing thumb, "and was just studyin' wildlife and tree growth and such, but she didn't like it."

"I still don't see," Kilmer said.

York gave the fire a small smile. "And the forest-fire look-out" — he moved his thumb again — "he climbed off his perch to exercise his legs, and she came rollin' out of the brush. He was lucky he could fly up to his tower, leavin' only the seat of his pants for her to remember him by."

York paused, still with his small smile, and went on. "Sour Sow, we began callin' her, but the nice game warden felt it fell shy of bein' quite proper, and besides, he stutters. By the time he'd got 'Sour Sow' off his tongue, he disremembered his lines. So now we call her Sweet Sue, though it doesn't help his stutterin' much."

Brobeck asked, "Did you ever see her?"

"Sure. Time or two."

"And didn't shoot?" It was Kilmer asking.

"I didn't shoot," York said and left the why unanswered.

"If you had," Brobeck put in, "she wouldn't be around now."

York looked at Brobeck. He might have nodded. He got up and said, "Time to bed down."

Lying face to the sky, Ben could imagine men like themselves gathered around the fire of the moon, hunters and nonhunters and lonely survivors under the felt weight of space. They would be talking about leaders and policies, about money wasted as against the saving of lives, about wilderness exploited or left pristine, about dreams versus practicality, and each would make a good case and leave judgment shaky. And they would be talking, or maybe just thinking, each man to himself, about sex and fidelity and justified exceptions to code, and here again, for reasons general or personal, revealed or kept secret, they would be divided, inside and out, and unsure in decision.

A great she-bear rose to the moon that his eyelids closed out and floated around it, and he asked moon and bear, "Where are the clean choices?"

23

THE MORNING COLD had lifted and was lifting still more as the sun climbed above the ragged wall of the mountains to eastward. The frost that earlier had bleached the grass had melted, and its hanging drops were little suns on the stems. All the same, as he washed navy beans, Ben's hands cramped in the water just brought up from the river.

York paused in his aimless strolling to say, "Don't look too good. I thought to hear shots by this time, or maybe the breeze ain't just right."

They had risen before dawn, York to bring in the horses, Ben to kindle a fire and prepare bacon and eggs. From his sleeping bag Brobeck had said, "Go to it, Ben. Keep up the good work. Us hunters need a wink of sleep more."

A little later the three had rolled out and, shivering, washed at the stream's edge and, having eaten, ridden away, Kilmer with only one pack horse, Brobeck and Green with two.

York sat down on a fallen log and filled his pipe. "You don't have to wash the face of every damn bean," he said.

"You tend to your horses."

"Tended to already. I'll keep 'em up for a while just in case. It don't hurt to get 'em used to the corral and a couple forkfuls of hay."

Ben drained off the wash water, put in fresh, added salt pork and nudged the pot into the fire.

"Reminds me," York said, taking the pipe from his teeth, "I knew a man hereabouts lived on sowbelly and beans. Used to drink the grease from the pan. It killed him."

"I'll throw these out."

"Nope. Steady diet, it was, and some damn disease so rare the doctors got onto it too late to save him."

"Pellagra, maybe?"

"That shows what wide readin' does for a man. Pellagra is right."

They were just filling in time, waiting on events, while, over and beyond and underneath what was said, York listened. No word, no tone of voice, Ben thought, could keep him from hearing.

York went about setting up the camp stove, saying, "Who hankers to circle round a damn fire so's to keep smoke out of his eyes? Should have done this before. We'll kindle her later." He sat down again and knocked out and filled his pipe, lighting it with a twig he had held in the fire.

When they fell silent, there was nothing to listen to except the voice of the stream and the occasional cries of a proud-crested Steller's jay, so vivid on his pine perch as to pale the sky. Silence closed them in, the great voice of silence, waiting for the fracture of gunshot. Save for the jay, there was no wildlife to see, no bird overhead, no creature below. The world lay open to settlement.

With a stick Ben nudged coals around the bean pot.

The mountains had marked York, Ben thought, the mountains and distance and solitude. There was little his eye would miss or his ear not hear, and, if neither functioned, he would still be aware, drawing on a sense most men lacked.

On impulse he asked, "Mind telling me how old you are, Jap?"

"Somewhere around fifty. Fifty-five, maybe. A man loses track."

"And already you're counting yourself as a relic."

"I been in the mountains, off and on, mostly on, since I was a pup. Let me see. Call it nineteen hundred or a little before. The outside don't have a hold on me, not now, not anymore, barrin' the whiskey sold there."

"It hasn't changed that much."

"So you say. Speakin' of whiskey, that reminds me." York got up, poured whiskey and water into a tin cup and offered the drink to Ben. He sat down with the cup after Ben had taken a sip.

"A man in town," York said, "he just sees strangers walkin' the street and goddamn radios playin' what he don't want to hear, and everybody yappin' for progress, and the air foul with engine farts. Give me the good smell of horseshit. Let me hear a coyote."

He didn't need to be reminded that they had heard them last night, in the early dark and at dawn, singing their laments to the sky.

Ben said, "You can't go back, Jap. Not today."

"That don't mean we have to be hell-bent for tomorrow."

"People, jobs, come ahead of things."

"That race is run, and no winners, when things play out."

"That's beyond any time we can see."

"My time, anyhow."

York went silent, the cup forgotten in his hand, and Ben got up and gathered more firewood. The knock of the ax sounded small.

He came back to the fire, fed it and sat down, and it was then that they heard the shot. It sounded as a faint boom and then gained volume and rolled through the hills.

"Brobeck?" Ben said.

"No, Kilmer. One shot. Listen."

But the one shot was all. The silence closed in again, like a great, muting hand.

York had his pipe going. He said along the stem, "He's not what I would call a dead shot. I've taken him in here before." He blew out a breath of smoke and added, as if he found one note of grace, "Well, shit, he pays me."

He rose, went to the corral, caught up a horse and threw a pack saddle on it. His own horse stood saddled, cinch loose. Returning, he said, "I gave that Kilmer just one pack horse, and that just to keep his pecker up, figurin' he wouldn't come back with no more than a rabbit that might get tromped on, but if he's lucked into an elk —" The words trailed off.

He sat down again and again knocked out and loaded his pipe and, smoking, waited; and it was as if he could endure time and development, minutes and hours and what was to come, as if he had learned patience from hills with no clocks. But Ben knew he was alert. He didn't need to flick his ears like an animal or sniff the wind or lift his head and stare.

Ben stirred the beans, made sure they were cooking and asked, "Coffee?"

"Not when there's whiskey. How about buildin' a cup?"

Ben did so and passed the drink, then took a small swallow himself and gave the cup back. He sat on the log with York.

Counted by the minute, time dawdled. By season and year it flashed by, leaving the fact of its passing incredible and memory confused in the mix of dates and events. Ben had heard someone say that, to pass a short winter, sign a promissory note that fell due in the spring. But time hurried on, note or no note. It did, save for now when they reckoned it minute by minute, half-hour by half-hour.

The sun had lagged up to high noon. A little breeze worried the campfire and went on. The horses in the corral were beginning to nose one another, to stamp hooves and switch tails as the warming day gave life to the flies.

A shot sounded among the hills, then, after a long, waiting moment, another, and York said, "That's Brobeck. Got an elk, you can bet. Second shot was a make-sure or maybe for mercy."

He was about to relight his pipe and relax but of a sudden held up. It was an instant before Ben could hear the pound of hooves and the flap of leather and the ring of horseshoes against stones. Kilmer galloped into the campground, pulled to a halt and swung from his horse.

York had risen and gone forward, Ben behind him. Kilmer said, "I shot me a bear, a big grizzly."

"Dead?"

"As good as. It got into the bushes."

"As good as! My ass."

Kilmer stepped toward York. He put both hands out. "Now wait a minute." The words came in a rush. "It's probably already dead, and I'm going back, but two guns are better than one in that cover, and I thought you'd want to come along as back-up."

"I told you we wasn't bear huntin'.""

"I know, but I rather surprised it, and it acted as if it might charge."

"Sweet Sue don't bluff. Where's the pack horse?"

"I left it."

"Just dandy. Now where at is the bear?"

"Where Stone Creek comes in. There's a point there."

"Shot just once, huh, just the once?"

"I was lucky to get one shot in."

"Shit! And her makin' for the thicket and all."

"You don't believe me?"

York didn't answer. He turned to Ben. "We'll saddle up, Ben. Can't leave her suffer, or for some poor bastard to stumble upon."

York made for the corral, and Kilmer ran up and tugged at his arm. "What the hell? I'm going along."

York shook off the hand and turned long enough to say, "Not on one of my horses, you ain't. Just see to the one you rode in."

"It's my bear."

"My horses. Come on, Ben."

He caught up a saddle horse and bridled it as Ben threw on a saddle. Then he bridled his own horse and tightened the cinch, led the way through the gate and closed it. They both mounted. York took the lead.

As they rode away, Ben looked toward Kilmer, standing slumped, the fret of his wrinkles set deep in an expression no longer puckish. Kilmer watched them go from the clearing.

York set a fast pace, not trot or gallop or lope, but the steady, long-striding walk that the trail called for and that only, Ben thought, a trained mountain man could get out of his mount. Now and then, falling behind, he had to set his horse to a jog to catch up.

Except for an infrequent, "Goddamn," that carried back, York was silent, though once he turned to say over his shoulder, "No guts. He spooked. That's Mr. Earl Kilmer."

The stony trail twisted among boulders, through spare stands of timber, and climbed high above the river, where it narrowed to a mere goat path along the side of a cliff, and wound down to bottom land and low growth. The sun, tipping far from its zenith, got in their eyes. Ahead, a horse whinnied — the pack horse, it must be, that Kilmer had left.

They came to it a quarter of a mile farther on. It was straining at its tie rope and swinging side to side but calmed down when it saw it had company.

"We'll tie up here," York said. "Don't want 'em spooked and breakin' away."

With the horses secured, York slid his rifle from the scabbard, saying as he did so, "Get your shootin' iron, Ben." The sight of it brought an exclamation. "By God, a peashooter."

"I should have told you. I'm not a hunter. I don't know why you brought me along."

"You better'n Kilmer." A smile without humor touched York's mouth. "I aimed to shame him, the son of a bitch. One lonesome bear, and he's got to shoot it and then run for papa."

Ben said, "Well?"

"Don't matter, your gun. It'll do as a come-on. Loaded?"

"Few shells in my pocket."

"Put 'em in," York said and examined his own rifle. "Let's go."

They mounted a small crest and angled down toward the river, and ahead, where another stream joined it, Ben could see a finger of land tangled with windfall, flood drift, willows, and dead high-grown weeds.

York watched right and left as he walked. He tested for breeze, tossing grass stems and pinches of duff into the air and watching which way they went. "Upwind is the ticket," he said. "A bear can't see worth a damn, so we let her smell us and see won't she charge on the bait. Only if worst comes to worst do I aim to fart around in that woodpile."

"Kilmer might have missed."

"Could be, and I hope so, but I'm bettin' different."

He came to a halt perhaps twenty-five yards from the nearest point of the tangle. "Two shots, easy, at this range if she charges, and that ought to change her mind, even allowin' that a grizzly can carry a cartload of lead. Now you stand over there, Ben, out of the way, and take pot shots into that jumble."

"Random, you mean?"

"Yeah. Look good first. Can't see her from here."

There was nothing to see, only the downed logs and the thicket of willows and the tall weeds. Nothing moved there. Ben levered a cartridge into the chamber and fired.

A second of waiting, and the willows thrashed and bent aside and out of them broke the bear, stretching and humping in an uneven run, the sun shining silver on the tips of her fur. Throat sounds came from her and the gut-rumble of strain. She headed for Ben.

Almost in the observing instant York's rifle cracked. The bullet jarred her. It set her back. She snorted a whoof and got a new hold on earth and came on, now veering toward York.

York was on one knee, his hands working at the breech of his rifle, working where it had jammed, his attention all on it as if the one problem absorbed him, bear or no bear, world or no world.

That much Ben had time to see before he swung up his rifle and fired. He fired again, seeing puffs where the bullets struck and the bear oblivious.

The bear reared and swiped at York. She knocked him over. She dropped and enveloped him.

Ben ran forward. He squatted for an eye or ear shot safe for York. The firing pin clicked on an empty chamber. He jerked up and reversed the rifle and slammed it against the great head of the bear and heard the crack of the stock and the mad throat sounds. York's rifle! Underneath. No chance!

A part of York's face wrenched free from the bear's bite, and one eye saw Ben, and the part and the eye disappeared, and the bear strangled out through its teeth, "Run for it! Run!"

The broken gun was a hindrance, carried forgetfully. Ben cast it to one side as he fled. The horses snorted and lunged at the sight of him, and he slowed down and spoke to them and untied his own animal. It was wild to be off and set out at a run when he got one foot in a stirrup. His right leg dangled until at last he could lift it over the cantle.

No time to spare the horse. No use to rein it. No excuse to

think about leg smashed against tree or a fall down a cliff. Hang on and let run. A stitch struck his side. The pace pounded him. He heard the wheeze of his breath.

Here was the campground, and there were Green and Kilmer and Brobeck, Brobeck bending down over a section of carcass. Their eyes lifted wide.

"York!" The word came out as a cry. "York!"

Brobeck strode to him, hunter's knife in his hand. "What, Ben? Easy, now."

The two others were coming up.

"It's York. Bear's killing him. Hurry!"

They stared, unbelieving, and then, believing without further talk, ran and caught horses and flung saddles on. They streamed out, single-file, Brobeck leading, and kicked their horses. Ben's followed, winded.

A nightmare under the pleasant sky. A dread dream among quiet bushes and trees and the peaceful windings of trail. A reaching cry, silent in silence. The stitch left his side.

There was no movement near the finger of land and no sound. At first sight there was only a big bear in a sprawl. The horses shied off from it, snorting.

Brobeck swung off. He said, "Hold the horses, Kilmer, Green, one of you." He went to the bear, gun at the ready, and poked her with the barrel. The bear lay as before. "York's underneath," he said, though Ben had seen. "Here, lend a hand, Ben."

Hands on hindfoot and forefoot, they dragged the bear off. A "Holy Jesus!" came out of Brobeck.

There lay York, or what once had been York. A flap of raw scalp covered most of his face. Punctures and cracks marked the bone of his skull. Brobeck felt for pulse on wrist and chest. Back to Ben, he lifted the flap of scalp and laid it again over the face, saying, "Don't look."

Of a sudden he rose. "You, Kilmer, Green, head for the ranger station. Get help. Get a doctor flown in, no matter he's dead."

"Both of us?" Kilmer asked.

"Both. You can't do anything here. Might help out there.

Take off!" He had assumed a tone of command, an air of command new to Ben. "Ben, tie up our horses."

As Ben started to go, Brobeck said, "Wait," and untied a yellow slicker from in back of his saddle. Kilmer and Green were leaving. The slicker, Ben saw on his return, covered York's face and part of his body. A couple of blowflies were investigating the bloody mouth of the bear.

Brobeck sat down on the ground close to York's body. One hand kept hitting at the gathering flies. The other held his rifle upright, butt down. He said, "Goddamn blowflies. They come out of nowhere at the smell, or whatever, of dead flesh, and they go back to nowhere when it cools off." His hand made another sweep. "Care to tell me how it all came about, Ben?"

Ben sat down beside him and told him in detail and ended up asking, "But what else could I do, Frank? What else?"

"Nothing. Not a God's thing. Now quit faulting yourself. Quit sounding, Ben, like a prayer for forgiveness. You did what most men wouldn't have done. There's nothing to forgive."

It was an idle thought, dodging in and out of mind, that Brobeck under strain, in the company of death, used proper language. His day-by-day speech was an accommodation to custom.

Brobeck's hand moved again. "In a way it is fitting. Two of a kind, you might say."

"And both kinds getting scarce."

"I guess York would have had it this way."

"If he had to go. He was a friend of the bear, if she only knew it."

"You can stretch it and say, maybe, that she was a friend of his. I won't, though. When a man like York goes, you can only damn life."

Ben offered cigarettes, and they smoked. The sun shafted through the thin screen of trees to the west. In silence they waited and drew on their cigarettes and rubbed them out under foot. The sun slid past the trees and rested on the crest of a mountain. The blowflies were fewer.

It had been a day of waiting, a long day of waiting, with York alive and then dead. York was still waiting if resurrection were more than a myth. He would have enough patience.

Dusk came on and night, a bright night with creeping chill in it. No longer did Brobeck have to fan away flies.

At last they arrived, Kilmer and Green and two men from the Forest Service, one of them leading a couple of pack mules.

"I'm Butler," the first of them said after dismounting. "This is Fairbury. A doctor's flying in in the morning. No use, though, from what I've been told."

Brobeck had risen. He shook hands and introduced Ben. "No use at all," he said, "except to make a report."

Butler stepped toward York's body. He took off his straight-brimmed Forest Service hat.

"Look if you want to," Brobeck told him. "I wouldn't, though."

Butler's eyes went to the bear. "One nuisance removed. More than a nuisance, a danger."

"High price to pay."

"Yeah. I guess so." Butler kneeled to feel the wrist of York's outflung hand. "Already cooling off," he said. "We'll take him to the station and fly him home in the morning."

Home. Where was York's home if not where he lay?

"We brought a litter and poles," Butler went on. "The mules are used to packing in tandem. Won't be one bump. Fairbury, you want to bring the tackle?"

"Sure thing."

Kilmer had wandered up the trail away from the rest. Maybe he had no stomach for blood and death and what had to be done. It was more likely, though, that he felt indrawn and blameworthy for what had happened. Ben had a quick touch of sympathy, feeling somehow guilty himself.

They fixed the poles between the pack animals, wrapped York's body in canvas, placed it on the litter and lifted and tied the litter to the poles.

"You'll be in to report?" Butler asked Brobeck after he'd mounted his horse.

"All of us in the morning."

Now, from up the trail to their camp, Kilmer's voice called. "Hey, Ben, I found your rifle. You must have fallen and broken it, getting away."

Ben could hear Brobeck say, under his breath, "Son of a bitch!" Then he spoke out. "All right. Let's go."

24

FRANK BROBECK woke up early. The alarm clock glowed in the creeping light and said five-thirty, but he hardly needed it to tell him the time. He could always guess within fifteen minutes of right. It was too early to have to get up, though his woman, an early riser, already was gone from the bed.

He could hear her in the kitchen, making biscuits or something, getting ready the hot breakfast he liked. A good wife, he had. She was his woman, and he was her man, faithful to her barring a time or two, long ago now, when he'd jumped the reservation and felt bad about it. Maybe she wasn't the knockout she once was, but, hell, when had he ever been?

He rolled over in bed. The day's work and worry would come soon enough. He would doze and think pleasant thoughts, not, for Christ's sake, about his friend, Ben Tate, whom people were looking at, their eyes questioning.

What they wanted to know was was it true that Ben had run away when Jap York was being mauled and chewed to death by the bear? Had he been scared shitless and turned tail and fallen and splintered the rifle he could have used?

You didn't have to look long to find the weasel in the woodpile there. You could hear Earl Kilmer saying something like, "I'm just telling what I saw, just the facts that I know. The broken rifle and all. I wasn't there at the actual time and don't claim I was, so don't get me wrong. I don't know what I would have done in Tate's place. Tackle that bear or get the hell away? Tackle, I hope, but a man never knows until the time comes. Anyhow, York's dead, and that's the end of that, and I don't want to say any more."

The sneaky bastard.

If he had had any sense, Brobeck thought, he wouldn't have let Ben junk the gun in the rocks that were covered by snow now, since winter came early and cold in the mountains. It would show it had been fired. It might have bear hair in the cracks of the stock. But Ben had said, "Useless!" and pitched it away as if mighty few things were of use. If he had had any sense, he would have skinned out that mangy old bear. The hide would show Ben had shot it. One hell of a thinker, the high sheriff was. One hell of a law officer, and one hell of a smart politician to boot.

Sure, at the time, with York torn up and dead, everyone was upset. Everything was a muddle. Who would have thought to save a bad-broken rifle that wasn't much good in the first place? Who would have thought to peel the shabby hide off the grizzly? But there was no excuse there for a man with a head on his shoulders. The only one with a head had been Kilmer. Fine doings, that!

He might as well get up and lay off the brain plague, but it was too early yet except for more of the same.

What in hell use were words against doubt? What use were his words? What use would Ben's be if he knew of the fix he was in and spoke out? To deny a thing was kind of to sow the seeds of it. And even people who thought well of Ben might have trouble in putting questions out of their minds. There were some who wouldn't try to do that much.

You had to know Ben before you passed judgment. You had to size him up careful. See his newspaper and look at the stands he took. Think about bracing that bear, and nothing to do it with but the club of an empty gun. Ask how he won a captaincy during the war and find out it wasn't by shuffling papers. Ben was a quiet man, or pretty quiet, quieter now than he used to be, and there was maybe a fault. Or was it a credit to him, what you might call the mark of the years?

It took a long time to grow up, Brobeck reflected, thinking far back to Ben in his crazy gunny-sack pants and himself with booze in his belly and a chip on his shoulder. Days of extra-high spirit and a man so full of piss and vinegar that he didn't have to stop and think, or thought he didn't. Young, dumb and all at sea, that's what they were though they wouldn't own up to it, fuzzy-heads trying to get their asses behind them. Time and happenings put their butts in place, more or less, and made their stands solider. But years and hindsight didn't make a man sure enough to be sure sure, not if he had any brains. Neither did the goddamn nature of things. So his ass was never quite fixed or at ease in one spot.

It was almost a relief when his bedside telephone rang, though the boys knew damn well not to call him except in emergencies. He lifted the receiver and, clearing his throat, got out "Brobeck."

"Skeeter Jerome here."

"All right."

"George was skittish about getting you out of bed."

"Good for him."

"You know Pinkie Adams, he gets up early to go to the station and see if there's anything hot on the wire and all that."

"I don't need a run-down on Pinkie. Get to it."

"Well, he went by Billie Gayle's place and saw the door open and peeked in, and there was Billie dead on the floor. He hustled down to the office. Pinkie, I mean."

"That's too damn bad."

"Worse to come. Billie was strangled. There's a wire around his neck."

At the end of his breath Brobeck said, "Jesus!"

"Thought you'd want to know."

"A goddamn mind reader, you are."

"Hold your horses. It wasn't me did it."

"You been there?"

"Right. I left George in charge."

"I'm on the way."

Brobeck lunged out of bed and hustled into his clothes. About to leave the room, he turned and went back to the phone. After three buzzes Tate's voice came on. "Ben," Brobeck said, "some son of a bitch throttled Billie — Billie Gayle — last night."

He heard a gasp. "He's dead?"

"In his club. I'm settin' out." He hung up before Tate could ask more.

"Just coffee, Stella," he said in the kitchen. "And damn quick, girl!"

She poured it before her face asked him what.

"Billie Gayle's dead. Murdered." He went to cool the coffee at the kitchen tap.

She was saying, "Oh, no, Frank! Now who in the world — ?"

Between gulps he told her, " 'Who?' is the question."

He slammed out the door.

It was a miracle of Jesus the way people gathered around violent death no matter the hour. It was as if some devil of curiosity aroused them from sleep or diverted them from their travels to work. Or was it just that murder was a welcome spice to workaday lives? Already, by the time he pulled up to the curb, there was a group around Billie Gayle's door.

He pushed through, heedless of questions, and met Deputy Chet George just inside the entrance. George said, "God, am I glad you're here!"

"Stand aside. Let me see."

George moved his big bulk. "You won't want to look twice."

Billie lay spraddled, face up. After a glance at the face and one away from it, Brobeck made himself look at the cord or wire that was almost invisible in the trench it had dug round the neck.

He said to George, "Get me a bar towel. Get a doctor. Get the coroner. You haven't moved him?"

"God, no. Not me."

Brobeck covered the face with the towel. He watched George go out. Then he went to the door and said to the gawkers, "Look, a man's been murdered, strangled. That's all I can say. That's all I know. Won't you move off now? Go about your business? There's not one earthly thing you can help with."

From the little crowd Pinkie Adams said, "I just happened to shy a glance in, and there he was."

"Yeah. I know. Move away and tell them about it."

They moved but not far.   Maybe his words would keep them out from under foot, though.   The group had increased.   Spence Green was the latest addition.   Now Tate made his way through.   "You can read all about it," Brobeck announced.   Three or four of the men stepped forward, as if where the press had a right to go, so did they.   "I'm deputizing Tate," Brobeck told them.   "All right, Ben."

He laid back the bar towel that covered Gayle's face.   He pointed to the wire.   "Waitin' on the coroner and doctor," he said.   "Have to, I guess."

In a voice that was more breath than tone, Tate said, "York. Now Billie Gayle."

Brobeck put the towel back.   "Once I figured nothin' could make Billie Gayle look any worse.   That goddamn wire."

Tate didn't answer.   There was a set around his mouth Brobeck hadn't seen there before.   He was pale.   Who in hell wouldn't be?

"Ben," he said, "you willin' to be my deputy?"

"More than."

"I don't know as I'll need you except ask some questions. That's your knack.   Now would you push them eager loafers back from the door?"

While Tate did so, Brobeck straightened and moved to the counter.   Should have done that before, he told himself, instead of making himself want to puke.   The cash drawer beyond the counter hung open.   It was robbery, then, robbery and murder for the sake of a few cents.   A dumb-headed act by whomever.   Except for the drawer, everything seemed in order.   Billie must have been ready to lock up for the night when someone came in, noosed his neck, took the cash and went out, leaving the door ajar.   A smart officer in a well-equipped office would be looking for fingerprints, he supposed.   But for whom and for what in a patronized place?   Besides, you couldn't try to match prints with everybody in town.

Doc Crabtree came in with his kit.   That was like him, old as he was.   First on the scene, whereas the two younger men in the local profession would have to shave and shower and eat a well-balanced breakfast. Doc's knees cracked as he stooped by the body. He took off the towel and felt of the flesh. "Dead quite a while," he said. "Late last night or very early this morning at a guess."

"I figured so."

"Strangling is quick." Doc shook his head slowly. "Just a moment of terror, agony, then nothing. Let's turn him over, Frank."

"Better than facing him," Brobeck said, lending a hand.

Doc's eyes came to him. "Frank, death isn't pretty. You can't make it pretty. Never mind. Undertakers can doll up a corpse." His eyes and hands moved to the wire where it was twisted. "I'll get this thing off."

It was haywire, common haywire, that anyone might find in a truck or a pickup. Holding it up, Doc said, "Catch the bastard."

Lawrence Chiles, undertaker who doubled as coroner, interrupted them, asking as he approached, "Now what have we here?"

"See for yourself," Doc answered. "He's all yours."

"Looks like it, sure enough. Someone really put the strangle on him."

"With this," Doc said and held out the wire.

"Help turn him over, will you? As coroner I got to see." Then, the body turned, he added, not as if fazed, "What I expected. Ever see a case before, Doc?"

"Suicides with a rope."

"Well," Chiles said, rising from his stoop, "in one way or another death comes to everybody."

"Not with a goddamn wire round your neck," Brobeck broke in. "Not when you're a cripple already. Not when you're goddamn unable to protect yourself."

"Now hold off, Frank. No offense meant. I was just saying we all got to die. A lot of survivors find comfort in that thought."

"Shit!"

"All right. All right. Don't blame you being upset. Doc, can I take him away now? I got the ambulance and everything outside."

"Any time."

"You'll report?"

"For what it's worth."

Chiles went out. In his place at the doorway Chet George appeared. "Give Chiles a hand, George," Brobeck said.

On the street the group had grown to twenty or twenty-five people, whom Tate was discouraging from closer approach. Voices asked: "What about it, Frank?" "Is he dead for a fact?" "I can't believe it's Billie."

He answered, "Billie Gayle. Stone dead. Somebody strangled him. That's all I can tell you. Let the coroner through, will you?"

"No one who knew Billie would do him in," Pinkie Adams announced.

Brobeck told the crowd, "I figure that's right. Any of you got a hunch? See a stranger? Suspect anybody?"

Silent, they looked one at another.

"If any of you call to mind anything — it don't matter, little or big — come tell me right off." Chiles and George came out with the body, covered by a sheet. "It's over. Make way, please. And let's go about our business." He halted George long enough to say, "You stick around, Chet. See they don't mess up the place."

He and Tate moved away.

"What next?" Tate asked.

"See if anyone had a car stolen, for one thing. No report at the office or I would've been told, but a man that would murder Billie for what he had in the till, he's not likely to have a machine of his own."

"I'd ask at the beer parlors, too."

"Any more great ideas, Ben? Sure, they're likely places. But a man wouldn't bust in on Billie for booze. He didn't handle it."

"For the price of booze, then, if he was dying for a drink. Or, perhaps already drunk, he just chanced on Billie and thought easy pickings."

"Maybe. Let's walk on down to the Arfive House and talk to Jim Sowder. He's the best bet."

"Yes, sir," Sowder answered to their questions. He stood behind the bar, a fat man with a mustache through which he'd strained plenty of beer. A half-empty glass of it rested close to his hand. "Just maybe I got something for you. But have a beer first, on the house, gents."

At their refusal he said, "Great waker-upper."

Brobeck asked, "Just what is it you have?"

"Well, I s'pose it boils down to nothin', but there was a stranger here yesterday. Said he was a barber and figured to set up shop. I don't know what with. He didn't have a damn dime."

"What did he look like?"

"Medium tall. Comin' on to middle age. No whiskers. No hat, and that was funny. Who you see with no hat? I ask you."

"Go on."

"His hair was climbin' back from his forehead, and his head was kind of flat on top." Sowder lifted his glass with a plump hand and drained it.

"Clothes?"

Sowder used the bar towel on his mustache. "Ordinary, like a workin' man. One of those jumper jackets. Denim, I guess. He was dark-complected."

"You should have reported him earlier."

"Christ, man, I just came down from upstairs. Ain't really open yet. First I knew was a minute ago someone told me Billie Gayle's dead."

"All right. Anything else?"

"Well, the stranger, he looked kind of dopey, like he'd spent many a day with a bottle. Tried to borrow the price of a bottle from me against what he'd make cuttin' hair. I staked him to a beer." Sowder drew a fresh one for himself.

"Tip me off if you remember any additions. Oh, anyone besides you get a look at him?"

"Quiet night. Jesus, a few more of them and I go belly up. The goddamn legislature ought to quit fuckin' around and let a man sell whiskey and such by the drink."

"Anyone else, I asked."

"There was a couple of machine operators. I know 'em but not by name. They're workin' up north, diggin' a canal or something. They aimed to get back on the job early."

Two other bartenders said yes, they'd seen such a stranger. He was trying to bum drinks but didn't seem drunk, just maybe drying out after one hell of a spree. Yeah, he looked pretty much like Jim Sowder said.

Outside, Brobeck said, "We got some kind of a suspect, Ben, and description enough to alert towns around. So back to the office for me. You might keep diggin' if you have the time?"

"Time enough, but —"

"But what?"

"Oh, nothing."

"Nothing, huh? Now see here, you look like you've got an idea in your head."

"Maybe the beginning of one. It's too far-fetched, though. Forget it."

"I don't want you chasin' some wild-assed shot in the dark. Not alone. You're my deputy, remember."

Tate gave him a tight grin. "A deputy without pay ought to be given some privileges. If I go out on a fool's errand, let me be the fool. You have your hands full."

"Well, but you take care. Hear?"

Brobeck walked to his car. As he drove it toward the courthouse, he saw Tate, standing still at the curb, lost maybe in thought.

25

BEN WAITED until Brobeck's car was well down the street. Then he walked back toward Jim Sowder's place. There were comings and goings on the sidewalk, early though it was, people wanting to know more than was known. He answered briefly and went on.

Sowder was alone with his beer. He said, "Here again, huh? Thought better about suds on the house?"

"No more than a short one, then. Thanks." He swallowed and said, "Jim, about that man you saw?"

"What about him? I told all I know."

"Would you call him a hobo type?"

Sowder considered while he dried his mustache. "Could be, but how do I know? Hobos ain't twins, or quads or quints, or whatever you call it. Excuse me, but I kind of got to swamp out, Ben. Place is a mess." Without enthusiasm Sowder walked down the counter and took a push broom from a corner. "I can talk, though."

Ben sipped at his beer. The far-out possibility that he wouldn't mention to Brobeck kept pecking at him. If the man were a hobo, he wouldn't wait here for a train. If he had any sense at all, he would head for the main line of the railroad and its stopping point thirty miles to the east, there to lose himself on a freight train among a small army of bums. Once aboard, it was goodbye to the scene of the crime.

Sowder was saying while he rested the broom, "Know what, Ben? Good people won't stand for it. Once that man is corralled, they'll run for a rope, me along with them."

"Don't. It won't do, Jim. No lynching."

"You can ask anybody. There's a lot to be said for it. Vigilantes, I mean. Damn right."

Sowder had swept some of the litter in a pile. He returned to the back of the bar as if for another beer and apparently thought better of it.

"About that hobo deal, Ben. Hell, we don't have 'em here. Like you know, passenger traffic, it's nothin', and freights just once in a while to pick up wheat or cattle or sheep."

"There was a freight train through yesterday."

"Yep. Up to the end of the line and right back. Nothin' unusual, or Pinkie Adams would have said so. Hobos, they want to be where trains are goin' and comin' — on the hour, you might say."

Ben finished his beer. "I suppose you're right," he said. "Well, just a wild idea."

"It don't hurt to ask, foolish or not."

Ben went out and walked toward the office, wondering if the idea was wild, asking himself whether he had kept it from Brobeck because it was wild. Or was it that he hoped to prove something, against the rumors of cowardice he had heard in the wind? What did it matter?

At the office he typed a note for Mary Jess, telling her he was out on the Billie Gayle story.

He drove his car to a gas station and had it filled. It was idle and apart from the business at hand to reflect how many stations had come into being, where once there were only a couple, owned by garages. Now there were eight or so, some of them on the best corners, operated by men who might know enough of mechanics to change a fan belt.

He headed east, up the hill from the valley and out on the flats. Away from the graveled road, right and left, stretched fields of stubble and summer fallow and occasional pasture, so open to sight as to reveal any creatures larger than mice. Ahead, the way lay empty. The sun, two yards up from the skyline, glared at him, and he pulled down the visor, squinting hard. The day would be mild. Late September. Mellow September.

A prudent man would have brought along a revolver or rifle or shotgun — some means of defense or capture. But the suspect was middle-aged by report and unarmed apparently, a stultified addict to alcohol. And this search, as Brobeck would say, was wild-assed in the first place.

Ahead, far ahead now, was a glimmer of something under the eye of the sun. It came to be two somethings, a pickup and a car at the side of the road. He speeded up and arrived and came to a halt. A man — Duke Blakely, he recognized now — was working on a tire at the rear of the pickup. "Trouble, Duke?" he asked.

Blakely came over to him, lug wrench in hand. He was sweating. "Wouldn't you reckon? Yes, suh, Ben." He raised the wrench for emphasis. It trembled to the tremble of his arm. "Some sorry son of a bitch made off with my pickup last night. Right on Main Street, I swear it was."

"Stolen last night?"

"And a good tire ruint. No spare in back, so I reckon I was in luck, or the outfit might be in Dakota." He lowered the wrench. A whiff of him told that it was whiskey sweat that he sweated.

"Did you report it?"

"No dang telephone. I was fixin' to report it in town when I come on it right here."

"What time last night, Duke?"

"That's a question that don't allow for an answer. No, suh." He smiled uncertainly. "I don't work at it, Ben. A small man like me and sometimes ailin' to boot shouldn't ought to take on a load, but last night some of the boys and me kind of babied up to a jug, and time I looked for my pickup it wasn't there. I just figured my young'n had got tired and took it. He's independent-minded, he is. So one of the boys brought me home." He pointed to the other machine. "That old wreck of mine ain't fit to drive."

"How late, though, Duke?"

"I swear I don't know. Time I got home and located the bed, I just laid down to sleep off the liquor, like a man will, and 'twasn't till after sunup I see I was robbed." He brought a dirty hand to the sweat on his forehead. "By God, suh, bottle fever's bad enough but thievin' makes it more miserable."

"What about your son?"

"He caught a ride earlier. Gone off to give old man Mose a hand by the time I got up."

"All right, Duke. You can manage the tire?"

"That's kindly to think of. Sure I can. But say, Ben, mind tellin' me why all the questions?"

"Billie Gayle was strangled last night. Now don't get excited. I'm on a wild-goose chase."

Blakely's eyes showed red when they went wide. "My land! Strangled to death! Billie Gayle!" Then, "Want I should chase the goose with you?"

"You have troubles enough, and I can handle any goose I can't find."

"Well —" Blakely, perhaps relieved at the answer, drew the word out. "I'll go back to the house soon's I fix the tire. Need help, I'll be there, bottle fever or not."

Once again the road was open, save for one car, bound for town, that passed by and rolled up a cloud of slow dust. The sun rose above the windshield, no longer glaring inside. How far could a man walk in how many hours? How far from the pickup? How far a hurrying man? He might have taken to the fields, scanty though the cover was. He might have caught a ride.

But round a bend Ben saw him, striding along. The man didn't signal. He kept walking, eyes ahead. Ben braked and said, "Hey!"

The man stopped and turned slowly. He wore no hat. His half-bald head appeared flat. He was dusky of face. His eyes appeared lost, blank as the blank fields around him.

Ben got out and walked over. "Where you bound, mister?" The man didn't answer. "I asked where you're going. I'm a deputy sheriff."

Not until the man flung back his arm did Ben see he had a rock cupped in his hand. The rock glanced off his head. A fist swung and hit him. He scrambled on hands and knees in the gravel. He tried to shake the daze from his head. He couldn't see, and then he did see the man climbing into his car. He got his feet under him and lurched, still half-bent, and grabbed a leg and pulled the man out.

Of a sudden they came to him, the old tricks long forgotten. Of itself his left hand shot out and knocked the man's chin up, and the heel of his right hand came across and hit the exposed Adam's apple.

The man choked and gurgled and bent, and his hands clutched his throat.

Ben hit him again and left him lying. He opened the car trunk and scattered tools as he yanked at a length of clothesline bound around them to keep them from rattling. The man still was gasping when Ben pulled him upright and tied his unprotesting hands. He pushed him around the car, opened the door and said, "Get in!" The man couldn't, not without help.

Ben turned the car around. He wouldn't ask questions yet. The man couldn't answer. Later, maybe he wouldn't. Leave the interview to the sheriff. But remember what Jim Sowder had said. About the temper of the people. About a rope. About lynching. To take the man in now, in broad daylight, would be asking for trouble. He used his handkerchief on his face. It came away bloody.

He left the road in favor of Duke Blakely's turnoff. The man was breathing easier now, though his tied hands kept rubbing his windpipe. The fight had gone out of him. Just the one try, the final, wild effort, and he had given up when it failed.

At a honk of the horn Blakely appeared on the front porch, his expression inquiring. An old, baggy dog managed to take two steps from him and let out one bark. To the man Ben said, "Get out." With his hands tied, the man couldn't work the door catch. Ben stepped to the ground, worked it for him and pushed him forward. "You have company," he told Blakely.

Blakely's wide eyes were busy. They went from face to face and down to the roped hands. "Sure enough," he said. "Step yourselves up and come in." He led the way to a dusty living room crowded by overstuffed furniture. "Sit down, you all."

The man seemed reluctant or too numb to sit. Ben shoved him

into a chair and took one himself. "We'd like to wait here a while."

"First off, you ought to see to that head, Ben."

"It'll wait."

"I didn't get your friend's name."

"Tell us," Ben told the man.

For the first time, except for gasping and mumbling, the man spoke. "It don't matter." His voice was hoarse.

"I said tell us."

"Hoffman, then."

"First name?"

"Harry."

Blakely's gaze turned to Ben. "He's the one done it? Killed Gayle, pinched my pickup and all?"

"I haven't asked him."

"Just catched him after a fight, huh? He don't look like much for a fact, but him fightin' is a kind of a giveaway. Right?"

"The sheriff will find out."

"Are you the son of a bitch?" Blakely asked Hoffman.

Hoffman didn't seem to have heard.

"Ben, you must for certain patch up your face, I swear, suh. You're leakin' blood. Your friend here, it don't matter about him. Mostly just bruised."

Ben wiped his cheek and forehead with his bloody handkerchief.

"Or would you like a drink first? I been nursin' my bottle fever along. Feel better, too, a sight better."

"I could use a drink."

Hoffman looked up with a sort of sad expectancy, like a dog, Ben thought, that hoped for a crust.

Blakely had disappeared. He came back with an opened bottle and two mismatched glasses. He put them on a scarred table and went to the kitchen again and returned with a tin pitcher of water. His hands were steady as he poured. He sat down and drank and asked after a swallow, "Want we should leave out your friend?"

"Depends on you. I'd give him one."

"Dumb bastard looks like he needs it. But them hands, Ben, they're goin' to drop off."

It wasn't until then that Ben saw Hoffman's hands had grown pale and puffy from the tightness of clothesline. "You have a gun, Duke?"

"Sure thing. Old Betsy, right in the kitchen."

"You might bring it — and a glass for Hoffman."

"I'll untie him and pour him a drink," Ben said on Blakely's return. "You keep the gun on him, just in case, but, Duke, remember he goes to the sheriff alive."

"Hush. It would be like shootin' a cow."

Ben undid the clothesline. Hoffman had trouble holding the glass, but his eyes seemed to say thanks.

"All right, Duke. You hold him there, and I'll go tend to my face."

"Washroom off the kitchen. Basin and water there and maybe some stickin' tape."

The side of his forehead was bruised from the stone and had a gash in it. Blood was smeared down to his jaw. The bruise was swollen and would darken later. He used a washcloth and soap but couldn't find court plaster.

"I'm sorry it's going to be a long day," he told Blakely once he had washed up.

"So? Nobody here but us three, what with my missus dead and my kid workin' out. Chores can wait. Have another drink."

Ben fixed whiskey for the three of them while Blakely watched, gun in hand. Some kind of dim life seemed beginning to show in Hoffman's lost eyes.

"Pleased to have company, day or night," Blakely said, lifting his glass.

"I want to take him in after dark," Ben said, answering an unasked question. "People in town are worked up."

Blakely let out a long "Oh," then added, "a rope party maybe, you mean?"

"That's what I mean."

"By God, no good, suh. No good. I seen one down South. I

was sort of on the fringe of the mob, takin' part, you might say."

To their surprise Hoffman croaked, "What's the difference? A rope is a rope."

They waited for more, and, when it wasn't said, Blakely went on. "A nigger, it was, accused of rapin' a white girl. So we strung him up and shot him full of holes. I been thinkin' on that many a time."

"Wrong man?"

"Puny reasons. The girl — we called her that so's to buck up our cause — hell, she was a woman grown and an old whore to boot. Fuck anybody, black or white, for a price, and likely give him a dose in the bargain. See?"

"Yes?"

"Well, this nigger was kind of duded up, looked like he had the price, and I reckon she was drunk or anyhow lost her business sense, and she let him have it before collectin'. But, clothes or no clothes, he was broke, and when he couldn't pay she squawked to the sheriff, yellin' rape, so we had an excuse to stretch his neck." Blakely shook his head. "Excuse was all it was. It didn't take much there in them days. It turned out, though we never owned to it, that this nigger was a pretty well-turned young buck. Just a boy." The memory made him sigh. "It's been on my mind, I can tell you. So I don't hold with lynchin'. No, suh."

Hoffman had listened, not intently. It was as if the talk and the possibilities were remote from him, noise and shadows from another world.

The slow afternoon passed. Twice, while Ben held the gun, Blakely brought food — boiled beans and ham, bread and butter, coffee and canned milk. The gun was unneeded, except perhaps once when Hoffman had to go outside to relieve himself. For the rest, he just sat, answering, if he answered at all, in monosyllables. Often his gaze went to the bottle, which was less than half full in the first place and had been drunk empty since.

As darkness settled, Blakely said, "I can go with you. Act as guard if you want."

"No. I'll just tie his hands again, and that's probably a needless precaution."

It was curious, he thought as he bound the man's wrists, that they spoke of Hoffman as if he weren't there, a third person talked about in his absence. But not so curious, either. Hoffman wasn't there but in some dim region known, if it were known, to himself alone, a place of echoes and shades.

He drove his car to the rear of the courthouse. No one was watching. No one could see in this darkness. The back door gave onto a hallway, and here was the sheriff's inner office. He turned the knob and pushed Hoffman in.

Brobeck sat at his desk, his big face drawn. His eyes, as he lifted them, showed the red rims of worry and work. He said, "What!" and lurched to his feet.

"I think you'll want to question this man."

Brobeck's quick gaze had taken them in, from the gash on Ben's head to the tied hands of Hoffman. "So," he said. "Him?"

"Your case now."

"And a fight, huh?"

Ben nodded.

"Lock the door behind you, case of a run for it."

He went to Hoffman and untied his hands and set him down in a chair. He motioned Ben to sit and then sat himself. "Tell me, Ben."

Ben told him, and then Brobeck turned to Hoffman. "What's your name? Now, no playin' dumb. What's your name?"

"Harold Hoffman." At least the man's voice had grown clear.

"Where from?"

"All around."

"Were you here yesterday, last night, in town?"

"I guess so."

"What do you mean, you guess so?"

"Seems so."

"I'll call witnesses, if it comes to that."

Hoffman said, "Yeah," not as a question.

"What did you do here?"

"I left."

"Sure you left. Left after what?"

"I forget."

Ben said, "Give him a drink, Frank."

"Sure. All of us." He reached in the bottom drawer of his desk and got out a bottle and, after rummaging, three tin cups. Handing a cup to Hoffman, he said, "Here's for your memory."

He gave Hoffman time to gulp and time to collect himself if he ever could. Then he asked, "What did you do here yesterday?"

"Loafed around, I guess."

"You're always guessing. Do you remember killing a man, strangling a man with a wire? Did you do that?"

Hoffman gave a faint shrug.

Brobeck said, "Stand up. Turn out your pockets. Put the stuff on my desk."

From the pockets came nothing but a broken cigarette and five dollars and sixty-five cents in change.

"God Almighty," Brobeck said, mostly to himself. "For five dollars and sixty-five cents!" He faced Hoffman again, "Where did you get it?"

"I forget. From somebody."

"From somebody dead. From somebody you strangled. Speak up!"

"It's kind of hazy, I tell you."

"Not that hazy."

"It was whiskey."

"Didn't you know, when you killed and robbed the man, it was too late to buy whiskey?"

"I've been drinking so long, I didn't give that a thought, not until afterwards."

"So you're confessing. You did rob and kill a man?"

Hoffman's head dropped. He said in a breaking voice, "It was me. It was whiskey and me. I didn't aim to kill him. It was whiskey did that. He died so easy."

"Yeah. A poor cripple you picked on."

Hoffman spread his hands on his face. His lungs filled and emptied. Through his fingers he mumbled, "Oh, God, keep this from my mother." When his hands dropped, his eyes showed the glisten of tears.

Brobeck said, his words slow, "Jesus Christ, Ben!"

"I know. I know," Ben answered. "Poor damn fool. Poor damn everybody."

"Don't forget Billie Gayle. All right, I'll get Skeeter in here to take down a confession."

"Frank," Ben said, "you have to think about something more."

"What's that?"

"The temper of the town. That's why I brought him in after dark."

"A mob, a lynching, huh?"

"It wouldn't take much."

"I can hold 'em off."

"You might not. If we could get some dodgers distributed —"

"You're just thinkin' out loud, or tryin' to."

"I know now. Get the Boy Scouts. Get the postmaster. By early morning we can have dodgers on every doorstep, in every post office box. Not quite that, but enough."

Hoffman wasn't paying them any attention, though he'd quit crying.

"And what you goin' to say on these so-called dodgers?"

"I'll talk reason, that's all. Make people think twice if I can."

"You'll get 'em out, you and Okay Myers?"

"Myself. Not Myers. He's the vigilante type."

"And you already been in a fight, spent a long day and look like a coroner's case."

"It's important, Frank, damned important. Now, you'll get in touch with the postmaster and whoever leads the Scouts now?"

"Yeah. Yeah. And meantime have a confession typed out. See you when?"

"Not more than three hours."

Ben went out the back way, found his car and drove to the office.

He went directly to the Linotype, ignoring the typewriter, and thought how to begin and finally started working the keys, stopping often to find words most likely to cool passions. He had to hand-set the title and the improvised name of the source. But in thirty minutes by the clock on the wall he had the form on the job press and two hours later had run off two thousand copies.

He took them to the back door of the courthouse, noting as he drove that a gang of boys and a man or two had assembled out front.

Doc Crabtree sat in the office with Brobeck. "Thought Doc ought to look at your head," Brobeck said. "And your wife called."

"I forgot."

Brobeck smiled. "I told her her loved one would live." It wasn't meant as a dig, Ben realized.

"Let me look at that head," Doc Crabtree said.

"Read this first." Ben handed leaflets to both of them.

Brobeck frowned as he read, then asked, "Who's the Committee for Legal Justice?"

"I just appointed it. You and Doc Crabtree and I."

"And this here, where you say the prisoner could be got to only at the cost of my life?"

"Well?"

"Hell, Ben, it sounds pretty damn — what's the word? — pretty vainglorious. What's more, you don't mention yourself in the deal. Not at all."

"The credit goes to the sheriff's office."

"I'm afraid the real firebrands won't be affected," Doc Crabtree said, his old eyes lifting from the dodger.

"I'm ahead of you there, Doc," Brobeck answered. "There's Joe Burke, he's a hothead, and Jim Sowder, who's got a little bunch of ragtag disciples and himself is pretty easy fired up. So I called and enlisted them. They'll help on twenty-four-hour guard duty."

"Wolves in the fold," Doc Crabtree said, smiling.

"Now, Doc, don't josh me. I'll deputize them. They'll take the oath. They promised, and whatever they are they won't go back on it. Simple. They just want to take part in the game, so I played choose-up and picked 'em for my side."

"At first," Doc Crabtree said, "it seemed to me that you boys with your good intentions might just stir up the pot. Not so, though. Not at all so. With your language, Ben, and your strategy, Frank, well, you've aborted whatever might be. There'll be no mob action. Hundred to one."

From the front of the hallway somebody shouted, "Ready, Sheriff."

Rising, Brobeck said, "Must be fifty, seventy-five kids out there besides Green and Montgomery, that new teacher, and Sandusky, all three Scout leaders or whatever you call it." He picked up the bundle of dodgers. "The men have been layin' out blocks for the kids to cover, and someone will be at the post office to stuff the boxes." As he went out the door, he explained, "Got to make my pep talk."

Doc Crabtree creaked up, reached for his bag and came over to Ben. "Now for the noggin." His hands explored and his eyes examined. "No concussion I can detect, but you'll need a stitch or two." He cleaned the gash with alcohol, sprinkled it with some kind of powder and used his needle.

Brobeck had returned by the time he was through. He said, "More deputies. Young and enthusiastic ones, too, all for law and order and the workin's of court. There'll be dodgers under almost every damn door in town before sunup."

"No more I can do," Doc Crabtree said and picked up his bag. They both thanked him, and he gave a goodbye salute.

Brobeck sat down again and reached for his bottle. "Time for a drink. Long past time. Prisoner locked in his cell with Skeeter on guard and his relief comin'. Relax, Ben, and don't think on your sins, which look like some of 'em might have caught up with you."

With his cup in his hand he went on, "We got him, or you did, and hurrah for our side. Only, Hoffman's such a miserable bastard. Kind of upsets me, even when I call to mind Billie Gayle. How come, Ben?"

"What?"

"I don't feel any better but ought to. Got a right to."

Ben thought a minute, feeling too tired to think. "I guess you could say that, after the first taste, all victories turn sour."

"Where'd you pick that up?"

"It just came to me."

"Any more sayin's like that pop into your head, spit 'em out. I like to have my notions harnessed. Anyhow, Ben, at least and at last we got a sure sure."

"A sure sure?"

"Hoffman's guilty as hell, and he'll hang. Not sure but sure sure, which we ain't got enough of in this life. When can anybody be dead certain of anything, any time, no matter when or not? You got a sayin' for that?"

"You might put it that every course of action is attended by uncertainty."

"Good, but make it 'haunted by uncertainty,' and it comes out even better."

"All right. It doesn't work, though, Frank. The hell with it. Ideas like that just make for timidity. And what use is the timid man? Just a eunuch."

Brobeck sighed. "No balls at all, like some song goes. But it's plain to me you think on two sides of your head."

Now Ben had to sigh. "I suppose. What I do know is that I'm dead sitting here on my tail." He got up. "Good night, Frank."

Brobeck rose and put out his hand to be shaken. "Thanks, Ben. You know, goddamn it, hadn't been for you — "

"Good night."

26

"THERE WAS NO NEED for you to get up," Ben said, watching Mary Jess mix batter for hotcakes. "You'll be worn out by tonight, or earlier."

"And you?" she answered. "After some breakfast it will be trying enough. Thank God, I don't have to watch."

"I'm hoping it won't take long."

He looked at his watch again. Three forty-five A.M. The outside windows were black with night. They cast back the kitchen lights, as if the surrounding darkness would not tolerate penetration. The kitchen was a snug brightness, not to be ventured away from.

"I'll think about something else," he said as Mary Jess put a skillet on a burner. "I'll try to. And you do, too. Get your mind off it. Think about the new building we've put off too long."

"You're talking just to divert us, Ben."

"Why not? It's a good subject. I want an office big enough for you and me and at least another full-time helper, not to mention callers, and a shop where printers don't have to bump into one another. As it is, you do half your work at home. Of necessity."

"That Frank Brobeck," she said, ignoring him. "What's wrong with the man?"

"I've told you. People. What he thinks the electorate wants. What they think they want."

She shook her head and began separating slices of bacon.

His mind flitted back while he waited. He was in the sheriff's office again, and in his hand was a printed and personally signed invitation to witness the execution of Harold Hoffman at between four and eight o'clock on the morning of August 29. Brobeck sat behind his desk, a shuffle of papers before him. Skeeter Jerome occupied a chair near the door and was applying vaseline toward the end of a heavy coil of rope, at the very end of which was a loop and a huge knot, a hangman's knot, Ben supposed.

Ben held out the invitation. "Frank, how many of these did you mail?"

"Upwards of two hundred. Why?"

"God, Frank!"

"Why again?"

"I wish you had talked to me. Or, better yet, Mr. Collingsworth or someone like that."

"Don't tell me they don't want the man hanged."

Ben, in the lighted kitchen, saw himself in the sheriff's office shaking his head. He was saying; "That's not the point, Frank. They wouldn't want to make a spectacle of it, a carnival, a circus."

"That's not the way I see it. Barrin' death and accident, I bet every one of those I invited attends. And I sent cards just to responsible people."

Jerome interrupted to say, "Frank, look. This rope is getting to be slick as a greased pig. You won't have to worry it doesn't slide in the knot." His eyes returned to the rope, and he put on more vaseline, intent on his work.

"That's good, Skeeter," Brobeck said. "Now see here, Ben, the law says fifteen witnesses got to be present. That takes in law men, preachers, reporters, doctors and members of the family, if any. Adds up to quite a little circus in itself, don't it?"

"Not to two hundred."

"Ben, people elect me to do what they believe should be done. You won't hear 'em hollerin'. Was I to say no to everyone except them that the law specifies, what then?"

"They think they want to see it. That's as of now, just as of now. But I bet not a one of those you've invited would spring the trap. You'll have to pay for that, or do it yourself."

"Wrong again. I've got volunteers, quite a bunch. I gave the job to one who said he wanted the honor of doin' it. Clarence Rudey, it was."

"What the hell, Ben?" Jerome broke in. "Why make a fuss? It's got to be done. What difference if a lot or a few see him on the gallows? Reminds me, Frank, that gallows we had to borrow from Deer Lodge should be here today. There was a call earlier."

Brobeck nodded. "Plenty of time."

How answer Jerome, an honest and competent deputy, whose careful work with the rope, Ben imagined, stemmed not from an eagerness to see Hoffman hanged but from the determination to get the job done and done right?

"I just don't like it," Ben said.

"It won't make any difference to Hoffman," Brobeck told him. "He just sits quiet. Nothin' upsets him, not the Court of Appeals rulin' against him or the governor refusin' to butt in. Crowd or no crowd, he'll stay calm. That what's botherin' you, Ben? Because he just sits and takes easy what comes? A nice, quiet, peaceable man that killed Billie Gayle and damn near brained you? Think the public oughtn't to see how we treat such as him?"

Ben got up and said again, "I don't like it. No use to say why."

"Then we got to differ, Ben." A hanging look of regret showed on Brobeck's big face. "No lastin' matter, for God's sake?"

"No, Frank."

Mary Jess brought him back to the kitchen, to the darkness waiting outside, to the now and what was soon to be. "Bacon's done. How many hotcakes, Ben?"

"Just a couple. I'm not hungry."

"Now, Ben. That's not enough."

Her consideration, her solicitude, was not a new thing, he thought. It had always been there. It was new only in his tardy recognition of it, new in his guilty thanksgiving. Such loyalty overrode shortcomings, or ought to. And he had been blind to it, blind to her abiding regard until that night, nearly a year ago now, when he had come home after delivering Hoffman to Brobeck and listening to his confession.

Though it was late, she and her father had been waiting when he returned from the courthouse, spent and somehow depressed. They had been right here, in this kitchen, when he opened the back door. Her eyes flew wide, and a gasp came from her, and she was on her feet, running to him, before he could get the door closed.

"Ben, you're hurt!"

Her hands, her gentle hands, came to his forehead and cheek, and there was such a tenderness in her touch, such a fearful, unexpected concern in her eyes, that he was almost undone. He felt his mouth twist and his throat choke, and he turned his face down and away, seeking control.

"It's nothing much," he managed to say. "Doc Crabtree took care of it."

"Your forehead. Your cheek. Ben, sit down. Sit right here."

Mr. Collingsworth said, "You caught him, eh, boy?"

Mary Jess put in, "Frank Brobeck said that you did."

"Single-handed, too, boy?"

"It wasn't as much as you're making of it."

"That's as may be," Mr. Collingsworth said. "When you feel up to it, we hope that you'll tell us."

"Not now, Father. Not now. Ben, you look ready to drop. Don't you want to lie down? To sleep?"

"Not quite yet, Mary Jess."

She studied him and got up and went to the cupboard. "There's a bottle here somewhere," she said, moving boxes and sacks. "You bought it, Ben, once when we invited Mort Ewing to dinner. Here it is."

She took the bottle to the sink. "Tell me how you mix it. You're going to have a drink, I don't care what Father says. If anyone ever needed it, you do."

The rare smile that rested so well on Mr. Collingsworth's sober face touched it now. "I do declare, as they say," he said, "I do believe I'll have one, too."

A year ago, Ben thought, while Mary Jess brought food to the table. Almost a year ago. A year fled, lived month by fast month if a man waited for death on a rope. And though the winter had hindered construction, the dam was growing and both town and county still growing with it. From thirty-five hundred to eighty-five hundred — that was the estimated increase in county numbers and probably not far from right. And there was bus ser-

vice north and south from Arfive, and letters were being flown
from big city to city, and roads were being paved, and on the local
screen Greta Garbo and Harold Lloyd had appeared, and Will
Rogers, too. And during the year an oil field had been established
not far away, and a coal mine was being worked twenty-odd miles
to the north of town, and in Europe those jackasses, Mussolini
and Hitler, were kicking up dust that was none of America's business, and Helena suffered an earthquake, and March and April
had been very cold and a sheepherder had died in a blizzard.

All were marks of the months, all noted in news columns, and
all important enough to men not sentenced to die. Did Hoffman
take heed of them? Was outside life closed off from the inner life
soon to end?

Sometimes, when he thought of Hoffman, Ben almost wished
he hadn't caught him. The man ought to hang, but what was the
use? A worthless life taken in pay for a good one? Where was the
gain unless in the unlikely event it saved other lives? In that
mood he made himself see Billie Gayle again, Billie the good,
lying strangled, his birth-stricken face so tortured that a man sick-
ened on seeing it.

Mary Jess broke in, saying, "You've hardly eaten anything,
Ben."

"It's enough, and it was good. Thanks. Now it's time to be
going. Not long until dawn."

She came to him when he rose, and he kissed her.

"Goodbye," she said. "I'm glad it's business that takes you
there, not mere curiosity."

"I'd dodge it, but how would we look, not being represented
when so many out-of-town newspapers are?"

"No argument. At least you're one man who won't find satisfaction in going and seeing."

"Not much, anyhow." He felt her eyes on him as he went out
the door toward the car.

Low on the eastern horizon the day gave faint promise of being
born. Labor pains. Twilight sleep. Another day delivered, another man dead. But darkness hugged the ground, intruded on
here and there by lights in households that had risen early for the

big event. When a man took a life, he sacrificed the right to his own. Made sense. Gratified sensibilities.

He parked his car in front of the office and walked toward the courthouse, seeing cars clustering around it and men getting out, hurrying, though the time wasn't four o'clock yet. Be early and find places up front.

He walked around the courthouse, exchanging greetings, to the squat jail behind it. Brobeck had had a canvas tunnel or chute erected from the back door of the jail across to the county machine shed where the gallows presumably stood. A street light shone on the surroundings and them, and lights beamed dimly from the poorly shaded windows of the machine shed. A slit about midway of the tunnel allowed entry. Chet George stood there, making sure those wanting inside had their invitations in hand. There was an increasing crowd outside, many strangers included. Visiting officials, probably. Newspapermen. They began lining up, strangers, friends and acquaintances, and filing in. George was calling, "Better come in, folks. You don't want a last-minute jam."

Ben went through the back door of the courthouse and entered the sheriff's office. Brobeck was on his feet, pacing. Skeeter Jerome was standing, too. Brobeck came to a stop on seeing Ben. "Waitin' for a full house," he said. He looked at the clock on the wall. "Then the sooner, the better."

Jerome said, "Forget the fidgets, Frank. Hell. All in a lifetime."

"These goddamn sheriffs, ex-sheriffs, deputies and what not. They stormed the damn office, Ben. But Skeeter got names and titles for you, case you wanted them. I cleared 'em out just a minute ago. I can tell you there's no law in Montana today, except by God here."

"We're on the map," Jerome said and sat down. "Isn't that what you've always wanted Arfive to be, Ben? On the map?"

When Ben didn't answer, Brobeck spoke. "Reverend Hystrand is with Hoffman now. What can he say? Just tell me that."

"Repent and pray for forgiveness, I suppose."

"And we're all miserable goddamn sinners, anyhow, hell-bound because it took screwin' to bring us into the world. Shit! How's the crowd, Ben?"

Jerome got up and went to the back window while Ben answered, "Gathering. Going inside."

"I'll give 'em five, ten minutes more." Brobeck was pacing again.

From the window Jerome said, "Slash in the canvas that somebody cut. Gate crashers."

Brobeck went to look.

"No reason to get lathered up," Jerome reported. "County road boys are throwin' 'em out, and there's the town marshal."

The door opened, and Brobeck turned and said, "Hi, Rudey. I was waitin'. You know Ben Tate?"

"Sure." Rudey advanced and shook hands. He was a short, stocky man with more of a belly than doctors approved. His face was broad but foreshortened, marked by eyes that seemed to hold a slow comprehension.

"Rudey," Brobeck told him, "there's one thing I want you to be careful to do."

"What's that?"

"Spring the trap quick, unexpected, while Hoffman is waitin' for me to put the hood on him."

"Why in hell for?"

"So Hoffman won't know. To save him that last minute of thinkin'. Call it mercy, rememberin' mercy ain't so goddamn merciful in a hangin', not at the best."

"That son of a bitch don't deserve any mercy. I say let him suffer."

"Don't matter what you think. Hear! You spring that trap accordin' to me if you want to have the honor of doin' it."

"All right, Frank. I didn't set out to rile you. All right. Just like you say."

"You better get there then."

Rudey went out.

Brobeck said, "Ben, there's a press section, sort of. I doubt it holds out."

"I won't try for it."

"Come on, Skeeter. 'Bout time to escort the bride to the altar. See you, Ben."

Ben walked away and went toward the slit in the tunnel. The crowd had increased, grouped back from the entry and ranked along the tunnel. Someone had raised a ladder to a window of the building, and two men were trying to stand toward the top of it. But these obviously were people without invitations. Ben made his way through them to the slitted door, where Chet George waved him in.

For lack of chairs men stood inside, jammed toward the gallows that stood waiting its customer. The men smoked and talked and looked toward the mouth of the tunnel, and smoke layered the air, drifting like clouds under the stingy beams of lights in the ceiling. Soon they would quit talking, quit smoking, quit moving, all energy centralized in their eyes.

Ben edged in beside Mort Ewing. "Hi, Mort," he said and had to smile at what he was about to say next. "What brings you here?"

"Not such a fool question," Ewing answered. "I don't know. It wasn't really that I wanted to be in at the kill. Dingbats have been strung up before and me not there and no use if I was. You could say, I reckon, that Billie Gayle brought me here. Not much sense in that, either."

"I have some reason," Ben said and felt of the copy paper in his pocket.

"Yeah, but both of us got better ones. We're human beings. I reckon that's the curse of it. You take animals, they'd be long gone, unless it was mother and cub."

"No mother present," Ben said, passing time. "Hoffman didn't want her to know, but I hear she got word of it."

"Not a damn soul on the mourners' bench. It's all hallelujah." Ewing shrugged. "A man dies alone anyhow."

The gallows and platform seemed to rise tall. But Brobeck had said a drop equal to a man's height was enough to break his neck if the knot was tied right, add just a few inches for safety's sake. So the thing wasn't so tall. A man standing under it, arms raised, could touch the platform. It and the scaffolding over it just appeared to be high, beyond reach, as remote and as near as the doom restless men dreamed about.

Quiet crept on the crowd, and eyes turned toward the mouth of the tunnel. Out came Hoffman with Brobeck on one side of him and Jerome on the other. Hoffman's hands were tied together. They walked smartly, Hoffman without urging, as if for inspection.

Someone said in a soft hiss, "There's the pisshawk."

The three climbed the thirteen steps. "No help needed, thank you," Hoffman's carriage seemed to say. He looked for the trap and moved to it. Brobeck adjusted the noose while Jerome strapped the man's legs. Ben couldn't see Rudey. He made note of the time.

Brobeck stepped back. "Mr. Hoffman," he said, "does the condemned man have a final word to speak before the sentence of the court is complied with?"

The man's face might have moved, but no words came out.

"You want to say anything? You got something to say? Last chance if you do." Strain, that was what Brobeck was showing.

Hoffman stood silent, stood composed, his dull face impassive. Only his eyes turned, and his head appeared to incline toward it as Brobeck raised the black hood.

The trap fell open, and Hoffman plunged through.

A man might imagine he heard the crack of the neck bone as the body yanked to a stop. He could see the head canted and the limbs writhing and jerking in protest against this ultimate violation of being. The writhing and jerking gave way to small shiverings, which gave way to nothing. The tongue had protruded.

Doc Crabtree and young Dr. Roberts went forward and used their instruments. After a while they pronounced Hoffman dead. The time was eight minutes from drop to dissolution. Lawrence Chiles stood ready to cart off the body. He was always ready for death.

Outside, a red dawn was streaking the sky. A new day was born.

27

THE OFFICE seemed to crowd in on him. It was too small. It was disordered, no matter the pains taken to keep it tidy. There was the pile of exchange papers, catalogues, unread copies of *Editor & Publisher*, statement blanks, letters under paperweights that went unfiled for lack of space in file cases. Here was a typewriter, there another, both on stands beside copy paper, notes, and starts on editorials.

Actually, Ben thought, the place hadn't changed much since the old days of Macalester Cleveland. The town had grown, the paper had flourished, but the plant hadn't kept up. As of old, though the connecting door was closed, the thump of a job press in the shop and the chatter of the Linotype accompanied conversation in the office.

He had grown accustomed to crowding and clutter. It was only on occasion that he was acutely aware of them, occasions like this one with Jerry Stoneman occupying the one extra chair. Stoneman's calm gaze went from object to object, but if there was anything critical in his assessment, the fact didn't show on his face.

But Ben said, "You're thinking we've outgrown the place, and you're right. The town has topped us."

"Oh," Stoneman answered. "That's interesting." From a pocket he took a package of cigarettes, offered one to Ben and lit up. Ben found an ashtray under some papers.

Stoneman always dressed more or less cowpuncher fashion — boots, frontier pants, close-fitting shirt and short-waisted jacket. On his knee rested a stockman's Stetson. A working ranch hand might have faulted him for being over-immaculate if he weren't such a ready buyer of drinks. He could talk cowboy talk. He could walk like a cowboy.

"I just happened in to say hello," he said. "Good weather for driving."

Through the dusted window Ben could see trucks and cars passing. There was some foot traffic, though his office and shop were located at the head of the street and on the east and wrong side of it. As always these days, dust rose and rolled and sank and rose again.

"We're going to pave the streets, Main Street first," Ben said. He was just making conversation. He was just waiting.

"That's good. You have an up-and-coming town."

Ben drew on his cigarette.

"You're thinking of expanding, then?" Stoneman's tone was the tone of casual interest.

He had opened the subject himself, Ben thought, opened it because of suspected if unrevealed criticism, and now Stoneman had returned to it. "You've heard, then," he said, "but heard wrong if you believe it's expansion. I'm going to build a new and adequate building. I've bought a lot and drawn plans."

"Sounds fine."

"It will be. Right now I have three men in the shop and a devil to boot, and room just for two. Two extras, one just part-time, on the news staff. It's thick in here when we get together."

"Mrs. Tate?" Stoneman lifted an eyebrow.

"She often works at the house. She's there today."

"I see."

"There'll be no more of that, not in my new place."

"I imagine it will mean quite an outlay?"

"I have it figured."

Stoneman stubbed his cigarette carefully. Not a fleck of ash escaped the tray. "I can't say for sure, Ben, but I have an idea we would be willing to help with the financing. That, at least, is a possibility."

So there was the purpose of this casual visit, there the hook delicately baited and dangled. Ben said, "Thanks, but no."

"Oh, it wasn't an offer. Just a suggestion."

"Thanks again. I'm all set for the money."

"We like to help. That's all. Help communities, help independent enterprises like yours."

"But you wouldn't let me be independent, not the interests you represent. Besides, you own and control enough papers. All the dailies, almost."

"Say it's so, is it so bad, Ben? We stand, we've always stood, for the welfare of Montana. Where would the state be without us? No progress. Empty acres." Stoneman drew another slow cigarette from the pack and set a match to it. He was careful to put the dead match in the tray.

"Your 'we' means copper and power, one or the other or both. The twins. Am I right?"

"Does that matter?" Stoneman asked, breathing out a controlled shaft of smoke. "Our interests often coincide, to be sure, but they never are adverse to the interests of the state."

"I could argue that point."

"But let's not argue, Ben." Stoneman smiled a neat smile. "Let it ride. You have the financing, you say, so you have no need of us. If I were you, I'd make sure though, before closing the door." He thrust out his hand. It was firm and assured. "Goodbye for now."

Stoneman put on his clean hat with care, at an angle just short of jaunty, and let himself out.

He left a threat enclosed in the office. It circled and waved and focused, made sharp by his words. Make sure. Don't close the door. "Goodbye for now."

It had been a long time, yes, months, since Stanton Rivers had given assurance of support from the bank, of a loan to help erect a new building. Now there was greater reason than before that he grant it. The paper was even more prosperous. A look at the books would prove that. So make sure as suggested. See Rivers. And now. There was a deposit to make anyhow.

Ben stepped to the shop, asked Okay Myers to watch out for visitors and then gathered up checks and cash and the slip and took his hat. At the door he met Peter Sears' teenager, who covered high-school events. "I'll be back before long, Pete," he told him.

Stanton Rivers sat erect behind his barricade and nodded without smiling. The trim mustache on his dark face seemed to signify prudent management.

"I'd like to talk to you," Ben said.

Rivers nodded again.

"If you'll wait just a minute." Ben went to a window, made his deposit and returned.

Rivers said, "Come in." He indicated a chair.

Ben sat down. "It's about the new building. I'm ready to start and just wanted to clear things with you. Again, I mean."

Rivers' hands fiddled with a pencil, newly sharpened. His eyes were on it. "I remember," he said. "That was some time ago, though."

"And my business is better than ever. I can show you the books."

"Your business." Rivers sighed a sigh that seemed to breathe regret. "I must tell you, Ben, that the needs of the community have been almost too much for us."

Ben made himself smile. "Don't tell me you're broke."

Rivers raised a quick, protesting hand, as if Ben's words might cause a run on the bank. "Heavens, no! I meant we're extended."

"Overextended?"

"Extended as far as good banking practice allows. That and no more and no less than that."

"Which, no more and no less, means you're saying no to me?"

"Only because of that, Ben." Rivers raised his eyes. They might have been sad. They were unyielding. "I'm damn sorry."

"So am I." Ben quit his chair. "Disappointed in you, Rivers. I thought your word was good."

"Circumstances —"

Ben didn't wait for the rest. Outside the bank, he almost collided with Mort Ewing.

"Hey," Ewing said. "Whoa, now. Easy, boy."

"Sorry, Mort."

"Here." Ewing took his arm and moved to the side of the building. "Rest your butt on the window ledge. You ever heard that confession's good for the soul?"

"My soul's all right. It's my business."

"So?"

"The bank just shut me off. No new building, I guess."

"Say it again."

"It's tied up with Butte. Jerry Stoneman's in town. Two and two."

"Makes four, easy. So Stoneman saw Rivers, and that cracker-ass Rivers put the kibosh on you?"

"That seems to be it."

Ewing's hand went to his jaw and massaged it. "I do think I'll have a talk with that dude."

"Who?"

"Rivers. Rivers oughtn't to dry up like that, not without someone's thrown in a dam."

"Don't speak for me, Mort. Don't act on my account. It's not your business."

"It's Rivers I'm thinkin' of, not you. A good sermon might save that son of a bitch of a sinner. Be on my conscience if I didn't try. Missionary spirit I got. But, first, come have a drink with me."

"Thanks, no, Mort. You have a drink, and you'll think better of it. A man has to hoe his own row."

"Needs tools regardless. But so long, Ben. Me for a soothin' cup."

28

EWING MOVED as if to enter the Arfive House, but he didn't go in. He waited until Tate had gone on, then walked back to the bank. He told Rivers, who sat smiling beyond his little fence, "Want to jaw with you."

"Come in, Mort." Rivers put out his hand, as if they hadn't seen each other since Lewis and Clark traipsed over the mountains.

"Not here. Private. In your priest's hole."

"Surely." Rivers rose, his smile grown uncertain, motioned Ewing inside and led the way behind the cages to his office in the rear, where he waved toward a chair.

"All right, Mort. Open for business."

"I'm makin' some business mine. Somebody else's."

"Whatever you want to take up, Mort."

"I just got it out of Ben Tate that you said no deal on a loan."

"Since he told you himself, I can confirm it without impropriety. I had to refuse him. I regret that. But our ability to finance more undertakings is limited."

"Your piccolo is playing what sounds like horseshit to me."

Rivers wouldn't get mad. He couldn't afford to. He said, "Now, Mort, you're being extreme. Let me explain."

"Explain away."

"You know things are uncertain, Mort. Here's Roosevelt fiddling with the dollar, until we don't know from one day to the next what it's worth. He's throwing out money as if it came free, money the nation cannot afford. Look at all the handouts. Think about taxes. He has no business sense, that man, and so banks face uncertainties and difficulties. We don't know what to expect except trouble."

"Yeah. And bankers know, don't they? They went broke, knowin' so much, and it took a dumb feller that don't know his ass from an asset to save 'em."

"Oh, come on, Mort."

"Nope. I'm goin' on, though we're on a sidetrack. There ought to be a law that you smart moneymen post a big picture of Roosevelt in the lobby and fall down on your goddamn knees and give thanks every morning and on the half-hour every day. It was him saved your hides."

"We would have saved our own if Hoover and his advisers had been left alone."

"Sweet crucified Jesus!"

"It's true, Mort." Rivers gestured with a thin, pleading hand. "You know I wouldn't low-rate you, but you've been an outsider. You've not been involved as many of us have. You could afford to sit on the sidelines. Twice in twenty years you've had the luck to sell off your livestock before hard times hit us."

"Have it your way. Luck. Take this last time. It was just lucky I read about the Hawley-Smoot tariff that some of you wise men was so hell-bent for. It was just lucky I heard that London kicked back at us, and so foreign trade came to a stall. And the New York stock market, meantime and all along, was on its jubilee spree, the booze bein' supplied by you banker boys. Pure luck it was that it come to my notice."

"That's hindsight, Mort."

"Lucky I sold out when there was nothin' behind me to see. But get back to the subject, Rivers. Tate. Ben Tate and a loan you said no to."

"I've given the reason." Rivers' finger went to his mustache.

"Have you, now? Here's an honest man with a goin' business. Damn little risk. None, you might say. And you turn him down."

"If you could see the total we have out on loan —"

"No. No. We'll kind of round up the past so's to make it fresh in your mind. One bank went bust in this town, like you know. Like you know, yours could have, too, easy."

"I've always been grateful for what you did with the other depositors. Grateful you didn't close out your own account."

"For my own self, bad judgment. For the town and county, worth a gamble. That's the short and the long of it."

"Nevertheless, I'm grateful."

"Not grateful enough to help finance Ben Tate?"

Rivers leaned forward. Both hands came out, as if he carried a bowl to be filled. "Mort, please, you have to remember that we're a member bank."

"Mumbo jumbo, member bank."

"Seriously, we can't be altogether independent, oblivious of others."

"My bank would be."

"What are you saying?"

"Nothing, but I reckon another bank wouldn't hurt. An independent one."

"You're joking, of course."

"Sure thing. Now about that independence or shortage of same. Somebody, some mouthpiece, gave you the word. It don't take a crystal ball to tell who and for who."

"I'm telling you the truth about our being extended."

"Maybe so. Maybe. You know, Rivers, here in the cow counties we've kind of gone along with the big interests. They had their business, and we had ours, and no conflict — that's what we thought. But I wonder how it would be if it got out that the interests were callin' the shots right here in Arfive. Dumb we may be, but by God not flunkies to fat asses. 'Get out, leave us alone, fuck the bank!' Can't you hear the call loud and clear when people learn about Tate?"

Ewing got up.

"You're threatening me," Rivers said, rising slowly.

"Damn right I am. Let people know, that's my plank. Close my account and say do the same to my friends. New bank if it comes to that. Independence."

"Blackmail almost," Rivers said. His voice didn't sound strong.

"Sure, and the price is a little goddamn spunk in you and a loan to Ben Tate. No usury."

He heard Rivers sigh as he went out. He reckoned he'd done pretty good.

29

YOUNG PETE had gone from the office when Ben returned to it, and Mary Jess wasn't about. The door to the shop was half-open, left that way so that callers would feel free to enter if no one was outside to greet them. But Jerry Stoneman occupied the extra chair. It was as if he never had left it. His hat rested on his knee, he had a cigarette in his hand and had moved the ashtray within easy reach.

"Back again," he told Ben and deposited a bit of cigarette ash.

"So I see."

"I thought perhaps we ought to talk some more — that is, if you feel like it."

Here was the man, here the representative of the interests, who had told the bank what to do, what not to do. Here was the operator, here the enemy. Ben sank into his chair. Why no hot anger, then? Why no denunciation? Because Stoneman was only a tool, a seductive tool, and all men were tools, of desire and money and circumstance?

"Same subject as before, I suppose," Ben said.

"The same suggestion, at least."

"And more appealing, you think, now that you've put the brakes on the bank?"

Stoneman took time in seeing that his cigarette was extinguished. His hand waved the bank aside. "To quote you, Ben, the town has topped you."

"That's accurate enough. To keep up, I need not only a bigger building but new and added equipment. No secret there."

"With adequate facilities you could be putting out a semi-weekly. There's business enough, isn't there?"

"I've thought about it."

"As it is, you're inviting competition."

"Yours, you mean. You don't have to beat around the bush."

"Anybody's." With deliberation Stoneman offered Ben a cigarette and lit one himself. "Hell, Ben, business abhors a vacuum. Look the facts in the face. A newcomer, seeing opportunity here, would cut into your advertising and just could underbid you on the county printing."

"If it was willing to suffer the losses."

"Its backers might be, in the beginning, at least."

"Jerry, cut out the hints. Cut out the veiled language. We're not government diplomats. I know the whos, whats and whys."

Stoneman smiled. "Yes, I suppose." He drew on his cigarette. "I'm your friend, Ben, whatever you think."

"It would be nice to be able to believe so."

"I said we would see to the financing. That's certainly friendly." Stoneman leaned forward and used his cigarette as a pointer. "What's more, we wouldn't ask you to do one single thing for which a case couldn't be made. A good case. We're not fools, or rascals, either."

Ben had to smile in return. "Just greedy."

"Just as you do, Ben, we like profits. If there's something wrong with that, there's something wrong with America. Maybe Russia has a better idea, huh?"

"Don't be a fool, Jerry. Only fools throw in that communist business when a man disagrees with them."

"Take the pot, Ben. You're right. I know better than to tag you that way."

"To go on, then. What would you expect if I accepted your help? What positions would you demand?"

Stoneman's hands went out as if in exasperation. "No demands, Ben. Christ sake! Just understanding. Just considered sympathy. Just a kind of fellow-feeling, with allowances for some differences, if it came to that. Just a matter of using your head."

"Specifics. As Thoreau would have said, simplify, simplify, simplify."

"I've been to college, too," Stoneman replied, smiling again as he attended to his cigarette. "Let's take the duck pond first or, as your paper refers to it, the great dam on the Breast."

"What about it?"

"It's needless, Ben. It's make-work. No logic supports it. Flood control, hah!"

"But still better than starvation and revolution."

"It would never have come to that if the natural forces of economics had been allowed to operate."

"That's an unsupported opinion. Anyhow, there'll be irrigation later. I suppose you call that unproductive?"

"Irrigation maybe. But what will surely come about, unless people are alerted, is the generation of power." Stoneman leaned forward and jammed his cigarette out. "Public power, Ben. Socialism. Mussel Shoals, the Tennessee Valley, socialistic as hell. Foreign to American tradition. At odds with established and proven practice."

"Your side has always argued for private enterprise, which implies competition, though you hardly dare say so. Competition might be a good thing."

"You miss the point. Competition, yes. or monopoly if necessary and controlled. But not government competition, for God's sake. What individual industry, what associations of industry, can stand against the powers of the government? The massed powers? The bureaucratic powers? Hell, man, it's David against Goliath with David losing. His little slingshot against all the artillery! The only hope for him is the people, an informed people, Ben, a people made wise."

Stoneman straightened as if for breath, his position expounded and standing invulnerable. "We would hope," he went on, quietly now, "that you would take a firm stand against public power."

"Hope?"

"You asked for simplicities. That's one." Stoneman paused to pass cigarettes. When he had his own going, his eyes raised as if to find what effect his words had had.

"One simplicity," Ben said. "Name some more."

"A more general one, then," Stoneman answered, his head raised to the plume of smoke he blew out. "It concerns your Mr. Roosevelt." The name seemed to put a bad taste in his mouth.

"Mine?"

"Oh, not yours alone but yours nevertheless. Last year you promoted a big birthday celebration for him. A grand march, a dance, a great birthday cake, a public listening to his radio talk."

"As if we, the town, weren't part of a national celebration!"

"We could do with less adoration of Roosevelt."

"Next item."

"Yes," Stoneman said. "Right in your own backyard now." He paused as if waiting for a question and then went on. "Brobeck. Your friend, Frank Brobeck. He has political ambitions."

"Is it so wildly ambitious to think about the state senate?"

"Ambitious enough, and he wouldn't stop there."

"Who can tell? Anyhow, he's as good as elected. Your man, Kilmer, will run a poor second."

"As matters stand, yes, thanks in large part to you and your paper. I said, as matters stand now. They can change. They can be changed."

"I'm listening."

"Let me tell you a little story, Ben." The smile played on Stoneman's face. "Do you know how Joe Dixon was defeated for re-election as governor back in the twenties? What helped beat him?"

"That was just before my time here. I know your people opposed him. But tell me what."

"A golden gravy boat. A little damn gold gravy boat. He used it on the family table. It cost him votes."

"As a mark of the spoils of office, I suppose."

"Sure. And it wasn't golden at all. It was gilt and probably inexpensive at that. But the opposition found out about it and made it gold. Alchemists, they were, as well as smart politicians. They harped on it."

"You mean you did. The big interests."

"Personally I can't claim any credit. But once the story was out and repeated enough, no denials, no protests, worked. Gold it was, then, now, and forever. Amen."

"The story somehow applies to Brobeck, huh?"

"Not precisely, Ben. Not precisely. It was just meant as a word to the wise. He hasn't been elected yet."

"He will be."

"Remember the slip between the cup and the lip. There's time to go before the election, plenty of time for posters and pamphlets and letters to voters. Then we would hope that you would lie low, saying nothing either way in your editorial columns."

"It would have to be for a better reason than any I can imagine. But what and where is the fake gravy boat?"

"No fake this time. We would, or will, address ourselves to the fundamental decency of the people."

The word "decency" seemed to hang in the air, unattended and orphaned or beset by what had been spoken and what was to be. It mixed with the outland sounds from the shop, unnoticed till now.

Ben said, "The boat?"

"The boat would be Bloody Brobeck, the man who loved hanging, loved it so much that he made a public ceremony of stretching a neck. Revulsion, that's what good people will feel. And the people not invited to this glorious spectacle will be quick to agree Brobeck is brutal."

"Invited or not, people were all for the hanging."

"They were. They were. Past tense. Do they feel so good about it now? Will they when they read about how bloody-minded he proved himself? Why do you think all hands at the hanging climbed to the courtroom and got drunk after the big treat?"

"To drown their guilt, you would say."

"Wouldn't you?"

"I wasn't there." A man should be able to think of a stronger answer than that, but any defense was weak. Here was shaky ground, there a shameful proceeding; yet, exaggerated as circumstance and person might be, the political threat to Brobeck seemed small.

"That's a frail boat," Ben said. "It won't go far from shore."

"I wish you'd be reasonable, Ben. As your friend I wish it."

"You could shut up."

"No," Stoneman said slowly. His gaze fixed on Ben. His face seemed to harden. "You and Brobeck compose quite a team. Can't you see it, Bloody Brobeck and the brave editor, who ran from a bear and left a friend to be killed though he carried a rifle?"

Hold tight, Ben told himself. Hold tight. He said, "That's a damn lie."

"How would you prove it?"

"Get it straight! I'm for Brobeck. He would say stick your god-damn loan up your ass, and that's what I say. Goodbye."

"Not quite yet, my friend." Stoneman's face drew itself to a point. His eyes bored at Ben. A shine came to light in them. He said evenly, "There's the small matter of a chippie, name of Beulah Sanders. We have your note to her."

Ben kept still.

"Girls get confidential, girls in bed do, even girls who administer emergency relief, which seems to be what you got. Right? We get it in Butte now."

Ben didn't answer.

"I don't think you'd want those things whispered about. So, Ben, the loan —"

Ben went to the door and flung it open, ignoring what else was to be said. He came back and caught Stoneman by the collar and yanked him upright and seized the seat of his pants and threw him out. Stoneman's clean hat was on the floor. He threw it out, too.

Stoneman had fallen. He came to his feet and brushed off his knees and elbows, taking his time. He said, "Too bad, Ben," and, hat carefully placed on his head, started down the street. From across it Pinkie Adams was watching. Soon the whole town would have wind of a fight.

Ben closed the door and turning, saw Mary Jess at the entrance to the shop. "So you know," he said. "Eavesdropping."

"That's just what Father would have done," she said in a strange voice. "Yes, I heard. You were busy. I came in the back way. I saw you throw him out."

"The *Advocate* along with him, I guess."

Now he saw a glow in her eyes not seen before. To his astonishment she said, "To hell with the newspaper." She came to him. "Just like Father."

He would have construed the comparison as criticism, but her arm came up and went round his shoulder, and she kissed him.

He wasn't sure whether hug and kiss were maternal and protective or admiring and wifely. It seemed not to matter much.

PART III

30

"IT'S A GLORIOUS DAY, MORT," Julie said.

"No argument. But someone wrote about the hounds of spring bein' on winter's traces. Me, right now I think about the hounds of winter on autumn's traces."

"There's no reason we can't go to Arizona or California for the winter." Her tone was teasing. Not looking at him, she kept tooling the car along a dirt-and-gravel road.

Westward, from up here on the far bench, Ewing could see the mountains and Elephant Ear Butte standing clean and clear, defiant of time. It was a crazy notion that the spirit of Prof Collingsworth, who so often had gazed at the butte, might have penetrated and personalized rock. He answered as he knew she knew he would. "No flabby climate for me."

"Tough guy," she said, still teasing. "A soft winter might aid your convalescence."

"So might a good freeze. Anyhow, woman, I'm already healed up."

She didn't answer. She just drove along, her eyes fixed on the road's bumps and turnings, her hands quick on the wheel. For something to say, something true if not new to him, he said, "You're awful pretty."

One hand left the wheel and squeezed his. "You won't wear your glasses," she said.

But he saw well enough — the clean, gentle lines of her face, the trim lines of her figure. Thank God she hadn't grown round-shouldered and busty, the way most women did, given time.

"Shall I turn around when I can?" she asked. "I don't want you to get tired."

"As if I couldn't even ride a car!"

"No more broncs, Mort."

"I tell you that horse didn't spill me. I tell you again he slipped and fell on the sidehill."

"I know."

She was thinking, he knew, about the time he had barely crippled into the ranch house after the horse had rolled over him. She had hustled him to Doc Crabtree, and Doc Crabtree had hustled him into Great Falls. Ruptured spleen, broken ribs and assorted botherations, they had said there. When he didn't heal right after they'd carved on him, Julie had got him onto a damn airship, and together they'd torn off to the Mayo Clinic. But they'd been back in Arfive for a month and more now. He was as good as new, or almost.

They rolled through irrigation country, made possible by the dam on the Breast. Houses had gone up, small mostly, just as the holdings were small, kept that way by government restrictions on land ownership.

Shrubs and trees, with caragana and Russian olive predominating, were making a show of growing alongside the households. The fields had been harvested and lay bare or stubbled. Here and there little bunches of dairy cows stood listless or nosed at the ground, in any case looking sad. A hand-to-mouth living, these farmers had. Some day the damn government would find that the western grower couldn't make out with a postage stamp for a farm.

A cock pheasant, decked out like a big and gaudy trout fly, ran up the road and took wing, and a shot sounded from the bushes alongside a fence row, and the bird cumpled and fell. A man appeared from the bushes, shotgun in hand, and hurried to get it.

"That's Dee Berger," Ewing said. "Slow down and pull up."

"The scientific farmer?"

"That's him."

Berger had the dead cock in his hand by the time Julie brought the car to a stop. Ewing got out. "Clean shot, Dee," he said.

"Don't count the times I've missed. How are you, Mort?"

"Good. Fair to fine, anyhow."

They stood at the side of the car. Berger, Ewing thought, wore the look of toil. A short man and stringy, he had a face that a lot of weather had looked at. He carried his head bent, as if, when he wasn't studying soil, he was studying books.

"Looks like you're making out all right yourself," Ewing said.

"Work and worry, that's my dish."

"Worry?"

"This soil's getting boggy. Too much water and no run-off. We've got to have drainage ditches and soon."

"Not too surprisin', is it? They had to drain-ditch that Medicine country."

"It was to be expected, all right, but that's not all of it, Mort."

Ewing waited. Berger was a man who considered his words before letting them out.

"You know I do a good deal of dry-land farming, too, Mort. In fact it pays better than irrigation, though you can't diversify much."

"You're talkin' to an ignorant hay hand."

Berger smiled, "I know how ignorant you are."

"I doubt it."

Berger drew a breath and waited and spoke. "Did it ever occur to you that summer-fallowing is a sort of irrigation?"

"Nope. Not exactly."

"It is, though. Why let half your acreage lie fallow for the next season? Why root out every thirsty weed? Why keep the surface soil scratched fine?"

"I might make a guess."

"Sure. To preserve moisture." Berger hitched the shotgun that one arm held. With the other hand he made little swings with the bird. "That's close to irrigation. I'm not sure how much land and what kind of land can tolerate that much water. The mineral salts underneath come to the surface. No crop will grow on it."

"Like alkali?"

"Like alkali."

"Any evidence?"

"Some. You'll see a little, not much, even on irrigated land with drainage ditches. But it's on dry, summer-fallowed acres you see it most. Not a great deal yet, but I'm afraid there'll be more. We're just catching on to it."

"It's something to think about, I reckon. Long term, though. Don't let it pester you into the boneyard. Leave the torment to hell. It's got a corner on it."

The eyes of Berger's down-turned face rose, and a little smile came on and was gone. "All right." Berger moved the shotgun again. "Won't you and Mrs. Ewing come eat with us?"

"Thanks, no. We'll roll along."

They said goodbye. Berger looked at Julie, touched his hat and turned away, worry still seeming to ride him.

Julie steered the car round a curve and down into the valley of the Breast. The leaves had turned yellow here, and some were skittering loose, waving goodbye as the breeze gentled them down. Long since, the grass had turned tan, cured on the stem. Standing hay, it would make good winter graze at the ranch.

She came to a stop in front of the apartment they leased. "You're going to eat now," she said. "I'll see to it you eat well."

"Heil Hitler."

It took her just a few moments to make sandwiches and to pour a glass of milk that he would have put down the drain if she hadn't been watching.

After he'd eaten, he said, rising, "I got to see the town's running all right."

"A nap first."

"No damn nap. Now, Julie, hell."

He went to the door, where her voice stopped him. "Your cane, Mort."

"Oh, God's sake!"

She was smiling, his cane in her hand. Her eyes met his. "Mort, do you remember what you said first, right after you'd come out from under the anesthetic?"

"Some fool thing."

"You said to me, 'You didn't think I was going to leave my girl, did you?' "

"That was the simple, by-God truth."

"It's the simple, by-God truth she's not going to let you." She put the cane in his hand and kissed him.

The cane made a man feel like a cripple, an old codger whose pins had played out. Next stop, the rest home. Next thing, the loss of his mind like Prof. Collingsworth before finally he croaked. Some people said he'd worn out his brain just by thinking. He might have preserved it with some moderate drinking.

He swung the cane as he walked. Damn if he'd use it as if his steps were uncertain. Coming up from the side street that led to the Methodist church, a bunch of women were strung out. They were all hats and suits and old boobs and bound butts. If you made a pass at one, she'd simper or call the town marshal to prove she still had allure. He knew most of them but acted as if they escaped notice. Greeted by call or signal, one or more of them would want to tell him about the new preacher.

Fall days, he thought. Fall of 1945, end of the war, and things were settling back as near normal as ever they'd be. At the ranch cattle would be grazing, peaceful under a kind sun, watched by young Mort, who would be helped by his wife and helped or hindered by his two kids. And here, for his health's sake, he lived in an apartment, boxed in like a steer in a squeeze, safe, Julie would say, from the temptation of work.

What did a man out of work do? What did a man out of work in town do? He ate breakfast and read the *Great Falls Tribune* and maybe went for a ride and had lunch; and there was the rest of the day lying blank unless he could bring himself to listen to the damn radio, unless he had a good book, which he didn't. *The Egg and I* was the latest he'd read, and it was pretty mild fodder.

He went by Stan Rivers' bank. A couple of grandpas had their bent backs against it, waiting for someone to jaw with. To them he said, "Hi, got some business," and left them looking deprived.

He dropped in at the Maverick Bar. They were the entertainment now, the almost only entertainment, these bars and lounges that in franker days had been known as saloons. Every damn one of them had a music box in it, and some knucklehead was always feeding it coins, foreclosing all but yelled conversation.

But except for old Ruby Yont, who foreclosed conversation with her own jabber, the place was empty, barring Elmer Barns who drank a quart of his own goods every day when he didn't drink more.

Elmer waddled over to him. Too much of his intake had gone to his belly and liver. "Brandy, as usual?" he asked.

Ewing nodded. "Have one yourself."

"How about me?" Ruby asked, gazing up with pouched eyes. Under her fingers were some loose coins. "You ol' son of a bitch. Got plenty of money."

"Give her a drink."

She left her stool, coin in hand, and faced toward the juke box. "We'll have a little music to go with it."

"No damn din," Ewing said. "Choose up. Din or drink?"

She got back on her stool. "I just wanted to hear 'Don't Sit under the Apple Tree,' but all right. I like a man with no bullshit about him."

Ewing took his gaze away from her. She was like a lot of she-stuff these days, moochers and spenders, young and old, some of them living on welfare and sponging drinks when their money ran out. It wasn't so long ago that a saloon was a man's place. It wasn't so long ago that even the roughest cowpunchers watched their language in the presence of ladies. Now talk was likely to be unrestrained, and even the women customers with clean mouths seemed not to be fazed by coarse talk.

He drank his brandy and went out. He used to while away time playing solo, but who knew the game now? Men played pitch or cribbage or sometimes poker, none of them calling for the card savvy that solo did.

Milt Dearborn was taking the sun in front of his new-car sales-room, which stood vacant except for an antique number that had been spruced up and might run for a mile or two. Dearborn said, "Hi, Mort. How's the invalid?"

"In bed. Can't you see?"

"I see. Say, Mort, you'd better sign up for a new car. That old buggy of yours isn't long for this world."

"Last time I had it in, you said you'd got it fixed good as new."

"So I did, but there's just so much a mechanic can do. The new models will be rolling before you know it, and I could kind of juggle you up on the list. It's longer already than the telephone book."

"Forget it. I got a feeling them new models will be made out of tinfoil. Anyhow, why you pushin'? You made out fine, sellin' old cars and tinkerin' with buggies like mine."

Dearborn smiled a fat smile. "Times change," he said.

"That's a new thought."

Ewing eased up the street. The town had toned down since the big dam was built. It was smaller than it had been at its peak, bigger than it had been before it. No heavy machinery growled along now. No work crews jammed the place. Burtville and such outlying joints were vacant and ramshackle and looted of usable lumber. The streets were paved and not clouded with dust. A good-enough place. A kind of prosperous place. But not everything was for the better, he thought, walking along. Arfive didn't have a men's store anymore, not a good one. It didn't have a general mercantile company, where a man could buy anything from pickles to pants and a few yards of dry goods to take home along with a cheese wedge. And if the county had been helped, it had been hurt, too. For the war effort, for the benefits offered by government, too much good grazing land had been torn up to grow scanty crops, marginal land that native grasses would never return to. It would sprout tumbleweeds and Russian thistle and such.

He came to the Arfive House, where Jim Sowder was cultivating a good case of cirrhosis. It was too early for much in the way of trade. A stranger was nursing a hangover with a beer. In a corner a machine as big as a shed, lit up like the Fourth of July, asked for coins to find its voice with.

Ewing pointed to it and said, "That'll tickle the customers deef."

Sowder put out a fresh beer for the customer, made change and answered, "Newest thing. It's what people want."

"Not this people. Long as it's silent, give me a brandy."

He was sipping at the shot glass when Earl Kilmer came in. Kilmer gave a bobtailed hello and ordered straight gin. Centered in him was a pot as shaped as a prize Halloween pumpkin. It didn't like the belt that tried to surround it. Kilmer would have one drink here, one at the Maverick, one at the Broken Horn, and make the round again, thus convincing himself that people would think he didn't drink much. That hadn't worked with his wife. She had left him.

Like men who might have been important but had grown unimportant, Kilmer talked importantly. "Well, Mr. Mort Ewing," he said, "how do your thoughts flow now that you have a Pendergast man in the White House?"

Ewing gulped his drink, answered, "I shut off the faucet," and let himself out.

He passed a strange boy who walked with a limp, maybe given him by enemy fire.

The return to peace hadn't been as difficult as some had imagined. Or it wasn't being that difficult. Ex-soldiers were returning to old jobs. Ex-soldiers were returning to school, or planning to, taking with them, so Ewing had heard, an intent and interest and determination new to all campuses. The factories that had turned out war materials were turning to the scanted needs and demands of consumers.

Young Mort wasn't a veteran, and young Mort felt bad, not because he wanted more schooling but because he hadn't had a part in the big scene. He had wanted to go. Ewing hadn't argued one way or the other. He had excused himself from the draft board when young Mort's number came up, saying other members ought to pass on the case. Young Mort was married and had a kid and a second one on the way, but that consideration in itself wasn't decisive. What was was his classification as a necessary man, engaged in work important to victory.

Sound enough reason, Ewing thought. The ranch was too

much for him to operate single-handed. If old Dunc McDonald, his long-time foreman, had been alive, the two of them could have managed all right. But old Dunc was dead, and his like was not to be found except in young Mort. "I'm sorry, Son," he said to himself, knowing the boy brooded. "I'm damn sorry, but no one better ever tell me that you dodged."

Just off Main Street Ben Tate had his new building, which wasn't so new but still looked it. Ben was in plain sight at his desk, talking with Frank Brobeck, who was on his feet, as if about to take leave.

Ewing entered and said, "How, Ben? How, Senator? It's not my health, it's to keep harmony at home that I carry this goddamn stick."

"I was just sayin' so long," Brobeck answered, smiling. "Now I'll sure as hell go, seein' you don't know me by my first name. Good luck." He went out.

"Take a chair, Mort," Tate said. "How's Julie?"

"Up in the collar like always. Trompin' me underfoot. Been quite a while since I've run across Mary Jess."

"She's at home, probably working."

"I miss her pieces in the paper. Lots of folks do."

"I know, but the fact is she's too good for it."

"Yeah, I guess so. Sometimes I see her stuff in the *Atlantic* or *Harper's* or somewhere. Nice pieces."

"Nice, and at good prices, too." There was a touch of pride in Tate's voice, if a man could be proud of something beyond his own reach. "She can write rings around me. Always could."

Ewing offered Tate a cigarette and took one himself, Julie not being there to see him. It struck him that Tate was growing into middle age. Hell, he was already there, except in an old duffer's reckoning. His hair was half-gray, and his body had settled, giving him the look, not of flabbiness, but of solid assurance.

"It don't seem to bother you," Ewing said.

"Bother me, for heaven's sake! Her talent? Her national publication? Bother me!"

"Good for you."

"We've both found our niches."

"More power to you, Ben. So what else is with you?"

"Few brickbats in the air. Some people don't like it that I speak for the Indians."

"They got a shitty deal. Always have."

"Try convincing readers of that."

"And bein' treated shitty, they get pretty shitty themselves."

"That's in the nature of things, Mort. You tend to conform to your stereotype." Tate paused and went on. "I think the bars ought to close down at midnight."

"Or sooner maybe."

"Some people disagree violently. You'd be surprised."

"I doubt it. I see what you print, and I hear people talk."

"About birth control? About the editorial in favor of limiting families?"

"Sure."

"Delegations called on me. Fundamentalist preachers. Priests. Spokesmen for both. They didn't request, they demanded a reversal of attitude."

Ewing already knew about that. He knew that the demands had made Tate speak out stronger than ever. He knew how Tate had handled a couple of rough customers who had bitched about news stories and had come to the office to rough up the editor and had left with their tails dragging. Looking at him now, Ewing thought that Tate was no man to tangle with, not without just cause. What some people might take for timidity was simply reserve. Push it too far if you hankered for showdown.

"Think on it, Ben," Ewing said. "You're just ahead of your time."

"Shouldn't I be?"

"Suits me."

"I can handle the brickbats so long as I'm sure in my mind. Sure sure, Brobeck would say. There are more of them flying, now that I've said to give Harry Truman a chance." Tate leaned forward and put a hand to his chin. "I try to get out a good paper, Mort, the very best I know how to."

"It's your paper, Ben. It's burned with your brand. It's better than people deserve. Not that I wasn't always on your side, but I got to say now you've growed up. You're a man, boy, a by-God man."

For a minute Tate's face looked stricken, as if, unbeknownst to him before, he'd received word of an elevation in rank. "Thanks, Mort," he said softly. A thoughtful, sober expression came on him, something like that of Prof Collingsworth when he looked west to the butte. He put his cigarette out. "Did you ever think that all men owe debts?" He fell silent, not as if he expected an answer, and added, "I have debts I can never repay."

"Now, how's that?"

"Not money, Mort. Not that. Call it example. Call it help in being whatever I am. The best I can do is pay honest interest."

"I didn't come to hear a confession," Ewing said, "but just who are these Christly characters?"

"I'll name just three."

Like in the Trinity, Ewing thought in a corner of his mind. He kept still.

"They are old Macalester Cleveland, Benton Collingsworth and Mort Ewing."

Ewing said, "Shit!" and got up. "Quit it, Ben. Quit that calf talk."

On the street it occurred to him that he had been in a sore-assed mood all afternoon and now he wasn't. He found himself twirling his cane like an old fool. That goddamn kid name of Tate. That goddamn Ben.

He strode on. Julie would be anxious about him.

31

DOC CRABTREE cursed himself, cursed the years and cursed the long-time patients who didn't leave him time to curse his arthritis.

But there, by God, his shoelaces were tied, and the telephone had been silent all night. He got up and took the coffee pot from the hot plate and poured himself a cup. If he did say it himself, he made better coffee than he could buy. Better food, too, thanks to long practice and the recipes left by his wife in years almost forgotten. These days in restaurants a man was a master chef if he could fry hamburger and uncap a Coke. Wonderful diet for kids.

He put his coffee cup down, unscrewed a bottle cap and chased three aspirin tablets with a drink from the faucet. A splash of whiskey in the coffee wouldn't hurt, either. He had lost all taste for breakfast.

Physician, heal thyself. Yeah. But where was the man and where was the medicine that could conquer arthritis? Nowhere. That was where.

He let himself down in a chair by his oilcloth-covered table and sipped from his cup. In a little while his joints would ease up, but never enough. He couldn't use the knife anymore, no matter how he babied his fingers. Hell, sometimes he could hardly get his pecker out of his pants. In too many cases, not of arthritis alone, medicine stood helpless. Before the common cold, even, it wrung its hands and could offer no more than aspirin, liquids and bed rest, which had the single advantage of doing no harm.

You're feeling sorry for yourself, he thought. Great stuff! The stuff of a lot of murky philosophical writing that Prof Collingsworth had foisted on him, asking what he made of it since he couldn't make much himself. Take that Norwegian or Swede, Kierkegaard. A woe-is-me guy, he was, a lonely, suffering believer, who harped out something like: Alone, alone and tortured and sad, Lord, my God, in whom I put my whole self and trust, believing in You and You solely, though it appear that You treat me ill. No wonder the man never did an honest day's work in his life. He just enjoyed suffering. The wonder was that Ben Tate, reading more of him, found interesting a few bits of his wailings.

He had drained his cup when the telephone rang. The time was too early yet for the girl to be at the office or for Paul Whitaker, whom he had taken on as associate. More, the caller probably would insist on his services. He had a notion to let the thing ring off the wall but made himself get up and walk to it.

"Yes. Yes. Mrs. Anderson, you say? She's worse?"

"She wants to see you this morning if possible. You, not Dr. Whitaker."

Much good an associate did him! Old patients demanded old doctors.

"All right. All right. Directly." He hung up.

There wasn't one blessed thing he could do for old Mrs. Anderson except cheer her up and make sure she had her digitalis and nitroglycerin and pee pills. That heart of hers was on its last legs. A professional diagnosis, that! A fine figure of speech!

He went back to the kitchen and poured a half-cup of coffee. Not for the first time it struck him as he drank that he had never saved a life, never in his career. At his best he had merely staved off death, which had time to wait and in time would assert itself. Sometimes it was tardy. An old bastard like himself had lived too long already. He couldn't say the same of Mort Ewing. It took a roll under a horse to remind him he wasn't immortal, and even that didn't kill him by one hell of a sight. And even old Mrs. Anderson kept staring death down, that old gal, that old, gentle gal who was tempered like a cold chisel and wouldn't let even her own daughter know how sick she was. Why didn't she call one of the younger physicians, one without arthritis, who had a potful of faith in the magic of medicine?

He put on his hat and picked up his bag in the office. The day looked fair enough, and the drive up to the bench wouldn't hurt him.

As a matter of fact it was helping him, he thought as he drove toward the hill that led up from the valley. It was loosening him up even as his hands twinged on the wheel. The morning sun warmed old bones. And left and right and ahead and behind was the land that had claimed him. High plains, mountain and butte, dome of sky, crystal water — these fastened on a man. These held him captive. They had decided his future long ago, the future of doing the same old things. No advanced study for him, no big-city practice, no College of Surgeons, no name of renown. They had faded beyond ambition and reach while he worked content in captivity.

Content?

The car climbed the hill to the bench, and fields and pastures rolled by. They lay barren now or tanned by vanished heat. Branding and haying and harvest were over, and creature and earth, breathing September's sun, waited for winter and then the new time of creation. It was a season of catching breath, of tarrying, of lazily laying hope in the hope chest.

Content? The word was as good as any but left a margin of error. A man didn't lay dream aside without remembering it, without thinking of what might have been. Take Prof Collingsworth, dead and gone now, along with his smile and his furies. He might have been a great educator. Hell, he had been a great educator, too big for a little town. The land had claimed him, too. It was a mistress he couldn't live without or shake off. It had been maddening, that confining attachment, or it must have been, else why his dark moods and ready rages? Maybe he didn't quite know the reasons for them. Maybe nobody really did. Just put it down that Collingsworth had a hot temper. Allow again, though, for the idea that the land was his mistress, and he stayed in her bed, full of love and frustration.

Driving, lazing along alone, freed the mind. A man could think what he would. He could range as far as he wished. He could remember, rehearse and consider, with no fool on hand to offer a penny for what lay in his mind.

Prof Collingsworth had suffered two strokes, but it was cancer of the prostate that killed him. He had rallied from the strokes, you could say, if you spoke just of muscles and left out mentality. In time he could get about pretty well, but he couldn't think. He would look at you, a hunting, blank wonder in the blue eyes turned gray, as if he were seeking the lost pathways of mind. Sometimes he would recognize you, sometimes he wouldn't. Often, after starting a sentence, he would stumble, the track of thought gone, and then say, as if to cover embarrassment, "It doesn't matter." A pitiful goddamn state to be in, when you still had sense enough to know you didn't have any.

In the distance he could see his destination, a neat huddle of buildings standing against the far junction of earth and sky. No need to hurry. Out of old friendship he had been this way many times, only to do and say what he had done and said before.

It was after the first stroke, after Mary Jess had written Prof's resignation to the school board, that the cancer had made itself evident.

Doc Crabtree saw himself in his office, talking to young Whitaker, who had called on Collingsworth a few times. "Under the circumstances a major operation seems out of the question," Whitaker was saying.

A good boy, Paul was, gentle and earnest and able, not dedicated to the proposition that a medical degree entitled the holder to instant wealth.

"Agreed," Crabtree answered. "I thought that was settled. Useless in the first place and fatal in the second."

Whitaker nodded and went on slowly, as if venturing, "But a minor one?"

"I hope you're not thinking what I suspect."

"I suppose I am."

"A goddamn orchidectomy."

"Yes. The absence of the male hormone — well, Doctor Crabtree, you know better than I about that." Whitaker's hand came out in a little, asking gesture. "It figures to prolong his life."

"Good God Almighty, Paul. Prolong his life! What life?"

Whitaker appeared a trifle puzzled, as all young doctors would, Crabtree supposed. Keep the heart beating, keep the lungs breathing up to the last inescapable moment, no matter that the patient would be better off dead. Only old doctors knew enough to hold off on treatment when further treatment was cruel.

"You never got to know the real Collingsworth, did you?" Crabtree asked.

"No. Not when he was at himself."

"Not in his prime, Paul. Damn it, there was a man with balls, honest-to-God balls, and I be goddamned if we send him to his grave without 'em. Son of a bitch, boy! Castrate Collingsworth!"

The Anderson house stood clearer, the house once owned by old Mr. Greenwood, now safe in the arms of the socialist Jesus. She would meet him at the door if she were able, a frail old lady who hated frailty.

In his mind he was again at the Collingsworth house when Prof Collingsworth died. He heard the last of the snoring breath of coma and closed the dead eyes and brought up the sheet. Mary Jess was holding a dead hand. "It's all over," he said to the stricken face. It struck him afresh that, despite the show of strain, she was an uncommonly pretty woman. Her fine-drawn features retained much of the look of her little-girlhood.

"I wish Ben could have been here," she said in a voice like a leaf's rustle. "He wouldn't have gone if he hadn't felt sure Father would last until he got back."

"I felt sure, too. I encouraged him to go to Helena for that meeting."

"I have to wire Charles," she said, as if that small task oppressed her.

For an instant, memory slipped forward to Charles Collingsworth, who had come and gone after the funeral, an agreeable and gentle but rather sad young man who had been in the war, not as a combatant, but as a member of a musical group that entertained troops. A man? Whatever he was, it was just as well he had returned to New York. Arfive was no place for him.

Thought was a queer and wandering process. It was bits and pieces and jumps foward and back, while the eye only half-saw the road and the skunk that ambled into the bushes. So he was back at Prof's bedside again, and he motioned toward the door and said, "Come on, Mary Jess. Come on now."

She followed him into the living room and perched on a chair as if about to take wing while he stood. "I'll see to arrangements, immediate ones," he told her. "You'll want Lawrence Chiles, I suppose."

"Yes, but not yet, please, Doctor." With the tip of her tongue she wet her dry-looking lips. "That's the same room in which Mother died. You know. You were there."

"Yes. Yes. But now to other things, Mary Jess. Whom do you want to stay with you?"

"No one. I'm all right."

"Look here. You're not going to wait here alone until Ben can reach home. I'll tell you that. I'll call the Ewings."

She gazed at him without speaking. It was as if there were no life in that fine face, only the life of remembrance. She was a little girl again, standing desolate just outside the door when her mother died.

"Father was so much a part of me," she said, still in that rustling voice. "So much a part of all the life that I know." A hint of challenge came into her tone. "He was a good man, Doctor Crabtree. You know he was a good man."

"You don't need a second to that sentiment. It should console you."

"But he died."

"As other good men have. The time comes sooner or later. Survivors adjust. Things go on."

"I tried to please him. I always tried."

Crabtree felt like shaking himself, like shaking her. "Everyone knows that. Good Lord, girl! It wouldn't have pleased him to live on with just half a mind left and hardly that."

"All along, I could hope."

He nodded and stepped forward and took one of her hands. "Of course. And now you have to be reconciled."

"I wish Ben were here."

"We'll try again to reach him. He'll get word, and he'll be on the way, don't you worry."

For the first time tears shone in her fine eyes. She didn't wipe them away. She said, "I need Ben," and then added as her thought shifted, "Poor Father."

"Mary Jess, dear, he's better off now. Think of his death as release. His release."

Her shimmering eyes rose to his, and her mouth shaped, "His release." Something came into her face, something of heightened bereavement or dawning knowledge, he couldn't tell what or which. She repeated, "Release."

Of itself his car had come to a halt in front of the Anderson home, like an old horse that knew where to stop. Now he'd go with his satchel and hold the old lady's hand.

32

IT WAS A WINTER, Ben reflected, the like of which even old-timers could hardly remember. They would think back for a worthy comparison and then shrug and perhaps say, "We've had it just as bad. Now let me see." Mort Ewing would shake his head and remark that you never could tell in Montana. The seasons came and went, never to be forecast from seasons before. Hell, even day by day you never could tell. The Weather Bureau itself was as likely to be wrong as right.

He sat in his office and looked, not at the waiting page in the typewriter, but at the big window that gave on the street. Little good it did him now, with snow sweeping across it and ice built up at the edges. No human figures passed by to be recognized only as shapes bundled and storm-bent. No business, not much anyhow, came through the door. People who got about gathered in bars or the lobbies of hotel and bank, a little boastful and glad that they had dared face the weather. Outside they would squint toward the west, toward the mountains, snow-mantled, from beyond which, surely sometime, the chinook wind would blow.

In its place, he thought as his mind tried to fiddle with words to be put into print, came more snow and more cold — fifty below one night — and the land lay stiff, and the house mourned in the night. So it had been since early November, week after week of snowfall, wind and, after it, still nights with the frigid stars flaming. The winter solstice came and passed, and so did Christmas, and left the weather unchanged.

Except for one day, one single day, when the chinook blew, and the hopeful said the backbone of winter was broken, only to speak differently when morning came.

He pushed the typewriter aside and went into the shop. Okay Myers, bent with years and soured by the weather, was readying type for the little job press. Young Myers, himself not young anymore, was back at the Linotype. Okay said, "That squirt hasn't shown up. Some shop, with no printer's devil."

"How you fixed otherwise?"

"Fair. Just fair." Myers' eyes were accusing. "Not much job work left. Not enough copy to put out the paper."

"Don't worry," Ben said and turned back. Myers was both an old mother hen and a good man, as fussy about the fortunes of publishing as the owner himself. A lot fussier. Needlessly fussy.

He returned to the office and sat down before the typewriter, saw what he had written, tore it from the machine and rolled in a fresh page. His subject was the killing winter of 1886–87, now dim in the memory of the oldest Montanan, revived, when it was, largely through reports and books written years back and by a celebrated postcard picture painted by Charlie Russell in his young cowboy days before fame overtook him. Make it light, Ben told himself. Make it cheerful. Start with a bullet lead, maybe, "We've lived through worse." He typed for a few minutes, consulting notes he had taken, and felt satisfied, though his mind kept trailing away.

He and Mary Jess would get up in the morning and try to peer through a window layered with ice to get the thermometer reading, and then, in order to get it, he would dodge outside, where the cold stiffened nostrils and mouth and burned his lungs.

Seldom would the car start. On days when it wouldn't, he would get into storm coat, overshoes and mittens and leave to Mary Jess, who insisted on this bit of help, the business of tying a muffler to cover his lower face. Cap over his ears, he would plough and slide to the office.

"I feel guilty," Mary Jess would say, kissing him goodbye before she adjusted the muffler. "I get to stay in a warm house while you have to fight weather."

"You're not to worry. Hear?" he would answer. "You have your work, I have mine, and that's good." He would smile. "I wouldn't let you go out today. Oh, do you need anything?"

If she required much in the way of supplies, he would take it to Hanson's Garage and get a ride home. If it was little, he carried it, first in one hand, then in the other, and arrived with fingers clinched to the package.

The front door opened, letting in both a cloud of frost and young Bob Perry, whom he had employed as reporter less than a year ago. "A lot of cattle are starving," Bob said needlessly, shedding his wraps. He was all youthful enthusiasm, bucked up by emergency. "They're flying hay in. Going to drop it."

"Late recognition, too late for some cattle," Ben answered. "I bet the Ewing ranch doesn't need help."

"How so?"

"You wouldn't ask if you knew Mort and young Mort better. But never mind. The printers need copy."

Bob went to the rear of the office and sat down at his typewriter. The keys began to tap.

He had forgotten his own story, neglected it as he wouldn't want Bob to do. He fixed his eyes on the page and his notes. Fifty-percent losses in cattle here, seventy-five-percent losses there, total losses elsewhere — those were the reports that had come in when ranchers could get about to assess herds after that bitter winter of long ago. The hard lesson learned was that cows had to be winter-fed in Montana and states adjoining. No more trusting to nature to bring them through. Without hay, no sure survival.

He finished a page, inserted another and sat staring at it, knowing his mind was divided, knowing he couldn't quite make it single.

It was in weather like this weather was, more than a month ago, that old Mrs. Anderson died. Somehow Doc Crabtree had made it to her house, though too late to save her. In all likelihood the trip, if managed earlier, would have been fruitless, but, anyhow, there was old Doc for you, faithful to call. Come rain or shine, hell or high water, boil point or subzero, there he was somehow.

The postal service, instead of bragging on itself, might admire and pursue his example.

Mattie Murchison came from Minnesota for the funeral, arriving tardily at Great Falls on a train that had been held up by snowdrifts. With the help of snowplows Lawrence Chiles had managed to meet her and bring her to Arfive.

"Want to look over this?" Bob Perry asked from his typewriter seat.

Ben moved aside to the copy desk and took the three pages. He edited and headlined the story and said, "Take it back to Okay. Nice story, but you might remember there are two *m*'s in 'accommodate.' "

"Yes, sir, and thanks. Then get back on my beat?"

"Such as it is. Remember, the mayor has something for us. Probably an original message that the hour is darkest just before dawn."

"In other words, if you'll excuse me, bullshit." The boy looked timidly hopeful of approval.

"It takes a certain amount, whatever you choose to call it, to nourish a newspaper."

Bob smiled, and Ben smiled back at him, and Bob said, "Yes, sir." He went into the shop, returned almost immediately, put on his wraps and walked out into the storm.

Ben went back to his typewriter. He was as good as done with his story now, and Okay wasn't so shy on copy as he made it appear.

Mary Jess and he had wired for flowers for the funeral, had attended church services and gone to the cemetery in the car he had had to have towed beforehand to get the engine to fire. It was the graveyard scene that came most often to mind — the frozen clods of earth under the false grass carpet the undertaker had laid, the little group, pallbearers included, exhaling the white smoke of frost, the chilled preacher who believed in Lordly benevolence. He couldn't tell much about Mattie, who stood with her head bent, burdened with wraps. He could imagine the chunks of earth thudding on the casket as the grave was closed, the little crowd gone now, the sense of loss rolling to the more comfortable climate of home fires, the old body left to unkind mother earth.

He shook himself and completed his story and put it aside and let his mind drift.

Mary Jess and he had made a courtesy call that evening, churning up the hill to the bench to the clank of chains, a homemade cake resting between them.

Mattie herself met them at the door, thanked them for the cake and saw them in. Seated in the living room were Frank Brobeck and the long-time tenants, the Broquists, who had managed the farm for old Mr. Greenwood and, later, for Mrs. Anderson. They all rose and exchanged greetings and sat down again, stiff as waiting-room patients, as distant from one another as if no common language existed.

Only Mattie managed a show of sociability. She asked them, please, to find chairs, put the cake on a table already crowded and turned back to say, "If you're hungry, for heaven's sake help yourselves to the good things people have brought."

No one moved, and she added, "Later, then. You needn't hold back. Friends have been so generous."

Scrap by scrap the conversation got going. Ben listened and looked. Time had been good to Mattie. It might have shortened a trifle that old, free stride, but it had left her face almost unlined, her figure straight, her body obviously vigorous.

And yet it was as if he were observing somebody new to him, somebody old and somebody new, with only the threads of unspoken awareness relating them to him. He thought he saw that awareness in her eyes, in the smiles she smiled at them all. Underneath the chatter was his memory of the old Tuesday nights, of his education in sex, of their lying side by side satisfied. Yet it wasn't he who had lain so, not himself now, but some strange version worked on by the years, recognized only dimly, accepted with something of — right word — rue.

Mattie's remembered words came to his ears. "Mike — my son, you know — will be mustered out before long. Thank the Lord, he survived those flying missions. He's still in England."

Then, in answer to somebody's question, "Yes, I'm thinking of moving back and living here on the farm."

The Ewings, in force, had arrived then and, soon afterwards, some other friends from country and town. After a bite to eat, Mary Jess and he had taken their leave.

He tapped out a headline for his storm story, took the copy into the shop and came back and sat down again. There was still an editorial to write, and Bob's unwritten copy to edit later before the time came to knock off. He flicked on a light, for the early dark was settling in, or unsettling in, worried by the whip of the winter wind. Another bitter night in store.

But something could be said for the long cold. There was the final coziness of home, the sense of safe shelter from all the furies. He and Mary Jess would talk good talk while he drew on the pipe he had taken to. Or they would read or listen to music while reading. No matter. The worries of the day were outside, along with the cold and the wind.

Later they would go to bed and sleep close, the two of them against desolation, and they would murmur a word or two, warm body to body, and sleep would flow over them, sleep that didn't need to knit the ravels of care.

Once, after her brother had come and gone from their father's funeral, she had stirred in bed and asked, "Ben, what did you really make of Charles?"

"He was pleasant enough."

"You're avoiding the question."

"Am I?"

"Out of consideration for me?"

"That would be a good reason, dear."

"He is one of them, isn't he? You know what I mean."

"He's a sad man, but your worry won't help him."

She gave him a sudden hug and pressed closer, facing him. It was all right, he had thought. It had been all right for a long time. He supposed, like all men, he would always speculate about other women, about good-looking girls, but speculation was idle when love at last had brought understanding, and it, in turn, the final commitment.

"Oh, Ben," she had said into his thoughts, "I'm so glad you're a whole man. I'm so glad you're you."

"It's mine to be glad that you're you," he said and kissed her, and his hand brought up her nightgown.

The door flung open to a great puff of vapor, and Bob Perry said, "You were right about the mayor," and there was the editorial yet to be written.

33

APRIL COULD BE and usually was a harsh month in Montana, Mary Jess reflected as she rode along with Ben at the wheel. All the spring months, including May, could be harsh, months of wind and snow flurries and rain that was almost snow. Even so, she thought, remembering, they were better than the months just passed. With hardly a pause the bitter, winter weather had held until almost the last of February and then had yielded to a windy, fretful, and unpredictable March.

Today was clear and not too cold. Under the force of the wind and occasional touches of warmth the snow drifts had shrunken. Like veins, runners of blown dirt threaded their surfaces. But to the west the mountains rose pure, a ragged, walled white that narrowed the eye. The lowering sun lit the top of Ear Mountain.

Ben was silent, and for this little time she chose to be. They often were. They didn't need speech as a lubricant. They crossed the bridge over the Breast. The river was edged with white ice. Between its frozen shores the stream ran dark.

At last she asked, "We won't be late, Ben?"

"Plenty of time," he answered, yet consulted his wrist watch. "Maybe half an hour for drinks, even."

"You might be disappointed," she said, just for amusement.

"Not with Mort there. You think young Mort wouldn't have a bottle for his father?"

"You have to learn to call him Phil." The full name ran in her head: Morton Phillip Ewing, Jr. "He shouldn't have to live as a shoot, growing in the shadow of Mort."

Ben said, "Yes, ma'am," and smiled.

He steered off the highway onto the dirt road that led to the Ewing ranch. Wheels had worn and skidded ruts in it, leaving shoulders of mud that were stiffening as the half-hearted sun sank. The car lurched along.

On a slope, before the house came in sight, cattle nosed for the wisps of hay overlooked when first they were fed. Young calves mingled with them, pushing for udders when the cows halted.

"Good condition," Ben said and added, "you'd expect it."

Then the house came into view. Not one house but two, and barns and a corral and outbuildings. The smaller house, she knew, once sheltered Mort's old ranch foreman. Sometimes it served as a bunkhouse these days, replacing the cabin used formerly. Smoke climbed from a chimney, straight in the still air.

As Ben braked to a stop, a big dog ran out, barking a welcome that his tail seconded. Mort opened the house door before they could knock. "Come in and get the chill off," he said. "Stay outside there, Tip."

When they entered, Phil stepped up to shake hands with Ben. Julie greeted them, and, after her, Mabel. The Ewings' two boys, one hardly more than a toddler, squirmed through to mix with the company. A fire flamed in the big fireplace.

Phil took their wraps and told them to find seats. Over his shoulder he said, "Dad, you're the bartender. Can't you see these people need saving?"

"I was waitin' till they fell over," Mort answered. "But all right. I know the poison they got a taste for." He went through the open doorway into the kitchen.

By the time he returned, a glass in each hand, little Tony had climbed onto Ben's knee, and Ben was giving Baby Jon a hand up. They were like that with Ben, more so than with others. As she took the glass that Mort offered her, it came to her mind how little it was that young people, small or big, had entered their lives. Almost not at all, save for these two Ewing children. To be sure, Ben engaged high-schoolers to help in the shop or gather personal items, and rather recently he had hired a young editorial assistant, whom he liked — but beyond that?

"Mort," Julie was saying as Mort gave Ben his glass, "won't you ever learn to use a tray?"

"Look out there, young'ns," Mort said. "Leave the man one hand free, anyhow."

"He's Uncle Ben," Tony told him. "Aren't you my Uncle Ben?"

Ben answered, "You betcha."

"Now as to a tray," Mort said, turning toward Julie, "I'm not servin' tea."

Julie laughed and started to rise, saying, "You could save yourself steps," but Mabel jumped up. "Let me," she told Julie. She and Mort went into the kitchen and returned with drinks on a tray that Mabel carried.

Mabel, Mary Jess thought as the drinks were being served and talk flowed around her. Mabel, an old-fashioned name suitable to a stocky and unpretending woman who seemed cut out to be a ranch wife. No condescension there in that thought. No derogation. Recognition, rather, and more than a touch of admiration. Had Mabel conceived and carried the babies in her body without that wild terror of childbirth she herself had once known? Had Mabel given birth to these children without qualms about what might be in store for them? With no misgivings about the world and the lives they would be forced to live? Probably she hadn't considered. She was too healthy for fear of the future, too natural. The present was dear beyond any anxiety about the dim years ahead.

Mort, standing, lifted his glass. "Here's to peace and prosperity," he said. After they had drunk to his toast, he went on. "A bad-matched team there, Ben. Peace and prosperity. Ever enter your noggin they don't pull together?"

Phil answered for Ben. "Aw, cut it out, Dad. This isn't a wake."

"Just wanted to keep talk flowin' free," Mort said, seating himself. "On the bright side, then. I'm pleasured to be in good company." He waved his glass around. "And double glad to be back at the ranch."

"That goes for all of us," Phil said.

"Come a real break in the weather," Mort continued, looking toward Mary Jess, "we're movin' from the dang town."

She supposed his language was restrained because of the children. "Do you find town so bad?" she asked.

"Worse'n that. Course, if you got something to do, like Ben, I reckon it's tolable. But for an old fool like me, I tell you it's torment. Nowhere to go but to saloons. Nothin' to do but drink, and not much of that because Julie rides herd on me."

Julie smiled. Ben was doing simple finger tricks for the children.

"We could use a good man," Phil said, looking at his father.

"Comin' up," Mort answered. "Be here for brandin'. What I figure," he went on, now looking at Ben, "is to redo the other house, or maybe build a new shack entirely. Eh, Julie?"

"Whatever you say." She added, "When I'm sure you're well enough."

"What a man has to put up with! What a well man has to put up with!" Mort's eyes went to the others, away from Julie. "She knows I'm finer'n frog hair. It's just she likes high society."

"I like you better," Julie said, her smile indulgent.

"We have time for another," Mabel told them. She gathered the glasses on the tray, went to the kitchen and returned with refills. She went out again, saying before she left, "Excuse me. A few last-minute things."

Mary Jess told her, "I'll help. Let me," but Mabel shook her head. "Julie's already been more help than I could ask."

They were called soon to dinner, or supper as Mort would have called it, into a dining room of linen and candlelight.

"That's a noble roast," Ben said, seeing it.

Mabel saw to seating them and said to Mort, "Dad, don't you want to carve?"

"Just because the Injuns taught me to chunk meat, I'm an expert, I am."

He was an expert. The plates went around and were added to from side dishes of potatoes, mashed rutabagas, hot biscuits and gravy. For a salad there were spiced peaches and cottage cheese on lettuce leaves.

The little boys sat on either side of Phil, who cut their meat for them and helped the smaller one with spoon feeding.

The conversation was idle — praise of the food, comments on weather, chit-chat about people in town, talk of the calf crop, the market and later prospects. At one point Mort said, "I haven't been around long enough to see so much snow in the mountains before. God himself hasn't, I reckon. Must surprise Him, seein' the woods covered over and every dang canyon choked up to the rim."

"Means plenty of irrigation water," Phil answered.

"Yup. Plenty. God's plenty."

They had hardly finished the dessert of chocolate pie with whipped cream than little Tony said, "Playtime."

Phil groaned and replied, "Hold up a minute there, boy. Coffee and smokes come before that. Don't you see that big people have rights?"

Mort answered, saying with a smile, "Nope."

"No," Mabel said to Julie and Mary Jess. "We'll leave the dishes. Please."

When they were seated again in the living room, Tony announced to his father, "We'll play bucking horse."

"Will we now? Who says so?"

"Please, Dad. Pretty please. Look at Jon. He wants to, too."

Pretending reluctance, Phil left his chair and lowered himself to hands and knees, and Tony straddled his back. Phil let him ride there, making only a show of bucking while the boy hung on, crowing. Smiling, Jon waited his turn.

Mort looked on with grandfatherly indulgence. It was hard to think of him as a grandfather. It was impossible to think of him as old. His eye was still bright, his face lined by weather rather than years, and, when he walked, he walked straight and sure, not with the duck-foot and high-knee action of age.

Mary Jess let her eyes rest on Ben. He was grinning, his teeth showing through his pleased smile. He sat on the edge of his chair. With a little encouragement, Mary Jess thought, he would play horse himself.

Phil dislodged Tony with a sudden drop of a shoulder. He had to lie flat to let Jon get on. After a tour of the room, Jon fell off happily.

They had another turn each before Mabel said, "All right, boys. Fun's over. Bedtime."

They insisted first on going around to kiss everybody good night, then let themselves be shooed away.

Outside, the night's chill pressed against them as they went to the car after saying goodbye. The sky showed no star and no moon. The headlights cut an uncertain path through the dark. The mud had frozen, and the hard lumps of it, carved and mis-shapen by light, jolted them.

They rode without speaking until they reached the turn to the highway. There Ben slowed and looked close at her, and his hand reached for hers.

"Something on your mind?" he said. "Something upset you, made you feel sad?"

She squeezed his hand. "After such a good evening? Sad? Of course not," she answered, feeling sad for Ben, for herself who had failed him, sad somehow for everyone in the world.

34

"THIS STATE is like some goddamn drunk," Mort Ewing said, "one of those jokers that's got his arm around you one minute and his fists in your face the next." A smile appeared on his weathered face, paled somewhat by his long months in town. "Only it's been one hell of a spell between hugs."

He and Ben Tate sat at a table in a corner of Jim Sowder's bar, both damp from the rain that was pelting outside. In this weather Sowder had few customers. Those coming and going had left wet trails from door to bar stools.

"June in Montana," Ben answered. "Typical, only more so." He sipped at the drink he had decided to have before going home. "No sign of a break. The weather reports call for more."

"Never say typical here. What's typical is — what's the word, Ben?"

"Atypical."

"That's it." Ewing stretched and sighed and picked up his glass. "Sure, the rain will help many a crop and pasture, and the lucky ones are thanking the Lord, but I don't like it."

"You're not alone. Neither do I."

Ewing went on as if to himself. "All this rain, and the snow pack in the mountains deeper and higher'n Christ can remember. Every damn stream will be runnin' over its banks if it ain't over already." He looked up. "You seen the Breast?"

"Even last night I could hear it from the house."

"I went to the ranch yesterday. Furloughed, you might say, by Julie. Came in an hour ago. Crossin' by the bridge, I sure noticed." He shrugged. "Worst that can happen at the ranch is my ditch might wash out, but Jesus!"

"In the paper last week I tried to put people on the alert. It was too early then for a real warning."

Ewing signaled for a refill, and Sowder came puffing with the drinks. "Wet enough for you?" he asked, putting them down.

"Why, now, is it raining?" Ewing said. He looked at the window and added, "Oh, shitaree."

Sowder laughed and puffed back to the bar and resumed the game of cribbage he was playing with Clarence Landusky.

"Got a great sense of humor, that man," Ewing said, low-voiced, and went to work on his drink. Then he said, "Ben, there's them too dumb to know what may be in store."

"I've thought about that, too. I guess none of us are prepared, dumb or not."

"Build an ark and put on board two of each kind."

"Be serious, Mort."

"I am, kind of." His expression grew serious. "I've outgrowed my time, Ben. Once I would have been talkin' to Prof Collingsworth, figurin' things out best we could. But even was he alive, we wouldn't be the head and the hoof and the haunch and the hump anymore, like old Macalester Cleveland said. Know who is?"

"Nobody, Mort."

"Wrong. You and Frank Brobeck, that's who. Prof and I pass the goddamn torch to you, boy."

"There's the mayor and members of the Chamber of Commerce and plenty of others."

"Don't shit me."

"All right. Thanks. Go on."

"You got to allow for the fact the dam might go out. Then where are you? Where is Arfive?"

"That's been on my mind, too."

"Uh-huh. Caught you. You been plannin' already. Just what now?"

"Just notes in my mind."

"Reel 'em off."

"Appoint captains. Assign districts and households to them. Gather boats and what motors we can. Arrange for a distress telephone. Have food ready to take up to the hill towards the bench. All that's for starters. It's all for emergency."

"Good boy. Add sandbags, if there's time. Any reports on the dam? Aerial survey? Forest Service ought to know."

"I checked. One aborted flight. Poor visibility."

Ewing nodded. "The sky would be hangin' too low there. What about the dam people themselves?"

"Nothing. They're keeping mum."

"That figures. They wouldn't admit that their baby might go down the drain."

Ben called for two more drinks. Sowder didn't comment this time.

Ewing went on. "The Breast is too dinky a stream for figures on flood stage, rate of flow, likely crest, and all that. But, Ben, who knows for sure? It could come in a day or so, three or four at the outside. We could be washed down to the big water with nary a thing saved but our nightshirts."

"Tomorrow I'm going to drive up to the dam and see for myself."

"If you can get there. Stay on the high road. Take Brobeck with you. I'll go along if Julie'll let me." Ewing smiled. "She wants to save me for some goddamn museum."

Ewing finished his drink, got up and said, "Call me, Ben." They both put on raincoats. Ben followed him out. The rain was still falling. Ben's car sputtered and died and sputtered again until finally all cylinders fired.

At dinner Mary Jess said, "Won't this rain ever stop? What's the prediction? What do you hear? Ben, you're not listening."

"Sorry," he answered. "I was just thinking."

Rain drummed on the roof of the kitchen, where they often ate when alone. The flow and gurgle of downspouts sounded from outside.

"Let me in on it," she asked.

"You'll be safe in this house. We're high enough. Please stay in it, Mary Jess."

"You're not very illuminating, but I suppose you're thinking of the danger of flood?"

"Every dry swale, every wrinkle of land between here and town is running water. In low spots it's over the road."

"So?"

"Same everywhere, Mary Jess, and it will be worse."

"How worse? Now come on, Ben."

He shrugged. "God knows." He hadn't wanted to tell her, had wanted to spare her any anxiety about him, but their tie, one to another, demanded he speak. "The worst is that the big dam might go out. I must have a look at it."

"Oh, no, Ben. Please don't. It's frightening." The look in her eyes was enough. She need not have spoken.

He reached over and patted her hand. "There's no cause for upset, Sweetheart. Frank Brobeck will go along, and probably Mort."

"How? Any car would get stuck."

"We'll borrow a truck from the sheriff or the road department. Now please don't worry. There's nothing to worry about." He smiled into the still-anxious face. "Remember, I'm a newspaper-man."

"And lots more than that," she said, yielding. "I can't stand in the way of what you feel you have to do."

He helped her with the dishes, then they read for a while and later went to sleep to the sound of rain, muted because the house was two-storied but still distinct and incessant and pleasant but for thoughts of what might be.

◆

Even with chains on, the truck skidded and floundered, and Brobeck, driving, had to peer through the windshield that the wipers couldn't keep clear.

"If we get there at all," Brobeck said, "it will be by this old road. North bank's clean out of the question. Wish Skeeter Jerome could have scrounged up a four-wheel drive. Still, he done his best, and thanks to him."

"It's his thanks to you," Ewing said. "He wouldn't be sheriff if you hadn't backed him."

"Nuts."

Ben, wedged in the middle of the single seat, kept silent. From horizon to closed-in horizon was one steady weeping. The close sky shut them in. The sun was lost. The road, little more than a wagon trail, wound through untilled grazing land though no livestock was in sight. The homesteads that the dam watered were lower down on the benchlands.

"Up this hill, if we can make it," Brobeck said as the tires ground for purchase, "and we'll see what we can see. Must be within five miles of the dam."

The truck spun to a halt, and Brobeck managed to back up and take a run at the trail, which wasn't a trail so much as a stream hurrying down over gravel and mud. Like a boat in rough water, the truck rocked to the top.

There Ewing said, squinting through the windshield, "Looks like our road has taken to the water. Got a submarine handy, Frank?"

Brobeck had braked to a stop. They pulled down their hats, drew slickers around them and got out and walked, skidding, down to the river's edge. By turns the river was a torrent and a wide sweep of water. Uprooted willows, spring-colored and budded, ran with it, along with a tree, and a boulder rose and rolled, its grating audible above the voice of the stream and the rain.

"Ever seen it higher, Mort?" Brobeck asked.

"Maybe as high. No higher. Goddamn rain."

"At least the dam's holding," Ben said.

"Or we wouldn't be here," Ewing answered. A patch of red showed in the water and made itself into a drowned cow. It moved along with weeds and willows and topsoil that muddied the flow. "Dam goes out," Ewing went on, "the whole valley will be a river, hill to hill, wide as the Mississippi low down."

"No way to tell how it's holding, not on this road. One hell of a roundabout by another route, and no sayin' we'd get there even then. What say, Ben?"

"Back to town. What else?"

They crowded, wet, into the truck. The rain kept a curtain around them.

"I had a sneaking hunch that goddamn dam never should have been built in the first place," Brobeck said after turning the truck around. "Flood control, they called it."

"Yep," Ewing answered. "You might say it's a washout, washed out or not."

"That's not the whole of it, not the sole reason," Ben said.

Brobeck asked, "That so?"

"You have to allow for overgrazing and overcropping and timber up on the headwaters that never should have been cut. So, quick run-off. So, big water."

"Yes to all that," Ewing said. "At every turn, sometimes it seems to me, man fucks himself."

When they crossed the bridge close to town, Ewing eyed the stream. "Up by a foot or more. Goodbye bridge."

It was still raining when they reached the office.

"Come in," Ben said. "There's a bottle in my desk."

"What's the time?" Ewing asked. "Can't tell by a sun that don't show."

Brobeck answered, "Comin' on to four o'clock."

"We'll call it six and quittin' time, and I'm due a drink."

Bob Perry was waiting inside. He said eagerly, "The sheriff wants one of you to call. He's asked three times."

But also waiting was the Reverend Mr. Jackson Moody, pastor of the First Methodist Church. He rose from his chair and asked Ben, "May I give you a story first, Mr. Tate?" His voice had the tone of the pulpit.

"Of course. Bob here will take it."

"I thought it best to see you. You can give it its proper importance, its right emphasis."

Ben nodded, not wanting to. "I'll write the story from Bob's notes. Oh, Bob, bring another chair from the back, please."

They seated themselves, all but Brobeck. Mr. Moody, a tall man, impressive of face, took his time sitting down. It struck Ben, watching, that religion had had little part in his own life, even though Mr. Collingsworth had taught the Bible class for twenty-five years. Organized religion wasn't for him or for Mary Jess, but the question flitted again into his mind. Where, but from churches with all their superstitions, would come a commitment to ethics?

"I fancy myself rather a climatologist, with due respect for the unforeseen decisions of God," Mr. Moody began.

"Yes," Ben said. Ewing was looking amused.

"Beyond science, beyond our efforts to understand, is God. Science may predict, but God wills."

"Yes."

"We are in danger of flood, is it not so?"

"Yes."

"So I am calling a meeting, a big meeting, a community meeting for men and women of all denominations or no denominations whatever. It will be a prayer meeting, Mr. Tate, a united appeal for the cessation of rain."

Bob Perry, taking notes, asked, "When?"

"Unless the rain ceases, Friday at eight in the evening, the day after the paper comes out."

"You better start praying now, Reverend," Ewing said. "Postpone it, and your message might not reach God before we're washed out."

"You sound rather irreverent, sir."

"How so? You want to inform God, don't you? The sooner the better, I say."

"God already knows."

Brobeck was smiling behind his hand.

"Well, then," Ewing began.

Before he could go on, Ben cut in, "All right, Mr. Moody. At your church, of course. We'll give the story due prominence."

Mr. Moody had hardly closed the door before Bob Perry said, "The sheriff, Mr. Tate. He said what he had was important."

Brobeck went to the phone and rang and listened. He hung up the receiver with slow gravity and turned to say, "The water's overflowin' the dam. Dam-tender, if that's what he's called, said so. He skedaddled to town. Says he'd go to hell before he'd stay up there, the way things are."

Ben swept his desk clear. "No time to waste," he told Ewing and Brobeck. "You're staying to help?"

Ewing nodded, and Bob chipped in with "Me, too," and Brobeck said, "Let me call my old lady."

35

"Disaster center," Ben said into the telephone.

"Ben," Skeeter Jerome answered from the sheriff's office at the courthouse, "you better haul ass up the hill. Just received a delayed report from the Forest Service. They finally got a plane up over the dam. Say it's likely to go out any minute."

"I've heard that before."

"But not official. Not so recent. Brobeck'll come get you."

"You're staying."

"But I have two stories to climb to, a regular crow's nest if I'm drowned out below."

"Tell Brobeck to wait."

"Don't be a damn mule. Calls here have dribbled down to nothin'. Same with you, sure as hell."

"You can't tell."

He hung up the phone and looked out the dark window. It was clouded with mist and spatters. Beyond it the beams of a street light were divided and fractured by the rain still penciling down. The flood water was rising. It had found a way through the sand-bags at the front of the office and was exploring the floor.

He made a move to put on the gum boots at the side of his desk, then sat back, leaving them there. Time enough to put them on when he had to.

Time. What was the correct time, if it mattered? The clock on the wall would tell him, if he cared to consult it. What was time, anyhow? Night and gray daylight and dark again, unmarked by hours, measured by preparations, households checked, calls received and succor sent in the float of night into day into night.

The town plat on his desk was a blur, until he made his eyes focus. It bore the locations of households and the names of householders. He had crossed out the places vacated. Even without looking, he knew that almost all of them had been, either by the owners' volition or with urging and help from the volunteer crews. Those not crossed out were being seen to. Beyond full report were the premises up the valley beyond the town limits. Like his own, a few places on the northern fringe were safe enough. In his eyes the plat and the names flowed together, leaving the thought of Mary Jess alone in the house.

There flowed together, too, the preparations that he and Mort Ewing and Frank Brobeck had made in a time that seemed long ago now. He forced himself to review them.

Crews. They had mustered men to give warning and aid, if needed.

Communications. He had cleared his telephone for emergency calls. A couple of boats had radios, borrowed from the sheriff's office, and could send messages to Skeeter Jerome.

His eyes lifted at the sound of the inner door opening, and Bob Perry floated into view. "I've got the stock up off the floor best I could, Mr. Tate," he said.

The stock seemed not to matter, but he heard himself saying, "Good, Bob. Now it's high time for you to get out. I'll phone for a boat."

"What about you?"

"Time enough."

"Pardon me, Mr. Tate, but you look all done in." He added, "No wonder."

"I'm all right."

"Then so am I," the boy said. "I'll stick." He sat down.

His gaze wandered back to the list. Boats, outboard motors, food — these had been volunteered or appropriated at God knew whose expense.

Shelter, a tardy consideration, but the shack of a clubhouse on what was coming to be known as golf-course hill was too small by far. So tents it was, offered freely or borrowed of necessity.

Firewood, almost a last thought, seen to by Mort Ewing.

Sanitary arrangements, since the privy that graced the hill wouldn't suffice. Old Doc Crabtree was in charge of them.

"I figure we're in pretty good shape, Bob, but — " he was saying when the door burst open, letting in a gush of water. Dripping, Frank Brobeck, in slicker, rain hat and hip boots, entered and strode forward. "Goddamn you, Ben," he said, "Come on now."

"Some people —"

"Forget it. They're safe. Ingwald Jorgenson, he kicked like a steer, but we wrestled him and his missus and kid into a boat."

"The McIntoshes?"

"I got good reason to think she took off sudden with an oil-company lease hound, and he set out after them."

Ben looked at the plat and said, "But —"

"All seen to, for God's sake, and if you're not at the end of your tether, I never seen a pooped man. Get your duds on."

"You look bushed yourself," Ben answered but bent for his gum boots.

"Leave 'em. Not high enough. Got to wade on account of there's shoal water between here and the boat. It's across Main Street."

"Come on, Bob," Ben said to Perry. They began putting on rain gear.

"Shake a leg!" Brobeck said. "I got a very special passenger, and she's damn impatient." A big grin transformed his tired face.

Ben looked at him and said, "No — ?"

"Yes. The same pretty party."

"She was safe enough at the house. I asked her to stay there."

"So I understand," Brobeck said and grinned again.

◆

Like most of the other men and some of the women Ben sat on the brow of the hill, heedless of the warm wet, and looked down in the direction of town. It was still there. The flickering street lights proved that much, as they wouldn't if the dam broke. No

eye could penetrate the dark and the mist and the still-falling rain
and see the long bowl of the valley.

The watchers sat on the tails of their slickers or on patches of
canvas. A few had umbrellas. Brobeck was on one side of him,
Mary Jess on the other. Most of the children had been put to bed
under the shelter of tents, and with them most of the dogs had retired.

Back of him, Ben knew, bonfires tried to burn, and flashlights
and lanterns glowed. Light. That was one thing he had forgotten
but others hadn't. The tents would be showing changing patterns
of shadow. Behind them trucks and cars, driven up the hill by
lucky early-comers, were spotted unevenly, all with chains on.
The camp was silent, save for the sounds of movement, occasional
voices pitched low, and the sometimes-heard voice of the Reverend Jackson Moody, who for the time being had appropriated a
tent and was holding a prayer meeting probably attended by few.

It struck Ben that these people, the larger part of them, may not
have wanted an answer to prayer. Here was an event, a big event,
a spectacle to be seen and appreciated and, if worst came to worst,
a clean start on a new life. The atmosphere was one of expectancy, not doom.

"You must get some sleep, Ben," Mary Jess said. "Frank, too."

"With a couple of drinks, thanks to Mort Ewing, and food in
my stomach, I'm a new man."

"Same here," Brobeck put in.

"Humph to you both."

They had chugged to the base of the hill earlier, seeing before
them the fitful bonfires, the off-and-on eyes of flashlights and the
passing whites of tents. Arrived, they might have come to a picnic. Women bustled, men spoke and laughed, children shouted,
complained and played, and dogs joined the fun. All the dogs in
the county, it seemed. A million dogs, give or take a half-dozen.

Mort Ewing had showed them to a tent, humped inside with
bedrolls. "Figured you wouldn't mind sharin' it with Julie and
me," he said. "A no-thanks job, gettin' people parceled out.
Glad I don't run a hotel come a convention of Elks. Grub's in the

clubhouse, plenty of it. First, though —" He fumbled inside his slicker and took out a bottle.

In a canvas bag Mary Jess had brought dry clothes along, and he changed socks, trousers and shoes, feeling better for them though they'd be wet soon enough. Then he had gone to the clubhouse and eaten and spoken to Julie, noting on his way there that Doc Crabtree had managed to have latrine trenches dug, separated, men and ladies, by canvas sidewalls.

As they sat on the hill, Ewing plodded up to them through the mud. Before he spoke, the voice of the minister sounded in prayer. He listened and raised his face to the rain and, lowering it, said, "Looks like the man of God has lost touch with headquarters."

Even in the dark his face showed long fatigue, though, as always, he stood straight. Mary Jess said, "You look dead tired, Mort."

"That so? Feelin' fine, but, come to that, who of us isn't played out? Doc Crabtree needs a doctor himself, the old fool. When that arthritis bites him, he just bites back."

"Get to bed, all of you," Mary Jess said.

"And miss the parade, beggin' your pardon, for God's sake!" Ewing sat down beside them and waved an encompassing arm. "Biggest treat in their lives, this here catastrophe is."

"So I was just thinking," Ben said.

"I been here a long time and never saw the like of it. Know what? Gopher holes on the ranch are spoutin' water. My boy told me so on the phone. They're fountains, regular fountains, and that's what I call a miracle. The boy's safe at the ranch and no work he can do, so he keeps track of the wonders of nature."

"But your work is done now." Mary Jess was persistent.

"Know another thing, Ben?" Ewing continued, as if she hadn't spoken. "We damn near forgot water or even a tub or barrel to collect the rain in. But who would think of it when the air's all water itself?"

Ben said without thinking, "There's running water in the clubhouse."

"Yeah. One cold spigot. Can't you see a passel of people in line, waitin' to draw water or wash up, and, come his turn, each splatterin' the grub?"

Mary Jess laughed. That was an ability — to laugh at discomfort and even affliction — that had grown with the years. "You won't listen to me," she said.

"You not included, Mary Jess, but I been listenin' to bellyaches: 'Can't I have this tent? Can't I have that?' 'Why not quarter me with my neighbor?' 'We brought a whole ham, and it's done already gone.' A big bellyache from that Ingwald Jorgenson: What's the idea, draggin' him and his family up here when the water wasn't more'n ankle-deep in the kitchen?" Ewing let out a breath. "I come close to wishin' you'd let him drown, Frank."

"Me, too, the knot-head."

Mary Jess rose, saying, "Come on, Ben." She looked at the other two. "I'll sic Julie on you, Mort, and your wife, too, Frank."

"Not while there's kitchen duties. Not Julie."

"Or while my missus plays nurse for Doc Crabtree while he tends to a couple of sniffly kids," Brobeck said.

She took Ben to their tent, where he took off his slicker and shoes while she unrolled his bed. He fell on it and slept.

He woke up to the sound of rain on the tent roof. Some of it had oozed or sprayed through the canvas and was still doing so, and he felt as if he had spent the night in a mist. Mary Jess and the Ewings had risen and gone. In the cheerless gray of the morning he pulled on the boots that Mary Jess had brought in her bag, struggled into his slicker, put on his rain hat and went out, bound first for the latrine and next for the clubhouse.

The long day dragged by. Gone was the holiday spirit. Men and women were restless. How long, they were thinking, how long? Children complained, having exhausted the small novelty of novel environment. Even the dogs looked dejected, cast down by the unceasing rain, by the mud that caked feet and fur. Like children and dogs, everybody was muddy, some more and some less but all muddy.

From the brow of the hill the eye could make out the town below. An old-world town, Ben thought, squinting to see through the rain, a town like pictured Venice or some Holland village. From this distance the water seemed not so much to flow as to rise, inch by inch, he imagined, clapboard by clapboard, brick by brick. But the dam was holding. That much was sure.

In the afternoon a small airplane flew over low, and Ben and Brobeck signaled an "all right" with waves and thumbs up. It dropped a bundle that Doc Crabtree hobbled over to claim.

"Drugs," he told them. "I ordered a lot of stuff out of Great Falls before I came up, water purifier included."

"Rain water's pure enough," Brobeck said as if just to keep the conversation going.

"I'm thinking of the town later."

"If the town stands."

"Let it stand, and we could have sickness, much sickness, a plague in your language." Crabtree looked around to make sure no women were listening. "Every goddam corral, every goddam shithouse up the valley has been dumped on the town." He took the bundle to the shelter of the clubhouse.

The minister held another prayer meeting, more largely attended because it was better entertainment than nothing.

The slow afternoon passed, and early evening came on, and Ben stood with Mary Jess and Ewing and looked down on the town. Mary Jess, who had been telling stories to some of the young fry, appeared funny and dear in her dripping raincoat, muddy boots and borrowed rain hat from which some straggles of hair escaped.

"Ben," Ewing said slowly, "I reckon that the dam will hold, havin' held so far, but I don't know that it's such a blessing."

"No?"

"Flood control, huh? All it did was hold back a fast run-off, meantime scarin' the daylights out of a lot of poor devils. It blocked the water all right but still fed plenty to us, as it's goin' to do for some time, I figure. Maybe it's better to have a quick flood and be shut of it and no fiddle-faddle. Maybe."

"I hadn't thought about that."

"Don't matter." Ewing lifted his face to the dripping sky and after a moment said, "The preacher made contact, I'm thinking."

"What makes you think that?" Ben asked.

"I got psychic powers."

"Now come on, Mort," Mary Jess said.

"Me and weather been together a long spell. It's under my skin and in my eye and burrowed into my soul, beggin' the minister's pardon."

"What's it now?" Ben asked. "What say your skin and your eye and your soul?"

"It all inkles that it'll clear off come midnight or sooner."

Looking at the other people ranked on the hill, seeing behind him the women miserable and the children and dogs, hearing the querulous voices and, more than all, feeling the rain on his slicker and hat, Ben could only shake his head and answer, "I hope you're right."

It turned out that he was, Ben was glad to admit. Gradually the rain dwindled and ceased, and, as night fell, the clouds blew off to eastward, driven by a fresh wind. In their stead a full moon appeared, brighter than all the flashlights and lanterns and sizzling bonfires.

"Praise God! Praise God!" Mr. Moody kept crying. It was a sentiment, Ben thought, with which all were in general sympathy, though some might believe the thanks should go elsewhere.

Advised, supported and appointed by Ewing, Brobeck and Doc Crabtree, Ben, as reluctant chairman, called a meeting to announce that the real danger seemed over and probably, with daylight, the move back to town could begin. A big task lay ahead of them, he said, the task of cleaning up while at the same time taking precautions against infection. Doctor Crabtree had supplies that would be distributed to other physicians. Some houses — who could say how many? — wouldn't be habitable yet, but the fortunate, everyone knew, would take in the unfortunate.

They applauded him. Under the rainless sky, under the bright moon, the atmosphere of picnic returned. Men talked in strong voices and women chattered. Even the children and dogs seemed to sense improved feeling. Someone with a revolver fired a joyful shot at the sky. Men forged through the muck to cars and trucks and began sounding horns.

Ben eased away from the crowd to stand again on the rim of the hill. Mary Jess was with him, and later Ewing, Julie, Doc Crabtree and Brobeck joined them.

Even by night the town could be seen now, not so much by the gleams of the street lights as by the glow of the moon. It sat there in the valley, solid enough, the water of its streets shining silver. Those gathered stood without speaking, thankful and tired, with no words, it seemed to Ben, to express the shifting mix of their thoughts.

But a voice behind them broke in. "Big, big thing, huh? Big men!"

Ingwald Jorgenson stood there. His was one of the few voices left that betrayed Scandinavian origin. "Push me from my home out. My vife, too. My kid. Vat for? Nothing. Little vater in the kitchen. That is all. Yah. Big thing. Big men."

Doc Crabtree said, "You goddamn big fool, that vat you are. Home go now. Cook food in vater."

Jorgenson stepped toward Doc Crabtree, a fist at the end of one arm, but Brobeck pushed foward. "Beat it!" he said. His quick glance toward the ladies was one of apology. "Beat it or get knocked on your butt. Hear me, Swede?"

Jorgenson hesitated, then turned away muttering. Watching him go, Brobeck said, "That's thanks for you."

A smile touched Ewing's mouth. "That's politics. That's the why of political parties. You can't fool all of the people all of the time, but a fool stays a fool no matter what."

36

SATURDAY AFTERNOON and a good time to write one or two editorials, Ben thought as he seated himself before the typewriter. The shop was silent. Callers would be few if any. What with hustling advertising, attending to job work, gathering news and readying for paper day, the working week allowed little time for considered reflection, even with the help of a good boy like Bob Perry. Of course there was Sunday, but he and Mary Jess liked to keep that day free, for visits, for company and for leisurely drives that usually took them in the direction of Elephant Ear Butte. Mr. Collingsworth would have liked that. He would have demurred, at least, had they called it Ear Mountain.

The afternoon sun slanted through the window. June, having shown what it could do, had turned kind as if for forgiveness. No. It was like an erratic parent, who, having been unreasonable, had switched to sweet reason, with the cunning knowledge that it would be all the sweeter and winning by contrast.

As he looked at the blank page in the machine, he reviewed possible subjects. He could write about the spirit of a people who had cheerfully and industriously cleaned up the muck of adversity. Except for occasional small piles of sand deposited at curbs and street corners, the town might never have known a flood. But he had lauded that spirit before. It was old stuff.

He could comment on a presumably authoritative report that floods such as this last one occurred only once every five hundred years. Which wasn't the same as saying they couldn't occur in successive years. But why dwell on that remote possibility?

The bomb. The atomic bomb, dropped on Japan perhaps with

good reason. But a terror had been loosed nonetheless, and those who found comfort in America's sole control of it surely were shortsighted or blind. What the nation could do, so could others in time. He could see the new generation, maybe many generations, living under the shadow of doom, until at last maybe the long fear would numb people. Could the young hope of life, the gay spirit, the confidence in the promise of being, could they continue under the hovering threat?

A big topic for a small paper. Let bigger ones tackle it. Let science — if you could trust the very profession that had found and exploited a dread secret of nature — find an opposing or restricting secret, and meantime give warning and say public prayers in repentance.

Closer home, of more local interest, was Montana's monopoly control of liquor purchases and retail distribution and sale. An indifferent operation there, one shabby since the beginning, marked by political patronage, favoritism and waste and surely some degree of corruption.

He began to write.

He had tapped out a few lines when the door opened. A young man, by appearance shortly out of the service, stood in the entrance. He asked, "Mr. Tate?"

"Yes. Come in, won't you?"

The boy took off his hat and advanced, his hand out. "I'm Mike Murchison." He had a nice smile.

Ben pushed the typewriter out of his way, rose and took the outstretched hand. "Well, Mattie's boy! Welcome. I'm happy to meet you."

"Same here, sir. Wanted to, a long time."

"Just out of the service?"

"Yes, sir. All done with flying."

"Please sit down."

"But you're working."

"Not that much."

The boy sat.

"You going to live here, Mike?"

"I wish I could, after being around less than a week."

"I know. We had an item in the paper."

"I've never seen the like of Montana. It gets hold of you, doesn't it?"

"Not everybody, thank God." Ben hurried to add, "But it's too bad you can't stay."

"I'll be here just long enough to see that Mother gets settled. Afterwards, after a few years, I can't tell."

"I don't quite follow."

"I'm going to take advantage of the GI Bill and go to college. You see, sir, I volunteered before I was eighteen. Mother kicked but finally agreed." He went on as if his lack of years called for apology. "I'm not quite twenty-one yet."

"How did you like the service, like flying?"

"All right. I liked it well enough, all things considered. It had to be done."

Ben nodded. It had to be done, sure enough, though a man had a right to reservations about wars in general.

Ben filled and lighted his pipe and said, "Sorry. I don't have cigarettes."

The boy shook his head, disclaiming the habit.

"What school are you thinking of?"

"I've seen Columbia. I've saved some money. Now I'd like to visit Missouri."

"Not Montana?"

"Montana, too. You see, sir, I'm going to major in journalism."

The words threw Ben back, back more than twenty years, and he occupied Mike's place, a young man just come from a war, and faced old Macalester Cleveland. It was age and youth again now, except that he sat in both chairs. What say to the Mike who was the young Ben? He said, "You won't get rich as a newspaperman."

"I know that much. Does it matter?"

"No. It hasn't to me, anyhow. I simply mentioned it."

Mike said, his eyes asking for confirmation, "A newspaper can do so much good. A good newspaper can."

He was so open, so damned earnest and hopeful. Fitting for a green boy, strange and unexpected in one who had dropped bombs or helped drop them. In his mind, enlarging on old experience, Ben could see the bombs bursting. He could imagine blood and entrails, dismemberments, screams and stink and ruin. Yet this boy seemed to have remained innocent, untouched, remote from the destruction that followed his flights.

"You don't agree, sir?" Mike asked. "About the value of a good newspaper? About it and the public interest?"

"Yes, of course, but I'm thinking that an editor must remember mistakes."

"Oh?"

"I hate to count mine. Hell, Mike, I was an isolationist. I thought we could live by ourselves. Fortress America. All that stuff. All that nonsense. I wish I could erase what I wrote in those days."

"But a lot of people thought that way once."

"Sure. We learned better."

"If that's all —"

"It isn't by a long shot. I used to be a town booster."

"What's wrong with that?" The smile on the boy's face had grown uncertain.

"Just that size doesn't mean quality. Bigger by itself isn't better. American tradition has it that way. So did I once. No more, though."

"But —"

"I was all for the big dam on the Breast River. I would be again if men couldn't find jobs and families were starving."

Mike interrupted to say, "They're going to reinforce the dam, I hear."

"Yes, and install generators. The power people aren't kicking about that now, not since they've found they can buy dump power at a bargain. That's not the point."

"I'm sorry."

"We know now that the dam can't prevent floods. I don't know that I ever did believe it. Besides jobs, I was for it for another reason. Irrigation."

Ben relighted his pipe, letting Mike wait. Then he said, "The dam did bring in farmers. It increased productivity. But the homesteader lives a hard, stingy life. All work, no play. That's partly or mostly because the government limits his acreage. No man can make a decent living from a quarter-section of land, not in the West. And not every acre of any homestead is irrigated, either — not by far."

"I wouldn't call that your fault."

"No? Call it uninformed enthusiasm. It was my fault I didn't know better and so didn't work for a better deal. Now I can only hope that deaths and transfers and a relaxed policy will make life easier."

Mike moved in his chair as if uncomfortable, and Ben went on, "I plugged for good roads, too. A mixed blessing there. Fine if you're driving, but good roads drain small towns — in our case to Great Falls, or from there, by plane, to Spokane. Try to find a good suit in this town or a first-rate pair of shoes."

"You had to choose, just the same," Mike answered with only a trace of his smile.

"That's the trouble with choices. They're never clean, almost never. Take sides, and you'll come to know regret or misgiving. That's the hell of it."

"Go on," Mike said, his gaze lowered.

"One more thing then. Summer fallowing. You savvy the term?"

"Do I know what it means? No."

"It's letting one piece of land lie fallow so as to store moisture for next season's crop. That seemed the answer for semiarid land, and maybe it is. I'm praying so. The paper promoted it, and it's been a saving thing for dry-landers, but —"

"But what?"

"There's saline seep, which you probably never heard of either. On certain types of land — we can't tell how much yet — fallowing sterilizes the soil. The stored moisture is unnatural. It brings mineral salts to the surface. Not much is known about it, and only God knows the outcome."

The boy raised his head now, the smile all gone and in its place a set stubbornness. "You'll excuse me, sir, but you talk as if everything came to nothing, that even a good press was always on the wrong side. I won't go for it."

In that same manner, Ben thought, might he himself have responded to Macalester Cleveland had there been reason for it in that dim time. Maybe he had spoken out. Memories got smeared. "I was only remembering," he said.

"So I noticed."

There was personality behind that still-boyish face. Personality, that quality hard to accept, or recognize in the young male. In support of himself, Ben had a quick notion to paraphrase Kierkegaard. How did it go? That the man who fought the future made a dangerous enemy. That the future didn't exist but took its strength from the man and then appeared as his foe.

In the waiting silence he knocked out his pipe and reloaded it. The fact had been in the back of his mind all the time, but now it pushed to the front, there to be examined and finally acknowledged. He had been speaking out of perversity, maybe even out of the shadow of envy. He had been contrary, almost consciously so. Innocence, he thought. Yeah, innocence. Confronted by it, experience wanted to wipe the smile from its face and so find the sour satisfaction of diminishment. Youth versus age. Faith versus actuality. The bright hope versus the realistic expectation. The bright hope ought to win. And here he was opposing it, estranging Mattie's boy.

Of itself a smile came to his mouth. He said, "I apologize, Mike. I'm not really gloomy. I wouldn't be here if I thought my work came to nothing."

Mike said, his face unrevealing, "All the time Mother was away, Grandmother forwarded the paper to her. She read it through every week. My mother, I mean."

"Wait. I haven't even asked how your mother is!"

"She's just fine. Glad to be back."

"She's a fine woman, Mike — not because she read my paper. I want to swear at God when I think of her life. Two husbands, and both dead, for the Lord's sake!"

Mike said, his tone flat, "I never knew either of them. I feel I know my father, though. I carry his picture around. He was a second cousin to her first husband. You know that."

"Yes. Might I look at the picture, Mike? Would you care to show me?"

Mike took a wallet from his pocket and from it a snapshot he handed over.

The print was fuzzy but the face plain enough. It was a square face, a good face, with straight eyes and a mouth that looked as if it knew how to laugh.

Ben nodded and said, "Good," and asked, looking at Mike, "Do I detect a resemblance in you?"

"Mother says so."

Mike put the snapshot away. He leaned forward. "I was talking about Mother and your paper. I'll tell you how she would answer you, if you want to hear." Without waiting for an answer, he went on, "The new library, it wouldn't be here but for Ben Tate. Same with the new rest home and the new hospital and a lot of other improvements. The paper always took the lead. Ben Tate did." The smile began to show again. "Doesn't that demolish what you said?"

"Allow for old friendship."

"Just the same," Mike answered, his eyes lifting to Ben's, "you're the main reason I want to be a newspaperman."

"Good Lord, boy!"

"You were the main reason, maybe I better say. That's why I wanted to talk to you. To get your ideas."

Ben took time lighting his pipe while Mike fingered his hat. "And I've been discouraging you," he said and shook his head. "All right, Mike. As that song goes, let's 'accentuate the positive.' "

Mike was leaning forward, waiting.

"Have you read Robert Frost?"

"A little, I guess."

"He wrote that the land was ours before we were the land's. A nice sentiment but not true as I see it. The land doesn't possess us. Hell, we abuse it every day so long as abuse brings a profit."

"Yes, sir?"

"We still have to learn to love and cherish and protect it. We're crazy. We can't keep digging and cutting and polluting. We can't keep poisoning and exhausting our topsoil or giving it to the wind. We can't if we want to survive."

"As the song you mentioned goes, you haven't 'eliminated the negative.'" The smile appeared about to be replaced.

"Hold on, now. I'm coming to that. Just remember that the earth is all we have. Her riches are limited. When she goes, we go. That's plain to see, or should be. But in the name of progress we keep drawing on an account that can be overdrawn. Progress. Progress be damned! Progress leaves us no retreat. What is called progress doesn't."

"So, then?"

"So here's the positive. Here's a coming, great role of a good and free press. Here's what you can do and I can try to do as long as I last."

"Yes, sir. I see, I think."

"Good. Educate. Inform. Look to the years ahead. Make people think. Speak from knowledge and concern for the future. That's not all you can do, but it's one hell of a challenge, and you'll have to fight." It struck Ben that he had been speaking with heat. He felt the heat go. "If only we can get people to love the earth."

He saw Mike's eyes were on him. The boy said, almost as if to himself, "To protect and preserve it. To be careful of it." Of a sudden, the bright, full smile came to his face.

"I'm glad I'm an editor, Mike."

"We had a rocky start, anyhow for me, sir, but you make me glad."

Mike stood up. He held out his hand, his gaze meeting Ben's. "Call me a convert. And thanks, sir."

"Remember me to your mother. We hope to see her soon."

Mike reached in his coat pocket. "She asked me to deliver this note, and I almost forgot." He held out an envelope.

After Mike had left, Ben sat back and fiddled with the unopened envelope. He felt drained and uncertain of the wisdom of what he had said. It was true enough, as true as he knew, but was it right for young Mike? Should he have opened up as he had? To a kid wanting encouragement, wanting certainty? The only certainty was that Mike was a good boy.

He straightened in his chair and opened the envelope and read:

Dear Ben:

Without any embarrassment to you, could I see you alone here at the farm? There's no rush, but tonight, any hour, would be a good time, for Mike plans to go to some country dance. Don't bother to phone and please don't apologize if you can't come conveniently. I will understand.

Fondly,
Mattie

37

BEN PUSHED BACK from the supper table, rose, gathered his soiled dishes, scraped them and took them to the sink, where he started rinsing them.

Seated behind him, Mary Jess said, "You don't have to do that, for goodness' sake. You worked all afternoon." She hurried to get up.

"Only if you call talking work." She began getting out dish-pans. "Young Mike Murchison visited me. I tried to put my wisdom in a capsule."

"Did you like him?"

"He's all right. You bet I liked him."

"And your wisdom?"

"My so-called wisdom. I should have doled it out. Take one tablet three times a day until symptoms disappear."

Mary Jess laughed as she ran hot water into a pan. "What were the symptoms? Move aside, Ben."

"He wants to be a newspaperman."

"Is that so bad?"

"Desperate."

She laughed again. "Do get out of my way, Ben. I don't want help. Go rest."

"I have to go out."

"Oh?"

"To see Mattie Murchison. Young Mike left a note."

"I'd be happy to see her, too." There was a question there.

"She wants to see me alone."

He knew her eyes were on him as he stared out the window. She asked, "What in the world?"

"I don't know, Mary Jess. I swear I don't know."

She was silent for a moment. He could almost feel her frown. The long light lay soft on the field behind the house, on the sturdy Breast River growth that had stood against the flood. Elephant Ear Butte rose in patches of shadow and light.

Her question broke into the scene. "You were close to her once, weren't you?"

"Yes." How close? she might ask next, though she wasn't given to prying. He braced himself. It would be wrong either to lie or to tell the truth. Best turn the question aside if he could. "I really don't want to go." There was no lie.

She turned and took his sleeve and got him to face her. Her hand was damp. If she had frowned before, now she was smiling. "Of course you must go," she said. She raised her head. Her mouth asked to be kissed.

He put an arm over her shoulders and kissed her. "I suppose so."

After he had got in the car and started out on the road that climbed between golf course and cemetery and flattened out on the bench, he wondered, as he had wondered since reading the note. Could Mattie be hoping to resume the old, secret coupling? He would be embarrassed if so. Cad was the word. He would feel like a cad in refusing, while all the time some part of him would remember those old Tuesday nights and want to go back. But, he told himself, Mattie wasn't like that. She couldn't be. Not Mattie. It was an insult to her to entertain the idea.

He let the car idle along. From the bench he could look down on the valley, mellow and warm in the evening sun. Now might be the best time of the year, he thought, with the solstice just come and gone and the days still long.

He turned off the gravel road and drove to the point of rocks under which lay the bones of old Smoky Moreau. Just so had he and Mary Jess stopped here in that long ago, their eyes on the valley and the wall of mountains beyond it. He cut the engine. Lines ran in his head, lines of a poem that Mary Jess had found, and both had liked and remembered.

How warm a wind blew here about the ways!
And shadows on the hillside lay to slumber
During the long sun-sweetened summer days.

Aye, yie, in words remembered from Mr. Collingsworth's days. Aye, yie, and the years passed, the years that the locust had eaten, and Mattie of the locust years wanted to see him.

The sun was easing down to the rim of the Rockies, and one small cloud had caught fire. The farther slopes that led away from the valley and climbed to the mountains lay striped with the yellow-green of grain and the barren dark of summer fallow. The war years had brought the plow to those virgin and gravelly acres. The war years and the dam had enlarged the town. No longer did prairie chickens nest where they used to, within walking distance from Main Street. Their cover was gone, torn up and appropriated by homes and paving and gas stations, the last of the birds dropped by eager shotguns. No more could a man walk a mile or so west to the Breast and catch trout. The slowed and muddied stream held no more than suckers and chubs.

He looked at his watch. There was time enough yet, with the sun still in sight and summer's long twilight to follow. He had been young in those years remembered now, and the land had seemed young, ready for the shaping hand of man. Man had come and aged it, he thought, man the manager. He had managed its streams, managed its soil, no matter the waste or the prospect, and left his wearing hand on its face.

Or was it just that he was older and saw through older eyes? Was the country still young to young Mike Murchison? Could he ever look to the settled east and sing with Badger Clark?

Such as they never can understand
The way we have loved you, young, young land!

He started the engine, backed up to turn around and went on.

So had he and Mattie and Mrs. Anderson come, to the house where old Mr. Greenwood lay dead, saintly in death, his features blissful in assurance of a blissful beyond. Snow had lain on the country then.

It's cold abroad the country I remember.

But the evening light lay warm on the house when he braked to a stop. Mattie met him at the door and took his hand in both of hers. "I'm so glad you found time, Ben. Please come in."

The girl of old, he almost could believe, the girl of long-striding grace, of appetite and honesty. She had passed the edge of middle age, yet she hadn't. Her tragedies had left face and figure nearly untouched. So had the years. In that instant of greeting he saw that she hadn't dressed up or needed to. She wore a simple housedress.

The living room was as he remembered, except that it was fully carpeted now and furnished as Mr. Greenwood might have thought unnecessary and even wasteful for a simple man of God.

"Sit down, Ben, anywhere comfortable."

He chose a chair near a sofa that was new since he had been here last. For a minute before sitting down she stood before him, her face open and frank, as if, behind it, there could be nothing disguised or devious. "It was convenient for you to come?" she asked.

"Of course. You see I'm here."

She seated herself on the sofa near him. "Tell me, how is Mary Jess?"

"Just fine. She wants to see you, too."

"I want to see her." She added, "But not tonight."

"I gathered that, Mattie."

"You've had a good life, haven't you, Ben? You're having a good one?"

"Yes. Far better, I'm afraid, than I deserve."

"That's nonsense. Now don't you think we better start with a drink?"

"Fine."

She went to the kitchen. The light from the west window

rested on the carpet. It explored its pattern. She brought back whiskey, watered as he liked it, offered him a glass and sat down, holding her own.

"I wasn't sterile after all, Ben," she told him.

"The evidence on that score seems conclusive," he answered, making his tone light.

"Mike told me about your talk. He was full of it." She nodded her head as if in agreement with Mike. "He was impressed — almost overcome, you might say."

"I don't know when I've talked longer at one stretch."

"You liked him?" she asked, a note of eagerness in her voice.

"I wouldn't have talked so much if I hadn't. *Like* seems a weak word. I was taken by him."

"I'm so glad, Ben. I'm so glad. That you and he became friends so quickly."

She sipped her drink and lowered and looked at it as if thinking what next to say. "I suppose I'd better come out with it, though I don't know quite how. I wrote the note, meaning to." She paused and went on to say, "You're a good man, Ben Tate. Don't forget that."

He had no answer. He drank from his own glass and waited. She raised her eyes to his face. It was not, he said to himself, that she wanted him physically, though he felt the guilty, first stirring of desire in himself. It was as if she wanted some kind of assurance, some agreement of mind and heart, some common, embraced understanding.

Abruptly she straightened, her mind made up, and said, "You see, Ben, I never married again."

"You mean after Mike's father died?"

"No. I was married just once, long, long before Mike came along."

"Wait. The picture that Mike carries around?"

"That's a picture of my first, my only husband. I had to have the print tinkered with so no dated or revealing things showed."

"Then, of course, he doesn't know."

"He'll never know. He must never know. Promise me that."

"I promise."

"It took some doing, Ben," she said with no trace of self-pity. "It wasn't easy, keeping the facts from him and all others, even my own mother."

"You needn't have told me. It makes no difference to me that he's —"

"Don't say the dirty word. It doesn't apply."

He nodded slowly. "No more to him than to you. Not to either of you, I meant to say." He finished his drink. "I know it wasn't a cheap affair, Mattie. I know that much about you."

"Oh, it wasn't. I always thought it was right. I know it was." She fell silent. Thought shadowed her face. "You will believe me, Ben? You do believe me — in me?"

"Never doubt it."

"Let's have another drink, then."

She picked up the glasses, went to the kitchen and returned with refills. Seated, she leaned forward and took his free hand. Her own was warm, and he thought of their old nights together.

She said, as if his thoughts were her own, "No, Ben. Past is past. Gone is gone." She halted and then said, "And yet?"

"And yet what, Mattie?"

"I suppose I could say that gone is with us today."

"The remembrance of it."

She put her glass aside and reached to hold his hand in both of hers. "I would never lie to you, Ben." A wrench came to her face and settled into lines of strict earnestness. "I would rather die than do that."

"Now, Mattie," he said, not knowing anything better. "Now, Mattie."

"In all my life," she told him, her eyes open to his, "I've known only two men. Believe me, Ben."

"Two?"

"My first husband and you, Ben."

"Then —" The conclusion, the sole and only conclusion, delayed for an unbelieving instant, came bursting inside him. "Good God!"

"I thought you'd want to know after meeting Mike. I wanted you to like each other." She squeezed his hand hard. "Accept it. Accept it. Don't be so thunderstruck."

A father! A father unrecognized, always to go unrecognized. To be at a far remove from his son. To feel pride and concern, never spoken. To know the blood bond and hold the cherished truth tight, never admitting, never revealing, never comporting himself as more than a friend. Never father and son. And Mattie?

"All the time," he said. His speech came ragged to his ears. "All the time. You carried it all by yourself. You left here —"

" 'Pregnant' is the word, Ben."

"And never let me know."

"I did what was right. You were in love with Mary Jess. Rightly so. Can you think I would ever come whimpering to you?"

"My responsibility." The words still came jerkily. "My — my doing."

"No more than mine. Not as much, Ben. I initiated those Tuesday nights. I don't blame you."

"But if I'd only known!"

"Yes. You would have acted, as they say, honorably. That's one reason I left here."

"If you had only told me sometime. You got no help."

"Don't take on so and please don't take it that way. I'm not asking anything of you except understanding. I haven't and won't." She pressed his hand. "No self-reproach, Ben, for God's sake. No repentance."

He said, recognizing a humility not there before, "I'm knocked out, Mattie. I feel damned."

Tears bloomed and shone bright in her eyes. "Damned? You've seen Mike. You know what a fine boy he is."

"No thanks to me."

"Ben. Ben." She was crying out for the first time. "It was worth it. He was worth it all. Think what we wrought."

He couldn't keep his eyes on that honest and tearful face. He looked down. The last of daylight traced the weaving pattern of the carpet. "Yes," he said. He added, "Sure."

He got up and stepped toward the door, hearing himself say, "Thanks, Mattie."

She said, "Wait, Ben." Then, "Oh, your hat."

He turned and took it, meeting her eyes just once.

"Ben," she said, "you wouldn't — I know you won't —"

"Not a thing. No. Nothing. Nothing at all."

At the car he halted, his hand on the door handle, knowing she watched him. The mountains stood steady, sharp-outlined by the dying blaze of the day, their fronts blurred in the gathering dusk; and he was in his first days in the West again, in an open pasture since then parceled out for the small, domestic uses of men, and westward he had come free, like Thoreau, and a lone cow lifted her head, blind to the radiance in his face.

He straightened himself and squared his shoulders and took a deep breath as he looked. It was still his land, his, and let time or change or dispensation try to deny it.

He got in the car and started on the road. It pointed west toward the mountains, to the valley, to home.